The (R)Evolution By Night Book 2

UNHOLY WAR:
Rage and Redemption

Matt R. Jones

The giant typewriter's metal frame was an unyielding barricade pressing hard against my leather jacket, and as the covies closed in, keeping the smoking barrels of their guns on me, I glared at them defiantly. If I was gonna check out, they weren't gonna get shit outta me.

"Fuck your Goddess and fuck you," I growled, throwing them the finger.

"Tell her yourself. You'll be meeting her in just a moment... my little chickadee," sneered Wanda, pulling the trigger. All three opened fire, and as much as I hate to admit it, I did indeed close my eyes.

But nothing happened.

A long, low hiss came from above, dripping with menace and unfiltered hatred.

I opened my eyes to the sight of the three covies gaping at something above me, their guns glowing with a soft purple light. I pushed away from the typewriter's frame and looked up, relief washing through me. Relief and just a dash of trepidation...

Donita looked like Hell itself.

The gypsy half-vampire's hair was a wild, tangled mess, her eyes were blazing bright red with rage, and her mouth was twisted into a fanged snarl of fury. At that moment she wasn't the loudmouthed kid sister who made us all laugh, or the gentle soul who'd recently nursed an entire litter of orphaned baby rabbits to adulthood, or even the intimidating, hard-edged lead singer of Rapture. She was something sent up from the underworld, something born of pain and vengeance, out to drag her victims back down to the depths.

One of her hands was held out as she crouched atop the giant typewriter, a soft purple glow enveloping it as she used her magick to stop the covies' guns from firing, even as they fruitlessly tried to blast her.

"Why couldn't you have just left us alone?" she demanded, her voice ragged with emotion. With a roar, she threw herself at the covies.

They didn't stand a chance.

Mystique Press is an imprint of Crossroad Press Publishing

Copyright © 2015 by Matt R. Jones
Cover Art by Daniël S. Hugo
Design by Aaron Rosenberg and David Dodd
ISBN 978-1-948929-40-0
For information address Crossroad Press at 141 Brayden Dr., Hertford, NC 27944
www.crossroadpress.com

First edition

Dedication

To Mom and Dad
The stories I wrote weren't always your cup of tea,
but you never stopped encouraging me, no matter how many
monsters, aliens, robots, ninjas, and yes, vampires I threw in.
Thank you.

Acknowledgements

This book (and the one before it) represents eighteen years of struggle, setbacks, and successes… I've had many, many helping hands supporting me along the way, and I'm grateful for every single one, whether it was advice, artwork, encouragement, or multiple book purchases.

If I've forgotten you, it wasn't on purpose—please do yell at me, and I'll make sure to include you next time. The *Unholy War* saga isn't just my story…it's yours as well, because you helped make this happen.

I couldn't have done it without all of you guys. *Thank you.*

If I wore a hat, it'd be off to…

Holly Jones (my beautiful and delightfully sarcastic wife), Mom and Dad, Uncle Joe (my first and biggest bad influence), Stephanie Jones, Nathaniel D Smith, Miss Pam (Suzy), Danny Barnes (Baldo), Kevin Steele, Brett Steele, Bob Long, Rob Miller, Tad Allard, Taylor Long, Todd Walker, Becky Bradway, Sonja Roudebush, Bill Leitze, Angie McKaig, Karen "Elmo" Diaz (thanks for the foreword, weirdo!), Victoria Howell, Chelle Ressler, Johnny Crypt, Derek (Not Drederick) Tatum, Gideon Culman, Dana Ouwehand, Samantha & Raven Landsberg, Sarah & Dylan Ray, Danita Mitchell, Dave Traeger (thanks for the shirt!), Chuck Wallace, Ryan Malcolm McGuinness, Don Lands, Scott Wirebaugh, Jack Ritchie, Joey Stantinopolis, Darkest Radio, Kanah & Aaryn Fuller, Jenna Anselmo, Martha Whitehorse, Philip Lewis, James R Tuck, Ryan Lebeck, Stacey Blades, Rob Sehr, Rosemary Moewe, Brian Babcock, the Drunken Zombie gang (Randy Witte, Bryan Wolford, Dave Gibson, and Wes Thompson), Lord Blood-Rah, Starsky Starcevich (bitchin' cane, dude), Stacy Peterson, the Peoria Public Library, David Youngquist (for taking a chance on the (R)Evolution By Night), Nerine Dorman (my intrepid editor, who kicked ass and made this book better than ever), and everybody who bought a copy of *Unholy War* when it was just a self-published indie book.

And then there's…

Stephen Lebeck—I don't know how many copies of the original editions of *Unholy War* you bought for yourself, your friends, your family, and how many people you've converted to the (R)Evolution By Night's cause, but damn…if I had a thousand more like you, I'd be bigger than Godzilla. I can't thank you enough for all the support over the years.

And finally, a salute to Sylvia Shults, who believed in *Unholy War* and fought for it tooth and nail, taking me down the path that ultimately led me to Crossroad Press. You're reading these very words because of her. If you love the (R)Evolution By Night and you ever see Sylvia out and about, you damned sure better thank her!

Foreword

There are times in our life when we meet people that change us forever. One of those people in my life is Matt R Jones.

Many years ago in an online newsletter for LA Guns, I read a story titled "Hollywood Vampires." I was drawn to it because firstly, it was well written and intense. Secondly it was about sleaze, rock 'n roll, and vampires—my favorite subjects. So moved, I immediately contacted the author to express my admiration. We started talking and he discovered I had been writing my own book secretly. Though our vamps are different, we both centered them around the music.

We wrote back and forth for several months, with him encouraging me to type up my secret world. He further encouraged me to send it to him to read. Surprisingly, he submitted it to another friend who ran a vampire website called *Pathway to Darkness*...I was shocked by the positive response I received. Single-handedly Matt had opened a new door for me—if not for him, my book would still be in a box in my closet on legal pad.

Over the years we kept in touch, helping each other. He has never given up, continuously developing his world and craft until there is a new genre—rock vamp. The (R)Evolution By Night is a dark, intriguing romp through the street with humorous points of life. The characters are so diverse and real, that you forget they're vampires. It's a world of love, music, and adventure that every wannabe rock star wants when they move to LA...and the love of music and their comrades that holds them together through all the escapades.

Music holds us all together through different times in our life. People who make that music are a strange, charismatic group; Matt captures that. He makes you feel like part of this merry band of gypsies—you can feel the joy they feel onstage playing their music, hear the love of the fans, and feel their pain during bad times. It is a rich, vibrant world you can get lost in.

So next time you go see a band, wonder if you see a glimpse of fangs. What mesmerizes your mind? The music? Or is there something else about that band that draws you in? That guitar player that is just a bit too pretty—is that natural? Perhaps there are vampires in our shadows, clubs, and music.

After fifteen years of talking on the internet, mailing stuff, and talking on the phone, I met Matt face to face. I was honored to attend his wedding, and it couldn't have been a better way to meet. I'm so proud of Matt for never giving up, for writing continuously, and bringing this world to us. You did good, weirdo.

Karen Diaz
Author, *Goodbye Nightbird*

Playlist

"Electric Wonderland"—Nasty Idols
"Under The Blade"—Twisted Sister
"Isolation"—Iggy Pop
"Restless"—Within Temptation
"Perish In Fire"—Monster Magnet
"Enter"—Within Temptation
 "Hallelujah"—Monster Magnet
"Change"—Ace Frehley
"Catharsis"—Anthrax
"Wake Up (The Sleeping Giant)"—Twisted Sister
 "Painkiller"—Backyard Babies
"Armorist"—Overkill
"Left Hook From Right Field"—Armored Saint
"If"—The Cult
"Wonderland"—The Cult
"Foolish Boy"—Mojo Gurus
"City Of Angels"—LA Guns

Part Five:

Spectres of the Past

Prologue

"Donita! Fucking get back here!" Brandi snarled as we pounded across the graveled rooftop, seven stories up. Fury radiated from her powerful six-foot-four-inch frame, her long, wild red hair streaming behind her in a messy ponytail.

Up ahead, the half-vampire gypsy—a whirl of purple skirt, flowing blouse, and tangled brunette-and-purple hair—stormed across the gravel, not even bothering to respond this time. Her hands were faintly glowing with purple magickal energy as she revved herself up for combat.

"*Donita!*" I growled, hoping to break through, but nothing. The normally cheerful half-blood was beyond us right now, focused on the dark, bestial shape springing from rooftop to rooftop up ahead.

When she reached the edge of the rooftop, Donita flung herself through the air, her skirt flapping like bats' wings. She barely reached the rooftop across the street, scrabbling for purchase before resuming the furious chase.

Brandi and I launched after her, skidding hard on the gravel of the other rooftop. My heart was pounding, my blood was hot, and my fangs were threatening to snap down into place as my body dumped adrenaline into itself. It had been two nights since we'd crushed the attempted coup of Los Angeles by *Covenant of Blood*-inspired zealots, and the wound dealt to our community was still raw, ragged, and bloody.

We were still counting our dead, repairing our world, and trying to figure out the best way to move forward. Some of us were having a much harder time than others.

Donita threw on a burst of speed, her bare feet a blur as she charged after the dark shape, closing the gap even as it increased its own velocity.

"Why's it running away?" Brandi demanded, her green eyes

narrowed. "It shouldn't be running away."

A tendril of fear wrapped around my heart and squeezed. *"Donita! Stop!"*

Something had been tearing up hobos on this end of town, something monstrous, and I'd figured some of us should check it out. We'd barely managed to keep the covy uprising under wraps, and we had dozens of vampires working around the clock to ensure the truth didn't come out. Politicians' palms had been greased, police departments had been fed mountains of false evidence, journalists had been persuaded to present their findings in just the right way, and a number of people had outright disappeared in the name of damage control.

The prevailing theory was that it had been a gang war gone completely out of control, and we were actively pushing the public perception in that direction. The last thing we needed was for somebody to stumble across some covy remnant mauling the homeless. So Brandi and I had set out to investigate, with Donita insisting on coming along.

Donita brought her hand up and there was a brief flash as she fired off a bolt of magickal energy at the fleeing form. The smell of ozone hit my nose, joining with the currents of exhaust and grime eddying around the rooftops. The gypsy's shot went wide, hitting an industrial air-conditioning unit atop the apartment building our target was galloping across, and the unit surged and sparked as it overloaded and shorted out.

It was late spring and the air was already thick and warm—some folks were gonna be pissed off when their AC went out tonight. Donita's enraged snarl told me she didn't really give a damn. The gypsy was out for blood tonight. To be honest, so was I. If I didn't have Donita on whom to focus, I might've been the idiot blindly running up front instead of her.

But we'd already lost one good friend; I'd be damned if we lost another. Especially since we already were losing Katheryne.

The gypsy sprang across the gap between rooftops, plunging through the acrid smoke billowing out of the ruined air-conditioning units. She fired off several more bolts, and from the roar of frustration, I knew she'd missed again. Brandi and I hit the rooftop, the stink of burnt metal and caustic coolant assaulting my nose as we tried to close the gap between Donita and ourselves.

"Fucking hell, we're both pushing two millennia and she's just a damned kid," Brandi growled. "Ought to be easier to catch her than this."

I grunted in agreement. Donita was hauling ass, and if our quarry hadn't already had such a big lead, she would've already run it down. I was thankful for that much, because if it was what I thought it was, our intrepid friend would've been in over her head. Donita was formidable as hell and had a bag of tricks a mile deep, but she was also hurting badly and wasn't thinking clearly—a sure recipe for disaster.

Brandi and I cleared the apartment rooftop, clambered up the side of an adjoining building, and caught Donita in the distance, spitting profanities and firing off more bolts as the dark shape leaped off the other side of the roof.

"She's right on top of it now," I said, my stomach churning. "If she hits it half-cocked and it gets hold of her, she's fucked."

"Then we'll just make sure—"

Brandi never finished her sentence as machine gun fire opened up on us, tearing apart the tarred roof. A bullet bit through my thigh before I had a chance to do anything, skewering the muscle with a red-hot rail-spike of pain, and I heard a sharp hiss from Brandi as she took on lead herself. The hell?

Up ahead, two black-robed figures jumped out from behind a couple of towering vents, hoods obscuring their faces as they kept the heat on us. Bullets whizzed past my head as I dodged, ducked, and rolled, biting my lip against the pain burning through my wounded leg. A vampire can withstand the damage of being shot, and heal it back up, a hell of a lot better than a mortal, but that didn't mean it didn't hurt. Especially when the bullet scraped the fucking bone. My leg was a throbbing mass of pain radiating out to my knee and my ass, and it was just made worse by the knowledge that we'd been suckered.

Sure, Donita had gone into business for herself and took off after the target without waiting for us, but Brandi and I were seasoned pros, and we *knew* Donita was emotionally compromised. The gypsy was fiery and temperamental on good days, and we should've known better than to let her go along with us tonight. The Valkyrie and I weren't exactly the coolest heads in the room, either, but if we'd done this our way, that big vicious piece of shit up ahead of us wouldn't have led us on a merry chase, right into an ambush.

"For the glory of the Goddess!" bellowed the asshole in the black robe closest to me.

"Oh, fuck you," I muttered as I ducked a hail of bullets. Religious nuts and guns were always a bad combination.

Brandi and I split up, going in opposite lateral directions, forcing the two covies to widen their field of fire, giving us both a lot more breathing room. I stumbled as my leg nearly buckled, and took a bullet in the side, but I kept going. The adrenaline would push the pain back, and I'd deal with it later. Then a bullet grazed my temple. The hot lead tore through my bandanna and sliced a furrow through my flesh, sending blood gushing down into my eye.

I'd deal with it if there *was* a later. Dammit.

I heard a scream from the other side of the roof and the racket of machine gun fire was abruptly cut in half. Then a bloodcurdling scream erupted from the other covy; out of the corner of my eye, I'm pretty sure I saw one of his arms go flying. It was enough to make the other covy hesitate, giving me a fleeting respite. "I got these cocksuckers!" Brandi roared. "You get Donita!"

The vent the covy was hiding behind was right around four feet tall, and with a grunt of pain I leaped up onto it, taking a split-second to kick the offending covy in the face before he could get a bead on me with his AK-47. It hurt my wounded leg like a motherfucker, but it was *so* worth it when I saw his teeth go flying like so many Chiclets. He staggered back with a squawk, firing blindly, but I was already well past him, hitting the roof in a roll before hopping back to my feet, a trifle less gracefully than I would've liked.

Ahead of me, Donita leaped off the building and dropped out of sight. Our fleeing friend was nowhere to be seen. Grinding my teeth against the mangled-drumstick pain of my leg, I picked up the pace. That damned kid. We were all hurting over Wade's death and terrified for Katheryne, but this was no way to deal with it… one doesn't deal with death by taking idiot chances and blindly throwing themselves at it like this. But even as I thought that, I wanted to sigh—yeah, I'd been four hundred once, too.

The ledge of the building came up fast, and what I saw made my heart hitch.

Donita was hanging off the edge of the old factory, dangling four stories up, while a revenant was snarling and swiping at her with its deadly claws. She was frantically moving hand-over-hand back and forth along the ledge, narrowly avoiding the beast's attacks, and it was going at her with such fury that she didn't have even a second to mount a counterattack or even get back up onto the roof.

Not that getting on the roof would've been a good idea. Standing at damned near seven feet tall and entirely made of solid monster muscle, the revenant was a fearsome opponent, hideously strong, disturbingly durable, and existing only to devour its victims. Fighting one was like going toe to toe with a tornado. I'd seen Donita take one out at close range during the Battle of Los Angeles, but she'd been clear-headed and had the advantage. If I didn't do something, she was fucked.

I snarled. I wasn't gonna lose another one of my friends to these assholes.

Hot blood cascaded down my leg as I galloped across the roof, my instinctive fear of the revenant pushed down by raw, naked fury. Behind me, the agonized screaming and wild machine gun fire reached a fever pitch, and I figured Brandi had things well in hand. I desperately hoped she did, because as much as I was determined to save Donita at any cost, I *really* didn't want to face another revenant.

I hit the ledge and hurled myself off the building, the blood pounding in my ears mercifully drowning out my groan of pain, and I sailed through the warm night air, over the trash-strewn alley far below, on a collision course with the miscreated monstrosity trying to kill one of my dearest friends. Donita may have been a pain in the ass, but she was *our* pain in the ass.

I leaned into it as I shot towards the revenant, intending to hit the fucker with fangs and claws and do as much damage as I could. With any luck, my momentum would carry us backward enough to give Donita time to get back up on the roof, and we could fight the savage prick off until Brandi caught up.

The milliseconds ticked away like drops in a Chinese water torture, and I could catch every detail of the revenant, even smell the corpse-stink of its tattered, soiled clothes and ragged, filthy skin. It had once been a male, with scraggly long hair and grimy beard, and it looked just like something off the racks at a Halloween store. It took another swipe at the cursing gypsy then fixed its blank, sightless eyes on me, giving me a chill that crystallized my marrow. Revenants were empathic trackers, homing in on the emotions of its victims, and it had doubtless sensed the storm of emotions roiling through me.

But I was too close for it to make a difference. I *had* to be! If that fucker clawed me out of the air...

Then the revenant said, "Oh shit."

I hit the bastard like a moon-rocket, expecting to hit a brick wall of flesh and bone, but he may as well have been made out of papier-mâché. I smashed through him, and we slammed into the rotten roof of the long-forgotten typewriter factory with all the subtlety of Khrushchev's shoe on a table at the UN...and kept right on going. Timbers screeched, I snarled, and the revenant howled. This was gonna suck so bad.

We dove through a sea of decaying wood, tarpaper, and rusty ventilation shafts, getting sliced, stabbed, and gouged the whole merry way. It felt like we'd pissed the building off and it had decided to exact its revenge by chewing us up like something out of a Stephen King novel. There was a brief moment where we fell through empty space, probably what had once been the offices, but rain damage and age had long ago weakened the floor to the point of zero resistance. We just went right on through and got chewed on again.

We both gasped as we hit something solid, our momentum painfully arrested, and as I stared cross-eyed into the fright-mask of the revenant's face for those couple of seconds, I did the only thing I could think of—I hit the asshole.

Though the monster certainly yowled in pain, it turned out it wasn't one of the brightest things I'd ever done. With an ear-splitting wail of ripping metal, the inner ceiling of the factory gave way and we plummeted again. Thankfully, it was through empty space this time, so we didn't get chewed. Not so thankfully, it was a long fucking drop.

We bounced off something unyielding and metallic then ended

up falling off the side of that...down to a similarly unyielding and metallic surface, where I banged my head with an unsettling *crack!* before managing to grab on and stop myself. The revenant kept right on going, crashing into debris on the way down and starting a mini-avalanche of junk. Thank the stars. I needed a moment to feel sorry for myself before I was ready for another round of this.

I lay there on my back for a few blessed seconds, gasping like a fish, trembling like a junkie in detox, and trying not to scream. I'm pretty sure it would've hurt less to have been run over by a steamroller.

"Fuck anybody who ever bought a typewriter from this shithole," I groaned as I painfully sat back up, my abused muscles and bones creaking in protest. As much as I wanted to sit for a while longer and sulk, I didn't have that luxury. I got back to my feet, my further-mauled leg sparking pain in protest, and scanned the shadowy interior of the factory.

It was musty, dusty, and smelled like ancient oil in here, and it was a damned maze, to boot. Some of the old machinery had toppled over, turning the assembly lines into a convoluted devil's highway, while chunks of the ceiling had collapsed and blocked off entire sections. The hair on the back of my neck stood on end—this was *not* the place to be stuck with a revenant on the loose.

Then the pained moan sounded out from somewhere down below, and I whipped toward it, peering through the gloom, trying to catch sight of the revenant...which didn't sound like a revenant. Revenants roared, growled, snarled, and even groaned, but there was a decidedly un-bestial quality to that sound of distress. Not only that, but there was what it had said right before I plowed into it way back up on the roof. Revenants didn't talk, either.

I glanced upward and shivered a little when I'd seen how far we'd fallen. Four stories. If we hadn't gotten tangled up in so much shit on the way down, we would've been splattered all over the floor. I probably would've survived it, though the healing would've been so protracted and painful I would've preferred death. Ugh.

Taking in my surroundings, I realized with a start what we'd landed on. "Holy shit," I muttered, a small part of me thrilled at the discovery. This was the old Axis Typemaster plant, which used to have a giant typewriter on the lawn out in front, just this huge monstrosity that was as big as a bunch of semi trailers stacked together. Bigger, even. It had disappeared sometime in the early 1980s, when the factory had shuttered, and I'd figured it had been hauled off for scrap. Nope, they'd just brought it inside the plant proper, where it had almost killed me.

Standing atop the nine key, which was big as a restaurant table, I looked at the vast keyboard sprawling downward, like the tiers of a stadium. Even covered in pieces of ceiling, twisted assembly line, and a multitude of other crap, it was still impressive. I couldn't wait to tell Stacey what I'd found—he'd always thought this stupid thing was cool as hell. It'd make him feel better after Dorian had ripped his pants off and thrown him through a plate-glass window in retribution for wrecking his beloved Mustang during the Battle of Los Angeles.

There was another moan, and I tossed my delight at my discovery aside. I carefully started down the littered keyboard, shaking off the pain of the meat-grinder descent and letting my anger salve my wounds. I was getting the distinct feeling we'd been had.

Somewhere, down in the tangle of twisted and fallen machinery, I heard the revenant—or reasonable facsimile thereof—staggering to its feet. I picked up my pace, my fangs sliding down into place as I scanned for him. I wanted to barrel down after the bastard, but we'd already been suckered once tonight. No sense making things too easy for these fuckwads.

That turned out to be the right move, as a commotion rose from the other side of the cavernous room, and I heard what sounded like a door being torn off its hinges. "For the glory of the Goddess!" a woman bellowed from the darkness, and the tromp of at least three pairs of booted feet thundered across the concrete floor below.

"He's up there somewhere!" cried a pained voice, which I assumed belonged to the faux revenant. Thanks, jerkoff.

I could get up on top of the typewriter, possibly even get inside of it, but where would I go from there? Nope. I stood a better chance of finding cover under all the debris littering the typewriter, especially if these covies were armed. In a big factory like this, it theoretically shouldn't be too hard to hit and run my pursuers until they were all iced, though I wanted to take at least one alive for questioning. The thought of another uprising made me want to purge.

I darted across the keyboard, intending to drop down behind a mangled mass of rusty ductwork, but a spray of hot lead stitched up the keys toward me, chewing up the old metal and spitting shrapnel in all directions. If I'd been an eyeblink slower, my ankles would've been ripped to shreds. As it was, I took a bullet straight through my calf when I dodged backward, and I stumbled.

Between the bullet through my calf and the one I'd taken on the rooftop, I was slowed down enough that several vampires with machine guns could indeed get the drop on me. I started in the other direction, but a rain of gunfire against the front of the typewriter, tearing apart the faded Axis logo, stopped me in my tracks.

"Hold it right there!" snapped the female, and I turned toward my captors.

Out of the shadows, three red-robed covies packing AK-47s and a big vampire in a bedraggled revenant disguise strode up the keys, their eyes glittering in wary triumph. The leader of the group was a relatively young vampiress named Wanda, who used to play keyboards with the Turbofoxes back in the 1980s; we'd even done an LA-wide club tour with them at one point. Wanda was smart, funny, and did a wicked WC Fields impersonation that always had Stacey and me rolling. One of the hardest parts of this whole thing had been seeing how many old friends and acquaintances had been sucked up by the hoary old bullshit scrawled down in the *Covenant of Blood*.

With a motion from Wanda, the other two covies—whom I'd also seen around town—fanned out to keep me better covered, while the faux revenant looked like he wanted to pass out. If I recognized him right, the would-be revenant was named Elizalde, and was damned good with metal sculpture. Guess he'd found better ways to pass the time.

"Cute, Wanda," I said. "So what are—"

The single shot blasted through my shoulder, grazing the bone and shredding the muscle. I instinctively turned and took a second bullet through my already-wounded side for my trouble. I snarled and backed up against the front of the typewriter, fighting down the pain and trying to figure out how to get out of this. These fuckers had the drop on me, but good.

Speaking of drop, I barely hit the deck in time to avoid another spray of gunfire from Wanda, who clearly wasn't kidding around here. As a matter of fact, I got the feeling this wasn't going to be the classic James Bond situation where the villains yakked the hero's ear off—like I said, Wanda was smart. Not smart enough to not buy into the *Covenent of Blood*'s nonsense, but hey. Time to get outta here.

I sprang to my feet, intending to scramble up and over the front of the typewriter and get behind it, but my wounded legs slowed me down. It wasn't much. A mortal wouldn't have even noticed. But it was enough that a vampire could press the advantage. So I got shot right in the guts.

It wasn't fatal. It was something I could heal up from in less than a day's time. But it hurt like a motherfucker as a supernova of pain erupted in my stomach and radiated up through my lungs and heart, out through my spine, and down into my groin. It was only a few bullets, but it felt like I'd gotta hit by a bazooka.

I fell back against the typewriter, cracking my head against the damned thing *again*, and landed on my ass like a ragdoll. Not my finest hour. The typewriter's metal frame was an unyielding barricade pressing hard against my leather jacket, and as the covies closed in, keeping the smoking barrels of their guns on me, I glared at them defiantly. If I was gonna check out, they weren't gonna get shit outta me.

"Fuck your Goddess and fuck *you*," I growled, throwing them the finger.

"Tell her yourself. You'll be meeting her in just a moment...my little chickadee," sneered Wanda, pulling the trigger. All three opened fire, and as much as I hate to admit it, I did indeed close my eyes.

But nothing happened.

A long, low hiss came from above, dripping with menace and unfiltered hatred.

I opened my eyes to the sight of the three covies gaping at something above me, their guns glowing with a soft purple light. I pushed away from the typewriter's frame and looked up, relief washing through me. Relief and just a dash of trepidation...

Donita looked like Hell itself.

The gypsy half-vampire's hair was a wild, tangled mess, her eyes were blazing bright red with rage, and her mouth was twisted into a fanged snarl of fury. At that moment she wasn't the loudmouthed kid sister who made us all laugh, or the gentle soul who'd recently nursed an entire litter of orphaned baby rabbits to adulthood, or even the intimidating, hard-edged lead singer of Rapture. She was something sent up from the underworld, something born of pain and vengeance, out to drag her victims back down to the depths.

One of her hands was held out as she crouched atop the giant typewriter, a soft purple glow enveloping it as she used her magick to stop the covies' guns from firing, even as they fruitlessly tried to blast her.

"Why couldn't you have just left us *alone?*" she demanded, her voice ragged with emotion. With a roar, she threw herself at the covies.

They didn't stand a chance.

Using nothing more than her fangs, claws, and magick, Donita ripped them to pieces. Bones were broken, limbs were severed, flesh was burnt, and blood sprayed in all directions. Ignoring the searing fire in my guts, I climbed up on top of the typewriter just to get away from it. I almost felt sorry for them. Then I put my hands to my shredded abdomen, feeling a wave of dizziness wash over me as my body kicked into overdrive as it worked to heal the worst of the wound as quickly as possible, and any pity I might've felt left the room.

A heavy pair of boots clomped down on the metal next to me. "You all right, bub?"

"I've been better," I said.

"I'll pass you some blood here in a few," said Brandi, "Just topped off the tank, myself."

In one hand she held one of the rooftop covies by the scruff of his neck. Both were liberally spattered with blood, though he looked like he'd been ran over by a tank. Which I'm sure he had been.

"Got some info while I was filling up too," she said. "This was a sleeper cell, set to go off in case anything happened to Barzai. When Willie took him down, these guys went into action. Whittle away at our numbers by setting up traps like this, and start recruiting wherever they could, until they had the numbers to roll over the top of us. Basically restart the whole thing from the ground up."

A leg went flying past us to thud wetly somewhere behind the typewriter.

"Son of a bitch." I sighed. "Any others?"

"Dunno," she replied. *"As far as they know, they were acting alone, but who knows?"*

"Anything about Barzai himself? We never did find out who he was or where he came from." That didn't sit well on my mind, and the fact that this bunch of *Covenant*-obsessed fuckheads used the symbology of the long-dead Crimson Order bugged the hell out of me in quieter moments.

"Nada."

"Great." Whoever Barzai had been, he'd covered his tracks well; none of the covies had known much of anything beyond battle plans and a fanatical devotion to the Goddess of the *Covenant.*

"The G-Goddess will r-rise and purify this c-city with her holy f-fire," moaned the twitching covy in Brandi's hand.

"Oh fuck you," Brandi growled, giving him a bone-rattling shake. "When you meet your Goddess, you tell her if I ever get my hands on her, I'm beating the shit outta her, you got me?" Before he could reply, Brandi hoisted him over her head. *"Hey Donita!"*

The gypsy, looking like Sissy Spacek at the end of *Carrie*, whirled around, ripping Wanda's face off with a swipe of her clawed hand. As the mutilated vampiress fell screaming to the N key, Brandi flung her prize to the half-vampire, who pulled a dagger from somewhere within her blood-soaked blouse and skewered him straight through the guts, her arm coming out of his back all the way up to the elbow. Then he caught on fire.

The screaming and stench from below us was sickening, but neither Brandi nor I turned away.

"I wish Katheryne would do something like this," I said. "She needs to get this out of her, just like Donita."

Brandi sighed. "Donita blames the covies for what happened to Wade, and what's happening to Katheryne. She's getting a chance to take that poison out on them, or what's left of them. Katheryne doesn't have that option."

"Because she blames nobody but herself."

"And she's slowly taking it out on herself." Brandi shrugged. "Revenge isn't what Katheryne needs, anyway. She's too good of a soul. You, me, Donita...we've got enough darkness in us that murdering the shit outta somebody in retribution does the job. But

Katheryne, that sweet kid...she needs something else, something better." She paused. "She needs redemption."

I nodded in agreement. "Yeah, but...how does she get it?"

Brandi looked grim. "Fucked if I know."

As we watched the slaughter, Donita's words rang through my head. Why *couldn't* they have just left us alone? The whole point of our community in Los Angeles was to mind our own business and live our lives without bothering anybody. Yet the covies had damned near ruined it...and for what reason? Because we believed differently from them? The lives of so many vampires who wanted nothing more than to be left alone and be happy had been ended, and there were others like Katheryne who might never recover from what had happened to them that night.

Those assholes below us had been offered a home, safety, and acceptance, and they returned the favor by trying to destroy us. They were getting exactly what they deserved.

I

Well, it could've been worse.

A little over a week after the attempted takeover of Los Angeles by religious jackoffs, we'd taken in the sum total of what they'd done to us, and it was depressing. Repairs to LA itself were already beginning, with many of our tireless half-bloods keeping watchful eyes on the whole process, not only keeping the work from getting tangled in red tape, but taking care to continue the program of misinformation already deeply entrenched with the police and media.

We were burying the truth and burying it deeply. Relentlessly, even. The covies wanted to expose vampires to the world in order to "earn" the hatred of the mortal populace and thus fulfill one of the Goddess' commandments; each shovelful of dirt we threw on the truth was another victory, however small, against the covies.

It was an absolute frenzy down in the Catacombs, which had taken heavy damage in many areas, and some of the vampires who resided more or less permanently underground had started work mere hours after the Battle of Los Angeles had been won. Not only would we rebuild the city, but we'd make it even better than before, and we'd make sure nobody ever found out what really happened… if only to spite the covies.

The last time Stacey and I had encountered this kind of senseless madness had been at Runquist, a little village in eastern France; it had been an absolute massacre. Nothing had been left standing, and we'd been helpless against the might of those zealot bastards. We'd narrowly escaped death, and in the end, there'd been nothing but ashes and ruin. As much as I hated to see the damage done to LA, it was heartening to know that damage would be repaired. We'd mourn for the dead, rebuild our *community*, both above and below ground, and continue as we had before.

There were quite a few older vampires in the LA community, and we'd spent much of our lives rebuilding in the wake of destruction, so for many of us, this was old hat. We knew the score and got on with it, especially since it was the best way to cope.

We'd lost a full third of our vampire population to the covies, between killings and conversions. There wasn't a vampire in the city who hadn't lost friends to the covies, and as much as death is a part of the life of a vampire, losing a friend is never easy, especially if that loss is prefaced by betrayal.

The death of friends for an immortal is different than it is for any mortal. When we make friends with mortals, we go into the friendship knowing full well we'll outlive them and prepare for it from the beginning. But when you're immortal, you assume—hope—other immortals you befriend will be around forever.

I fully expect Stacey to be my constant companion and tag-along idiot well into the next millennium and beyond, and I refuse to even consider the idea of losing Clarisse. When one of the people you expect to be part of your existence forever suddenly disappears, it can be even more wrenching than it is for mortals. Paradoxically, we can deal with the grief and continue forth with our existence better than most mortals can—a benefit of our long experience—though it doesn't hurt any less.

One person who was hurting most keenly was Katheryne.

We were all deeply worried about her, and to be frank, there were times I wondered whether she'd survived the Battle of Los Angeles with her sanity intact. In the days following the battle, she became painfully silent, withdrawn and brooding, locking herself in some personal hell she couldn't get out of.

I was at a loss as to what to do. I'd never seen her like this before; she was always quiet, but not to this extreme. Katheryne was so bound up in her own mind and emotions that even Clarisse had a hard time touching upon anything other than a tremendous, unrelenting feeling of guilt threatening to crush her completely. But Clarisse didn't need to tell Donita that.

Though tearing apart the covy sleeper cell had been good for the gypsy, it had only been good for emptying out some of her rage. With each passing night, she worried herself sicker and sicker over her longtime best friend and lover, and was a seething mass of nerves, never resting, never feeding, and never doing anything but despairing over Katheryne. If this kept up, we were going to lose both of them.

After Dorian and I had departed from the cavern, Katheryne and Donita had stood silently in there for hour after hour, as if waiting for Wade to pop up from behind a rock and yell, "Surprise!"

That never happened.

After the sun had gone down, Katheryne had stepped up to the inky black hole in the wall of the cavern and had called out Wade's name, softly at first, but with increasing fervor until she was wailing it over and over at the top of her lungs. Then she had opened up with her magick on the cavern wall above the hole, and blasted down a huge pile of rock that completely blocked the entryway to subterranean depths unknown.

I heard this from one of the vampires standing guard outside the cavern, but even then it gave me a chill, especially when she told me that Katheryne kept screaming "It's my fault!" over and over while she was hammering at the rock. After that, Katheryne and Donita had left the cavern, which had in turn been sealed with explosives by the vampire guards, and Katheryne had slipped into her nearly comatose silence.

Since then, we hadn't left her alone. Not because of fear of suicide, but rather out of a fear she might withdraw from the world completely, something of which Donita was acutely afraid. Katheryne had largely overcome her guilt from what had happened to her in the past through Donita's love and acceptance, but this had brought it all back and, from what Donita said, Katheryne was even more withdrawn and morose than she'd been when she'd first met her.

The two had met during a gathering of magick-users who'd come together to combat an ancient evil known as Croatoan during the days prior to the Salem witch trials. Previous to that, Katheryne had lived as a recluse, only coming out of her hiding in the forests to occasionally feed. Donita feared Katheryne might end up doing that again, as she knew that Katheryne now thought herself to be a threat to us.

To the gentle half-vampire, Wade's death only served to confirm what she'd once believed about herself after the deaths of her family. Donita was afraid Katheryne might forever leave us *because* she loved us and wanted us to remain safe and sound. The witch had so much magick power boiling inside of her that she couldn't control it, beyond using it like a hammer. Donita had once told us that if she really wanted to, Katheryne could probably level a city block in a single blast. That much power and so little control over it had left Katheryne with the perpetual fear that she'd hurt somebody she cared about.

She'd made so much progress in working her way through that fear, in letting herself relax and simply be herself—and the covies had fucked up all those decades, those centuries, of effort in a single night.

So we stayed with Katheryne. Not only to keep an eye on her, but also to let her know we didn't blame her for anything. What had happened was a tragic accident and nothing more.

Other than what poor Katheryne was going through, and the rebuilding of the city and the Catacombs, things were rather peaceful around LA in the days following the battle. For those of us who weren't actively involved with the reconstruction or misinformation management, it was a time of rest, which we needed. We all took turns sitting with Katheryne and taking her with us wherever we went—she always went along without protest, but never added anything, either. She simply sat or followed along wordlessly, and there was something about her silence that disturbed me.

It wasn't the silence of one who was catatonic or unable to speak, but rather that of one who saw, heard, and was fully aware of everything around her, but wouldn't allow herself to become part of it. For Katheryne to do that around her friends—whom she'd always cherished in the past—gave me chills.

That fearful feeling went through me yet again as I watched Katheryne sitting on the ledge of the long-abandoned office building she, Clarisse, and I were atop. She was only a few feet from us, but she may as well have been a million light-years away. Clarisse and I had taken Katheryne hunting, hoping that some fresh blood might perk her up a bit. Not only that, she hadn't had anything in days, not since before the night of the battle, and she was looking pale, even for her.

Thus far, the prospect of a hunt and fresh blood hadn't gotten much of a reaction out of her. She'd followed Clarisse and me, but she'd shown no interest in any of the potential victims we'd eyed, and hadn't even said a word since we'd left the Catacombs.

Against the bright lighting of a neon sign on a hotel across the street, Katheryne, in silhouette, looked like a person-shaped black hole...an unsettling comparison.

Clarisse had her arms crossed and was biting her lip as she watched the witch sit on the ledge. "No matter how hard I try, all I can feel in her is guilt," Clarisse murmured. "It's like who she is is being eaten up by it, and when it's done, there won't be anything left."

I said nothing. What was there to say?

Donita had told Katheryne endlessly that what happened wasn't her fault and that nobody blamed her, just like what had happened to her family hadn't been her fault, but Katheryne wasn't buying it. What was worse was that she was even beating herself up over the loss of her family again, which Donita had thought the other half-blood had finally gotten over years ago.

I'd been there during one of the times that Donita was pleading with her to snap out of it, and when the gypsy had told her none of it was her fault, Katheryne replied with, "If I hadn't been there, none of them would have died."

I hated to admit it, but that did hold some harsh truth to it. Katheryne's family had been killed by a rival clan of magick-users when they'd found out how powerful Katheryne had become when she'd been turned into a half-vampire. As for Wade... The circumstances in both cases were beyond cruel.

Donita was right: it wasn't Katheryne's fault just because she had been there or because she had been trying to save a friend's life. I couldn't understand why Katheryne kept punishing herself for what had happened on both occasions, when it was so obvious that she wasn't to blame.

Maybe it wasn't so obvious to her, or her heart. I clenched my fist tightly, not even knowing who or what to be angry at for what Katheryne was feeling.

Clarisse put her hand on my shoulder. "If only every problem was something that you could beat up, huh?" she asked, and I grunted.

If only. I remembered Brandi's words from the other night... what Katheryne needed was redemption. But the covies were dead and gone. So was Wade. How in the hell could I give Katheryne what she needed?

Then a thought hit me. I couldn't give her redemption, but maybe I could give her something else.

I gave Clarisse a kiss on the cheek, then walked over to Katheryne and sat on the ledge next to her, taking in the view of this section of the city. It was somewhat run-down and garish, but still very much a part of the Los Angeles I loved.

Clarisse quietly stood back while Katheryne and I sat, and after I'd been next to the witch for a few minutes, I turned to her. The red neon of the sign across the street lit up the smooth features of Katheryne's face as she watched the activity in the streets below. Or at least it looked like she was watching. Her eyes didn't move as she sat, and I knew that what she saw wasn't what was in the streets below, but inside of her.

"Immortality carries a price," I said, watching her. "We watch friends, comrades, and lovers all die while we live on, and the older we get, the more it piles up. Those who can't handle it usually die by their own hand or do something stupid to get themselves killed. Those that can...we pass through the ages, we do, see, and know things nobody else can dream of, and we weather challenges that'd destroy any mortal. The price is heavy, but what we get in return is more than worth it. I think you know that."

Katheryne said nothing and made no indication she'd heard me, but I continued, "Maybe you curse yourself for what you are right now, you think you're a freak, you're a danger to us, but you're not. We don't blame you for what happened, nor do we love you any less. We're not holding anything against you—*you're* holding you against you because you failed at something."

I hated to use the word "failed," but I didn't want to treat her like a child either by softening up what I said, so I forged onward.

"You can't do that," I said. "You're wasting your gift of immortality and you're wasting yourself."

Katheryne didn't look at me, but she very softly murmured, "What happened is my fault."

"So because Wade didn't make it out of the cavern you're going to just give up?" I leaned closer. "You're going to let what you still have slip by?"

She said nothing.

This was the first chance I'd had to talk to her one on one since Wade's death and I was determined to make the most of it. I couldn't just stand by and watch someone I loved slip into a living death; I couldn't let her go without trying.

"When life takes something from you—whether it's your fault or not—you learn how to stop it from happening again. You dig in and hold on to what you still have more tightly than ever, and fight twice as fiercely as before, and you keep going. No matter how much it hurts, you grow and adapt and you push the pain back and never let up. As soon as you let up, you're dead and gone. You haven't given up yet, or otherwise you wouldn't still be here."

"Maybe I should," she whispered, her soft voice breaking.

"Because of something that you think is your fault? Because you didn't perform how you thought you should when it counted? You'd give it up because of that?" I asked her, my voice hard. "That's bullshit."

"Easy for you to say," she replied, still staring off at nothing. This was the most I'd heard her say in days, and I was hoping that maybe I'd reached something within her.

I laughed at her words, letting an edge of bitterness creep into my voice. Though I was more than happy with my life, there had been plenty of pain to endure in my time, and it wasn't all that hard to reach down and dredge some of it up.

"Easy?" I asked. "Surely you don't think my entire existence has been spent getting into trouble with Stacey and laughing about it afterward. It hasn't all been fun. I've bled and cried more than my share in my days, and I've had more than a couple of failures. I was lamenting over my various screw-ups long before you were ever even thought of."

"You?" Katheryne asked, turning to look at me at long last. Behind the sadness and guilt in her eyes there was desperation, an undying hunger to be loved and to be accepted, and it was so earnest and intense that my own heart ached for her. She looked tired, more so than I'd ever seen her, but her eyes burned bright. "But you're untouchable," she whispered, "Nobody can do anything to you. You just laugh it off or you knock them out of your way."

"I'm far from untouchable and I'm far from perfect," I said gently. "I just hide it and get around it better than most."

"Truthfully?" she asked. Her desperation had moved to her voice as well, and I could feel the sheer intensity of it within her as she leaned closer to me, like a drowning victim reaching for a lifeline.

I pumped every iota of sincerity I had into my tone as I spoke the next words. "You're my friend; I'd never lie to you."

The witch's eyes became huge, and I felt a thrill within me as I realized that maybe I'd made some progress with her.

I hesitated for a moment then said, "It wasn't all that long ago that people I loved dearly died because I couldn't react fast enough."

Katheryne simply stared in disbelief. I met her gaze, and her disbelief rapidly dissipated.

"How—" she began, but a high-pitched cry cut through the air, and Katheryne, Clarisse, and I all perked up instantly, looking around wildly. That hadn't been just any cry: it had been that of a small child, and it had very clearly shouted for help.

One of the rules in Los Angeles was that no vampire would ever, *ever* raise a fang or nail against a child for any reason, would never even look at a child threateningly, and if a child was in peril, they would do whatever was in their power to save said child. We cherished children and defended and watched out for them in every way we could. Children—even the obnoxious little twerps—were the future, as trite as that may sound, and they hadn't learned to hate or deal out mindless cruelty and destruction like so many adults, and were innocent and not worthy of our wrath or our hunger.

The child's cry came from the other side of the building, down in the alley, and the three of us all hurried across the gravel of the rooftop at blinding speed. When we looked over the side of the building, Clarisse audibly gasped at the sight two stories below, and I snarled with such ferocity I surprised even myself.

"*Frizz!*" I roared. He'd really done it this time!

Down in the alley below, the electric-haired vampire I'd grown to loathe was holding a young Asian girl who had to be less than eight years old. She was struggling madly in his grasp, now unable to scream for help, as he had a hand over her mouth.

When we'd first hit the edge of the rooftop, he'd had his mouth next to her neck, but at my shout, he'd looked upward, first in surprise then growing horror as he realized exactly what sort of trouble he'd gotten himself into and who it was who had caught him. He was fucked and he knew it.

"*Put. Her. Down,*" I growled from the roof.

As soon as the little girl was safely out of his arms, I was going to kill him. Finally, finally he'd screwed up hugely and I was the one to catch him. At long last, I had all the justification I needed to rub him off the face of this planet. That incompetent, low-life, *son of a bitch.* There was plenty of other, much more suitable prey out in the LA night—what the fuck was he doing looking to feed on a kid?

I was nearly trembling with rage, and my eyes were probably glowing brighter than any stoplight in the city. When I was through with Frizz, there wouldn't be enough left of him for a decent bowl of dog food.

"Wait, I didn't do anything!" Frizz screeched, defensively holding the frightened girl, who was dressed in footed pink pajamas, in front of him. "I didn't feed from her, honest!"

I didn't want to hear it. I pointed to the girl. "*Put her down.*"

The poor kid was completely terrified, and that made me even angrier than I already was. She was probably scared to death of me too—at that moment I was definitely a damned scary sight with fully bared fangs, hands bent into claws, and burning red eyes. Those same eyes never went off of Frizz for a split second, even though he kept looking away from me.

Frizz was starting to look as terrified as the girl, and with damned good reason. "But wait, hold on," he gibbered, "I didn't do anything!"

Katheryne leaped down into the alley across from Frizz, who nearly jumped out of his skin, screaming in surprise. She held out her arms and motioned toward the girl, "Give her to me please," she asked so softly I could hardly hear her. "Don't take her from her family. Please."

Despite the situation, it was wonderful to see Katheryne doing something besides sitting and brooding. Frizz regarded Katheryne with considerably less fear than he did me, and maybe even a hint of disgust. Or maybe it was just one of those odd expressions he always seemed to wear. The gawky vampire looked first to Katheryne then to me.

"Do it," I snapped, "Your existence depends on it. Do it and I won't kill you."

"You won't?" he asked, his eyes wide.

"Do it and I won't kill you," I repeated.

After several long seconds of indecision, Frizz set the little girl down onto the ground, who ran away from him and headlong into Katheryne's arms. The blond half-blood grabbed hold of the child and held her tightly, and relief descended on me. I hadn't realized how worked up I was over the little girl until she was in Katheryne's arms. Now it was time to get down to business.

When I started to jump off the building, Clarisse—who'd been strangely quiet the entire time—put her hand on my shoulder. "Wait a second, there's some—"

"Not now," I said then I leaped.

If Frizz had been a mortal, he would have pissed his pants as I was coming down through the night air toward him, guaranteed.

"Nooo!" he squawked out in the brief seconds he had before impact. "You said you wouldn't kill me!"

If only I could have taken a picture of his expression and framed it somewhere nice.

I landed on him, *hard*, and knocked the little bastard to the ground with twin blows from my fists. Then I dragged him to his feet by his collar and held him up in front of me, just to savor the moment.

"I lied," I snarled, giving him my widest fanged grin. "Not only are you an incompetent idiot and a total waste of skin, you're also *stupid!*"

I cocked back a fist and hit him in the face, and he went flying down to the other end of the dirty alley, away from Katheryne and the little girl. Though I hadn't turned around since I'd landed, Katheryne already had turned her back to the violence so she could shield the little girl from witnessing it. The would-be child-killer slammed into a dumpster, his momentum creating a massive dent in the side of it, then fell to the ground on his hands and knees, looking every bit the pitiful wreck he was.

"I can explain!" he cried, shaking his head and trying to regain his bearings.

"Steele!" Clarisse yelled at me. I ignored her.

"Ask me if I care," I said as I stomped down the alley toward Frizz. The first punch was purely for my own pleasure, and when I got hold of him again, he was going to be dead before I let go. I'm sure Frizz knew it too. He staggered to his feet and started to stumble away from me. I kept going at the same pace, a relentless killing machine, unstoppable and unswayable. As far as Frizz was concerned, that was the most flawless analogy in the world.

Clarisse's voice was lost amid the roar of unleashed anger, and I made my way down the alley after Frizz, who turned and ran like hell. I laughed and took off, leaving Clarisse, Katheryne, and the child behind.

One thing I grudgingly had to give Frizz was that he was fast. He managed to keep ahead of me as we ran through the twisting gamut of back alleys, leaping over fences, plowing through trashcans, and splashing through puddles. I didn't yell after Frizz as I chased him, wanting my silence to eat at him and cause him to make a mistake so I could run him down and rip him apart.

If not for the maze of alleys, I would have snagged him almost immediately, but all the turns and twists gave him a decent lead. No matter, he'd be dead soon enough—he couldn't run from me forever. I was enjoying myself immensely. My heart was pumping like a drum, my blood was red hot, and my muscles were singing the praises of the workout I was giving them. There was nothing like a good hunt to make a vampire feel great.

As I ran after Frizz, I thought that maybe this was just what I needed to take the remaining bad taste of the battle out of my mouth—hunting down and killing one of the annoyances of my life, forever ending his foolish antics and sloppy feeding techniques. This was to be a good night, with my having made some headway with Katheryne and the upcoming execution of Frizz, as well as helping to save the life of a little girl. A fine night indeed.

The wretch made a sudden turn down a side alley, and let out a bloodcurdling scream as soon as he was gone from my sight. I slowed down slightly and when I made the corner, a familiar smell hit me and I almost ran right into Frizz, who was screaming bloody murder, caught in the clutches of nothing less than a revenant.

Seriously?

I'd wondered about the presence of more covy sleeper cells in the city, as a few disturbances down in the Catacombs had been reported. It had seemed as though someone or something had been trying to get into the sealed tunnels leading to the hole where Wade had met his untimely demise. Some vampires had reported sounds of rocks shifting around and some of the rubble looked to have been moved around, but nothing definitive. Until now.

"Oh right, like I'm *that* fucking stupid," I said as I charged the "revenant." These morons really needed to get a new schtick.

Without even dropping Frizz, the revenant lashed out with one of its frying-pan-sized hands and hit me hard enough that I actually blacked out. It wasn't for very long—maybe a couple of seconds—but I woke facedown on the broken asphalt and dirt of the alley floor, blood trickling out of my ear and feeling like I'd had a bus dropped on my head.

Okay, maybe I *was* that fucking stupid.

The revenant roared, jerking me back to full awareness. Instinct kicked in and I scuttled backward, taking a glancing blow from the revenant across my shoulders, bouncing my head off ground. But my leather jacket took the brunt of the hit, and I drunkenly got back to my feet, backpedaling the whole way.

Frizz had been tossed aside, forgotten in favor of more interesting prey. He was busy trying to extricate himself from a pile of garbage cans as the revenant advanced on me...my luck, the dick would run free while I got my ass kicked again. Fuck that. I had to get outta here and find Clarisse and Katheryne.

Hell, maybe if Katheryne saved my ass my vaporizing a revenant, it'd help her snap out of her funk. That thought in mind, I turned and ran—

Right into another revenant.

I barely had time to get out a heartfelt, "Oh, fuck *me*," before one of its big hands swatted me upside the head, tossed me through the air and slammed me into a wall hard enough to make my world spin.

I tried to push myself up onto my knees, but before I could even move more than a few inches, the revenant was on me again, pounding on me with his huge fists like a piledriver, over and over again. I managed to get one of my own fists into the action, and popped the revenant a good, solid shot to the face. That drew a surprised grunt that quickly turned into an angry snarl, which was in turn cut off by my other fist hitting it in the throat.

I swept one of my legs out and came close to knocking the vampiric mockery off its feet, which caused it to stumble mightily. I slammed the heel of my hand into its kneecap, and drove forward with as much force as I could muster from my awkward position. I heard a satisfying crack followed by a scream of pain. The big bastard hit the ground as its leg gave out underneath it. A few more frantic kicks and I'd shoved it away from me and I was back onto my feet again, ready to run.

I didn't get the chance to take more than three steps, however, as *another* revenant came charging out of the side alley, hit me like a linebacker and slammed me against the alley wall. My head got hit again, and I grayed out. The revenant pulled me away from the wall and flung me against the ground, and the world faded away to black silence.

One night around a week after the Battle of Los Angeles, Clarisse and I headed out to a less-urbanized area in Pasadena within spitting distance of Mount Wilson. It was a preternaturally clear night out, and the full moon shone down upon the landscape, bathing it with an ethereal silver coating.

I parked my Chevelle up on a nice rock outcropping reaching out from a wooded area with a passable road running through it and small picnic areas scattered liberally around. It was reminiscent of any number of places where people would go park, and there were times when we came here that Clarisse swore up and down she'd seen this place in some movie once where it was used for just that purpose, though she couldn't remember which one.

Out here, we were deliciously alone. Like stupid kids, we chased each other around in the moonlight, reveling in nature and each other. As I chased her through the edge of the woods, she rolled, flipped, and did a lightning fast about-face. From there, she tackled me to the ground and nipped at my neck as we twirled around on top of the dirt.

She was my angel, my Clarisse, and I'd never let her go.

I had loved Alena long before I had first set my eyes on Clarisse, and though a part of me would always love her, Clarisse fulfilled a need within my heart and soul nobody else could. She was fierce and determined, yet soft and soothing. She was intelligent and cunning, but never cold and calculating. She had a childlike quality to her, tempered by her years of experience and maturity. She was forever young, yet wiser than many twice her age. She was all I wanted in a woman, and far more than I'd ever hoped to find again. I would walk through fire for her and fight a thousand armies if I had to, as long as she stayed by my side forever.

"Did I ever tell you that I love you?" I asked her as we lay side by side, looking up at the stars.

She laughed softly. "Only several times a day, and it never gets old. If you promise to never stop telling me that, I'll never quit telling you that I love you too." She reached over, laid her arm across my chest, and curled up next to me. I leaned my head over and rested my cheek on her soft hair, which had the same scent as a warm spring day out in the country. Even after all these years, I still remembered what that was like.

We lay in silence, listening to the barely audible hum of the city in the distance and the wind softly rustling through the trees. "How are you?" Clarisse asked me quietly.

I knew what she meant. Though I'd been relaxing somewhat over the course of the week following the attack, I'd still been strung pretty tightly, wondering about the covies and whether they'd be back. I was able to enjoy myself for the most part, though the voice at the back of my head kept whispering about the future. I also wasn't fully at peace with Wade's death... Wouldn't be for a long time.

"I'm managing."

"Liar," she said, snuggling closer to me. "You're as worried about whether there's another shoe to drop as Famine is whenever it's time for a bath. Like I've told you before, lover, you can't hide anything from me. I love you too much not to notice."

There were times it seemed she knew how I was feeling better than I did, and she was right, as always. I said nothing, kissed her, and gently ran my fingers through her hair.

"Good reply," she whispered after our lips broke contact. She softly kissed my jawbone and slowly moved down along it, toward my neck, sending the old familiar tingle along my spine. "I can't fix the problems of the world, but I can make them go away for a while," she murmured to me. This angel definitely had a pair of horns and a pointy tail to go with her wings.

She sank her fangs into my neck, and I exhaled sharply as she drank of me. My mind start to slip into hers, our essences entwining. We'd been feeding from one another heavily over the past week, developing quite an affinity for each other at close range. The outside world stopped existing, washed away by the rush of my blood in my ears and the beat of our hearts pounding in sync. Clarisse slid her fangs from my neck, rolled over on top of me, and kissed me fiercely, the fingers of our hands locked together.

As soon as the kiss ended, I put my hands on her shoulders, and pulled her neck to my lips. I kissed her neck gently then with more energy, finally breaking through her flesh with my fangs and taking her blood into me. She gasped, holding my shoulders with a grip of steel, and with a sudden, swift move, we rolled, and I ended up on top of her.

"I love you," she whispered, reaching up beneath my jacket and running her nails down my back in the manner she knew I loved.

I drew my fangs from her neck and gazed into her sapphire eyes. "Never leave me," I said. "There's no one out there like you."

She smiled warmly. "I wouldn't leave you for the world," she replied as she encircled me with her arms. "Never stop loving me."

"Promise," I said, and we kissed again. Within moments, I was feeding from her again, and she sighed so softly I barely heard her.

This mutual feeding always had a powerful effect, and I felt her surge through my consciousness as I absorbed her blood. She flowed into my mind like liquid warmth, further separating me from the rest of the world. I surged through her, letting myself get carried away in the surge and throb of our love.

We wrapped around each other, physically, mentally, and emotionally, and we ceased to exist as separate individuals, becoming one. Everything was lost under the hot haze of our bond, and we were happy.

Then the heat began to fade, and I tried to reach out and hold onto it, but it was flowing away like quicksilver through my hands.

When I called out to Clarisse, I couldn't feel her in my mind anymore. She was there, but she was a distant presence, and what I could feel of her was strongly edged with fear. I had the terrible idea that the covies had captured Clarisse and were taking her away from me, and I fought against the darkness, which only moments before had been glowing, loving warmth. This couldn't happen again, not like what they had done to Alena.

No matter how much I struggled and clawed at the blackness, I couldn't escape it, and it wrapped around me like a suffocating blanket. I felt like I was trying to swim in cement at the bottom of some primeval cavern that had never seen the light of day, and it was so cold and black my blood began to freeze solid within my veins.

As even my own thoughts began to slow, I could still feel Clarisse and her fear. I summoned every last bit of strength and resolve I had to fight against the freezing cold and infinite black, and I screamed her name before the iciness ensnared me.

"Clarisse!"

"Steele?" The voice reached down to me in the cold and the dark, penetrating even the icy depths of infinity, and I stirred.

Clarisse? Had that been her? How had she found me?

As I heard the almost musical sound of her speak my name again, I realized the ice had melted during my slumber. I now only felt coolness on my skin, and a soft, steady rocking motion like that of the ocean's waves. I lay in the darkness for a time, riding on the waves, and became aware I was no longer in that frozen cave—the scents of the forest tickled my nose and I could hear the crackle of brush being moved.

I also heard grunts and an occasional low growl, and the clean smell of the forest was cut with a darker, cloying aroma every now and then. It was as though I were among a gathering of animals, but animals never had that scent of death about them. As I tried to piece all of this together, I wondered where Clarisse was, if she was all right wherever she was at, and just as I did, I heard her voice again.

"Steele? Are you there?"

After she'd spoken, I felt a soft kiss on my cheek and inhaled the gentle fragrance of my lover's hair, and everything came rushing back to me. With a start I remembered the rooftop, the little girl, Frizz, and the revenants in the alley, and my eyes flew open as I gasped Clarisse's name. With my acute night vision I saw branches and leaves above me, with patches of stars shining through, and I turned my head to the side when I heard Clarisse's voice again. As soon as I turned, I saw her beautiful face looking back at me with a mixture of concern and relief.

"Finally!" she softly exclaimed as our eyes met, and leaned forward to kiss me.

After the all-too-brief kiss, I realized Clarisse was carrying me in her arms as she walked through the forest, and when I glanced around to take in the rest of the surroundings, I saw Katheryne walking along ahead of us, and ahead of her...

When I saw the revenant plodding along, accompanied by a revenant master on one side and a werewolf on the other, an extraordinarily bad feeling ran through me. It got even worse when I heard the footsteps and crunching of foliage coming from behind Clarisse. I returned my eyes to her, and she nodded, knowing exactly what I was thinking.

"We hadn't run them out of LA as entirely as we thought," she said, sounding more annoyed than anything else now that she knew I was okay. "And now that they've got us, they're apparently going to take us to visit their home, since they've already seen ours."

Their home? For a few seconds, I wasn't in Clarisse's arms at all, but in the back of the cart in which the Crimson Order had transported Stacey and myself when they'd taken us to their keep. I could hear the revenant guard growling at us, barely held in check by its master, and feel the cart moving over the rough road and the clatter of the horses' hooves as they hauled the cart along to its destination. Mercifully, it only lasted a few seconds, and I was in Clarisse's arms once more.

"Put me down," I told her softly. "I still feel woozy and I need to walk the rest of this off."

My head still rang like the bells of a cathedral. The revenants must have really pummeled the tar out of me, as I felt almost as bad as I had following the extermination of the sleeper cell. Then again, what was happening around me wasn't exactly the most comforting thing in the world to wake to.

"Yeah, you're woozy, but that normally doesn't make people shudder, especially vampires, and especially you," Clarisse said so quietly even I could barely hear her, and our gazes met. I wasn't even aware I'd shuddered, but I knew she wouldn't have made it up, and it didn't really surprise me I'd reacted to my remembrance in such a way. "What is it?"

"Spectres from the past," I murmured. This was neither the time nor the place to tell her about what I'd remembered. I'd never shared the story with anybody, and the only other person who knew what had happened during that terrible time was Stacey. Clarisse knew our village had been destroyed, that my lover had been killed, and that Stacey and I had been captured. We'd clawed our way out of it, but beyond those details, she knew nothing.

It wasn't that I was hiding it from her; it was just that I'd never had a reason to tell the tale. Seeing as how I hated even recalling it, I'd never seen the point in telling it to anybody. I'd been about to share it with Katheryne to try help draw her out of her shell and come to terms with herself, but Frizz's idiocy had interrupted that but good. And speaking of Frizz...

"Where's Frizz?" I asked, and Clarisse shrugged.

"Pretty messed up the last time I saw him, and probably dead by now," she said. "When Katheryne and I caught up with you, one of the revenants was tossing you around while its master was trying to get it under control, and another two masters were carrying Frizz away. I didn't see much, but it looked like one of the other revenants nearly tore him apart—he was an absolute bloody mess. Everything happened so fast. We were running after you one second, then the next we were in the middle of a covy convention, with two other revenants and three or four werewolves snarling at us, while the master trying to stop your revenant was yelling at us to stay put."

Though she didn't say it, I could sense the lingering shreds of the fear she'd felt earlier, and I held her just a little bit tighter to help reassure her I was all right now. She gave me a peck on the cheek and one of her beautiful smiles. "Right about that time, this tall, baldheaded vampire in a red robe and one of those scarlet medallions hanging from his neck stepped right into the middle of all of this and got it under control with only a few sentences. I don't know who he is, but everybody around here seems to listen to him."

"Where is he?" I craned my head and tried to catch a glimpse of this character.

"Up front, leading our little party," answered Clarisse. "Once he had everything organized, he herded us all into the back of a moving truck and had us all taken out of town as fast as possible. After we'd driven for a while, we came to a stop on the side of the road by the woods, pretty much in the middle of nowhere, and Baldy had everybody but the driver get out and follow him. We've been marching for well over an hour now."

"Where are we?" I was bothered by the knowledge that so much had happened while I'd been knocked out. It wasn't comforting to have been thrown into unconsciousness for so long, either, not when one was approaching two millennia in age. It was one thing to get my ass kicked; it was another to be taken out of the game entirely. That nagged at me.

"Somewhere by Mount Wilson is my best guess," Clarisse said. "I didn't get much of a chance to look for landmarks, but that's what my instincts are muttering, so I'm going to trust them until I see something that tells me otherwise."

Now I leaned close to Clarisse's ear. "How's Katheryne?" I nodded toward the witch in front of us, who was silently treading along without so much as a sidelong glance.

"Dead quiet. She took the time to run out into the street, flag down a police car, and hand the little girl to the cop before she ran after and caught up with me, just a few seconds before we ran into the covies. But she hasn't spoken a word since she asked Frizz to give the little girl to her." Clarisse shook her head. "I feel so bad for her. This is one of the worst possible things that could have happened. I can't feel much of her, but her guilt's gone way back up again. I think she's somehow blaming herself for us being caught."

"What?" How the hell was that her fault? If it was anybody's fault we'd been captured, it was mine because I didn't get out of the way of the revenants in time.

"Because she didn't use her magick to blast the covies before they had us surrounded, because she wasn't able to pull a rabbit out of her hat when Baldy told us that if we tried anything funny, he'd have the revenant master's pet tear you to shreds. Because she's locked herself into a vicious cycle where everything that goes wrong is her fault in her eyes, I guess," Clarisse said, dismay in her voice. She shut her eyes for a second and bit her lip. "I just don't know. The only thing I do know is that she's hurting right now, and she's just piling it up on herself even higher as the time passes."

I watched Katheryne walk along for a moment, then said, "Put me down, for real this time. I need to get on my feet again—it'll help clear my thoughts."

She nodded. "I'm setting him back onto his feet now," Clarisse said loudly, drawing the attention of our escorts. "So don't any of you morons take this as an escape attempt."

Several of the revenants growled menacingly, as did the werewolves, while the one revenant master turned as he walked and looked at us warningly. The sheer cockiness and complete confidence on his rough-hewn face made me want to kill him right then and there. We weren't holding any of the cards at the moment, so I contented myself with merely glaring back at him.

"The male heretic is awake and is going to be back on his feet in a moment," the revenant master called out when he'd taken his eyes off me.

A male from somewhere ahead of Katheryne—who glanced back at me when she'd heard I was awake again, then guiltily looked away—replied, "You would do well to keep an eye on him, Wilkesdon, for he has quite the reputation as a troublemaker." The voice was rough, commanding, and sounded mildly familiar to me, though I couldn't place it.

I shook my head. More covies, more converts. How many of those pricks were left, anyway? These guys were worse than herpes. Murderous, religious herpes, at that.

"Don't worry about it," the revenant master known as Wilkesdon said, looking back at me and grinning. "They're not going anywhere but where we want them to."

Clarisse eased me to the ground as she walked, not slowing down, and when she dropped me on my feet, I immediately picked up the pace and stayed even with her, taking her hand and holding it tightly. My legs felt weak for the first few steps, but I rapidly regained my steadiness, and less than a minute later I felt more or less back to normal.

As I walked, I tried to get a glimpse of who this Baldy was, but the view was blocked by Katheryne, the werewolf, the revenant, and his master. I could see a few other revenants and masters up in front of them, and behind us were several werewolves, plus another revenant bringing up the rear. We were totally outnumbered.

Running definitely wouldn't be an especially bright thing to do. If this rough path was on the way to their home base, then they knew these woods far better than us. Not only that, werewolves were master hunter-killers in the wilds, regardless of whether they were familiar with the area in question. As much as I hated it, we'd have to bide our time.

Not only that, but the longer I was awake, the less desire I had to run. It was an odd feeling, as though there was a certain... inevitability to what was happening. No matter what I did, I wasn't going to escape it. I was once again being taken to the home and hearth of a group of mad covies, and what was going to happen would happen, and I accepted it.

I didn't know if this was fatalism on my part, but it calmed me as we walked through the woods, Clarisse and I linked by our hands. I worried about her and Katheryne and what the covies would do to them, but for myself I felt little concern.

It was as if I'd been living on borrowed time since I'd escaped the Crimson Order in the past, and now this new group of covies, who ignorantly carried the emblem of the Order, would try to finish what the Order had started. It was like fate was playing an ironic little joke on me, and I snorted at that idea.

I don't believe in fate, my life is my own and the choices I make are mine—no cosmic force guides my actions or thoughts. Still, as we trudged along, I couldn't shake the feeling that this was supposed to happen, that the plans for what was occurring now had been laid down and predetermined a long time ago, and after all of this time, it was coming together at long last.

As I thought about this, I began to ponder why the covies hadn't simply killed us when they'd caught us. Taking prisoners certainly hadn't been in their game plan when they'd invaded Los Angeles, and if they thought taking hostages would get them leverage against the vampires of LA, they were going to be sorely disappointed. The community wouldn't be bullied by pussy terrorist tactics, and wouldn't back down if the covies threatened our deaths.

They'd try to rescue us, I was certain of that, but if it came down to the survival of the Los Angeles vampire community and the three of us, the community would let us go. They wouldn't like it, but they knew full well we wouldn't want them to sacrifice the entire vampire population of the city for the sake of three. Mr. Spock had gotten it right in *The Wrath Of Khan*—the needs of the many outweighed the needs of the few or the one. It was cruel arithmetic, but survival was a harsh mistress.

The more I thought about it, the more I became convinced we were being taken hostage. The unseen voice had mentioned my "reputation as a troublemaker," so they obviously knew who we were. If they knew that, they'd know we were highly regarded in the community and therefore would hypothetically make good bargaining chips. The fuckers. They couldn't beat us outright, so they were going to resort to cowardly tactics to try to take the city—tactics that were going to blow up in their faces. We might die, but the community as a whole would survive…and avenge us. I hoped I was still alive to see it blow up in their faces.

"Incompetents, the whole sorry lot of them," I muttered, and Clarisse gave my hand a squeeze.

"True enough, lover," she murmured back, "but for the moment they've got us outgunned."

"It's times like this that I hate you for your rationality and level head," I said, not without humor. "Moments like this are when I wish I had Stacey and his love of smashing, bashing, and utter mayhem. It'd be suicide, yes, but at least I wouldn't have to sit back and wait to see what was next."

"You two talk too damned much!" Wilkesdon barked back at us with a malevolent scowl. "Shut up before I have to separate you!"

I fixed gazes with Wilkesdon and regarded him with infinite calm and an equal measure of contempt. "How long since you turned?" I asked softly. "A week? Two? I've worn my fangs since before the Romans were in their graves. If it weren't for all of your buddies around you, you'd already be dead by my hand."

As soon as I started to speak, Clarisse gripped my hand hard enough to crush steel, no pun intended, but I pressed on. If it was one thing I hated in this universe, it was nothings who thought themselves deities just because they were surrounded by armed compatriots. There was only so much a vampire could take at times.

"Oh yeah?" Wilkesdon gave me a sneer born of overconfidence.

"The way I see it, you'd be dead right now if I hadn't have called my beasties off you."

I narrowed my eyes, and he chuckled.

"It was my two that beat you down like you were a kitten and they were a pair of gorillas. You just remember not to cross me or otherwise I'll sic 'em on you and let 'em finish what they started."

He raised an eyebrow at me, and the revenant next to him growled deeply, as did one of the monsters behind me, and I could guess which ones were his "beasties." The one next to him craned its neck to look at me while it walked, and I felt its blank white eyes boring into me like a diamond-bit drill. I didn't take my gaze off Wilkesdon, though—I wouldn't give him the satisfaction.

He seemed to realize that, and his grin grew oilier. "Or perhaps," he said, clearly relishing the moment, "I'll just sic 'em on this pretty little thing right here, and let you suffer the consequences of that." As soon as he said "pretty little thing" he pointed at Katheryne. "It's not like it'd matter if she was gone or not. She's not even a proper vampire, just some *freak*."

Katheryne said absolutely nothing, and continued to walk as though nothing had happened, but I'd seen the soft slump of her shoulders at Wilkesdon's words, and it had been a needle to my heart.

"*You son of a bitch*," I hissed, "You cold *bastard*." Clarisse held my hand like a vise grip, but that didn't mean a whit to me. "Let's go right now," I snarled, my eyes glowing, "You and me, and bring your pets if you want to—they won't be able to help you one fucking bit when I'm ripping your throat out with my teeth!"

I hissed at him with all of my fury, leaning forward as if to charge, and he stopped short, his revenant with him. The entire group came to a sudden halt as Wilkesdon and I glared each other down. His revenants' growling filled the air, and the one behind me sounded as loud as a jet engine, but I really couldn't have cared less at the moment.

In all of my years, I'd made many improvements to myself and gotten rid of a lot of bad characteristics that had gotten me into trouble in the past, but one thing that I'd never been able to get out of me was my temper. The calmness and feeling of inevitability from earlier was gone now, replaced by a stomping, raging storm of anger that demanded my full, immediate attention, which it got. In a way, it was fascinating how swiftly I could go from feeling like a temple of level-headedness to a snapping, snarling punk of a vampire looking for a fight. Nobody's perfect, I guess.

"Why don't you leave her the hell alone and fuck with someone who *wants* to fight?"

Wilkesdon took a few steps forward to close the gap between us, but he wasn't quite as stupid as I thought he was, as he took care to make sure he wasn't in my immediate lunge range. He was still far enough away he could get behind the nearest revenant if things got ugly.

"You'd better shut your mouth right here and right now!" Wilkesdon bellowed in universal tones of a bully, and I would have bet my life that before becoming a covy, Wilkesdon had been a barroom thug who liked to prey on those weaker than him. "You wouldn't want me to get mad at you!"

"I've fought bigger, badder, and better than you and I've won every time!" I strained to move forward a step, but Clarisse had both hands on my wrist and was pulling back on it as hard as she could, digging her heels into the ground.

Katheryne had also turned to watch the battle, a look of distress on her face, and I felt a pang when I realized she was probably blaming this fight on herself, since I was standing up for her. I couldn't help it, though—she was a good friend and a damned good person, and I couldn't stand by and let her take the abuse.

By now all the werewolves, revenants, and other hooded covies I hadn't seen before were moving in closer to get a view on the action, and the werewolves were grunting and growling in anticipation of a good fight. If I got my hands on Wilkesdon, I'd be disappointing them, because there wouldn't be a fight at all...a slaughter, oh yes, but no fight.

"You couldn't stand up to me or my revenants, *bad-boy,*" Wilkesdon sneered, nodding toward Clarisse. "Even your woman knows that, otherwise she wouldn't be holding you back so much!"

"Clarisse, let me go," I said in a remarkably even tone considering my current state. I gave my wrist a tug to underline my words. "*Now.*"

Her reply was calm and firm. "Don't you tell me to do *anything,*

Steele. You know damned well I don't take orders from anybody but myself."

"Let me go," I repeated, anger seeping back into my voice again. "No."

"Let him go!" Wilkesdon yelled, stomping his foot. The werewolves all let out a howl of agreement with him, while the revenants continued their constant snarling. "Let's see what he can do!"

"Let me go!" I snarled, yanking on my wrist.

Just as I was about to break free, a loud voice split the air. *"Cease this!"* It was a voice of unmistakable and genuine authority, unlike Wilkesdon's, and immediately everybody quieted down, even the werewolves. I got my wrist free, but when I looked toward Wilkesdon, I saw a face behind him that made me stop dead in my tracks.

The red robe and medallion were as I remembered from a century ago, and though the hair on the head was gone and there was a set of three scars passing across one eye, with another across the throat, the face was the same as the one seared into my memory.

"Akrath," I rasped, not believing my eyes.

Akrath didn't quite smile as he nodded. "Indeed," he replied coolly. "I'm honored you remember me—I certainly could never forget you." He reached up to briefly touch the scars above and below his eye. "The last time I actually set my eyes upon your raggedy face, I was burning alive. Thankfully, your attempt on my life was for naught. I advise you, the next time you're out to kill somebody, make certain you perform the task right the first time. Things have a way of—" And now he did smile, the bastard. "Coming back to haunt you."

He was content to let me stare for a few more moments as he turned and scowled at Wilkesdon. "You may be a controller of revenants, Wilkesdon, but that gives you no right to create problems. You follow my orders, and do no more. One as young as you has absolutely no business whatsoever displaying this level of impudence—do *not* incur my wrath, Wilkesdon. You will not find it a pleasant thing to weather..."

Akrath's voice trailed off to a savage whisper and fire in his eyes froze into solid ice. His enraged yet sub-zero countenance was almost enough to make me shiver. Akrath apparently hadn't mellowed over the years, and that didn't bode well for me, nor Clarisse and Katheryne, who were certainly guilty by association.

Wilkesdon—so full of piss and vinegar just a few moments ago—wilted under Akrath's gaze. He mumbled an apology of some sort then took his place by the revenant he'd been walking next to earlier, avoiding further eye contact with the baldheaded vampire. After Akrath had decided the revenant master had been put in his place, he said, "Never forget who is in control. You are only a cog in the great clockwork that is the Order, and just as a faulty cog can be replaced, so can you. I will not repeat myself. If you cross the line again, you will die.

"Now that that particular piece of business has been taken care of." Akrath looked back at me, where I still stood from my aborted charge. "I'll ask you and your friends to foment no further disruptions, unless you'd prefer to have one of your female companions disposed of by one of the revenants or werewolves." His smile made my skin crawl.

"You coward," I hissed.

He shrugged. "Call it what you want, but I dare say it will achieve the results I desire. You are problematic, to put it mildly, but predictable in your own way."

I backed up to stand by Clarisse again, and Katheryne remained where she was, not even looking at Akrath, but staring off in the woods somewhere. "What do you want with us?"

"It's not so much what I want of you," Akrath answered. "If I had my preference, you'd be dead right now, but someone else demands your presence. Someone you'd marked for dead, as a matter of fact. You and your ilk aren't as adept at killing your foes as you like to think. But I shan't go into that now, for we must be on our way before the toxic rays of dawn outrace us to our lair."

Akrath paused then added, with a great deal of relish, "You're now the guests of the Crimson Order. Enjoy our hospitality."

And there it was.

II

I glared at the cell door as it clanked shut in its stone frame, wishing I could fire lasers out of my eyes. I would have shot Akrath directly in the face as he peered in at us through the door's little barred window.

"Just keep this in mind if you're thinking of causing any trouble: the threat I made out in the wooded area still stands. It's in your best interests, and your companions', that you behave yourselves. I shall return in due time, and please keep the noise down, if you will."

Akrath smiled darkly, clearly enjoying himself, then disappeared from view. I could hear his footsteps as he walked down the stone hallway deep inside the Crimson Order's lair.

From the forest, we'd been led into a concealed tunnel hewn into the side of a large hill, and that tunnel led to many more. It was part of an entire network of caves and passages, almost like the Order's version of our Catacombs. Akrath had made mention that this place had once been a warren for werewolves, and that they'd graciously allowed the Order to take up residence in it, as its location was an ideal distance from Los Angeles.

I thought we'd be led underground, but for the most part the tunnels had either stayed level or had gone upwards. I had a feeling the hill the first tunnel had been in was only part of a far larger formation of rock and earth, its size concealed by the trees and other vegetation growing on it. Either which way, we were stuck.

As we'd been taken through the tunnels, I'd seen a sizable number of werewolves and other vampires moving about, and I had the unsettling realization that the Crimson Order had more manpower under its belt in addition to what it had recruited in LA. Not only that, I kept feeling déjà vu as I walked the tunnels.

It was almost like the first time, back in the keep, except for the different geography, presence of werewolves, and not having Stacey with me. Other than that, it was the same, with Akrath and a group of the Order's soldiers taking me off to my cell to await punishment of some form. Except this time, Akrath had managed to get me into my cell without trouble, unlike the original go-round. I smiled for a moment at the memory—by the stars, we'd gotten him good.

Then the smile faded as I remembered it hadn't been enough, and Akrath was still around. Akrath and somebody else I'd thought to be dead. But I didn't want to think about that, for if it was Azon...

I think I'd disappointed Akrath when I hadn't acted too shocked at his announcement that we were guests of the Crimson Order; I think he'd been hoping for jaw-dropping horror. However, the revelation wasn't all that shocking considering the medallions worn by the Order's minions, and Akrath's appearance more or less clinched things.

Looking back on it, I would have been more surprised had he *not* said anything about the Crimson Order. The part that bothered me the most was that the Order had been able to establish themselves a nice little colony here close to the most enlightened vampires I knew of. Then again, maybe that shouldn't have been so surprising since there had been numerous *Covenant* converts among the Los Angeles vampire populace.

No, not surprising, just...troubling.

"So who is Baldy, or Akrath, or whatever you want to call him, anyway?" Clarisse asked me as she sat on the little plain wooden table that was the only furniture in our dark and otherwise bare cell. "You two have got a lot of history, I'd say."

I moved over the door, put my hands on the bars, and looked out into the hallway, which had been formed of a dark stone. In the bright torchlight, I could clearly see two werewolves standing watch on either side of the door when I peered to the left and right. I'd figured as much, but it was still an unsettling thing to see. I wished Akrath had been more like an old movie serial villain and had left some sort of escape route that could have been exploited with a little bit of ingenuity. As things stood, we weren't going anywhere until the situation changed.

I stepped away from the bars, not wanting to attract the

werewolves' attention, and settled on the floor by the table, positioning myself so I could see both Clarisse and Katheryne, who'd moved to the corner of the cell and was sitting in the shadows, mute. There was nothing now but time, and how much of that there was, I didn't know, but I was determined to take advantage of it. I needed to share a part of my life with Clarisse I never had before, and to give Katheryne something to think about that could maybe help her come to terms with herself and her supposed failures.

"Akrath was a part of the original Crimson Order," I said, "and someone Stacey and I got the better of in a rather brutal way. It's no wonder he holds a grudge against me. If I were him, I would have hunted me down to the ends of the Earth."

"Ooh, naughty!" Clarisse giggled and poked at my shoulder with the toe of her boot.

A smile of genuine warmth crossed my face at the way she was able to keep her spirits up even in the guts of the Crimson Order's home base.

"Do tell."

I turned my gaze to Katheryne. "It might do you well to listen to this too. It's what I was going to tell you earlier, about a failure of mine in the past and how I dealt with it."

Clarisse turned on the table and held out her hand to the blond witch. "Come on, we won't bite. Come sit."

Katheryne looked like a little lost child sitting in the corner with her arms wrapped around her knees, and I hoped that what I had to say would make a difference for her. At Clarisse's words, she started a little, as if not expecting an invitation, and she remained where she was.

"Come on, Katheryne," whispered Clarisse. "I'd walk through the sunlight for you at this very moment if I had to, so just come sit with me. Would you?"

Clarisse's tone was gentle and soft, with none of her usual lilt, from one dear friend to another. Katheryne stirred then slowly rose and walked the few steps between the corner and the table. Once she'd reached the table, she stopped and stood there silently, as if not sure what to do next, and Clarisse took her hand and scooted over on the table.

"Here, next to me," she said. "Stories are always better when you've got a friend to share them with."

The look of gratitude in Katheryne's eyes at Clarisse's words struck me deeply, and when she sat on the table next to Clarisse, I felt a strong flush of love for my redheaded princess. I'd never fail her, I promised myself yet again, and even if I didn't make it out of here in one piece, she would, no matter what.

"It was about one hundred and eighty years ago, just before Stacey and I left for America, back when we were a couple of ne'er-do-wells who went by the names of Brom and Jules," I began, and not for the first time nor for the last time, the present slipped away and my past lived once again.

AD 1820 Runquist, a small farming village of about a hundred people in Eastern France

"You're the consummate showoff," I said, watching Jules gracefully jump his horse over the bales of hay he'd set out in the yard.

"I've got plenty of reason to be," he replied as he wheeled Llefelys, his trusty steed, around for another gallop through the yard. It was gorgeous out tonight, and though there were clouds in the sky, the moon and stars shone through clearly. I loved spring nights like this. I sat on the steps of the porch, with Alena directly behind me, her arms around my chest and her chin on my right shoulder.

"Let him show off if he wants to," she murmured into my ear. "At least he's not inciting any fights, like the last time we went into Dumas."

I laughed, thinking back to two nights ago, when we'd visited the little town ten miles west of Runquist. While Alena and I were enjoying ourselves talking with some people we'd met in a tavern, Jules had been busy swindling several roughnecks at various card games. After he'd won everything except for the shirts off their backs, they'd decided they'd had enough and attempted to retrieve their belongings from Jules. Bad idea.

A fight had broken out, and Jules and me had a great time pulverizing the thugs, while Alena had watched and shaken her head in amusement. I was going to have to talk her into joining one of our fights...she was missing out on a lot of fun.

"That boy is going to break his neck someday," Alena's father,

Thaddeus, said from where he sat in his chair, his back to the house. His legs were stretched out in front of him, feet resting comfortably on the planks of the porch and his pipe in hand. "Then I'll be out one of my helpers."

Alena giggled and said, for the thousandth time since we'd first come into their lives, "He can't break his neck, Father, he's a vampire."

Actually, we *could* get our necks broken, but it wouldn't slow us down for long. As old as Jules and me were, there wouldn't be too much of an effect. Mostly he'd be stuck in bed whining for a few hours to a day, depending on how bad it was.

"I *know* he's a vampire, Alena," Thaddeus groused, puffing on his pipe. The rich smell of his tobacco filled the spring air. "I know Brom is a vampire and I know you're a vampire, but that doesn't mean you shouldn't be careful when you're on a horse. I've seen men twice Brom's size felled by a nasty drop from the back of a horse. Or what if Llefelys were to step on his head? What then, my wise and worldly daughter? Even a vampire's no good without a head."

Alena groaned and I laughed. Thaddeus was one in a million, as was his daughter, and I was again grateful Jules and I had come into their lives, over ten years ago. It had been a chance happening, but it had worked out nicely, and it had been a lovely decade for all parties involved.

Jules and I had been passing through the village of Runquist in the winter months during one of our aimless, wandering journeys around Europe. While cutting through a field, our ever-sharp vampire ears had picked up the sounds of a struggle coming from the farmhouse. Either someone was getting robbed or there was a fight. Regardless of which it was, it meant we'd get to feed and/or rescue someone, so we investigated.

We'd gone back the way we came through the field and had circled around, hiding in the shadow of the barn so we wouldn't be seen in the bright moonlight. Someone had lit the lantern in the kitchen, and in the dim light we saw two burly men—scarves over their mouths and knives in their hands—watching a third of their number struggling with an older man. The two spectators seemed to be waiting for a good opening to stab the farmer, who was holding his own against the thug.

I inched along the shadow to get a better view, and I caught a glimpse of beauty.

I had always preferred redheads, but this was the most beautiful blond woman I'd seen in my long life. She had perfect, flawless skin, eyes like emeralds, and lips the color of blood. She was dressed in a thick woolen sleeping gown that had a certain dignity and elegance despite its obvious age and humbleness.

In fact, everything about this woman had simple, elegant charm, even though she'd clearly been woken in the middle of the night and was now anxiously watching her father slug it out with the intruders. I'd planned on helping the man anyway, but seeing his daughter sealed the deal.

"Jules," I said, "A good deed's in the cards tonight."

"Hmph," he replied, "Methinks ye spy a comely lass ye desire."

"That's one of the incentives, and stop it with that Old English," I told him, "You sound like a bloody asylum inmate."

He gave me his most lopsided smile. "And ye sound like a peasant."

"Shut up and let's go."

We sprinted across the front yard and positioned ourselves on either side of the door. Jules started to meow frantically in the manner of a cat pursued by an overzealous child with an axe. I then stomped on the wooden porch several times for effect.

The struggling inside abruptly ceased, and one of the bandits demanded, "Whut tha' bloody 'ell is that?"

"Mebbe you better go'n check," another said.

"Me? Why do I always gotta be tha' one'at checks? Why don'tchew do it fer a change?"

"Becuz I'm bigger'n you, that's why. You 'n Philly go check outside 'n see whut that bloody cat's screamin' 'bout."

The other two grumbled, but footsteps approached, and the heavy wooden door creaked open. The two thugs stepped out onto the porch, side by side, and looked in their respective directions. Both of them got a good view of a vampire standing at the ready.

"Meow," Jules said then leveled his guy with a crunching punch to the snout. One problem down.

I went straight for my thug's throat, looking for a nice snack to curb my hunger. Within minutes, both them were quite dead, and

Jules and I quite satisfied. Nothing like hot blood to warm a chilly vampire on a cold winter's night.

We left the bodies on the porch and walked right on into the small farmhouse. We turned the corner and stepped into the kitchen, where the remaining thug now held the woman at knifepoint, ordering the farmer to tell him where he kept his money. What a fool. As if a farmer in a tiny village would have an excess of cash.

The bandit, a fat, dirty fellow with thick stubble on his round cheeks, stopped and stared when Jules and I appeared in the doorway.

Both of us were dressed in long black leather coats and pants, our long black hair down on our shoulders. In the low, flickering light in the kitchen, we looked like dark spirits, and our angry expressions didn't help the bandit's confidence any.

"You shouldn't threaten a lady," I said softly and dangerously. "It could prove fatal."

Moving faster than his eye could track, I shot my arm out and tore the knife from his hand. His mouth dropped open and he first looked at his empty hand in shock then at me in fear as I idly twirled the knife about.

On the other hand, the woman looked more interested than afraid. Her father didn't know what to say or think, so he just stood and watched, agape. I smiled at the would-be thief and held his knife up in front of my face.

"You are in serious trouble now, my friend." I let my fangs show to put even more fear into him.

"Vampire!" He gasped.

"He's gifted with a mind like a steel trap," Jules commented.

The bandit pushed the woman aside, over to her father, and dug around in his grubby shirt. He produced a filthy gold crucifix—likely stolen—and held it up. I nearly laughed at the old wives' tale being trotted out yet again.

Jules *did* laugh and unbuttoned the first three buttons on his tunic. He pulled out a shiny Celtic cross made of platinum—his good-luck piece—and showed it to the bandit. "Mine's a lot nicer than yours," he said. "Platinum. Want to try and take it from me?"

"But the cross should scare you away!" the man cried in fear.

"You've been reading too many stories, my friend." Jules turned to me. "Do you want him or do I have the honors?"

"Go ahead," I told him. "The one I got on the porch was fatter than the one you had."

He gave me a mock bow and saluted. "You are a prince among men." He turned back to the bandit and said, "Well, big boy, time to find out if there really is a God."

He pounced on the thug, who let out an impressively high-pitched shriek as he hit the floor, but it didn't last very long—my friend was quite hungry. While Jules was feeding, I turned to the farmer and his daughter and bowed my head.

"You are vampires," the daughter said, eyeing me with fascination.

"Yes," I replied. "We mean you no harm. We were passing through when we heard the struggle. My name is Brom and my addled little friend on the floor is Jules."

"I'm *not* little!" Jules called up from the floor in between draughts of the thug's blood.

Thus began our long-term relationship with the farmer Thaddeus and his daughter Alena. They were open-minded, tolerant people, especially for country folk, and after they'd gotten over their initial surprise and been convinced Jules and I weren't going to kill them, they bid us stay for a time.

Thaddeus, a big man who took great delight in pestering people, was not the youngest man in the world and had a bad leg besides—he needed help during the growing season, and didn't have enough money to hire hands. It didn't take much convincing to get us to stay for a while, especially since Thaddeus promised to let Jules take care of the horses. That did it for Jules—he loved horses with a passion, especially troublesome ones that were difficult to ride. Nobody could sweet-talk a bastard horse like Jules.

We were originally going to stay just for a growing season, but we grew close to the father and his daughter, and one season grew into two then three. As Thaddeus grew older and weaker—but no less feisty—Jules and I took care of more and more of the work. After being all over the world and seeing so many strange, fantastic things, sometimes even an adventurous vampire started to crave a simple, satisfying routine; even hungered for a comfortable place to hang his hat, if only for a while. Working on the farm was good for

Jules and I, and we enjoyed our respite from wandering the world.

Then during the third winter, Alena took ill with consumption.

As she grew weaker and more frail with each passing day, I debated whether to turn her. When I spoke to her, I never brought it up—I didn't want to seem to be forcing it upon her. She was comfortable with my vampiric nature, but she'd never expressed a desire to be one.

But one evening, when Jules and I awoke from our rest in the barn loft, we found Thaddeus waiting for us.

"Alena is dying," he said, his voice hitching. "I know she's not going to get better, and she knows it too. Please make her one of you. I asked her today if she would allow this, and she agreed in a heartbeat. Make her live forever. It would do this old man's heart a world of good to know his daughter will remain young and beautiful for all time. Please."

Alena had regained her strength and vigor with blinding swiftness that night, and Thaddeus danced with delight—as much as he could with his bum leg—after his daughter literally lifted him off his feet in a warm embrace.

Naturally, we offered Thaddeus the chance to become a vampire, too. Why not? But though Thaddeus was growing older and weaker as the years passed, he refused our offers to become a vampire too. He said he'd had a good, long life, and immortality just wasn't what he wanted. He told us that when he finally died, it would be with peace in his heart, as he knew his daughter would be youthful and strong for eternity.

The friendship Alena and I had naturally blossomed into a deep, abiding love, and life settled into a comfortable, leisurely pace out in the farmhouse on the edge of Runquist.

Alena was a wonderful companion, open-minded and intelligent, though she was a bit old-fashioned; she tended to baby me, which truthfully didn't bother me. There was a certain charm to being well over a millennium old and able to lift up a horse trough with ease, but still having a woman who constantly warned you not to work too hard and would bring me water while Jules and I were working in the field. Alena spoiled me. Hell, I *let* her spoil me.

Jules and I watched out for each other constantly—though I was reasonably sure one of his misadventures was going to ultimately spell my doom—but there was a difference between Jules shoving me out of the way of a falling boulder and Alena fretting over whether my meat was cooked the way I liked it. I never asked these things of her: she offered her care and love to me freely, and didn't ask for anything in return, and I loved her fiercely for it.

And dear old Thaddeus. He was like a father to Jules and I both, and the three of us would often sit and talk for hours about our lives and views on the world in the manner of fathers and sons, and we actually enjoyed listening to him grump at us whenever we became mischievous. Thaddeus and Alena's household was a warm, joyful place, and the simple years there were the happiest we'd had in many a century.

Jules, Alena, and I took care of all of the difficult farm work at night, while Thaddeus did as much as he could during the day. After a time, he had taken to working at night alongside us, though he had to set up torches to see properly.

The other villagers commented on eccentric old Thaddeus, his strange daughter, and the two farm helpers who only showed their faces at night. Thaddeus and Alena had always been regarded as odd by the people of Runquist, so our nocturnal behavior didn't concern them much, especially since we produced such good crops and livestock, and often gave out gifts of our surplus to the people who hadn't done as well as us. We were strange, but we were kindhearted, so they merely shook their heads and let us be.

We only fed from the villagers of Runquist occasionally then only a few pints from the largest, strongest members of the community, so they wouldn't notice much when they woke the next morning. The three of us would travel to Dumas once or twice a week to feed from the townspeople there; though Alena had considerable strength thanks to my powerful old blood, she still had to feed quite often, as was common with fledglings. Mostly the trip was for Alena to feed while Jules and I would be along for the ride.

Any number of undesirable or just plain stupid types could be found for us to drain, and it was a good arrangement: Dumas had its criminal and moron element kept in check, and we got plenty of blood to keep us satisfied. Everything just *worked* so well in those years.

I leaned back in Alena's arms and she rested her chin on my

head, at ease with the world. Life was good.

After jumping the hay bales a few more times, Jules and Llefelys came trotting over to the porch and Jules said, "Let's go for a ride. Llefelys's feeling full of oats tonight, and the moonlight's perfect. Nights like this are meant for a ride out in the country."

I looked up at the sky—the sparse clouds were starting to thicken. I would probably have said no if it hadn't been so early in the night; the darkness had only been really prevalent for a half hour or so.

"I think I'll take you up on that," I said. "We probably shouldn't stray too far, though. We might get rained on."

Jules cackled. "Since when does rain bother you? Is this pastoral life making you soft? You hear that, Llefelys? Brom's domesticated!"

The horse snorted and made a noise that suspiciously sounded like a chuckle.

"I'll show you domesticated!" I hopped up, gave Alena a hug and a long kiss then hurried over to the barn.

Within a minute I was back out in the yard again, riding bareback on the horse I'd taken as my own—a young, rambunctious coal-black steed I'd named Lludd. I reared Lludd up on his hind legs and whooped as loudly as I could. Lludd whinnied in accompaniment, and I took off out of the yard like a lightning bolt, with Jules hot on my tail.

"We'll be back in a couple of hours!" I yelled back.

"Don't break your necks. We've got work to do tonight!" Thaddeus called after us.

"And don't get lost!" Alena shouted, laughing along with her father.

Lludd and I maintained the lead for a good distance, totally outpacing Jules and Llefelys. "That'll teach him to call me domesticated," I told Lludd as we barreled down a lushly vegetated hillside. The horse picked up his speed even further, and I was pretty sure he'd caught the gist of what I'd said.

The spring wind streaming through my hair felt good, and I was glad Jules had goaded me into this. Lludd's hooves thundered across the grass, and I bent low over him, holding as close to him as I could without actually melting into him.

Lludd and Llefelys could see exceptionally well at night, thanks to a few drops of our blood in their feed now and again. It also gave them increased strength, speed, and endurance, letting them conquer courses that would've been the doom of any regular horse. Though we were careful not to overdo it...we didn't need a couple of blood-addicted horses running around biting villagers.

The moon and starlight coming through the breaks in the deepening clouds lit up the rolling hills with an otherworldly light, transforming them into a fantasy dreamscape. I had not a care in the world as Lludd and I galloped across the land, Jules and Llefelys well behind us. Over the rumble of Lludd's hooves and the heavy pant of his breathing, I could hear Jules calling out insults after us. I laughed.

Some time later, we finally let Jules and Llefelys catch up to us when we came to a stream flowing out of the nearby mountains and crossed through a wooded area on the edge of the plains and hills. As Lludd was gulping down his well-deserved water, Jules and his horse came galloping up. Llefelys wore the same look of disgust that his rider had. I grinned. "Domesticated, eh?"

Llefelys hurried over to the stream for his drink while Jules scowled at me. "I let you get ahead of us so you'd feel better about being a house vampire."

I roared with laughter, and Lludd wetly snorted at Jules between drinks. "My thoughts exactly," I said, patting Lludd on his heavily muscled neck.

"Hell, the way life is around that house, and if I were with a woman like Alena, I'd become a lazy, contented bum after a time," Jules said. "It's nice for the wandering gypsy to have a warm home to come back to at daybreak."

He was right. We'd been wandering more or less constantly since we'd become vampires, and even though our spirits still loved adventure, we were getting to the point where a more firmly based life was starting to become attractive. I knew we wouldn't be here forever. When Thaddeus passed away, the three of us would likely pick up and move on. Though to where, I didn't know.

I'd been entertaining thoughts of crossing the ocean to America, to a place of huge, unexplored tracts of wilderness and brave people living out their lives on the frontier. America was young and bursting with life and new possibilities, and the spirit of the people was indomitable, if the tales coming back from sailors were to be believed. Besides, any people who had the temerity to not only stand up to but also successfully hold off the British Empire had my respect. Now if Alena could be convinced to leave her beloved Europe…

Jules looked up at the sky, where the clouds were pulling together into a thick blanket, shutting out the stars and the moon.

"Storm coming," he said. "Looks like we could be in for a few days of rain. Wouldn't be bad for the crops."

I eyed him and smirked. "Storm coming? Wouldn't be bad for the crops? Now who's the domesticated one, Farmer Jules? I may be a house vampire, but you're a grubby dirt vampire!"

He shook his head in disgust, and Lludd snorted at him.

"That's right, boy," I said. "He's a dirt vampire, working his immortality away in the fields, aren't you, Jules?

"You're a bloody baboon!" Jules barked, jumping off of Llefelys and throwing himself at me. "Defend thyself, ye petty house vampire! Prepare to feel the righteous wrath of the unconquerable dirt vampire! Yaaah!"

As Jules slammed into me, Lludd shifted his weight to minimize the effect to himself—a very smart move on the horse's part—which threw *my* weight off and sent the two of us sprawling onto the ground, rolling over and over through the dirt and grass.

"I'll stuff thy head up thy ass, ye ass!" Jules cackled.

"You'll be facedown in Lludd's manure pile before that ever happens!" I retorted while trying to get a good hold of him. He was faster than me, but I was stronger. If he held still for a second, I could get him, but he kept slithering around like a greased snake. "Slippery bastard!"

"You shan't get the upper hand on the wily dirt vampire, knave!" Jules said, rolling us both over so he was on top of me. "The dirt vampire gains the edge! Do you yield, house vampire?"

"Not in this lifetime!' I planted my feet firmly onto the ground and flipped both of us, and now I was on top of him. I snaked my arms around his, getting a solid grip, and squeezed my knees together on either side of his midsection, giving him a good dose of pressure. "Now who's got who, you dirt-eater?"

Whatever he said next was forever lost to me as a spike of pain shot through my head, causing everything to red out. I think I screamed, but I wasn't sure. I had my hands to the sides of my head, trying to keep my mind from exploding.

Molten lead shot into my skull deep into my brain; the pain was unbelievable, and I lost all coherent thought and sense of awareness for seconds. All I could see was an undulating curtain of red in front of my eyes, but I could smell thick smoke and I heard what sounded like the screams of the damned. For a few moments, it seemed as though I had been dropped into the fabled depths of Hell.

Alena.

Through our bond, I felt her pain and fear.

Something had happened back in Runquist, something hideous.

We had to get back, *now*.

As I slowly crawled back to full consciousness I heard Jules yelling at me and felt him shaking me like a madman. "Wake up, you idiot!" he demanded, more concerned than I'd heard him in years. "What the blazes happened to you? Come on, *wake up!*"

He stopped shaking me when my eyes opened. I was flat on my back in the grass and Jules was leaning over next to me, worry in his eyes. "What was that?" he asked as I struggled to my feet.

"We have to get back to Runquist," I said, leaning on his shoulder and shaking my head, trying to put my scattered senses back together. "Alena's in trouble!"

"*What?*" Jules demanded then understanding dawned. "Your bond..."

I nodded, transferring all my weight to my feet again. "We have to go *now*. She needs us." I looked to the south where, above the trees and hills, an unnaturally bright glow came from the direction of Runquist. "No," I whispered. "*No!*"

Jules stared. "What the bloody hell is happening?"

"I don't know!" I cried, panic rising in my chest. "We don't have time to take the horses back, and they'd probably just get killed in whatever's happening, anyway. We've got to fly there."

The horses were as fast as any I'd ever met, but flying was the quickest way back to Runquist, where I knew we were needed desperately. The village was populated entirely by peaceful peasant farmers and their families; nobody there but Jules and I knew anything about fighting. Runquist's two resident warriors had gone out for a spring ride when they'd been needed the most.

Jules nodded, knowing that we had no choice but to leave our beloved horses behind. He quickly removed Llefelys's saddle, and sadly patted the horse on his neck.

"I'm sorry, old buddy," he said, looking into his horse's eyes. Then he put his arms around Llefelys's neck and hugged him long and hard.

"You're smart," I said to Lludd as I hugged him. "You two will be all right. I wish we didn't have to do this, but we must." Lludd whinnied softly, and nudged my shoulder with his nose, as if he was telling me to get moving. "Goodbye, my friend. We'll be back if we can." I gave the horse one final squeeze around his neck.

With some difficulty, I separated myself from the powerful steed I'd raised from a shaky colt and turned to Jules. "Ready?"

He nodded, looking unsettled. Jules wasn't the best flyer in the world; he could manage, but he preferred to have both of his feet on the ground. He'd have to make do tonight. Without another word, we lifted off the ground and took off for Runquist. The horses both whinnied in unison, as if to say goodbye.

We rose above the treetops, and within moments we were out over the open plains again, heading in a straight line toward the foreboding glow of Runquist. We were moving faster than we could have managed on Lludd and Llefelys, though it wasn't fast enough for me, not nearly enough.

Jules was starting to fall behind—I was pushing our pace hard, beyond his limits. For him to have kept up with me for this long was a testament to his determination. I slowed slightly and maneuvered myself through the air so I was flying directly above Jules.

"Hold on," I yelled over the roar of the wind rushing past our ears, and I grabbed the back of his heavy work tunic with my hands, up by his shoulders. I lowered myself down even more closely, trying to cut down the wind resistance, and I went back up to my full speed again.

The glow to the south was getting brighter as we drew closer, and the smell of smoke was thick in the air. My heart kept beating faster. We had to get there in time, we *had* to.

Through our bond, I could feel Alena's pain and fright, though they were muted now, and starting to fade. My lovely Alena was dying. If only we could get there in time.

We passed over the tall hill on the outskirts of Runquist, and after we had cleared it, we gaped in shock at what we saw. The peaceful village was ablaze, a heavy cloud of smoke looming over the burning houses, obscuring our vision. Through the thick shroud we could see dark shapes darting around in the simple paths that passed for Runquist's streets, and above the rumble of the flames, we could hear screams.

The worst part was that we recognized all the voices crying out from the holocaust below us. My heart ached to help the people that had been good to us for so long, but I had to find Alena.

Jules and I dropped to the ground a short distance from the burning barn that had been home to Lludd and Llefelys just hours before, and we broke into a dead run toward the house. We could scarcely see a thing through the choking smoke, but as Jules and I got closer to the house, we saw the roof was on fire.

"You find Alena, I'll get Thaddeus!" Jules yelled, rushing toward the house. I didn't need to look for Alena—I was close enough now that I could track her through the smoke.

I found her by the well on the side of the house; it looked like she'd been cut down while trying to get water to put out either the barn or the house. There was another body not far from her, this one was dressed in a darkly colored outfit that wasn't something one of the villagers of Runquist would wear. I ignored the body as I ran to Alena.

She was lying on her side, curled up and clutching her midsection. I gasped when I saw how much blood she'd lost; she was lying within a spreading stain of her life's essence. Her workclothes were cut and burnt in countless places, and her hair soiled with soot and her own blood. It was awful, and an unbidden sob wrenched from my chest. My beautiful, shining jewel, so full of love and life and understanding, with centuries and millennia ahead of her to learn and grow and explore, who never had an unkind word for anybody... She'd nearly been torn to pieces.

The damage to her was so terrible I doubted it would have made a difference if I'd given her all my blood at that very moment. If only she'd been older, if only we'd had more time for her to grow stronger, I could have saved her. If only *if onlies* worked.

"Alena..." I murmured, kneeling down beside her.

"Brom?" she answered so softly I could barely hear her. Her eyes fluttered open. She was paler than a sheet. "Brom." She reached out to me, and I could see her nails were encrusted with blood.

I took hold of her shoulders and pulled her up next to me. She put her arms around my neck and held on with all of her remaining strength. "I'm sorry," I whispered, tears flowing from my eyes. "I'm so sorry. I loved you and I wasn't here for you. I failed you. *I'm sorry.*"

She fixed me with the same emerald eyes that'd captivated me the first time I'd seen her; those magickal eyes were clouded and glassy now. "You didn't know," she said slowly, haltingly. She let go of my neck with one of her hands and wiped a tear from my face. "It's not your fault," she whispered, which made the tears come even more fiercely. "I love you."

"I love you so much," I said to her, holding her as tightly as I dared. The fire, the smoke, the screams, everything faded into the background as I held my beautiful Alena during her last moments on this earth.

Alena started coughing, but it quickly subsided, and a phantom smile formed on her lips. "I fought them," she whispered. "I tore one of their hearts out just like how you told me. I really did it."

At least the blood on her fingers and nails wasn't her own. Sweet, gentle Alena had ripped out the heart of one of her attackers. She'd fought back. Despite the agony of my grief, I felt a small thrill of pride for my beloved.

I kissed her softly on her lips, and stroked her cheek. "You did good," I told her, and her nod was barely perceptible.

"Thank you," she rasped. "You gave me years of life I couldn't have had without you. Thank you." She paused, then whispered, "Make them pay, Brom, don't let them do this to anybody else ever again. Do it for me. Don't let them hurt any other lovers like this."

I held her tightly, and she returned my embrace as best as she could. "I love you," I said, and though her eyes closed, she smiled. "I'll avenge you, I promise. The monsters who did this to you won't escape me. I swear to you… I won't fail you in this."

I felt her presence in my mind starting to fade, and I trembled like a leaf in a tornado. A tidal wave of grief washed over me, bringing with it a growing madness.

Could I save her? Could I steal her from death twice? She was so young, but I was old and strong. If I gave her most of my blood, I could possibly hold off death long enough for her to heal herself. Revenants were usually created from older vampires, and as young as Alena was, I didn't think it was possible for her to become one.

Did I dare? How could I not?

Only dimly aware of what was going on around me, I bit into my wrist with my fangs, letting the blood flow. I heard Jules's voice behind me, and it sounded like he was shouting. There were also several other voices that I didn't know, but I paid them no mind. I put my wrist to Alena's lips.

"Drink," I urged her, and I felt her lips move slightly beneath my wrist. At first they barely moved, but gained strength ever so slightly, and I knew she was drawing blood from me. "Please live," I urged. "I'll never leave you again. Please."

A hand with a grip of iron snapped down on my shoulder and jerked me away from Alena. "No! I can save her!" I shrieked as she fell from my warm grasp to the ground, her eyes still shut.

"Back off him, you bastard!" Jules roared, and the grip on my shoulder disappeared as the sound of a punch exploded behind my head. I dropped and tried to make it back to Alena, but a savage kick slammed into my chest and threw me onto my side.

"I can save her!" I cried, springing to my feet and blindly striking out at everything around me. Figures dressed in black and brown moved around us, though how many there were, I didn't know.

As one rushed toward me, I slashed out with my fingers and felt them sink into the bastard's eyes, tearing them to useless tatters of flesh. He screamed, and I threw myself on him, intent on beating him into nothing but bloody chunks of meat. I'd kill anyone and everyone who kept me back from Alena, and if I had to kill them all, I would.

"Alena!" I howled. "Hold on!"

As I tore apart the bastard whose eyes I'd ripped out, I felt a rain of blows hammer down on me, and I heard Jules cry out in pain. I lashed out with my fists and feet, ripping and tearing into everyone that I made contact with.

These monsters had nearly killed Alena, and now they were trying to kill Jules, and I was going to make them suffer. I managed to get back to my feet again and pounced on another of the darkly clad attackers, ripping his throat out. I screamed in rage as I pummeled another one with my fists and tore at him with my fangs.

"Alena!" I clawed and shredded another, and another, and they kept coming. Bones broke beneath my fists and blood dripped from my nails and fangs as I fought them. I wouldn't stop until they were all dead. *"Alena!"*

I kept getting hit from all sides, and though I felt no pain through the berserker rage burning through me, I started to fog out. As I slowed, I got hit harder and harder and harder. Fighting back became difficult then impossible. I staggered, stumbled, and fell into unconsciousness.

III

The telling of my tale came to a halt as shouting erupted from the corridor outside our cell. A *lot* of shouting. As soon as we heard the voice behind the racket, we all exchanged looks of surprise and worry.

But not *that* much worry...at least not yet.

"You just wait until my girlfriend finds out about this, you sorry bunch of fucks!" the individual howled in protest. "She's gonna rip you in half like a phonebook, pal! And she'll turn *you* into a shag carpet, buddy boy! Yeah, go right ahead and snap at me! She'll take your whole damn muzzle, rip it off, polish it up real nice, turn it sideways and *shove it straight up your monkey ass!* Lemme go! Ohhh, you're all gonna be sooo sorry! *Sooo* sorry!"

The three of us hurried over to the bars of our cell door, trying to see as much as we could through the small opening. It was hard with three heads vying for space, but I managed to get a view of several Order vampires and a werewolf dragging a struggling form towards the cell.

A very *noisy* struggling form.

"Put me down!" he yelled. "You have absolutely no idea who you're fucking with! My girlfriend could kill all of you inside of a minute and walk away without even a broken nail, and you're gonna piss her off so much when she finds out the way you assholes manhandled me! Dumb sons of bitches, don't say I didn't warn you!"

"Doesn't he ever shut up?" Clarisse asked, rhetorically I assumed. Considering the situation, I felt compelled to respond anyway.

"I'd be a lot more worried if his mouth wasn't running a mile a minute right now," I said, glad my friend was at least still in one piece.

As the group moved closer, I got a better view. Though disheveled, Stacey looked to be in good shape overall. He was surrounded on all sides by vampires in black robes, with a pair of revenants bringing up the rear. A werewolf had his arms wrapped right around my friend's chest, holding him like a living vise-grip—the werewolf was so big that Stacey's legs dangled like a little kid's.

Stacey, apparently, had had enough. All of a sudden, he lifted both legs and started flailing all around in the werewolf's grasp, kicking at anything that got near him.

"Yaaah!" he screamed, and though there was anger in his eyes, he was also—on some level—enjoying himself. Yep, that's my little buddy.

"Yaaah!" Stacey yelled again as he managed to catch one of his captors in the face with a boot. He then slammed his head backward, trying to nail the werewolf with his rock-hard skull as the annoyed werewolf snarled and snapped. *"Put me down, you hirsute bastard!"*

By this time, the two werewolf guards were moving in, just in case the loudmouthed vampire got free. Neither looked happy, and I honestly couldn't blame them. Dealing with Stacey in this state was a pain in the ass.

The slim vampire put up a tremendous fight, and from what I could see, he was getting close to slipping out of the werewolf's arms. I silently cheered him on, not wanting to call out for fear of distracting him. Next to me Clarisse whispered words of encouragement, one of her hands nearly crushing my own in her excitement.

I glanced at Katheryne and saw, to my surprise, that she wasn't looking at the tussle at all, but rather out the bars toward the floor.

Following her gaze, I saw a large brown rat sitting on its haunches on the stone floor. From the way the rat was sitting, it appeared to be looking right back at Katheryne, with its little hands held to its chest and its whiskers twitching in the cool air of the hallway. Despite the ruckus just a short distance away, I couldn't help but watch the rat, too, trying to figure out why Katheryne was so interested in it.

But I didn't look long—a crimson flash shot past the rat and my field of vision. It was Akrath striding purposefully down the hallway toward the struggle, his mouth a hard thin line.

"Enough of this!" he bellowed

Like before, everybody froze thanks to the tone of sheer authority in his voice. Everybody except for Stacey—voices of authority just set him off even more. Stacey slithered away from the distracted werewolf's grasp and started to make a break down the hallway. He didn't get far, though, as he nearly ran headlong into Akrath, where he skidded to a stop at the last second.

The two stared at each other, Stacey's eyes growing wide as recognition clicked into place. I couldn't see Akrath's face from where I was, but I was willing to bet he was sporting that same look of confident contempt he'd worn with me.

"Well I'll be a monkey's uncle," Stacey exclaimed after a few moments. "Last time I saw you, you were busy doing your best impression of a torch, like one of those assholes on *The Gong Show.*"

"Believe me, I recall that all too well, you addled fool," Akrath replied smoothly, raising his hand up to touch his scars.

Though vampires could heal up nearly any wound inflicted upon them, they could develop scars just as mortals did, especially if the wounds were particularly deep or brutal. There were also cases where a vampire would let a wound heal, but do nothing to repair or remove the scar, choosing to retain a keepsake of damages visited upon them in the past for any number of reasons, ranging from vanity to madness.

I suspected Akrath's scars were partly because of the severity of the wounds we'd dealt him and partly because he wanted to keep them around as perverse badges of honor. Even though Stacey and I had wrecked the Order, we'd been unable to kill him.

"I know you are, but what am I?" Stacey blithely shot back, acting totally unimpressed with Akrath now.

"Doomed," Akrath replied.

"Surely you jest," shot back my friend, the picture of confidence. He'd folded his arms over his chest and was standing in a rather relaxed posture, tapping his foot against the floor softly. From looking at him, one would think he was discussing the weather with the baldheaded Crimson Order vampire

Akrath shook his head. "Not in the least. I speak only the truth, and one thing I should advise you is that if you make one foolish move, a pair of your friends shall cease to exist."

"What? My balls?" Stacey snorted. "Solid brass, motherfucker. I ain't scared of you, and neither are they."

Akrath chuckled. "Keep making jokes, and the females wind up dead."

"Say what?" asked Stacey, a momentary crease forming on his forehead: Akrath had hit a nerve. "You're full of it, you asshole."

"Oh am I?" asked Akrath. Without turning, he pointed toward our cell.

Stacey's gaze followed then met mine a second later. The slim vampire blinked as he took in my face, as well as that of Clarisse and Katheryne.

"D'oh!"

"So am I 'full of it,' now?" inquired Akrath.

Stacey threw him the bird without saying anything else.

"Or have you finally found out the Crimson Order holds all the cards now?"

My friend was first silent following Akrath's words, then he matter-of-factly stated, "Well, you're *totally* dead now. Brandi's going to *really* come down on you guys when she finds out you've fucked with me *and* Red. You may as well go out and wait for the sun to come up—it's going to be a much more peaceful death than the one you idiots have signed yourselves up for. Way to go."

"So much bravado." Akrath clucked and motioned for the two werewolf guards to take Stacey's arms.

Stacey actually held out his arms agreeably and smiled pleasantly.

For the moment, at least, Akrath had him—about the only thing that gave an individual any sort of power over Stacey was threatening the life of someone he cared about. He'd bide his time, as would I, until the moment came when we could strike out at the Order once again, and when that happened, a thousand deities wouldn't save them.

"You and Steele are so much alike it's endearing in an oddly misguided way," Akrath sneered. "We'll see how much bluster you two conjure up when you're face to face with the Goddess Herself."

"Just read me my rights and toss me in the slammer already." Stacey grunted. "If I wanted to hear an idiot preach nonsense, I'd watch the religion channel."

"Is it nonsense when it's the truth?" murmured Akrath, running a finger over the scar on his throat. He and Stacey stared one another down briefly then Akrath tilted his head toward the cell. "Place him with the others. He'll learn soon enough."

The werewolves escorted Stacey over to the cell, and Akrath produced a key from within the folds of his robe. The three of us already in the cell backed away from the door when it opened, and a few seconds later, Stacey was in our midst, sullen but no worse for the wear.

I embraced him as the door slammed shut, and he returned it, slapping me on the back a few times before we let go. "Getting a sense of déjà vu, old man?" I asked.

"Not quite," he replied. "They didn't even get us locked up in the dungeon the first time. They better enjoy it while it lasts."

Clarisse gave him a hug, and he waggled his eyebrows at her.

"Why Red, I never knew you cared!"

She gave him a smack on the chest and said, "Don't flatter yourself too much, motormouth."

Stacey chuckled then turned to Katheryne, who was standing back from the rest of us, her arms wrapped around herself. My longtime friend held out his arms to her.

"C'mon, Blondie, gimme a hug so I know you're okay." The witch hesitated then stepped forward, looking almost sheepish, and when Stacey hugged her and ruffled her hair, he said, "Don't worry, we'll be out of here in no time. The organization that can bring me and Steele down hasn't been formed yet, and probably never will. Just hang in there and everything'll turn out just fine."

Akrath's soft laughter floated into the dark cell. "Tell yourselves anything and everything you want to—it will all pale in the light of the Goddess," he said before his face disappeared from the barred window. His footsteps grew softer as he strode down the corridor, followed by the shuffling and stomping of the crew that'd brought Stacey in.

"Isn't he just the cheerful fellow?" Stacey grunted as he let go of Katheryne. She walked over to the door and peered out into the hallway for a few moments before rejoining us.

Clarisse scowled. "A genu-swine laugh a minute, let me tell you. Just wait until you meet Wilkesdon—you'll like him even less."

"Naw, nobody will quite take the place in my heart Akrath has," replied Stacey. "I'm gonna finish what we started back in the keep before this is all said and done, and I'm gonna see him burn for good if it's the last thing I do."

"So did you get the same spiel about someone we'd thought was dead wanting to see us?" I asked as we all moved farther back into the cell. Clarisse and Katheryne reclaimed their spots on the table, while Stacey and I dropped to the floor, and Stacey nodded.

"Yup, one of the revenant masters yapped it at me while I was getting dragged in here. That guy wouldn't shut up until I got a lucky shot in and kicked him in the mouth, heh. Somehow I get the feeling he meant Azon," said the slim vampire. "Though that should be completely impossible."

"I'm not giving it much thought, myself," I said. "For all we know, it's a bluff to play with our minds. They want us to sit in here and stew in our own juices for a while, hoping we'll go buggy and be that much easier to toss around whenever they decide it's time to introduce us to our 'mysterious host.'"

"Nothing doing," said Stacey. "I'm buggy enough as is, and nothing they do is gonna make me any worse. Fuck that psychological warfare shit. After all, just the two of us took them down before, and this time we've got four."

"The only problem is Akrath keeps threatening Clarisse and Katheryne every time I act even the smallest bit rowdy," I said. "And you heard what he said out there in the corridor. He assumes he's got us right where he wants us because he's got a couple of hostages."

"I don't take too kindly to being a hostage," Clarisse growled, cracking the knuckles on one of her hands. "He seems really hot to trot to make sure no harm comes to either one of you, at least for the time being.

"When he got the revenants off you in the alley," she said, looking toward me, "he gave you a quick check-over and told the masters to make sure the revenants didn't do any further damage. That's why I ended up carrying you. From what I could read off him, he didn't trust the revenants or their masters enough to not hurt you while we were on our way here."

"Yeah," Stacey said, nodding slowly, his hand on his chin. "The revenant master who was riding herd when they jumped me was real worried one of the revenants or the werewolf would get out of line and take me down before they got back home.

"I was riding my bike through one of the sluiceways, minding my own fucking business for once, just doing some thinking before I met up with Brandi at the Rango Drive-In for an Argento double-feature. All of a sudden something takes me completely out of my seat. After we've bounced about a dozen times I figured out it was one of those damned revenants... cocksucker was still holding onto me! He took the worst of it, though—all I got was a few scratches and scrapes, but I don't even want to *think* of what happened to poor Jocko!" Stacey moaned, shaking his head.

After taking a mournful breath, he continued, "When we stopped rolling, the revenant's pals had fun playing soccer with my head until I finally passed out. When I came to, that damned werewolf was carrying me along through the woods, sniffing and poking at me with his cold wet nose every couple of minutes. That little cretin revenant master was walking along right next to us, constantly asking if I was okay. I kept telling him to fuck off, which I guess he took as me being fine, but he was still fidgety as all hell the whole way back here. Little fucker wouldn't shut up for even thirty seconds," Stacey grumbled.

"I'm surprised you didn't run, seeing as how they didn't have anybody to try to hang over your head," Clarisse said.

Even before he replied, I knew why Stacey hadn't tried to flee. He shrugged. "I suppose I could have, but after I came to, the revenant master told me I was on my way to see the head of the Crimson Order and that the mistakes of the past wouldn't be repeated and yadda yadda yah, blah blah blah. As soon as he said Crimson Order, I couldn't shake the feeling I needed to go where they wanted me to go. Destiny's a bunch of shit, sure, but if I got hauled off to their secret base, I could wreak hellacious havoc in it, and then escape back to LA and come back with the cavalry. I was one half of the dynamic duo who took them down in the nineteenth century, and since this bunch of covies are calling themselves the Crimson Order, I kinda felt responsible. Like I'd started work on something that needed to be finished. Maybe I'm just getting responsible in my old age."

"I think we're just both crazy," I said, aimlessly dragging a fingertip along the stone floor.

"Yeah, and crazy's gotten us out of more things than either one of us can remember," Stacey said firmly, "And it's gonna get us out of this bit too. I, for one, don't plan on cashing in my chips any time in the next couple of thousand years. These fucks think they're in control, but they're gonna have to work around us again."

"I was telling them about the last time," I said, "And I'd just gotten to the part where they snagged us, but not to the part where we started getting revenge. Want to help me finish?"

My friend gave me a grin tinged with the emotion of remembrance. "Sure—may as well spin the yarn of how two plucky young vampires stood up against the forces of ignorance and spit in its collective eye."

And the telling of Brom and Jules's tale resumed...

The day following the destruction of Runquist, somewhere on the edge of the mountains, fifteen minutes after sunset.

I awoke to the rough motions of a horse-drawn cart swiftly jolting down the road, and when I pried open my gritty eyes, I could see several figures sitting along the sides and rear of the cart. The cart had a covering over it, though I doubted it was tall enough to stand up in, if my peripheral vision was correct.

Jules was next to me, and as I pushed myself up off the side of my face, he silently helped me upright again. I was stiff, sore, and felt like I'd been trampled by the horses. Judging from the stiffness, I'd been in mild torpor since last night—the thought of being unconscious and at these bastards' mercy for so long made me shiver.

The five dark figures in the back of the cart watched us quietly, their eyes glittering in the gathering gloom—more vampires. Backlit by the fading light of the day coming in through the back of the cart, they could see us far better than we could see them. One of the shapes was large, brawny, and ragged-looking, and it started growling a moment after I sat up. I shivered again...a revenant. Jules and I were in the front end of the cart, separated from the driver by a wall. We were boxed in.

"Welcome back to reality," one of the figures said in a heavy English accent. "Just so you know, you're now a prisoner of the Crimson Order. Any move to escape will be dealt with appropriately. Do *not* cross us."

The Crimson Order? They were the most feared group of vampires in Europe, and had been responsible for the deaths of thousands of vampires, werewolves, ogres, and mortals. Their power had been waning over the past few centuries, but they still remained a deadly force whose name sent chills through vampiric blood. Once upon a time, they'd been an army of the night, marching across the land and creating so much havoc they'd helped plunge Europe into the Dark Ages. Nowadays they were more a bogeyman spoken of in fearful whispers, striking from the shadows—smaller-scale, but as terrifying as ever.

I hadn't heard much from them within the years we'd been back in Europe following our travels to Africa, and I'd hoped they'd finally begun to give up the ghost. So much for that.

"They gave me the same bucket of bilge when I woke up earlier, while we were in a cave," Jules said, and concern crept into his voice. "How are you? They really beat the stuffing out of you last night." He then chuckled softly. "Of course, you left seven of their men dead before they could bring you down. I think they were wondering if they could even stop you at all."

"Alena?" I asked, though I knew the answer.

Jules turned his eyes away. "I'm sorry," he said, a slight tremor in his otherwise strong voice. "I couldn't get to her. They got me just like they got you: they jumped on me all at once and hit me until I went under." He looked toward the back of the cart and said loudly, "Now that's *real* fighting for you!"

The revenant growled, and though the sound put a tension in our bones, we didn't show it.

"You would be wise not to anger me," the figure with the accent warned Jules. "I have my large friend here in check at the moment." He indicated the revenant. "But I could let him rip the two of you apart if I so desire."

"You could've torn us apart back in Runquist or any other time from the moment you first captured us, but you didn't," Jules retorted. "You're keeping us around for something, so you aren't going to do anything to us right now."

Despite the dire straits in which we were, I smiled at my friend's boldness. He was also right. They could easily have killed us any time between now and last night, but we were still kicking. Something was afoot.

The revenant's growling got louder, and it started to shift around, but thankfully it stayed in place. Apparently that had been a warning from our host, who made no verbal comment to Jules's jab.

"Just wait," Jules murmured. "You'll get yours, you arrogant bastard."

Jules then told me we were part of a small procession of about twenty vampires—there'd been thirty-five to begin with, but Jules, Alena, and myself had taken our toll—with two revenants in addition. Apparently, the rumors of the Order gaining marginal control of revenants through the use of powerful, telepathically trained vampires were true. Wonderful.

We didn't say much else for the duration of the trip, though Jules cursed continually, partly to relieve tension on his end and partly to irritate our silent captors. Thunder rumbled and crackled in the distance, and the wind picked up. A storm was brewing, both outside the cart and inside me.

We stopped occasionally to trade horses, but other than that, we kept a steady, rapid pace. The sound of the driver's scratchy voice as he pushed his horses forward grated on me, but it was a petty concern at worst, so I ignored him as best I could.

Physically, I was in decent shape; my brief torpor must have done the trick. I felt like hell and had a beast of a headache, but once I got a chance to move around again, I'd be good. Jules seemed to be in a condition similar to my own, which reassured me. When the time came, we would both be ready to make our move.

The pain of Alena's death seared through me like molten lava, and not a minute went by that I didn't think of her. I hadn't hurt like this for centuries. Though the years with Alena had only been a wink in the grand scheme of my total existence, they had been some of the most wonderful I'd ever had, and their legacy would forever remain with my heart. Even if it hurt.

Jules hadn't said anything about Thaddeus, so I didn't ask. To tell the truth, I didn't want to know; things were bad enough as it was. It seemed absurd the Order would slaughter an entire village just to capture two vampires. We meant something to them, obviously, or otherwise we'd be dead now. If they wanted to capture the vampires of Runquist, why did they kill Alena? What made us so special to the Order?

The thoughts and unanswered questions compounded my grief, so I stopped myself from the painful dwelling. I sat with my back against the wall of the cart, trying to pretend I was just fine.

After hour upon tense hour of monotonous riding, the accented member of the Order said, "Look ahead of us, and see our lair. This is where you'll begin the ends of your disgusting existences."

Jules and I both moved over to the side of the cart and looked through a tear in the canvas, trying to get a glimpse of what was ahead.

Through the inky blackness of the heavily clouded night, we got a pretty good view of the grim, castle-like building during flashes of lightning. Though its architecture was imposing, it wasn't very large, especially where castles were concerned. But then, all of the evils of the world had supposedly come out of Pandora's little box, so size didn't mean much where unpleasantness was concerned. It was very much a miniature of the castles seen in illustrated stories, sitting among the crags, looking almost a part of the mountains themselves.

"You'll be suitably impressed when we arrive, I'm certain. Azon runs a tight ship," the Order member said, pride in his voice.

Jules met my gaze. We both laughed at the arrogant little bastard then sat back down in our original positions, refusing to look at the keep anymore, mostly just to annoy him.

However, the mention of the name Azon sent a chill up my spine. According to legend, Azon was the creator of the Crimson Order, cruel, clever, and unstoppable. If he was half as bad as the whispered tales made him out to be, Jules and I were in serious trouble.

The perfect day just kept getting better.

The breakneck pace of the cart slowed, and our guards fidgeted in anticipation. Even for an immortal, a long ride in a horse-drawn cart was tiresome.

After what felt like a decade, the cart came to a stop and our guards fluidly leaped out. As they stood outside the cart, we noticed several of them wore swords on their belts. Just great.

"We've got to go meet the master, my charges. Come on, now," our captor ordered.

After a calculated hesitation, Jules and I rose from where we sat and stiffly clambered out onto the ground. Our muscles were creaky, but as we marched across the hard-packed dirt of what looked to be the Order's stables—the neatest, most well-organized I'd ever seen—it felt good to be in motion again. The four guards formed a diamond around us, with the accented bastard at point. The revenant brought up the rear, an anticipatory growl escaping it every now and then.

Up close, the keep looked much bigger than it had from the wagon. But it wasn't the size of the keep that concerned me: it was what was contained within. This was the home base of an ignorant vampiric scourge that'd racked up a considerable body count over the centuries, and we were about to be ushered into it. I'd seen and been in much bigger structures over the years, but none this foreboding.

As we were swiftly marched across the stables, Jules and I saw the rest of the small procession unloading wooden crates and burlap sacks from five or six carts similar to the one we'd rode in. They moved with military precision and speed, no unnecessary talk or even friendly gestures. Azon ran a tight ship indeed. Lovely.

I tried to get a better look at what the order's minions were unloading from the carts, and the guard to my right gave me a shove and verbal warning to keep my eyes forward. The one with the accent turned his head back toward us and said, "No, it's all right. Those supplies came from their village after all. You two may be pleased to know the spoils of your village will be put to good use, keeping us supplied for a good time to come."

So they weren't just content to destroy Runquist: they'd gutted it as well. "Bastards," I whispered, clenching my fist.

"You'll regret the day you ever crossed us," Jules murmured so quietly only I could hear him. Lightning cracked across the sky, a jagged split in pitch-black sackcloth. Behind us, several of the horses whinnied in fright.

"It's going to be rather nasty out here soon." Our host laughed as we reached a wooden door eight feet square set into the dark stone of the keep. "You should appreciate our hospitality."

As he sharply rapped on the door, I muttered, "Only after you've enjoyed our hostility."

Jules grunted in agreement.

The door rapidly rose from the ground, revealing a torchlit corridor leading into the lair of the Crimson Order. The burly vampire operating the crank that raised the door gave us a small, predatory smile, and our accented host said, "Welcome to the keep of the Crimson Order. Feel honored. You two are members of a select few who ever get to see our home base."

"I'm not impressed," Jules replied, sounding bored. "The stable was much more interesting."

The host, a slim vampire with long, blond hair, sharp, aristocratic features and a hawk-like nose, turned and pinned us with piercing eyes. "I think you are—you're just afraid to admit it."

"You think too much," I sneered. Our fear increased as the minutes passed, and Jules and I both resorted to wisecracks when we were frightened. At this rate, we'd be putting the best court jesters to shame within the next hour.

He regarded us in the same manner a cat contemplated a mouse it was about to pounce. "Laugh while you can. Your time left on this plane of existence is very short. We can see to it that your last moments are absolute hell on Earth."

"Can I stay up late to hear another bedtime story, Father?" Jules asked. He laughed—a short, bitter sound. "You don't scare us."

It was a lie, and we both knew it, but we'd be damned if we let them know that. I didn't know if any of the Order's men had much in the way of empathic ability, but I was keeping a tight rein on my emotions, holding them as close to my soul as possible, no matter how intense they were. I didn't want to die—neither of us did.

Vampires like Jules and I clung to our lives with fanatical tenacity—we were scared shitless of the reaper. Most vampires who lived to be our age tended to be like that, so in love with life that we were more terrified of death than most mortals.

We'll fight when all hope is gone, we'll fight when we've got nothing left to give, and we'll fight when death is an absolute certainty. We'll bite, claw, and scream for just one more minute—one more *second*—of precious life.

We regularly risk our lives in the name of fun and adventure, sure—what's the point of living forever if you're not willing to put your ass on the line? We'll also gladly sacrifice ourselves to save someone we love, or even those we don't know, when it has to be done… Sometimes life has to be given so other life can continue.

Sooner or later, our number would be up. That's the way it is.

But a cornered vampire—especially an older one—faced with a meaningless death was one of the most dangerous things on the planet… Because we're so scared of death we're a little crazy. Just because we know we're going to die eventually doesn't mean we're not gonna *fight*.

The host snorted derisively then led us into the keep. I was immediately struck by how well furnished the corridor was, much nicer than any castle I'd ever been in; there were even thick rugs covering most of the floor.

Torches lined the walls at regular intervals, illuminating the countless tapestries and crests decorating the walls. I recognized many as belonging to myriad clans and families from all parts of Europe. Apparently, the Order liked to keep reminders of their conquests around.

Jules and I couldn't stop craning our necks around to look at the multitude of treasures that were everywhere. There were small tables with little carved stone statues atop them, swords and shields hung on the wall, along with busts of people I didn't recognize, paintings of all descriptions, and countless other artifacts. An art collector would have simply *killed* to possess just half of the items we'd seen so far.

"We have assembled quite a collection over the years, haven't we?" the host asked us, and Jules and I couldn't argue this point. "Azon saw no point in putting our prizes into storage where no one could see them. He has a great appreciation for the arts, and makes sure our collection is displayed where every member of the Order can see it and feel pride in their accomplishments. If we are to anger the mortals in order to draw their wrath, then we may as well be able to enjoy their art and aesthetic accomplishments. I doubt the Goddess would find anything wrong with that."

"I was always under the impression you fools were much more ascetic than this. Since you've fallen below the mortals and can't be a part of their society, isn't there something wrong with collecting all their artwork and walking on their soft rugs?" I asked.

Our host gave me a half-shrug. "Just because we're fallen doesn't mean that we can't appreciate the mortals' art."

Jules spoke up. "That's not what I've heard. I've ran into covies like you in the past, and one of them told me the *only* way to do it was like a monastery—completely ascetic, since you aren't worthy of enjoying beauty created by mortals. He was banging his fist on his copy of the *Covenant* the entire time, so he *had* to be right."

I remembered that particular run-in, back in Spain, when we'd encountered a covy praying to the Goddess in a graveyard. He'd raved at us for a while, which was pretty funny, but then he'd threatened to report us to some of his covy cronies. We'd killed him and buried him deep.

What I'd found ironic was that immediately after he'd told us about how we should be "gracious to our fellows," he told us we were going to be killed by the "Goddess-fearing vampires" for our heathen ways. Go figure.

"Thou must not emulate the ways of the Living, for the Damned are not worthy of their ways," Jules added, waggling his eyebrows.

The Crimson Order vampire shrugged again. "You do not understand our ways, nor do we expect you to. Azon warned us about that. You have forsaken the Goddess and her love, choosing to live out your existences as heretics. For that you'll be punished severely."

"You do not understand our ways," I mocked. "Is that the best you can give us? Can't you even think for yourself enough to explain why you can play so fast and loose with your interpretations of the word of the Goddess? Can't you even tell us what *you* think, or are you just going to parrot everything Azon's told you?"

The host gave us a haughty look. "Azon is our closest link to the Goddess here on Earth and thus he's always right. To question him would mean to question the Goddess, and that simply isn't done."

Jules scrutinized him so intently that the aristocratically featured bastard asked, "What the bloody hell are you looking at?"

Jules shrugged. "I'm just trying to see where your strings are attached, puppet."

The host's eyes narrowed, and his smile disappeared. My friend returned the withering gaze. "I will take great pleasure in watching you die."

Behind us, the revenant growled.

"Oh, you're such a good covy, aren't you?" Jules asked. "Love your fellow vampire, but delight in his death after he's argued with you. That really makes a whole lot of sense, you turd."

The host ground his teeth and I had the feeling the verbal fencing would have escalated even further were it not for the entrance of a tall, long-haired vampire dressed in robes of crimson.

The vampire—a big wheel in the Order judging from his walk and bearing—came down the flight of stairs we'd been heading towards and said, "Perhaps I had better take command of this group now, Timos, before you come to blows."

Like the other Order minions we'd seen, he was lean. With his hands hidden in the sleeves of his robes, he had something of the appearance of an Asian monk, though the image was disturbed by his long, flowing blond hair. A shiny medallion hung round his neck, the hated insignia of the Order inscribed upon it. This was a symbol synonymous with death for so many of us.

The newcomer's voice was hard as iron, and he clearly expected to be obeyed. "It is very unbecoming for one of the Order to behave in such a manner, Timos. You should be ashamed."

Chastened, our host cast down his gaze. "Aye, Akrath. You shall have the honor of leading us to Azon, and I shall silence my tongue." Talk about whipped.

Akrath turned his attention to us, inclining his head in greeting. "I am Akrath. I am Azon's second-in-command, and I shall accompany you throughout your stay, brief as it may be."

"Oh, lovely," Jules sneered. "Instead of being led about by a snotty little prig with Azon's hand up his bum, we get a high-speaking, long-haired schoolmarm. I don't know about you, Brom, but I'm just having the time of my life."

"I'm feeling exceptionally privileged, myself," I replied, rolling my eyes. "Perhaps I'd feel even better if Akrath here would take a spear and shove it through his eyesockets, thus saving us the trouble of doing it later."

Instead of glaring at us like Timos would have, Akrath merely smiled. "I'm sure Azon will find your wit amusing. My colleagues have informed me my sense of humor is somewhat lacking, so I am unable to appreciate your barbs. Please follow me."

Akrath turned around and began to walk up the steps. Timos followed close behind, and we fell in place as well.

I looked at Jules, and he returned it. "Well, how do you like that?" he muttered as our group marched up the stairs.

I didn't like it at all. Jules and I had gotten ourselves out of difficult spots in the past by being so infuriating our captors slipped up—that was the idea with Timos. Then Akrath had showed up, and I got the feeling he wasn't going to go for the bait. I was hating this situation more and more.

"Akrath, could you put the hood of your robe up, please?" Jules asked very politely as we ascended the stairs.

"Why, may I ask?" Akrath inquired without turning to look at us.

"The shine of your lovely flaxen hair is blinding me," Jules replied, "you mangy jackass."

"My hood stays where it is," Akrath answered calmly. "Your friend can assist you in climbing the stairs if you need it. Be sure not to fall—the sudden movement might cause the revenant to lash out, and I'm not certain if Timos can maintain control in such a situation. I have my doubts about him."

Ouch. The ice in Akrath's voice was almost enough to sting *me,* and I hadn't said anything for the last minute or so.

"*Damn,*" Jules growled. "Now *I'm* starting to get annoyed."

I nodded. We continued up the stairs, crossed landings, and went up even more stairs, all the while tossing insults at the Order's second-in-command. No luck. Even though taunting Akrath did us no good, we kept at it, mostly to distract ourselves.

Everywhere we went, the décor was the same—the keep was jammed to the gills with treasures stolen from those who'd fallen before the Order. How many other villages had been crushed beneath their boot heel? How many other lives had been destroyed in the name of the "Goddess?" My stomach was a roiling sea of anxiety and fear.

After what seemed like a century, we reached our destination. Akrath knocked on a massive set of ornately carved double doors, and they smoothly slid open to reveal an impressive chamber that was a veritable museum of statues, tapestries, and other works of art. Our eyes widened at the elegant opulence of the high-ceilinged room, which was filled nearly to bursting with items of all description. It was a European version of a scene from *1001 Arabian*

Nights, opulent without overdoing it. Obviously, Azon took great care in his decoration; even mass murderers could have appreciation for aesthetics.

At the back of the room was a throne that would have made King Arthur at his peak feel inadequate. Constructed from high-quality polished wood and beaten gold, it gleamed on a hulking stone dais that raised it well above the rest of the room. Two guards, dressed in black, were posted on either side of the dais.

On the throne sat a black-haired vampire dressed in robes like Akrath's, except trimmed with gold and cut from better cloth. Around his neck was a golden medallion bearing the symbol of the Order. Azon, we presumed.

On the steps leading up to the throne were two people: one dressed in the typical uniform of the Crimson Order, while the other was a large, dirty figure dressed in ragged clothes. The latter was currently engaged in an argument with Azon. Well, *argument* was a misrepresentation: the man was shouting at Azon, who merely sat and watched with a vaguely amused expression.

As we stepped inside the room, the man stopped yelling and turned to look at us. It didn't take him long to figure out we weren't affiliated with the Order, and faint hope washed across his roughly hewn face. "Brothers!" he cried, his eyes slightly wild. "Are you also being punished for having the ability to think for yourselves? They captured me several—"

"Do not speak to them. They are not your concern. *I* am. Face me," Azon said in a voice that, while it was deep, flowed like liquid silver. It was a voice unaccustomed to disobedience.

"I am not your puppet! You cannot control me!" the man said, keeping his back to Azon.

A bare second later, the man's feet were several inches off the steps, and his neck was firmly in Azon's grasp. He struggled against the hand clutching his neck, but despite being brawnier than Azon, it was a lost cause.

"I don't wish to control you," Azon said, looking up at him with a smile. "You are a heretic, contaminated by the ways of mortals and utterly ignorant of the glory of the Goddess, and I cannot profit from your continued existence. Therefore, you are nothing to me. I am hungry, however, and Ramset here informed me you are very strong.

You killed a number of my men when they captured you. Strength is a quality I seek to cultivate in myself, and you will aid me in this."

Without a further word, Azon jerked the man forward and plunged his fangs into the poor soul's neck.

I began to protest, but the words died in my mouth as Azon brutally slammed the man to the steps and roared, "This is a *half-life!* How *dare* you bring me an unclean offering!"

Now the other vampire—Ramset, I presumed—was on the receiving end of Azon's grip, and he fought against his master's hand to no avail. The scraggly half-vampire was effortlessly pinned to the steps by Azon's foot on his chest.

"I did not know!" Ramset frantically protested, terror surging across his face. "He was so strong I assumed he could not have been a half-life! You have always said how weak they are—"

"They *are* weak, and you are a fool!" Azon snarled, his voice dropping to a feline growl. "Due to your incompetence, impure blood has crossed my fangs, and I must now cleanse them with the blood of a true vampire, however stupid that one may be!"

Ramset shrieked and twisted around as Azon bit into his neck, but his master held him firm, and his struggles rapidly weakened. Less than a minute later, his inanimate body lay at Azon's feet, horror forever etched on his now-still features.

"I do not suffer fools gladly, and may the Goddess find it in her heart to forgive your foolishness," Azon remarked to the corpse. He then reached down and roughly hoisted the half-vampire to his feet. "You are an abomination, my friend—neither vampire nor mortal," he said to the quivering man. "You know I cannot allow your continued existence."

"I have a right to be!" the half-vampire cried. "You can't condemn me just because I'm different from you!"

"Yes, I can, the Goddess has empowered me to do so." Azon ripped through the man's chest with the sound of tearing meat and crunching bone, and moments later, Azon held the man's shuddering heart in his gore-soaked hand. The man stared in twitching horror at Azon's acquisition as he gasped away his last few moments of life. "You disgust me and the Goddess both—to Terminus with you."

The half-vampire's body joined Ramset's, and Azon dropped the heart onto it.

"Remove these vermin from here," Azon ordered the guards, who quickly grabbed the bodies and scuttled out of sight. This was easily the most repugnant, vulgar display of power I'd seen in ages, and I longed to crush Azon's bones beneath my fists.

Akrath clucked his tongue as he stepped away from us, produced a crimson rag from within his robes, and handed it to his master. "Ramset should have tested the half-life himself to make sure of the purity of the blood," he said as Azon wiped the blood from his hand. "Mistakes such as this are growing too common these days."

Azon nodded, and handed the rag back to Akrath. It promptly disappeared back into his robe. "These mistakes will be coming to an end very soon, one way or another, I assure you." He looked over toward us and smiled. "Back to business."

"Come forth," he said, and stepped forward as we approached him.

He was slightly less lean than Akrath and a little shorter, though more powerfully built. His hair was even longer and blacker than mine, with skin like ivory and searing blue eyes burning with keen intellect and extreme cruelty. He exuded an air of command and control like few others I'd encountered before. I had a feeling that most, if not all, of his men would willingly follow him outside at high noon if he asked it of them.

This was the vampire who'd created the Crimson Order and killed countless vampires, mortals, and werewolves in senseless massacres. It was this vampire who called for the destruction of all who didn't fit the *Covenant of Blood*'s view of how the world worked, and did everything in his power to destroy the "heretics." It was this monster who had given the orders that burnt Runquist to the ground. It was because of this scum that Alena and Thaddeus were dead.

I probably would have been impressed if I hadn't been so enraged. I spat on the rug in contempt.

Azon tilted his head to one side, causing his waterfall of ebony hair to flow over his shoulders. "That rug is over five hundred years old," he said.

"I could not possibly care less," Jules said. He purged the contents of his stomach right there on the spot, to the visible horror of everyone assembled except for Azon and Akrath. I followed suit.

"That's what I think of you and your foul Order," I hissed, spitting the last of the slimy purge from my mouth.

Azon crossed his arms over his chest and eyed us like a school headmaster. "Eating is something not condoned by the Goddess. Not only that, it is a filthy habit," he informed us, holding out his hand, indicating the mess we'd made on his rug. He shook his head and regarded us with apparent regret. "You two are so old and so strong it is a genuine waste you have corrupted your vampirehood with ignorance."

"I like how I am," I growled at Azon with such open anger that the guards around Jules and I drew a little closer, and Akrath gave me a sharp look of warning. "You've no right to dictate to me what I should be."

"Oh, but I do," Azon told me, as if the "truth" should have been self-evident to me from the beginning. "Through me the Goddess speaks, and what I say is the verbal expression of her will. Vampires as a whole are too lazy and frivolous to bother coming to terms with their heritage. They deny the existence of the Goddess, and refuse to pay penance for their sins, so groups such as the Crimson Order come into being. We do not like what we do, but do it we must—it is the will of the Goddess. To disobey the Goddess is folly, guaranteeing one an eternal stay in the cold blackness of Terminus."

His eyes blazed while he told us this, and though there was no doubting his intellect, he was also a damned fanatic. Unfortunately, he was a highly effective fanatic.

"The *Covenant* states that vampires are not to kill one another, and to treat their fellows with love and graciousness," I said, trying to keep my voice level. "Those words are from the supposed Goddess herself, and now you turn around and tell us it's her will that you do the things you do: killing and slaughtering innocent vampires as though they were cattle?" I bit my bottom lip and did my best to maintain my composure, though it threatened to jerk away from me like a nervous horse.

Azon gave me a slight smile, a smile that reminded me of a snake. "It is true we are to treat our fellow vampires with love and graciousness, and to never strike out against them...*unless* they stray from the path of the Goddess. At that point we must do our best to convert them. If we cannot, we kill them rather than allow them to continue their wickedness and blasphemy against the Goddess. Better to condemn them to Terminus early instead of letting them run wild through the countryside, corrupting and perverting what a vampire should properly be. It cannot be helped sometimes."

"You didn't even try to convert Alena," I barked. "You simply killed her outright. You're murderers, pure and simple. You're just trying to put a good cover over it. Trying to legitimize yourselves by claiming to perform the will of some mythical deity taken from a book of lies written by madmen!"

I was seething now—dealing with religious types had always been frustrating almost to the point of being painful. This *was* painful. These monsters had destroyed my entire life from the past ten years and two people I'd loved dearly, and they had Jules and me at their mercy. It was all I could do to stop myself from charging Azon, the guards and revenant be damned. "You're wasting your immortality on nothing but *lies!*" I growled, my vision taking on a gently reddish cast, telling me my eyes were softly glowing red.

"You are so deluded, it saddens me," Akrath said, shaking his head.

"As it does me," Azon added.

"You're both a couple of jackasses," Jules growled.

Timos shot him a glare dripping with hate. The revenant snarled, and the guards around us shifted their weight uneasily. Both Azon and Akrath laughed softly.

"Who are these people, Azon?" a woman purred from my left.

From out of the collection of statues and ornate pieces of furniture slithered a woman dressed in flowing black silk robes. Her hair was the darkest shade of black I had ever seen, the skin covering her finely boned face was so pale it almost glowed. The woman's gray eyes were half shut as she watched Jules and myself, a faint smile on her scarlet lips. She seemed to glide across the floor like a spirit, sidling up next to Azon, who put his arm around her slim shoulders.

"These are Brom and Jules," he told her. "They are the heretics who lived in the village of Runquist." He turned his gaze back to us. "This is Tempestia, my consort."

Translated, that meant Tempestia was around because she amused him and gave him someone to feed from whenever he felt like it. This was the closest thing to affection that existed in the world of the Order and vampires who believed in the "proper way of things." I remembered cuddling up next to Alena on cold winter days and kissing her infinitely soft lips, and was disgusted at the empty gestures of "affection" Tempestia and Azon showed for each other.

"Oh, you mean your whore, eh?" Jules needled.

"Bitch," I corrected him.

Tempestia nodded slowly as she looked at us, her eyes still half-lidded. "You were right about them, Azon. They are the most ill-mannered, scruffy-looking heathens I have ever seen."

"You're not bad-looking yourself, wench," Jules leered. "Drop those silks of yours and let's have ourselves a nice show!"

Before Tempestia could reply, I fixed my gaze on Azon and said, "I thought the Order was against relationships like this. After all, aren't the ways of mortals—consorts included—forever denied you due to the decree of the Goddess? Doesn't the great and mighty Azon practice what he preaches?" I gave a haughty bow to Azon, and Jules mirrored me, though he wiggled his backside when he did.

Azon's eyes looked somewhat fuzzy for a brief second, as if his thoughts were somewhere else. "Tempestia is a special case," he said after a momentary hesitation. Tempestia looked pleased, though Akrath looked slightly embarrassed. These uppity-ups so hated it when their flaws were pointed out, especially little hypocrisies such as this.

"Oh, sure!" Jules said lecherously. "I can see she's a very special case, especially when I take a look at her saskatoons." He'd used a word we'd once heard from a Turkish trader. "So sweet! I can see why you'd give up the life of celibacy, Azon!"

Tempestia's narrowed eyes closed further, displeasure crossing her features. "I'm glad your village burned," she said. "Your people got what they deserved." She turned to me and snidely declared, "I'm glad your woman is dead too."

I bared my fangs at the hateful bitch. "Just wait," I said slowly and dangerously. "Just wait."

Tempestia giggled and stepped away from Azon. "You're a fool," she said to me. "You can't do anything to me."

"She's right," Azon said. "You're in no position to make any threats, and it's a waste of your time and ours to do so."

"What the hell is this about?" Jules demanded while I fumed at Tempestia. "Why so much trouble to bring us here?"

"To make examples of you," Azon flatly stated. "Our power has been slipping as of late. We had to leave Europe to make a short crusade to deal with another group of heretics, and we haven't been able to effectively reestablish ourselves since then. It was the first time most of us had ever left this country, and I think the uprooting and fighting in foreign conditions had a negative effect on my men. However, we intend to reestablish our influence more strongly than ever before. You two are the beginning.

"The both of you are the oldest vampires within a hundred mile radius, and you chose to live among mortals, scratching your living out of the dirt like a common peasant, emulating the ways of the mortals, the ways you have been expressly forbidden to follow. We will *not* stand for that. News of the destruction of Runquist will spread rapidly among both vampires and mortals alike, though only the vampires will realize the full impact. Word gets around very quickly among vampires in this part of the country, you know. That is how we learned of your mockery of proper vampirehood in Runquist. When it becomes common knowledge we razed an entire village to capture two heretics, it will make larger heretical vampire groups reconsider their way of life. If we would go that far to stop *two* heretics, what might happen if there were more?

"Once the news of the razing of Runquist is thoroughly disseminated, we will execute you in the usual manner, though I haven't yet decided on whether to burn you at the stake or crucify you. I admit I'm leaning in the direction of crucifixion, but I may surprise you. I am also debating about keeping one of you to feed from. Both of you are quite old and rather strong besides. It would be a shame to let all of your powerful blood go to waste. However, a double execution could be twice as effective as a single one… Hmmm. We are going to have to discuss this matter further, Akrath. This will have to be very carefully calculated—we cannot leave anything to chance," Azon said, rubbing his chin.

Akrath nodded at his master. "Yes. The general emotional

climate among the vampires at the time would definitely be a factor in the decision, my lord."

"Yes..." Azon said thoughtfully. He gave a slight shake of his head, and focused his attention on the present again. "In the meantime, the both of you shall be our guests—in the lower levels of the keep, though. The upper levels are reserved for more pious and proper vampires," he said with a chuckle. Tempestia joined him, while Akrath merely smiled.

I fixed Azon's gaze with my own. "I want to know one thing," I growled.

Azon spread his hands in a hollow gesture of generosity and said, "Certainly."

"Why did you kill Alena? You kept us in one piece, so why did she have to die? Tell me," I demanded, stopping myself from trembling only through an effort of sheer will.

"She was too corrupted by yourselves to be converted and too young to have been of any use to us," he answered. "You two are useful because of the potency of your blood and your age, which is also very significant in a symbolic sense. Her blood was the thin, weak gruel of the young, and her age would mean nothing to other vampires. She was just as useless as the mortals of the village and a heretic besides. It was best to consign her to Terminus."

"Alena was a greater vampire than you'll ever be, you bastard," I snarled. Jules grabbed my arm, realizing how close I was to blindly attacking. "I'll see you dead, Azon. I'll kill you. I swear by the blood of Alena you'll die by my hand."

Azon laughed at me and shook his head. "Such misguided energy. You would have gone far in the Order, Brom, had you not succumbed to your own foolishness. Of course, perhaps it is better this way—had you gone in a more proper direction, I might be competing with you for my job."

"Surely not, my lord," Akrath said.

"Your confidence in me is most reassuring, Akrath," Azon said to his lackey. "I was most wise when I chose you."

Akrath momentarily bowed his head in respect and said, "It was, and is, my ultimate honor."

Jules made loud kissing sounds, but he was ignored.

"Take them away." Azon pointed toward the door. "I grow tired of their presence. I will see them again at a time and place of my choosing." He gave Jules and me a significant look. "You are mine now and your fates will be determined by the will of the Goddess."

We both bared our fangs, but he didn't seem impressed.

"Escort them to the lower levels, Akrath," Azon commanded. "Put them in the same area where we keep the revenants. We'll see how easily they rest surrounded by the sounds of the most savage members of our force. I would say it was a pleasure meeting you, gentlemen, but I'd be lying."

"Come with me," Akrath said, leading us out of Azon's throne room, through the tall, ornately carved doors, back out into the corridors of the keep.

"Have a pleasant stay," Azon called after us.

"Die," Jules replied.

The doors of the throne room slammed shut behind us, and our small procession followed Akrath down the stairs and through an array of elaborately decorated corridors. "Don't you have any shame at all?" Jules asked Akrath. "His boots must have a mirror-sheen on them from all the licking you do."

"I serve Azon in the best capacity of which I'm capable," Akrath answered evenly. "I do as he sees fit."

"You're a sheep," Jules informed him. "The day an independent thought goes through your mind is the day your head explodes."

"I will not fail Azon," Akrath replied, sounding not the least bit annoyed by Jules's constant prodding.

We went down a steep flight of stairs, and picked up the sounds of growling from below. We were getting close to our new place of residence. I felt like a marauding lion cornered by the cunning African tribal warriors Jules and I had observed more than thirty years ago. My heart kept racing as we stepped off the stairs and into a corridor.

The revenant at the rear of our procession growled deeply and fidgeted as he heard the sounds of his kind. "We should move quickly," Timos whispered to Akrath, thinking we couldn't hear him. "It's going to be harder for me to control him the longer we're down here—the other revenants make him very restless."

"I realize that," Akrath replied softly. "But we must maintain our appearance in front of them."

Timos grumbled, but didn't argue any further. The growling of the other revenants grew louder, and Timos's revenant kept getting noisier as the seconds passed.

We stepped out of the corridor into a larger room with doorways opening onto other corridors on three of its walls, not counting the one through which we'd just come. There was a heavy oak desk here and tapestries depicting battles covered the walls. Two nervous-looking vampires stood watch by the desk.

A quick glance down the corridors confirmed my suspicions—each corridor was a dead-end lined with doors. The sounds of angry revenants emanated from all three corridors. This was a guardroom for the revenant section of the keep. The Order must have had to spread them out while still keeping them in a relatively small area; revenants didn't take well to each other's company.

"Place Brom in the east corridor, and the other in the west corridor," Akrath ordered the guards. "It is in our best interest to keep them separated."

From out of nowhere, Jules lunged and threw a vicious punch to Akrath's nose. The Order's second-in-command staggered back, holding his hands to his face. The guards leaped at us, having expected a move like this, but not in such a brainless and sudden manner. Luckily for us, that's what Jules excelled in.

I grabbed Timos and bit into his neck, savagely drawing blood from him as I hammered him with punch after punch. Screaming, he pulled free of my teeth, leaving a chunk of his neck in my mouth, which I promptly spat out, gut-punching him at the same time.

The revenant shrieked in rage as Timos's telepathic control faltered, and the grotesque monster grabbed the closest guard, biting into him with two-inch fangs and tearing him with unforgiving claws. Good. I headbutted Timos, knocked him down, and stepped on his face while I leaped at another guard, going for his eyes.

A scream from the corner told me Jules was busy at work, and I drove my thumbs directly into my guard's eyes then slammed his head against the near wall with a resounding *crack*. I tore the sword from his belt and slashed open his stomach. It had been decades since I'd last held a sword, but my reflexes instantly returned, and I hacked off the guard's head for good measure.

The revenant was going berserk, tearing away at the guards

closest to it while Jules and I maintained our distance during the melee.

Jules had also acquired a sword, and he drove it through another guard's heart with malicious precision. Akrath leaped at Jules while he was pulling his sword out of the guard's body, and I slammed into Akrath's back, smashing him into a wall. Jules and I both laid into him with our fists and feet. Akrath was probably at least as old as us, which made him dangerous in the first place, and being Azon's right-hand man didn't enamor him to us either.

The lean vampire was tough, I had to give him that. While Jules took a few seconds to beat back another guard, Akrath landed several heavy punches on me, which slowed me down for a couple of moments, but didn't stop me.

I swung wildly with my hand, bending my fingers into claws, and Akrath let out a satisfying yell of pain as I opened up three bloody trails across one of his eyes, though I didn't succeed in actually taking out the eye itself. I kept pummeling Akrath until I remembered my sword, at which point I stepped back. When Akrath lunged, I let my experience guide me, and I sliced him neatly across his throat, letting his own momentum push him more deeply into the blade.

As blood sprayed from Akrath's throat—the gurgling vampire frantically clutching at it—Jules snatched a torch from the wall and set fire to Akrath's robes. I drove my sword through the chest of the now-flaming vampire then delivered a solid kick to the face which knocked him down one of the corridors and left him lying motionless on the floor, facedown.

Good riddance.

As I turned, the revenant was upon me, and I cut up my knuckles punching him in the mouth. "Get back!" I roared at him, and kicked him in the stomach.

Blood sprayed everywhere as Jules sliced off the monster's arm and I kicked his feet out from underneath him. My left arm suffered several rips as the beast dragged his claws across it when he fell. The two of us started kicking away at the revenant, which then grabbed hold of Jules's ankle and pulled him to the floor.

"No you don't!" I yelled, and drove my sword through the side of the creature's head. He screamed, but held firm to Jules's ankle.

"Lemme go!" Jules screamed at him, frantically slashing away with his sword. "Lemme go! *Lemme go!*" he yelled over and over again like a mantra, wildly slicing at the revenant as fast as he could.

A crimson rain flew through the air, spraying us, the walls, and everything else.

Following Jules's example from a moment earlier, I swiped a torch from the wall and set the revenant's filthy rags ablaze. The shrieks it made were unbelievable, and the monster let go of Jules's ankle.

Limping only slightly, Jules dropped his sword, hurried over to the desk, picked it up, and unceremoniously slammed it down on top of the revenant. That put a stop to the beast.

We glanced around the room—between ourselves and the downed revenant, all the guards had been taken care of. Things were starting to look up at last. Damn, it felt good to be in marginal control of the situation again.

The noise from the other revenants was deafening. They smelled the blood and heard—and probably felt—the turmoil going on in the guardroom. I could clearly hear them beating against the metal doors of their cells as they hissed and snarled in bestial rage, raising a chaotic cacophony that rattled the walls and frosted the blood.

"The natives are getting restless," I said to Jules, who grinned at me, looking quite proud of the damage we'd done. "Is your ankle hurt very badly?"

"'tis but a scratch. Your arm?"

I flexed my arm, and though it stung, it didn't bother me much. "I'll manage," I replied.

"You…can't win," someone burbled from the floor.

We both turned and saw the shredded face of Timos peering up at us with his one remaining eye. His face and neck hung in bloody tatters—he looked more like a hunk of meat ready for cooking than the cocky vampire he'd been ten minutes ago.

"Care to lay odds on that?" Jules asked then cleaved Timos's head with his sword. "We're not dead yet."

"Speaking of which, we need to get moving," I said to Jules as the clamor of the revenants increased another notch. "I don't want to be around when the revenants embrace their newfound freedom."

"My sentiments exactly," Jules replied, and he snatched the

remaining torch from where it was affixed to the wall. With several quick motions, he set the tapestries hanging on the walls ablaze, and helped the already-smoldering desk sitting on top of the dead revenant along. "This ought to make sure they don't stay down here where they can't give the Order any trouble."

Revenants hated fire with a passion, and if there was a fire blazing in the guardroom, they'd put as much distance between themselves and it as they possibly could.

"Let's move," I said. "I've got a promise to Alena to keep."

We both ran from the burning room, Jules still carrying the torch. The bellows of the revenants were reaching fever pitch, and I thought I heard the sound of metal scraping against stone—time we were gone.

Two more of the Order's henchmen dashed out of a side corridor in front of us, and we didn't even slow down. Blood flew, screams ripped the air, and Jules and I continued on our way, swords slicked with new blood.

When we reached the set of stairs down which Akrath had led us, we stopped and Jules said, "I've been smelling gunpowder since we've been down here, and I've got a honey of an idea. If the Order's got a cache of the stuff somewhere, all we've got to do is find it and put where it'll blow this place sky high. A big enough boom, and we could take the Order off at the knees. What say you, oh fearless compatriot?"

As he talked about the gunpowder, Jules got a gleam in his eyes I knew all too well. Jules madly adored explosions, and if he could create a gigantic one as a means of exacting revenge, he'd stop at nothing to make it happen.

I considered his proposition. On one hand, it was a great idea, but on the other, Azon might be able to escape in the chaos and start anew somewhere else. I had to see him dead by my hand—I wouldn't, couldn't rest until I'd killed him.

I'd failed to protect Alena from the Order, and I'd sooner kill myself than fail in exacting the revenge that I'd sworn to. But, beyond my own need for revenge, the Order's base had to be taken out, scattering them to the winds and sending a message that the Order wasn't invincible.

But I'd *promised* revenge, and that revenge revolved around the death of the conductor of this symphony of madness, Azon. Not only did I want to kill him for Alena and Thaddeus, but I also wanted to kill him for *myself.*

Jules could read my consternation. Even without his empathy, he knew me well enough to know what was going through my head. "What if we split up?" he asked, anxiously looking around. "I could go find the gunpowder while you tore your way through the Order flunkies, and as soon as I got everything in place, I'd catch up with you."

I thought about this. I didn't want to lose sight of him, not here in the belly of the beast. The Order had already taken Alena and Thaddeus away from me, and if something happened to Jules, I'd never forgive myself.

He was tough, not to mention extremely fast and wily. If anybody could survive in these lower levels with the Order looking for him and the revenants running loose, it was Jules.

"Somebody's got to get to Azon quickly, before the alarm spreads," Jules said. "It might even be better for you to go up against them alone—you'll have the element of surprise and won't have to worry about the safety of anybody but yourself. I'll get back with you as soon as I've made my mark." Again his eyes glimmered at the prospect of making a large, highly destructive explosion, and warmth for my longtime friend galvanized my will further.

I reached out, grabbed Jules by the shoulder, and pulled him to me in a brief, fierce embrace—one between blood brothers and eternal friends. When I let go, he gave me a grin. "Listen for the big blast, and you'll see me not long afterward. Just don't do anything stupid, and we'll get out of this in no time."

He handed me the torch, then without another word turned and ran off back down the corridor, swiftly and silently like a cat, sword at the ready. I watched him go, and hoped with all my heart it wasn't to be the last time I saw him. Then I threw all such thoughts out of my head except for one thing and one thing alone: vengeance.

The sinews of my body tensed, ready for the battle, and my senses sharpened to a razor's edge as I tightened my focus to a tiny point. It was now or never, time to live or die by the sword. Vengeance was to be mine, and if not, I'd die in the most spectacular fashion I possibly could.

With a low growl, I lunged up the stairs, torch in one hand and sword in the other, ready to bring as much death and mayhem to the Order I could manage.

IV

I set fire to everything I could as I ran through the corridors of the keep, setting alight priceless tapestries and antiques, the likes of which would never be seen again. There would be time to mourn their loss at some later date; for now I was concerned with only one thing, and that was the dismemberment of the Order.

I encountered several groups of Order soldiers during my mad rush through the keep, and I mindlessly threw myself into their midst again and again, slicing and hacking until I was the only one left standing.

Despite my fury, I was absolutely silent during my assaults. I wouldn't allow myself to scream, bellow, or even growl as I fought. It wasn't because I was afraid of being heard—if anything was going to give me away it was the howls of agony coming out of the Order's henchmen as I hacked them to ribbons. I wouldn't make a sound because I wanted every last bit of my rage to come out through my violence. There would be no outlet except for my sword and the pain and death I meted out.

The tightness of the corridors within the keep served me well—in their closed confines I had an advantage against the Order. While they were getting each other's way, I moved around neatly and easily, slicing and slashing at any opening I got, using my torch to set clothing and surroundings ablaze.

Not only that, but my great age and experience served me well, granting me speed, strength, and cunning far beyond what the Order's soldiers could muster. While they had me greatly outnumbered, they couldn't stop me.

I pressed every advantage I could, I pushed myself to the absolute limits of my abilities, and though I didn't emerge from the battles unscathed, I was the only one to walk away from them. My clothes, leftover from the farm, were so stained with blood they were more red than anything else, while my face was covered in soot and streaked with gore, both my own and that of my foes. I drank as much blood as I could, feeding from the dying, trying to keep up my strength and to replace what I lost through my wounds.

Every cell of my body screamed at me to slow down, to take a breath, if only for a moment, but I couldn't stop. I had to keep going, I had to get to Azon and put an end to the Crimson Order, exacting my revenge and fulfilling my promise to both Alena and myself.

The Order had destroyed my life through their love of the supposed Goddess, something that didn't even exist, and now I did everything I could to destroy them through my love of Alena. She'd been brutally ripped from me, I could never hold her, I could never feel her soft skin, I could never kiss her again, and now I expressed my love for her the only way I had left—avenging her death by slaying her murderers.

Would she have been pleased with the death and destruction I wrought in her name? No, at her heart of hearts, she wouldn't have. Despite urging me to destroy the Order, Alena was never one to celebrate death in any form.

As I struggled with a revenant, dropping my sword and torch in the process, an image of her holding the body of her beloved pet rabbit Samuel, weeping at his death several years ago, entered my mind. Even as I smashed in the face of the revenant with repeated blows of my forehead, crimson tears ran freely down my cheeks.

Alena would have found all of this death distressing. At least the death in and of itself, but she would have understood and approved of what it represented: no more innocent lives being rent to pieces by the Order and no more lovers being taken from one another by these ignorant monsters. That was what she'd wanted when she'd asked me to avenge her. She hadn't so much wanted the deaths of the Crimson Order as she'd wanted the lives of other vampires, other people, and other lovers to be safe and free of the oppression of the covy fanatics.

My beautiful Alena…some might have called her view of the world naïve, but she meant it with all her heart. Naïve or not, she was noble in her conviction, and I would fulfill her final wish or die trying.

The revenant I was brawling with went low then tore through my tunic and flesh with an upward slash of its claws that cut deep. Through the haze of pain that invaded the clarity of my rage, I could feel a sudden flood of wetness splatter over the front of my body—I'd been hurt badly.

I blindly lashed out with my hand and tore through the revenant's eye before I stumbled backward several steps and fell flat on my face. The revenant staggered away from me, screeching in pain then I heard a scraping thud as it fell to its knees.

I looked up from the floor, barely able to move, to where the revenant was clutching its wounded face with both of its huge hands. Though I'd slowed it down with my desperate shot, it wouldn't be long until it got back up and came after me. I tried to lift my arm as I felt my blood spilling out underneath me, leaving me in a spreading pool of my lifeforce, but it was useless. I could barely even move my hand.

I'd pushed myself to my limits and beyond during my mad charge through the keep, and now that I'd been hurt, I was paying the price for it. Even a vampire as old and as strong as I could only take so much before his body finally hit a brick wall.

How long had it been since Jules and I had parted ways? Half an hour? Maybe a little longer? I hadn't slowed down at all since then, after coming out of torpor just earlier this very day, without any truly proper feeding or rest. Despite not being in the best of shape to begin with, I'd been a one-man army, ripping through the ranks of the Order, but that hadn't been enough.

I clumsily clawed at the stone floor as I struggled to regain my strength. Was this how it was going to end, in this smoke-filled corridor, surrounded by the broken bodies of my enemies, my revenge and promise only partly fulfilled? Was this how the grand adventure of my life was going to end...in failure?

What about Jules? Was he all right? Would he also end up dying at the hands of the Order because I wasn't there to help him? As these thoughts ran through my head, I made a sound again as I lay on the floor of the corridor close to the top of the keep: a moan of despair.

"Brom."

That voice. It couldn't be.

With an effort, I looked down the corridor, toward that sweet, beautiful voice, and what my bleary eyes beheld astounded me.

"Alena!" I rasped, my throat rough with smoke and fatigue. My hand raised itself from the floor, almost of its own accord, reaching towards her.

She stood down at the end of the corridor in the blue kirtle that accented her hair and eyes so well, and her angelic face was flawless, despite the smoke hanging in the air from the burning tapestries and furniture at the other end of the corridor.

"Brom," she said, sadness in her voice.

"Help me," I whispered, my hand falling back to the floor, and Alena held out her own hand.

"Come to me," she murmured, "Come to me, my love, let me give you the strength you need."

I struggled mightily with my exhausted body, trying desperately to get my limbs to work correctly, fighting with everything I had against the massive blood loss I was suffering. My soul screamed at my flesh to obey its commands, and slowly, but surely, it did, and I was on my knees, painfully crawling toward Alena. I didn't know how it was that she was standing at the end of the corridor, and I didn't care. She was there and I was going to her.

"Your sword, don't forget your sword," Alena said, and I grabbed the hilt of my adopted blade as I crawled across the floor, taking it with me. "You won't fail, my love," she said, her voice as wonderful as always. "Stay strong and come to me."

I was so out of it I didn't even realize how close I was to the revenant until it lunged at me, snarling in wounded fury. Though the logical part of my mind was gone, my instincts weren't, and I desperately latched onto the beast and plunged my fangs into its neck as it tackled me. As we tumbled across the floor, I greedily downed as much of its blood as I possibly could.

It tasted horrible, but within the degenerate blood was great strength, and that was what I badly needed. I rammed my sword through its torso all the way to the hilt, drawing another shriek from it, and regardless of the blows it rained upon me, I wouldn't let go.

I drank deeply of its blood, draining it dry, and after what seemed like centuries, my mind cleared and I found myself lying on the floor, entangled in the revenant's corpse.

My body, reenergized by the infusion of the monster's blood, went into overdrive, furiously healing itself, making my flesh tingle and burn. Within moments I could stand again, and I lurched to my feet. I remembered Alena, and I looked to the end of the corridor, but she was gone.

"Alena," I whispered, holding my hand out toward the place where she had been then drawing it back to my chest, where the wound the revenant had dealt me was still repairing itself.

The monster's claws had torn clean through my tunic and flesh, cutting so deeply it gave me pause as I felt the wound. If it had gone any deeper, it would have gotten my heart, and that would've been the end of me. I shuddered, realizing how close I'd come to my own demise, and that served to strengthen my resolve to defeat the Order even further.

"Bastards," I hissed, shoving a handful of my sooty, blood-soaked hair out of my face, *"Bastards."*

Speaking of which, a group of covies, clad in the black caped robes I took to be the standard garb for run-of-the-mill members, came rushing down the flight of stairs at the end of the corridor, right by where Alena had been. One of them pointed at me and snarled, "You shall go no further, heretic! This madness ends here and now, I swear by the Goddess!"

The floor shook underneath us, and a dull roar emanated from the lower levels. The covies looked shocked and confused, not knowing what had happened, but I knew... Jules.

I smiled as I charged the covies and tore them to pieces.

Once I reached the stairway leading to the uppermost level of the keep, where I'd last seen Azon, I involuntarily leaned against the wall for a moment, unable to help myself. I'd never felt so bone-weary in all my years, even after what must have been buckets and buckets of blood I'd taken from my enemies as I slaughtered them.

The wound on my chest was mostly healed, though it had been torn open again a few times during my ascent, and I'd accumulated other wounds as well. My body was in torment, struggling to heal itself while fighting for its very existence. I was one huge, throbbing ache, but I maintained my focus: I wouldn't stop until Azon lay in a heap at my feet. Then, and only then, would I even consider anything resembling rest.

"Just a little more," I rasped to my body. "We're almost there."

"Almost isn't good enough!" cackled someone from further up the stairs, and a catlike shape hurtled through the air toward me.

It hit me and knocked me to the floor before I had a chance to raise my blade. I immediately felt the slash of sharp nails and punctures of fangs rending my already abused and tired flesh.

As I fought to regain my bearings, I realized this swift and vicious attacker was that little bitch Tempestia. She had her fangs sunk deeply into the shoulder of my sword-bearing arm while her nails raked at my torso, and I had to stop the mad wench before she hurt me even more than I already was.

Skipping finesse entirely, I hammered her in the side of the head with a punch from my free arm, which hurt me in the process; it caused her fangs to tear at the punctures she'd already made, but I didn't stop. I slammed her with my fist again and again, amazed she could hold on with such tenacity. A dozen frantic punches later, she yanked her head back from my shoulder and spat a mouthful of my own blood in my face, which enraged me to no end.

I smashed her across the jaw with a wild punch that knocked her off me entirely, throwing her to the floor. Before I could swing my sword on her, she'd sprung back up and flung herself into me again, and I dropped the blade as we tumbled around, the sound of her catlike hissing and spitting filling my ears. By the stars, she was stronger than she looked.

I held onto her wrists, trying to get her under control, and she snarled, "You got past the others, but you won't get past me! Azon will not fall before a scum heretic like you, so commands the Goddess!"

Her gray eyes were crazed, the blood dripping from her mouth making her look even crazier, and when she started to cackle at me, I wondered if Azon had found his consort in a madhouse.

I said nothing, put all my waning energy into keeping her fangs away from my flesh, and wished that I wasn't so depleted. If I'd been at full strength, I could've taken her easily, but I wasn't, so I had to make do with what I did have.

She had me almost flat on my back, straddling my torso while snapping at me and trying to get her wrists free. I kicked against the floor as hard as I could, moving across it a few inches with each kick, trying to get up against the wall. Tempestia seemed oblivious and kept right on laughing and snapping, which was what I was hoping for. If she wasn't all there mentally, perhaps she wasn't all that clever, either.

After what seemed like hours, I felt the top of my head graze a stone wall, and I lifted my head and kicked against the floor again, so the back of my head was now flush with the wall. A few more kicks later, and my shoulders were firmly against the wall, which was right where I wanted them. I let go of Tempestia's wrists and lunged forward as swiftly as I could, and felt a huge thrill of satisfaction as my fangs sank into her ivory neck.

I shoved against the wall as I wrapped my arms around her, and we changed positions, with me on top of Tempestia, at last getting the advantage. Her laughing came to an abrupt end as she started screaming and struggling in my grasp. I don't think she liked the game we were playing any longer.

Tough luck. Her blood—while slightly odd-tasting—was delicious, much better than the revenant's. I drank as much as I could, and I felt some of my strength returning, which made it easier for me to hold her down.

"Let go of me!" she shrieked. "The Goddess will not stand for this!"

I kept right on drinking, hoping I'd drain her dry soon so she'd shut up, but she surprised me. Even with all the strength I'd regained from feeding from her wild blood, she somehow slithered out of my grasp. My fangs came free of her and before I knew it, she was on her feet again.

I swept my leg out and knocked her back down again, then made a mad crawl across the floor for my sword. Tempestia saw what I was doing and did the same. I managed to beat her to it, and just as I grabbed the sword, another rumble shook the floor beneath us.

What the blazes was Jules doing down there?

I took no time to wonder, however, as the momentary tremor gave Tempestia enough pause for me to drive my sword home through her chest. She let out a wail of pain and frustration, clutching at her wound. After I pulled my sword out, I grabbed her by the arm and flung her against the wall.

Blood sprayed out of her mouth as her head cracked against the stone, and I held my sword at the ready, in case she charged again, but all she did was stare at me with eyes rapidly draining of life. "You'll pay for this," she hissed, blood pouring out of her mouth. "The Goddess will make you suffer ten thousand years for this. The Crimson Order will never fall."

My only response was when I spat on the floor and licked her blood from the blade of my sword, making her writhe in impotent fury. But all the rage she could muster wasn't enough to stand against the damage I'd dealt her.

Her head began to fall to the side, the light fading from her eyes all the more swiftly. "The Goddess will make you pay, yesss..." were her last words to me before she slumped over into a broken heap against the wall.

As soon as I saw Tempestia wasn't going to make a further annoyance of herself, I headed back up the corridor toward the stairs leading to Azon's little throne room. I took the stairs two at a time, hugging the wall as I ran up the curved, torchlit staircase, taking a second to snag one of the torches as I hurried past.

I reached the top to find the huge wooden doors closed, but with no guards present. When I tested the door, it was locked. No surprise.

I studied the wood in the torchlight, and from the look and scent of it, the doors were made of oak. Not the softest thing in the world, but no problem for me to break through. I put my ear to the door and listened, but couldn't discern any sounds from within. Whether an ambush was waiting for me or not, I was going to smash through and make a grand entrance. At the very least, the violence of my entry would give me a second or two to get a good view of what was in the room and adapt to it.

I backed up, positioning myself at the edge of the landing, and after taking a deep breath, launched myself at the doors. When I hit, a sharp jolt of pain went through my shoulder where Tempestia had bitten me, but I rode it out and made it work for me, hitting the door even harder. I heard a sharp snap as the bolt gave way and both doors flew open, crashing loudly as they made contact with the stone walls on either side of them.

What I saw surprised me: Azon was standing alone on the dais with his back to the doors and his hands clasped behind him. He didn't turn around or even flinch when I stumbled into the room, and continued to gaze out the huge window that overlooked the valley below the keep. I hadn't noticed the enormous window the first time I'd been in the room—it had been covered over with a black curtain, but was now pulled off to one side. The window was glassed in with a delicate framework of panels much like that of a stained glass window in a church, save with clear glass instead of colored.

Outside a violent storm was raging, with sheets of rain hammering against the window and vivid thunder and lightning. Now that I was actually in the room, I could hear the sounds of the storm, and I would have been rightly impressed if I hadn't been so focused on Azon, who hadn't even bothered to face me yet.

"The Goddess is angry on this night," Azon said as I slowly walked across the carpet of the lavish room, alert for any attackers hidden among the sculptures, statues, furniture, and other pieces of Azon's collection. "Your actions have not pleased Her at all, I fear."

I said nothing, drawing closer with each step. I wasn't here to speak, only to kill, and as far as I was concerned, he could face away from me the entire time. I'd happily stab him in the back—just so long as he was dead, I didn't care how it went down. I didn't expect him to grovel or plead for his life, and I couldn't have cared less if he did… The only thing he had to do tonight was die by my hand.

As I neared the dais, Azon finally turned and regarded me, shaking his head.

"By the Goddess, you're a mess," he said. "We are the Fallen, true enough, but the least you could do is conduct yourself with some dignity and comportment. Just because we are descended from the tainted bloodline of Brahman doesn't mean you have to take up the appearance of an uncivilized savage."

By this time I must have looked like a demon from the fabled depths of Hell. My clothes were tattered, bloodied rags and my hair was a tangled, clotted mass. My eyes burned with the unhallowed fire of vengeance, and my fangs were bloodstained and fully bared. I was probably something most mortals—probably many immortals—would have run away from upon first sight, but Azon didn't bat an eyelash.

I continued to approach, slowly and deliberately, my gaze locked on Azon, but every other sense reaching out around me, waiting for an ambush.

"I suppose you have killed Akrath," said Azon, his tone that of a scolding parent. "He was a fine vampire. He truly understood his place in the world—something so few of us do—and he will be missed. But the Goddess will care for him, I'm sure."

I said nothing. He shook his head. "I assume Tempestia also fell to you, even after I let her take some of my blood as her own to give her additional strength. She was a trifle odd in the head, but loyal to the Goddess and myself as well. I know she'll be taken care of, as well."

He eyed me carefully, looking me up and down. "Despite your crudeness, you impress me. You've made it all the way up here from the lower levels, and have managed to knock aside every obstacle in your path. I suspect matters would have been different if the majority of the revenants hadn't been down in the lowest part of our home, but that's irrelevant at this point. I see your friend isn't here, though to the best of my admittedly limited thought-viewing capabilities, you feel no grief for his loss, so either you don't care that he is dead, or he is not dead and still running loose somewhere, quite possibly the source of the explosions that seem to be plaguing the lower levels."

Regardless of how close I got, Azon still held his ground and didn't look the least bit concerned.

"You would have been a boon to the Order, my friend," Azon said softly. "It's a pity you chose the path you did. With your strength and determination, you could have been our very own avenging angel, defending us and the Word of the Goddess all over the continent. The heretical Circle of Magnus created something of that nature not all that long ago, something to be used against us, but the Goddess saw to it that it destroyed them and itself. No, you are no cobbled-together monstrosity. You were created whole and nearly perfect by the hand of the Goddess herself. You betrayed your destiny and spat in the face of the Goddess. For that you must perish."

I had almost reached Azon by then, and as soon as the last word had come from his mouth—before I even had a chance to blink—he was right up in my face, holding my wrists with an agonizingly powerful grip. He bared his fangs scant inches from my face, his eyes blazing red, and with a loud hiss, he flung me backward across the carpeted floor.

I held onto my sword but dropped my torch, and was barely able to roll away from Azon as he tried to deliver a kick to my ribs. I kicked him in the knee, causing him to stagger a step. When he did, I charged him like I had his doors, bowling him over backward and against the steps of the dais.

I tried to bring my sword up to slice at him, but he knocked me aside with a swat of his hand, throwing me through the air and making me land on my wounded shoulder. Another bolt of pain shot through my arm, but I ignored it and struggled into a crouching position, coiled and ready to spring. I'd underestimated Azon—he was far stronger than I'd taken him for, and would have been a challenge even if I'd been in top condition.

Azon stood smirking on the steps of the dais. "You cannot defeat me, you fool," he said with the utmost confidence. "The Goddess will not allow it. The deaths of the other members of the Crimson Order can come about, but mine will not. I have led the Order for centuries now, and I will continue to do so for centuries more. *That* is the decree of the Goddess, and a heathen such as yourself will not change that. The only way that you can hope to survive is to give yourself to the Goddess. Your sins can be paid for by spending the rest of your time in this world with dutiful and loyal service to the Goddess. Think about it. You will no longer be casting about pointlessly with your existence, you will have a purpose and a reason for being, and it will be a most righteous purpose!" Azon held his arms out above his head like a preacher enraptured with his lord.

"Join the Crimson Order," Azon commanded, his gaze locked on mine. "It's the only way for you to survive!"

"I'd rather die," I snarled, and spat on the carpet.

"Then so be it!" he declared, drawing back and gathering himself, and in the split second before he would have rushed me, I saw something in the window behind him. It was a dark silhouette, with two blazing red eyes, and it was flying right toward the window. I smiled.

Glass exploded into the room as Jules shot through the window at full speed, slamming into Azon with enough momentum built up that he carried Azon off the dais right toward me. The slim vampire showed that perhaps he was better at flying than I thought by stopping in midair to let Azon continue without him, but I was considerate enough to help stop Azon's unscheduled flight with my sword.

I did end up stabbing Azon in the back that night. He'd twisted in the air, and my sword entered his body just around his left shoulder blade and came out somewhere on his chest, either going right through the heart or taking a good slice along it on the way through.

I came close to being knocked off my feet by the out-of-control vampire's momentum, but I dug in my heels and stayed upright. Jules dropped to the carpet, pulled his own sword out of a scabbard he'd swiped somewhere along the line, and neatly skewered Azon through his abdomen, and the blade came out of the monster's back just a foot or so below where I'd ran him through.

Azon groaned and gurgled, weakly flailing around on our two blades. Jules met my gaze and we both let go of our swords. Azon fall to the ground, and we kicked the shit out of him.

I stomped on Azon's head and screamed at him, "That's for Runquist!"

I stomped again. "That's for Thaddeus!"

Again. And again. And again.

"That's for Alena!"

Again.

"That's for Jules!"

I kicked him in the side of the head, sending blood spraying out of his mouth.

"That's for me!"

Jules backed off as I grabbed Azon by the neck and lifted him up off the floor with one arm. I looked into his bloody, ruined face and laughed. I wondered if he could even still hear me. I didn't care.

I motioned for Jules to pull my sword out of Azon's back, while I pulled Jules's out of his abdomen and let it clatter to the floor. Azon groaned, and I met his eyes and said, "This is for everybody who's ever had to lose someone they loved because of your false gods and book of lies! *You make me sick!*" I roared at him.

Holding him with one hand, I jammed my hand through the flesh of his chest, smashed through his ribcage, and grabbed his weakly beating heart. With a twist, I ripped it free of the chest cavity. I held it up in front of Azon's now-ashen face and crushed it to pulp in my hand. "Your Goddess is nothing, and so are you. Vengeance is *mine!*"

Tossing his heart aside, I held Azon over my head, took a few steps, and flung him against his throne as hard as I could and smashed his pompous seat of power to pieces. The bastard didn't move, and never would again.

Jules and I looked at Azon's body for a few moments, then at each other. My friend was as much of a wreck as I was, though it looked like he'd crawled through a city's worth of chimneys and had then gone for a swim instead of rolling around in a slaughterhouse. We grinned broadly at each other as what we'd just accomplished made its full impact on us. For the first time since before I'd felt the first jolt of pain through the bond I'd once shared with Alena, I felt a part of me loosen.

"So what took you so long to catch up?" I asked.

"They had more explosives than I thought, so I scattered some about here and there, nice little caches, you see," he said gleefully. "And I set fires all over the place, fires that would eventually make it to the explosives, the gunpowder and such, and then I got the hell out of there. After blasting a hole in one of the outer walls so I could make good my escape and then freeing all the animals from their stables, of course."

Jules was talking a mile a minute now, and it felt good to listen to him babble after hearing nothing but screams, snarls, and the diatribes and threats of fools for so long. "Then I climbed up the side of the keep, hoping to find a way into one of the upper levels so I could come find you, and that's when I noticed the window, so I went up to take a peek in on it, and saw you in here with Azon, and I decided it was high time I entered the fray and saved your sorry tail once again!"

"And a damned fine job you did too," I said, and we had another quick embrace, each relieved the other was all right.

Only then did we notice that a great deal of the material piled up in the throne room had been caught on fire from my forgotten torch.

The fire was leaping high, feasting on all the assembled treasures, and the smoke was getting thick in the air, despite the hole in the window.

"Perhaps it's time that we made our exit. I think we're done here," I said.

"Indeed. It shouldn't be too much longer until some of my other caches get set off by one or other of the fires I started, so we should be gone before this place comes down," Jules said.

The two of us made our way over to the window, taking the time to stick our swords into Azon before we departed, as a parting gift to our host for his hospitality.

As Jules and I flew through the window of the burning throne room, I whispered, "Rest in peace, Alena. You have been avenged."

Jules and I sat on a crag not far from where the Crimson Order's keep burned in the night. As the keep had been built with no windows other than the one in Azon's throne room—so no daylight could get in whatsoever—the heat inside the keep kept building, and I imagined it was like an oven within the walls, even with the hole Jules had made in one of the outer walls.

The heavy rain pouring down couldn't do a thing to help anyone still running around in there, and after the two of us had run loose in there, I doubt there were all that many left. The Crimson Order was doomed.

Several explosions rocked the lower levels of the structure, Jules's caches finally igniting and doing their damage. An explosion hit the highest level of the keep too, not very far from where we had estimated Azon's throne room to be—the reason of which we were uncertain, since Jules hadn't left a cache there, but we didn't give it much thought as the keep started to crumble. We had won.

I sighed heavily. The rain soaked my weary body, cleaning the blood and soot from me, and the chill it brought helped take an edge off the heat of my wounds. Both Jules and I were aching and exhausted, both physically and emotionally, and we said little as we watched the base of the Crimson Order burn. I still keenly felt the pain of Alena's loss, but now at least there was closure, after a fashion.

I couldn't bring her back, but at least Jules and I had made sure there would be no more Runquists and no more massacres, at least at the hands of the Crimson Order. I didn't even want to think about the other fanatics in Europe. How many more of us would die as a result of vampires like Azon? How long until they learned? I shook my head. Too long.

"Where to now?" Jules asked as a lightning bolt ripped across the black sky.

"America," I said. "Where they don't have fools like Azon, or at least not as many. We can make a fresh start there. I've had enough of Europe to last me the rest of my days."

Jules nodded. "Sounds good. I've heard those American women have got some real kick to them."

"That's the spirit," I said, punching him on the shoulder. We sat in companionable silence for a time, watching the former home of the Crimson Order, now its funeral pyre.

The keep crumbled even further, and flames erupted from the massive fissures that opened in the sides of the structure, spitting out into the rain. As the keep tumbled to a pile of rubble and parts of it slid down the side of the peak, I said to Jules, "Let's get out of here."

"We made it back to Runquist two days later, and there wasn't anything left other than a burned-out ruin," I said. "We were in America six months later, and we haven't been to Europe since, and I never intend to go back. I don't even really know what the situation is like in Europe these days where vampires are concerned. I don't care, either. As long as I've got Hollywood and Los Angeles, I'm more than happy."

The hours had rolled by during the telling of the story, and though none of us wore a watch, my vampiric sense of time was telling me it was well past daybreak outside. The night was over, and now people other than Stacey and myself finally knew the tale. Though remembering and relating all of it had been an emotional roller coaster for me, it felt good to have shared it after all of the years gone by.

Clarisse and Katheryne had sat quietly while Stacey and I finished the tale, and they both looked slightly off balance by what had been said.

"I'd never realized," Clarisse said, looking at me with pride and love in her sapphire eyes. "I could feel through our bond it was something that had touched you deeply, and I'd known you'd loved a girl named Alena, but… Wow," she concluded, shaking her head.

I nodded.

There was no jealousy in Clarisse's voice where Alena was concerned. After all, it was a given that a vampire of my age would have had at least several lovers in his time, the same going for Clarisse, and we didn't feel petty jealousy over the past in the way many mortals did.

Instead she'd come away from the tale with a more profound understanding of why I was the way I was. Why I was so fiercely determined that no harm would ever come to her as long as I was alive and kicking. I think she also gained an understanding of why I wasn't all that concerned with getting myself out of the lair of this new Crimson Order.

I could see it in her eyes she was catching on that I'd already determined what my destiny was going to be, regardless of what the Crimson Order attempted, and that scared her a little. Stacey and I were in this until the very end, for better or worse. I know she didn't like that prospect, but at least she understood it.

As if she were reading my mind, Clarisse said, "At least this time you two won't be alone. I love you for your concern for me, but I'm not leaving here without you, even if I get the chance to escape. If I ran, I couldn't live with myself, no matter what happened."

I nodded again, not surprised. It would have been pointless to argue with her, as strong-willed as she was, and the steely look in her eyes broached no argument. I'd never seen her back down from anything in all the time I'd known her, and that was just one of the reasons she had my utmost respect.

Just as I'd loved Alena for her gentleness, I loved Clarisse for her strength. The Crimson Order may have found sweet Alena to be easy pickings for their cruelty, but they were going to find Clarisse an altogether different story.

I'd moved closer to her during the course of the tale and she reached toward me. I gave her my hand, which she squeezed tightly.

"I'm not gonna die on you, baby, I promise," she said, and I smiled at her.

"I'm holding you to that," I replied.

She smiled back, moving a finger over the left side of her chest. "Cross my heart and hope to die, stick a needle in my eye."

Stacey grunted. "Visceral fucking kid's rhyme. Buncha little eye-stabbing hoodlums, no wonder the world's in such a messy state." He snorted, eliciting a chuckle from Clarisse and myself, and even a faint grin from Katheryne.

Katheryne had listened with unbearably intense raptness during the tale, and now that it was done, it was as though some of the darkness surrounding her had been lifted. She still didn't look happy, but she didn't look defeated, either, and I took that as a good sign.

"Like the story?" I asked Katheryne as I tore my gaze away from Clarisse.

The blond witch slowly nodded. "Thank you," she whispered, and I could see from her eyes that she meant it with her entire soul. "I'll never forget it."

"Promise?" I asked softly.

She graced me with her little smile. "Promise."

"As much as it pains me to bring an end to such a touching display of love among friends, I fear I must interrupt," said someone from outside the cell. Akrath.

His scarred face watched us from the barred window of our cell door, and I again wished for laser-beam eyes.

"If you don't mind, this is a private party, no Akraths allowed," Stacey growled.

"It seems rather late to be informing me of that," Akrath said lightly, "as I have been out here listening for approximately ten minutes now. I had come to summon you, but I thought it polite to allow you to finish your tale. Though you are both in possession of some very unsavory qualities, I will have to say you are both rather engaging storytellers."

Stacey and I exchanged disgusted looks, annoyed that something as personal as what we'd just told to Clarisse and Katheryne had been heard by unwelcome ears, even if those ears had been attached to a vampire who'd been a part of the tale.

"Your thumbs-up review warms the cockles of my black little heart," I sneered at Akrath, and Stacey rolled his eyes.

"Yeah, all you need now is some big fat guy to be your counterpart and you can start going out and reviewing movies. It's either that or you can keep hanging around the Order and get killed by us," he said, looking dagger eyes at the bald-headed vampire, who looked unmoved.

"I doubt very much I will die by either of your hands," said Akrath. "You both tried, and failed. The Goddess saw to it I survived, and I will continue my service to the Goddess until the day She sees fit to remove me from this plane of existence. But enough of these pleasantries. Your presence has been requested by one of great importance, and I don't want to keep that one waiting much longer."

The four of us all made eye contact, then slowly got to our feet and started to move toward the door of the cell. Through the barred window, I caught glimpses of a pair of werewolves behind Akrath, and I could hear the grunting of a revenant somewhere out there too. It looked like the Crimson Order was making sure we had a good escort on our way to meet whoever was waiting for us.

"Still think it's Azon?" Clarisse whispered as we stood at the door and waited for one of the Order lackeys to unlock the door of our cell.

"I hope not," I replied. "But then again, I've also seen stranger things happen."

"Yeah," Stacey added, "Akrath is still around and being bothersome, even after we stomped him, sliced him, and set his shit on fire, so it wouldn't surprise me if ol' Azon hadn't found some way to cheat death and come back to annoy us for one more go-round."

Katheryne said nothing, but merely stood and waited for the cell door to be unlocked, her arms crossed over her chest, her face impassive.

Once the door of the cell had been unlocked, Akrath motioned us out into the hallway, where we found our escort was rather sizable. There were three werewolves, four revenants, plus two masters and several other "ordinary" Order members, dressed in the ubiquitous black robes.

"All of this for little ol' *us*?" Stacey asked in a mock Southern accent, looking flabbergasted. "Ah didn't think we all was so special to y'all!"

Akrath shrugged with one shoulder. "Personally, I do not find either one of you special at all, but then, I am not the one giving the orders around here, so I must abide by what I am told."

Stacey and I glanced at each other then started making rude kissing noises at Akrath. Unimpressed, he eyed us and said, "Remember...it would be wise for the two of you to behave yourselves in this context. This time around, we have a bit of, shall we say...*insurance*." He looked squarely at Clarisse and Katheryne, which made me shiver just the slightest bit.

Clarisse hissed loudly at the bald vampire, then slowly growled, "Don't you *dare* use me as a living shield, you pussy."

Akrath gave us a smile and replied, "A coward is what mindless berserkers call pragmatists. Oddly enough, it is the pragmatists who usually end up surviving the battles."

"Suck it," Stacey snapped.

Akrath didn't even dignify Stacey's request with a response. Instead he gave an order for the escort to surround us, which they did with an almost military quickness.

As we walked through the dimly lit tunnels, penned in by our enemies, we hung together in a tight knot, Clarisse and I holding hands. Occasionally we passed a few Order members here and there, but for the most part the corridors were empty.

After a time, I got the distinct feeling we were being taken the long way to our destination, a standard mind-game designed to raise tension. I didn't let it get to me. What was going to happen was going to happen regardless of how long it took to get there. When the shit hit the fan, we were going to take full advantage of it. Stacey and I had beaten the Crimson Order once, and we could do it again.

"There you are!" said a someone with a voice that sounded at once familiar and unfamiliar. We came to an abrupt halt as all of the Order lackeys stopped in their tracks. "I was beginning to think history was going to repeat itself!" The sound was coming from somewhere ahead of us, and the acoustics of the stone tunnel made the voice harder to identify.

"Not at all," said Akrath. "I was merely giving our guests time to prepare themselves."

"You truly are too kind," said the other speaker.

As I twisted around to see who it was, I thought I caught a glimpse of crimson robes similar to Akrath's, though the hood was up and I couldn't see the face.

"It's not Azon…is it?" asked Clarisse, trying to look around the two werewolves in front of us.

"I…don't know," I replied, trying to remember what Azon's voice sounded like, but my recollections were distorted by time. For all I knew, it could have been Azon up ahead of us.

But then again, something didn't seem right…and I'd ripped his heart out myself, after all. But like I'd told Stacey earlier, stranger things had happened. Where vampires are concerned, one should keep the idea of "never say never" in mind.

"Wait just a damn moment!" Clarisse squeaked, jolting. "I think I've—"

"So let me see our guests, Akrath," said the unidentified speaker. "Don't be so rude, let them cast their gaze upon the one who wanted to see them!"

Akrath was agreeable. "Of course, forgive me for my lack of manners, wise one." He ordered our escort to spread out slightly.

The two werewolves in the front of the group parted, and Akrath stepped aside, giving us a good look at the crimson-robed figure standing before us, his face obscured by his hood. The last time I'd seen the likes of him, he'd been standing on top of a building egging his covy pals on with promises of paradise, and had then been torn to pieces by a horde of angry vampires.

Or not.

"I am Barzai the Wise," said the figure as he stepped closer to us, "The mastermind behind the attack on your precious city and the engineer of your recent capture, though a few of my more bestial soldiers got a bit overly enthused with their duties. Welcome to the base of the Crimson Order, the last place you'll ever see before your deaths!" He let out a screeching, high-pitched laugh that made something in my head click.

"Barzai my ass!" Clarisse burst out, stomping her foot and pointing at the robed figure. "I've been around you before, you little shit!"

From the sputtering behind me, I think Stacey had reached the same conclusion Clarisse had. I was there too, but I sure didn't like it.

"Oh, I am Barzai, let me assure you!" said Barzai, and he started to reach up for his hood, "But I have also been known as…"

"Frizz!" I roared as the hood came back to reveal the useless piece of trash I'd last seen struggling with a revenant in a back alley.

The yellow-haired vampire laughed gleefully, his eyes shining with delight. "You did that perfectly!" he crowed, his eyes alight. "Just like in the movies! I was hoping you'd do that! It was perfect! Wasn't it perfect, Akrath?"

"Yes," replied Akrath simply.

Despite my surprise and anger, I noted Akrath didn't sound all that happy with the little runt of a vampire. He sounded obedient enough, but there was an undercurrent of displeasure. I didn't give it much thought...I was too busy trying to figure out the hows and whys of this little dickhead's collusion with my old enemies.

"Easy, champ, easy," said Stacey into my ear as I growled at the grinning Frizz. Clarisse held onto my arm tightly, a nonverbal command to stay put.

"In case you couldn't tell," Frizz said, obviously enjoying every word, "the reports of my demise have been greatly exaggerated. Both demises, actually!" Then he let fly with one of the most annoying donkey laughs I'd ever had the displeasure of hearing. The worst part of it was that he wasn't laughing like that to be especially obnoxious—it was his *natural* laugh.

Behind me, Stacey whispered to Akrath, "So you got your ass kicked by Steele and me, got burned up, lived to tell about it, and you're still serving the Order a century later, and you're playing second fiddle to that *geek*? You need to find a new line of work or something, dude—you're getting ripped off."

"I should've killed you when I had the chance!" I snarled at Frizz, who laughed again, pleased as punch.

"Killing me would have been a great disservice to vampires everywhere," he replied, and fanaticism lit up his eyes. "You would have destroyed the one who'll help lead the Crimson Order and vampirekind into a new age of understanding and piety to the Goddess. If you'd killed me, you could have doomed all vampires!"

"I highly doubt that," I sneered, wishing I could freeze everything in the entire world save Frizz and myself for five seconds—that's all I would've needed to completely wipe that little bastard out of existence. "The only thing doomed around here is the Crimson Order. With an incompetent like you at the helm, they're on the path straight to the junkheap… even Stacey and I aren't as dangerous as your own ineptitude."

At my words, Frizz's eyes narrowed, and the glee in his eyes faded, replaced by genuine anger. "I wouldn't say that if I were you, Steele. I wouldn't say that at all. After all, it was my idea to send out a double in my place during the Battle of Los Angeles. If I'd gone out there myself, I wouldn't be able to lead the Crimson Order now, would I? That's planning in advance for you. You could learn a thing or two from me," Frizz growled, like a nerd finally getting a chance to one-up a high-school tormentor. "And not only that, it was my idea that got you captured, wasn't it? It was *me* who thought of those two plans! You should respect my abilities!"

"What abilities?" I asked, my anger channeled away from out-and-out rage to something far more snide and slithering, and my voice dripped with scorn. "Your sloppy eating tendencies? A lack of killer instinct that drives you to try feeding off defenseless children?"

Thinking back to the battle and our encounter with Frizz in the parking garage, I made an educated guess then spat, "And if you think you're so brilliant, why the hell couldn't you round me or Stacey up back in the parking garage? Unless I miss my guess, which I so seldom do," I sneered. "You were going to try capturing us then and there with the cute little ambush, right after telling us something that would make us leave the garage as soon as possible. Then if you'd gotten a ride with Stacey, you would've tried to get his ass in the grinder too, one way or another. But you couldn't, could you? You thought you had a flawless plan right there, two vampires with one stake, huh? But you fucked it up, didn't you?"

Frizz was getting royally angry as I pressed on, my voice getting louder and cockier with each word. The glow of his grand revelation had gone straight down the *terlet*, as Archie Bunker would have said. I was enjoying watching him start to twitch in rage as I snapped away at him, and that just encouraged me to be even more of an asshole.

"You fucked it up like you fuck *everything* up, you dumb piece of shit! And not only that, I bet on the night of the first crucifixion, you tried to get me to go with you so you could have grabbed me and made me your trophy prisoner there too, eh? Hold me hostage so you and your boys could just waltz on into the city and take it? You're an idiot, Frizz, a total loser."

Frizz was shaking and quaking in anger, his eyes flickering red, and I could sense the tension building up in our escort. Akrath stepped over to Frizz. "Now is not the time for this, wise Barzai," he said. "We must—"

Frizzed thrashed around like he'd been jabbed in the ass with a cattle prod. "I wasn't trying to capture you that night!" he screamed at me, his arms flailing about wildly. "I was trying to get you to go with me to give you a chance to join us and realize the love and glory of the Goddess! I was trying to *save* you, Steele!"

I folded my arms over my chest and met his mad eyes. "If joining the Crimson Order is being saved, I'd rather die."

"Barzai, please, this is not—" Akrath began again.

"Shut up, Akrath!" Frizz yelled at the bald vampire and gave him a shove. He glared at me, one of his eyes twitching steadily. "Oh, you'll die all right," he whispered angrily. "If not your body, then your soul when you lay your eyes upon the Goddess and she opens your eyes to the reality of her love. After your soul has crumbled, she'll remake you into a proper vampire… Either which way, the heathen vampire you are now is going to die."

"Promises and threats, threats and promises," I sing-songed. "I couldn't give a tinker's damn about your Goddess. What I want to know is how a little nobody like you got this little army together and got the werewolves to cooperate. I don't care what you think of yourself or what these guys think of you, I know for a stone-cold fact you're an incompetent fucknut and you couldn't have done this by yourself. So who's using you as their figurehead? Who's the man behind the curtain?"

Murder in his eyes, Frizz hissed, lower and meaner than he ever had before. "Nobody's using me, you fool. I'm doing this on my own with the guidance of the Goddess. She handpicked me out of all of the vampires in Los Angeles to lead her followers, and then gave me everything I needed!"

"Yeah, horseshit." I snorted. "Welcome to the real world, Frizz. Stuff doesn't work like that, remember? Those revenants and other vampires came from somewhere, not to mention the werewolves, and you don't have enough going on to get a Boy Scout troop organized for a picnic. You can tell me all the pretty stories you want, but you're just clutching onto that shit because you think it validates your existence. You think it makes you out to be the good guy and me and my kind to be the uncaring jerks who pissed on you because we're assholes. Wrong-o, you punk-ass bitch. We pissed on you because you're a piece of shit and we don't suffer fools gladly, Frizz."

"Shut up," Frizz growled. "Just shut up."

I forged ahead. "You had every chance in the world, and got more tolerance from us than you deserved, but you kept fucking up and proving how worthless you are. If you think I or anybody else regrets the way we treated you because of the bind we're in now, you're fooling yourself. Even if I end up dying by your puny hand, I still won't regret treating you like the nothing you are because you got what you deserved. The only thing I'll regret is not killing you when I had the chance!"

As soon as I finished speaking, I spat on the floor, and my three companions all did the same. I gave Frizz my most slimy smile. "Your false goddess doesn't scare me, and neither do you."

Frizz looked ready to cry. His face was crumpled and his eyes were lost—he'd expected us to fall to our knees in fear or worship of him, and what he'd gotten was condemnation and collective contempt. As I stared him down, I felt no pity in my heart for him, not an iota, and I hoped that before I died, I'd feel my hands around his neck.

He took two steps toward me, and I straightened my stance even further, completely defiant. Frizz's frustration started to transmute into anger again, and I could see it welling up in him. If not for Akrath, I think the little peckerhead would have tried to jump me. A pity.

"Barzai, *please*," hissed Akrath, looking pained. "The Goddess awaits… Let's tarry no further. Arguing with him will get you nowhere. He is too firmly entrenched in his ways to be swayed or frightened with mere words. I know this from past experience. He must be witness to the Goddess."

Frizz continued to twitch and stare at me while I grinned back at him.

Clarisse then said, "You know, I can at least respect Akrath for his loyalty and integrity toward his beliefs, misguided as they are, but you Frizz… Man oh man, are you a piece of work, you little worm. I've seen fledglings who had their shit together better than you. If you're running things around here, I'm not the least bit afraid anymore. Bring it on, little man."

Her voice simultaneously purred and sneered, overflowing with contempt, and that angered Frizz even more. It was one thing to get shot down by the guy he had been trying to impress/scare. It was another thing to get shot down by his gorgeous girlfriend. The former sucked, the latter…hurt. At least for a guy.

"You bitch," he growled to Clarisse, his screechy voice sounding about as threatening as a housecat in heat. "I'll make you mine. When the Goddess breaks Steele, you'll be mine. She'll give you to me, I know she will, and then I'll make you scream, you whore!"

If this kept up much longer, Frizz was going to go completely to pieces—it was *great*. From the look of urgency on Akrath's face, he'd reached the same conclusion, though he didn't share my opinion. I didn't get why he just didn't yell at Frizz the same way he had the others. But then, I couldn't figure out why the blazes Akrath was playing second-in-command to a goof like Frizz in the first place.

"Yeah, I'd scream all right…in laughter. My usual reaction to dickless bitches like you," Clarisse shot back. "The Muppets are scarier than you are." That brought a loud guffaw from Stacey, who'd been a huge fan of the Muppets since the *Sam and Friends* days.

"Crazy Harry, motherfucker!" Stacey barked, throwing up the horns in Frizz's direction.

"This can go no further," Akrath said firmly, putting his hand on Frizz's trembling shoulder. "We must go to the Goddess now. Let it be." Frizz didn't look like he wanted to, and Akrath reiterated. *"Let it be."*

Thirty tense, twitchy seconds ticked by before Frizz said, "Very well, Akrath, very well." He swept his gaze over all of us then whispered, "You'll pay when you meet the Goddess, you'll see. You'll be begging for your existence very soon, Steele, and you'll regret everything you've ever done against the Goddess, and everything you ever did against *me*. You'll fall before the glory of the Goddess, I promise you."

Stacey snorted. "Shit, after you've drained as many acid-heads as I have, seeing gods is something you do when you've got a few minutes to kill," he said, and then added, "Boo yah!"

"You'll see," Frizz hissed as menacingly as he could, "You'll see."

Things fell back into order—no pun intended—and we were all ushered along through the corridors again toward... wherever.

We were supposedly on this little field trip to go see the Goddess, but I had my doubts. I was thinking more along the lines of them trying to make us repent our sins by threatening to stick us in the sun. After all, wasn't the Goddess supposed to be the sun itself? I'd heard of practices like that among various covy sects and it wouldn't have surprised me if Frizz dragged out that hoary old chestnut to try to get us to bow down and kiss his ass.

What I still couldn't figure out was how a little creep like him was leading the Crimson Order—unless Akrath was far more incompetent than I'd taken him for, but that didn't seem likely. As a matter of fact, it wouldn't have surprised me if Akrath wasn't somehow manipulating Frizz into doing what he wanted. He could use Frizz as the frontman of the Order, while letting Frizz take the center stage, making him a more likely target for any assassination or mutiny attempts.

I stood by my original assumption that Frizz was somebody else's puppet in this whole game. The world was a fucked-up place, sure, but it wasn't so fucked-up *Frizz* would be in charge of anything of note. Was it?

The seemingly endless tunnels finally came to an end and we were led out into a vast cavern the size of a major-league baseball stadium and lit with hundreds upon hundreds of flickering candles that gave it a dark, ancient feel. The black-clad vampires milling around saying prayers or chanting for the Goddess only enforced that. It felt as though we'd stepped back in time a few hundred years.

Many of the vampires stopped to watch us go by, and I took a rough mental count as we moved along. Between the odd ones we'd seen here and there in the tunnels and the ones in the cavern, I counted at least a hundred. I saw and heard quite a few who looked/sounded Russian, Slavic, Asian, and Indian, and I got the feeling the vampires here weren't the ones recruited from Los Angeles. These had likely come from across the sea with Akrath and whoever else had survived the destruction of the original Crimson Order. I suspected these vampires weren't going to be quite the pushovers the ones in the Battle of Los Angeles had been.

Thankfully, I didn't see all that many revenants—less than a dozen—and hoped there weren't more hidden somewhere else.

We all held our heads high as we were lead through the echoing, candlelit cavern, passing knots of covies sitting on rough benches and at crude tables, all apparently paying tribute of some sort to the Goddess. We ignored their stares and whispered admonitions, though it wasn't easy.

I *hated* the way that they looked at Katheryne. Word must have gotten out that she was a half-blood; their glares of disapproval and disgust were particularly strong toward her. Though difficult, I held myself in check, not wanting to give them the satisfaction of acknowledging their existence.

Frizz and Akrath led us toward what amounted to the back of the cavern, where the light was almost nonexistent and no other vampires present. As we drew closer, I kept looking up at the faraway ceiling, trying to discern any hatches that could have been pulled away to let in pillars of killing sunlight, but I couldn't see anything.

That didn't really mean jack—the Order could have just as easily led us out some doorway carved in the wall and put Clarisse, Stacey, and myself out onto some ledge where we'd burn up in the light of day.

Then again, that didn't really seem likely.

If Akrath really was the man behind the curtain—which I was growing more and more sure of with each passing minute—I doubted he'd just execute us and be done with it, not after all of this. Granted, that'd be the intelligent thing to do, and Akrath, despite his fanaticism, wasn't stupid.

But most times, people had to get cute when disposing of a nemesis, regardless of how intelligent they were or how many times they saw James Bond villains fuck it up.

Akrath still bore the scars of what Stacey and I had done to him, and that counted for something in the way of grudges and past torments remembered. Not only that, Frizz had mentioned the Goddess breaking our souls, which was *not* execution, I assumed.

While having killed us hours ago would've been the smartest thing to do, it wasn't going to happen; apparently they had something unpleasant waiting for us.

Our group stopped and the covies separated themselves into two halves on either side, leaving the four of us standing by ourselves. Akrath and Frizz stood in front of us, slowly raising their arms above their heads. Behind them was a large bronze saucer, at least ten feet in diameter, atop a cylindrical pedestal several feet high, which gleamed faintly in the candlelight. I'd only managed a quick look at the saucer and the odd symbols engraved on it when a huge wall of flame erupted upward from it in a withering blast of heat, light, and sound.

Behind us, all the covies let out oohs and aahs of wonder, like a bunch of rubes at a carnival freakshow…or perhaps the congregation at a particularly impressive church service.

After the cavern's previous dimness, the great burst of light momentarily blinded us. Next to me, Stacey cursed the sudden brightness, and I noisily echoed it.

When the roar of the great flames' ignition quieted, I heard for the first time that day the hateful giggle that grated on me like a cyclopean set of nails down a cosmic chalkboard. The sound emanated from the shadows high above the crackling flames and, when I looked up, I thought I saw a shape in the darkness, though the flames were playing havoc with my sight. Clarisse squeezed my hand tightly just as we heard the giggle again, and in front of us, Akrath and Frizz and dropped to their knees, eyes upward. They began to chant in an ancient vampiric tongue used by covies through the ages in their ceremonies.

Somewhere behind us, one of the covies yelled, "It is the Goddess! The heretics will now pay for their sins!"

"I've got a bad feeling about this, dude." Stacey squinted toward the ceiling. "A *real* bad feeling."

"You're not the only one," I muttered.

Whatever it was up there, it was descending. It was wrapped in flowing, brilliant white cloth, shimmering in the light of the flames, and the heat from the conflagration billowed the fabric out like a great windstorm. The giggle came yet again, and this time it lasted for a long time, growing louder and more manic the closer the shape got.

Frizz turned back with a huge grin and howled, *"Your life is over, Steele! Now is the time to suffer for your sins!"*

"Yeeessss," said a woman from above, in a voice that doubled and tripled and quadrupled onto itself into an unnverving chorus. "Thou must pay the price for forsaking thy Goddess and striking out against those who would give you their love. Just as I once damned Brahman so he saw the light, so shall it be with thee! Kneel before the Goddess, Fallen Ones, kneel and *repent!"*

The voice grew louder and louder as it spoke, unnaturally so, and it seemed to fill the entire cavern. That was imposing enough, but through the flames and billowing white fabric, I got a good look at who it was.

"Holy shit, *holy fucking shit*," exclaimed Stacey, his eyes huge. Mine were probably at least as big, if not bigger. Lucretia's words from back in the Catacombs came rushing back to me in a chilling flood...the sky had indeed fallen.

The woman, garbed in what I could now see was a simple but elegant white dress, accented with black leather wristbands and collar, lowered herself until she came to a stop in front of the flames, which created a hellish backdrop. Her glowing eyes raked over all of us as though we were nothing to her, and she smiled, revealing her ivory fangs.

"Yesss," she purred as she took everything in, "Now all is in readiness, the unhallowed age of the sinner is thusly finished in this world, and an age of unparalleled vampiric purity shall begin on this day, so declares the Goddess!"

She held her arms over her head as every vampire and werewolf in the cavern knelt before her—save for us four—hailing her as the Goddess. Many of the rank and file actually cried as they beheld her glory.

Tempestia had certainly gone up in the world since the last time I'd seen her. Yet again, I regretted not having totally dismembered someone when I'd had them at my mercy.

For once, both Stacey and I were at a loss for words.

However, Tempestia most certainly wasn't, and after she'd given us all the once-over, she turned her attention to Frizz.

"Rise Barzai the Wise," she said, holding her hand in his direction as she touched down on the cavern floor. Trembling, Frizz rose to his feet while Akrath remained where he was. "Thou hast delivered the sinners to me as thou had promised, and for that I am glad, yes."

"I-I-I did it f-f-for you, my Goddess," Frizz stammered excitedly. "Anything for you! Without you I would still be a lost soul in that city of sin and hate, not knowing who I was or what my place was! I have you to thank, my Goddess!"

His voice was thoroughly mad with fanaticism and love for his "Goddess," reminding me of the losers on those faith-healing television shows late at night and on Sunday mornings. Frizz was a believer to the core of his being.

"I know," Tempestia said softly, taking his chin in her hand. "And for that thou hast the eternal love and gratitude of thy Goddess. Now that thou hast fulfilled thine purpose to me in bringing the heretics Steele and Stacey, it is time for thee to receive thy ultimate reward. Art thou ready, Barzai?"

"Yes, my Goddess, yes!" Frizz nearly screamed, his entire body twitching as if it had been hit with a live wire. "I am ready!"

Tempestia smiled again and nodded slowly, her eyes glowing a soft, mellow red. "Very well then, wise Barzai, off to eternity with thee, where thou can rest for all time safely against my bosom."

With that, she plucked Frizz off the ground, wrapped her arms around him, and plunged her fangs into his neck.

The cavern erupted into cheers and even more weeping was heard. Cries of "Hail Barzai!" and "Hail the Goddess!" filled the air amid much clapping and the aforementioned cheering.

However, my eyes were on Frizz, who at first seemed surprised by Tempestia's embrace, and then accepting of it. But as I watched, it became apparent Tempestia was taking this to the very end, and panic bloomed on Frizz's face as his strength rapidly ebbed. His arms weakly pressed against Tempestia's shoulders, but it was too late.

The others saw his meek struggle before he died, but took it as excitement and perhaps even an attempt to embrace the Goddess he'd loved so much and served in life. They cheered all the more loudly for him.

Barely a minute later, it was over and Frizz collapsed bonelessly into Tempestia's arms. She gently held his body in her arms, looking out at everyone in the cavern. "Barzai the Wise has crossed over, my children, and he is now and forever a part of me, as thee all shall be someday. His soul shall know eternal paradise because of his loyal service to his Goddess, yes. Hail Barzai!"

Everyone in the cavern echoed the sentiment, and Tempestia held Frizz's body above her head for all to see for nearly a minute before turning and carefully setting it down in the flames.

A final cheer rose for Frizz as the flames began consuming his corpse, and now Tempestia turned her attention to Akrath, holding her hand out to him as she had Frizz. The bald vampire got to his feet with considerably more composure than Frizz had. I wondered if this was the last we'd see of Akrath.

This was not to be, and though my initial shock at the appearance of Tempestia was dissipating, what I saw next hit me even harder.

"Thou may assume leadership of the hallowed Crimson Order for the time being, most loyal Akrath, until the Dark One has been properly prepared to handle the yoke of power I shall soon bestow upon him, yes," she said, sounding as though she were doing him one hell of a favor.

"Thank you, my Goddess," said Akrath, bowing his head graciously.

Tempestia nodded in approval. "Thou art truly my most loyal follower, dear Akrath, yes. And for that, I have reserved a very special place for thee in the forever, which I shall grant to thee as soon as we have shown this world's vampires what their true birthright is. Not even the Dark One, as powerful and loyal as he will be, will hold the favor I show to thee. Know this and be glad, Akrath, and never let thy path falter, lest thee forfeit thy rightful place."

"I shall not, my Goddess." Akrath again bowed his head.

Tempestia looked quite pleased. "See that thou do not, no."

Then it was as if he wasn't there anymore, as she turned her attention to the four of us, smiling from ear to ear. "How long have I waited for this moment?" she asked. "Too long. I have waited for this day since before I came to this body, when it was inhabited by my loyal follower Tempestia. Dost thou remember when thee smote her down when she was attempting to defend Azon from thy wrongful wrath? But it has all turned out for the better. I have taken the body of pious Tempestia and have used it as my avatar on this plane, so that I may better ensure the vampires of this world turn their ways to the true path."

"Are you finished yet, you ponderous whore?" I asked Tempestia, my voice a razor of scorn.

The collective gasp in the cavern was that of a horrified giant, but Tempestia only laughed.

"I expected nothing less from the likes of thee, Steele, yes." She chuckled, her eyes still glowing that light shade of red. "But I suspect thee will be changing thy tune here in the very near future. Thou will be a part of the noble Crimson Order in one way or another before the night following this one. This I say with assurance, as I have seen into the future and seen what is to be, yes. But being the loving Goddess that I am, I shall give thee a choice. I shall give all of thee a choice, as a matter of fact…excepting the disgusting half-life."

The fucking bitch didn't even look at Katheryne, didn't even acknowledge her existence other than the slur, and I would have charged if not for Clarisse's hand holding tightly to mine.

"You may all willingly submit yourselves to me, wherein I shall reshape thee into mine own image, loyal and pious to the true path of the vampire. Or thee can be difficult and require me to open thy eyes myself. But, either way, thou shalt serve me. Thy lifeblood *will* be shared with the Dark One to awaken him from his healing slumber. It is thy choice entirely, and thou do not have to answer now. I am a merciful Goddess, and shall give thee the rest of the day to make thy decision. Once the moon is high in the sky tonight, thy decision shall have to be made, and thy fates will be sealed. I shall allow thee to choose thy own path, but thy destination will be the same regardless. That is the decree of the Goddess, yes."

"And who, pray tell, is this Dark One you keep crowing about, you cow?" Clarisse demanded. "If you're gonna tell me I've gotta donate my blood to some 'Dark One,' the least you could do is tell us who."

Tempestia shook her head at Clarisse. "Thou do not *have* to give thy blood to the Dark One. Thou shalt give the blood to the Dark One willingly. Thou shalt do it out of love."

"You still didn't answer my question," Clarisse pushed. "Who's this Dark One, bitch?"

The would-be Goddess laughed. "Thy ways are so coarse, but

thou dost have a valid question. In answer, I shall simply present him to you."

She turned slightly and held out her hand toward the flames, which immediately extinguished, throwing our part of the cavern into darkness. When the candles started to light by themselves on the wall a short distance ahead of us, I caught my first glimpse of the Dark One.

He was affixed to a large cross, attached to the rock wall of the cavern several feet off the floor, with candles set into niches in the wall surrounding him. As the candles lit up, they gave off an unearthly greenish light, and we all got a good look at Tempestia's Dark One.

He was dressed all in tattered black garments, ripped and torn with a score of wounds. Dried blood and dirt encrusted his clothing and visible skin, and his long, dark hair hung limply down onto his powerful chest as his head lay to one side, his all-too familiar features illuminated by the candles. I gasped and Tempestia giggled with intense glee. We all stared at the body on the wall, speechless.

All but one.

Katheryne, who hadn't said a word since we'd left the cell, screamed a single syllable—a syllable shot through with anguish from the very depths of her soul. *"Wade!"*

Part Six:

War

I

"Oh she's the Goddess all right, don't doubt that for a second," Caleb said earnestly from his spot on the table. His deep-set, dark green eyes gazed back at all of us from a roughly hewn face framed by long black hair, and I wondered if the British vampire was as mad as Tempestia. But then with a grin he added, "In her own mind and those of her followers, at least."

"We'd gathered that already, *duh*," Stacey replied. "Why don't you tell us something we *don't* know? Quit being an asshole, asshole."

Caleb laughed softly at this, seeming genuinely amused by Stacey's admonitions, and he slowly ran his gaze over us. We sat on the other side of the cell—Katheryne clinging to Clarisse and still wordlessly trembling—suspicious of our "guest."

Upon returning to our cell, we'd found him sitting on the table, clad in the tattered remains of an Order robe and looking weary. "You must forgive me," he said. "It's been so long since I've had someone to talk to besides brainwashed sheep that making any kind of a joke is a treat."

"This is no time to joke," I said quietly, my voice full of steel. "And if you think—"

"*Joke?*" Katheryne screeched, pulling away from Clarisse. "*Joke?*"

Instantaneously, she was across the cell and violently shaking Caleb by the front of his robe. "One of my closest friends is hanging on a cross out there and all you can do is *joke?*"

The thin vampire was shocked by this outburst from what had formerly been the quietest member of our little party and didn't have anything to say in his defense.

"Why don't you tell me how funny it is that Wade's on that cross?" Katheryne snarled. "Why don't you tell me how *fucking* funny it is that he's crucified by Tempestia and it's *my* fault? Tell me how funny it is!"

Caleb was flung against the opposite wall of the cell, where he hit with a painful *thud* and crashed to the ground. As Katheryne stood over him, quaking with who-knew-how-many emotions surging through her, her eyes began glowing a brilliant blue.

"Holy shit!" Stacey exclaimed as Clarisse and I gaped. Katheryne's eyes glowed like that when she was building up a tremendous amount of magickal energy, either consciously or unconsciously. If she let rip…

My lover and I exchanged glances. Clarisse quickly shook her head, meaning she hadn't even felt this coming from Katheryne until it had happened, but Clarisse didn't take long in reacting, stepping up behind Katheryne and putting her hands on her shoulders.

"Katheryne," she said into the blond witch's ear, but got no response.

"Laugh!" Katheryne shrieked at Caleb. "Ha ha ha! So fucking *funny!*" she howled, the light from her eyes bathing her end of the cell with electric blue. "Laugh, damn you, *laugh!*"

Caleb offered no resistance, but huddled against the wall, his gaze locked on Katheryne's. Even without empathy, I could tell he was scared out of his mind.

"Katheryne!" Clarisse yelled at the witch, shaking her. "Stop!"

Outside the cell, the two werewolf guards were peering through the door and snarling warningly at us.

"Difference of opinion," I informed them, though they didn't seem mollified by the answer. To hell with them. I'd only worry if they entered.

By now Clarisse was shaking Katheryne so hard the half-blood's hair was swaying, and out of the blue, the witch turned her attention from Caleb to Clarisse, her eyes shining like miniature stars.

"I've got to help Wade!" she cried. "*I've got to!*"

Her voice was desperate, but beneath it was diamond, unyielding and irresistible, born of her boundless love for us.

"We will," Clarisse said. "We will, as soon as we've got the right opportunity, don't worry. Not even you can blast through so many of them and still keep the rest of us safe, and Tempestia's a wild card—we don't even know what we're up against with her. Once we do know, then we get revenge...all of us."

Katheryne stared at Clarisse then nodded slowly. "And I'll rescue Wade," she said firmly, as if no other scenario were possible. In her mind, I knew she wouldn't accept any other. "I got him into this, and I'm gonna get him out." Her jaw was set and her eyes held intense determination—so much so I was surprised my wished-for laser beams weren't shooting out of them.

"But you don't know if you got him into this, Blondie," Stacey said, putting a hand on Katheryne's shoulder.

She turned to Stacey and myself. "Until I know otherwise, I'm taking responsibility. I was supposed to help him back in the cavern, but I messed up. Now he's hung on a cross instead of where he belongs. I've got to help him."

When Tempestia had shown Wade to us, I'd thought for certain the witch was going to go to pieces. She'd said nothing else after Tempestia's revelation, and had trembled all the way back to our cell, where we'd been carted back to immediately afterward. The change in Katheryne was dramatic; she seemed to have regained a sense of purpose and strength.

Now I heard Brandi's words echoing in my head...*she needs redemption*. This could be the very thing Katheryne needed to save herself. If we didn't all get killed in the process.

The blue-streaked blonde half-blood turned her attention back to Caleb. "You're going to tell me everything you know about how Wade got here. I *have* to know."

Caleb still looked wary of Katheryne, as though afraid she'd lash out at him again, but he straightened himself into a more comfortable sitting position. "Wade? You mean the Dark One?" he asked.

Katheryne nodded.

"Well, gather 'round, my friends," Caleb said, "And I'll happily tell you all I can about my esteemed former employers, especially if it's something that'll help tear them down."

We all sat down in a rough semicircle, Caleb still against the wall and us around him like a group of campers listening a spooky story on a crisp fall night. But the scares here weren't for fun.

"I wasn't there when they found him, you understand," said Caleb. "The Goddess...excuse me, *Tempestia* never let me out of her general vicinity, so I didn't get to go out on forays or anything. I think she'd long suspected my priorities weren't quite what they used to be, but had kept me around since I was the guy writing down her exploits in the *Covenant Novum*. Or at least I was until I tried to make my spectacularly unsuccessful break for it. But anyway, during a reconnaissance run to the city—to figure out what you were up to, Steele—Barzai, a couple of the revenant masters, and their pets found your friend in one of the local graveyards, out of his mind and trying to dig himself under."

"Mad?" Katheryne asked.

"From what they said, yes," replied the Crimson Order's former historian. "He acted more animal than vampire, and if he hadn't been in such bad shape, I doubt that the revenants would have been able to beat him into submission. As it was, they lost two of the four they brought. Your friend's a force to be reckoned with, even in a wounded capacity." He sounded impressed.

"You haven't seen my girl yet," Stacey said. "She's the best-looking tank you've ever seen, but Wade, yeah, he's one helluva tough son of a bitch."

"Acting like an animal and trying to dig himself under," I said, putting everything together in my head. "Torpor."

"Just what I was thinking, lover," Clarisse said, her brow creased. "Somehow or other he'd gotten out of the cavern and made it aboveground to dig himself into the dirt so he could heal…"

"And he was fucked up enough that he was crazed, running on autopilot. I bet *that's* what that disturbance in the sealed off sections of the tunnels was a few days ago… Someone wasn't trying to get *in*, but it was Wade getting *out*," I finished. "There's a cemetery not too far from where one of the outlets to the surface from the Catacombs is too."

Though torpor was akin to a deep coma, a vampire's natural survival instincts kicked in and violently turned him against anything attempting to move his body. This would go on until the interlopers were driven off or the vampire was sufficiently hurt enough that his body shut down to prevent further damage. There were ways around it—especially for those close to the vampire in question—but it was usually best to leave a sleeping vampire alone.

"So why are they calling him the Dark One?" Katheryne asked

softly. "What are they going to do to him?"

Caleb looked a little surprised. "She didn't tell you? I figured she would've lorded it over you in the most insufferable manner possible."

"She said something about us giving our blood to him, yeah," I said. "But she didn't say why."

Caleb nodded. "She intends to use your blood to restore him to health and strength. So he can serve as her right-hand man and—for lack of a better word—mate."

"What?" Katheryne screeched. "Wade will never do that!"

"From how highly you seem to regard him, I'd agree with you any other time. But once you add Tempestia into the mix, there's a good chance you're going to be proven wrong," Caleb said, flinching at the long, angry hiss Katheryne let out after his statement.

"What the hell kind of horrible drugs are you on?" Stacey demanded. "Wade don't kiss *anybody's* ass, no way, no how!"

"True enough," Caleb said. "But you don't know Tempestia. How else do you think she's got so many adoring converts when she's obviously crazy? A lot of them, the younger ones especially, buy into the whole *Covenant* philosophy without question, but how about the older ones? There are members here that are a good five or six hundred years old, and they follow Tempestia around like a pack of loving puppies."

He paused a moment to let that sink in then continued. "She's got a lot of power, sure, but she's had blunder upon folly upon disaster over the years. Believe me, I know—I've had to come up with plenty of good cover stories and excuses while writing the *Covenant Novum*. But even with all that under her skirts, everybody's still ready unquestionably to follow her to their deaths, which a lot of them already have. Tempestia's got herself insurance, and it isn't Akrath, either—though he's made a lot of saves in his time. No, it's not Tempestia's inspirational leadership that's gotten her followers… it's her blood."

"Her blood?" I asked, frowning.

"Yes," said Caleb. "If not for the particular chemistry of Tempestia's blood, she wouldn't be here today, and the Crimson Order wouldn't be a concern to you. Tempestia's a special case—she didn't get turned like the rest of us did. She was *designed*."

Clarisse's eyes went wide. She knew a great deal in the way of vampiric lore and half-forgotten myths and tales, more so than even Stacey or myself. Apparently Caleb had hit upon something at least vaguely familiar to her. "The experiments in blood alchemy..." she whispered, taking hold of my hand. "They're true, then?"

Caleb nodded approvingly. "So you've heard of them."

"I've read some, yes, but I never really gave them much consideration. In theory, I can see how they'd be a sound idea— possibly even work—but I never thought they were actually carried out." Clarisse's sudden surprise had already faded into the bright interest she always exhibited when presented with an interesting piece of history. "Tempestia's one of the experiments, then?"

"An experiment that didn't quite turn out the way that her creators had hoped," said the historian. "But then, psychological profiling and genetic mapping didn't exist back then, so I doubt they could have predicted how the experiments would...take with her."

I must have looked slightly surprised at Caleb's mention of psychological profiling and genetic mapping, because he gave me a wry smile. "Just because I've been stuck with the Order for so long doesn't mean I don't know about what goes on in the outside world. I'm a historian, and knowledge is my realm. I've spoken with almost every single convert, forced or otherwise, we've ever had and gleaned a lot of information about the happenings in the world. But as I was saying, Tempestia reacted much differently than they thought she would—"

"Hold up there a second, big money." Stacey beat me by a scant second. "Now you and Red over there may know what you're talking about, but me, Steele, and Blondie haven't been filled in by this blood alchemy shit you're gabbing about. Mind if you take a few seconds and fill us in?"

Katheryne said quietly, "I know what the blood alchemy experiments were. At least one of us is well read." Then, wonderfully, she graced Stacey with her slightest of smiles, the one she'd always give after making a little joke.

Stacey gave her the finger, which made her small smile just a little larger then she looked back down at the floor again, satisfied she'd made her point.

Clarisse, clearly delighted Katheryne was coming around, said, "The blood alchemy experiments were carried out from somewhere in the fourteen hundreds to around the end of the eighteen hundreds. They were attempts by various vampire groups to create enhanced vampire soldiers to carry out their bidding. It was all really hush-hush, and as far as I know, very few of them, if any, went as they were supposed to."

"What happened?" I asked.

"Madness, insanity," Katheryne said, still looking at the floor.

"Exactly," said Clarisse. "The experiments involved taking a vampire or a mortal—sometimes willing, sometimes not—and infusing him or her with blood taken or donated from other vampires, and sometimes even revenants and half-bloods, and seeing what would happen. They usually shot for sheer strength, but I've heard of some that actually attempted to give full vampires the magickal abilities of half-bloods. Those were the ones that went the most horribly wrong, from what I understand."

"Our blood doesn't mix well with that of full-bloods," added Katheryne. "Though we're called 'half-vampires,' the real truth is that we're two separate species—similar in many ways, but with enough differences to create problems on a cellular level. It's no problem to drink each other's blood—that's okay, because it's essentially just a food thing. But when you try to turn a half-blood into a full-blood, or vice-versa, it's like transplanting a chimp's liver into a human. That's what they were trying to do, and it always backfired."

"Not always," Caleb said almost apologetically. "Tempestia was a special case, the one-in-a-million shot where it actually worked. Her body accepted with no rejection, but it did something to her mind."

"Her mind was never sound to begin with," I said. "I fought the bitch when Stacey and I took down the Order the first time. She was already several bricks short of a good shithouse."

"True, but in those days she wasn't nearly as bad as she is now," said Caleb, leaning comfortably against the wall, seeming to enjoy the role of storyteller. "Compared to today, she was mildly eccentric. She was merely a foolish turncoat back then, instead of being the leader of a horde of vampire fanatics, revenants, and werewolves."

"Turncoat?" I asked, half-formed suspicions of Tempestia's origin rising and popping in my head like bubbles moving to the surface of a pool of water.

"Yes," confirmed Caleb. "She was a different case than the other candidates for these experiments, as she wasn't a full vampire...she was a half-blood."

Katheryne's head snapped up instantly, her eyes narrow and angry. "*What*?"

Caleb flinched, and after the way she'd tossed him around earlier, I couldn't blame him. Katheryne wasn't a woman to show her emotions very often, but when she really did, she made those times count. "She's a *half-blood*?"

"As much as you are, my dear," replied Caleb after a few seconds' hesitation. "Except you're not taken in by the *Covenant* like she was. She read the *Covenant* at some point during her early life as an immortal and bought every word of it. When one of the groups performing the blood alchemy experiments found her, a *Covenant*-inspired lot called the Servants of Midnight, she offered herself up as an experimental candidate. She felt it was her duty, the only way she could redeem herself in the eyes of the Goddess for being a half-vampire."

Katheryne was enraged. "Up until the time I met Donita, I spent my entire life running, fighting, and trying to stay out of the clutches of full vampires who would have *killed* me because of what I was. I bled, I sacrificed, I watched so many innocents die because of their half-vampire blood, and she just goes and *offers* herself up to them?"

Her eyes were taking on a bluish cast again, and small blue sparks popped and sputtered into existence in the air around her, each dying in less than a second. I wondered if it would have been wise to back up a little bit, but Katheryne pulled it back, containing her magick. Afterward, her eyes glittered with a light that had nothing to do with magick.

"I may be weak at times, I may not be the best person in the world either, but I'm not stupid, and I'll never, *ever* sell out my own kind. Never." She hissed softly to herself, slowly running her fingers up and down the arm of the raggedy old blue sweater she wore almost constantly.

"Katheryne?" Clarisse asked, leaning over towards her. "You all right?"

Half-bloods had a special kinship forged from the hardships they'd endured at the hands of full vampires. They were their own little subset of the vampire world, intensely loyal to one another through their shared experiences. They didn't always like one another, and would even kill each other if *absolutely* necessary, but needlessly killing another half-blood was anathema to them. I could only imagine how much Tempestia's defection, especially to a *Covenant*-inspired group, would offend Katheryne.

When it came to the wholesale killing of half-bloods, it was *Covenant* fanatics who were by and far the largest offenders. Many non-*Covenant* vampires showed plenty of hatred toward half-bloods over the years, but never to the insane levels the *Covenant* groups took it.

"Katheryne?" repeated Clarisse.

The half-blood made a slight brushing motion with her hand, not looking up. "I'm fine. Just keep going with the story," she said, and fell silent.

I nodded, and Caleb took his cue. "The Servants of Midnight weren't in total agreement with the Crimson Order, figuring their own interpretation of the *Covenant* was the right one."

"Well, golly jeepers, imagine that," Stacey sneered. "Disagreements among different sects of a wacko religion? By damn, that's a new one."

Caleb shrugged then went on, "The Servants only had a dozen or so members, lacking the power and sheer numbers the Order possessed, so now that they had a willing half-blood subject, they hatched a scheme to take over the Order and bend it to their own will.

"They'd already captured a vampiress powerful in both telepathic and empathic suggestion. She was said to have been able to convince the weak-minded of anything she wanted. They'd give her or do anything she asked after she'd had time to work on them. The Servants had apprehended her thinking she'd help them amass an army. She refused to cooperate, but couldn't use her abilities on them to escape, either. Therein was her weakness—her talents only worked on those unaware of her abilities. If you were prepared for it, you were safe. The Servants were stymied. That's where Tempestia came in.

"They starved the poor vampiress until she was mad with hunger then set her loose on Tempestia, letting her feed until Tempestia was nearly dead. Then they held the newly fed woman down, dragged Tempestia over to her, and let the half-vampire gorge herself on the woman's blood, which was now a combination of her own and Tempestia's. Tempestia drank the woman dry, gaining herself a new ability in the process. Basically, it was a very forced second turning for Tempestia."

"That wasn't a turning," Clarisse growled. "It was a rape."

"By any means necessary, as long as it's in the name of the Goddess," Caleb said dryly, and Clarisse spat on the floor. "It was a gamble for the Servants. They'd expected Tempestia to die during the process."

"Too bad she didn't," Stacey huffed.

"After she'd recovered, Tempestia was more of a believer than ever. She talked endlessly of how the Goddess had spoken to her during the second turning, forgiving Tempestia for being an abomination," Caleb said then winced when I hissed a warning at him. "Her words, not mine. The Servants let this quirk go, however—there was no question of where Tempestia's loyalties lay now—and they began preparing her to infiltrate the Crimson Order. She was to use her new ability to take over the Order from the inside, by gaining control of Azon himself."

Like a good storyteller, Caleb paused a moment and let this sink in. Though disgusting in its particulars, it wasn't a bad scheme.

"Get on with it, dude." Stacey made a winding motion with his hand. "This ain't *Lights Out* and you ain't Boris Karloff."

Caleb continued, "Though a half-vampire's makeup isn't really suited for empathy and telepathy, Tempestia'd developed an almost hypnotic power over the weak-minded and receptive. It wasn't nearly as deep as the vampiress's had been, *but* once Tempestia got her fangs into you, she almost always had you in her pocket. She insinuates herself through the close mental bond formed during vampire-to-vampire feeding, leaving behind any kind of suggestions she wants, ensuring her victims were in perpetual adoration of her. That's how she got a lot of the current members of the Crimson Order, as a matter of fact. She puts you off-guard, gets close, and once she's bit into you, it's all over."

"That's why Azon allowed her to be around even though she was a half-vampire—why he didn't even notice what she really was," I said.

"Exactly," said Caleb. "After she'd had time to hone her ability, the Servants of Midnights set Tempestia loose. Though not the most clear-headed person in the world, Tempestia was much more cunning back then than she is now, and she seduced her way into the Crimson Order, carefully working up to Azon, who took her as his 'consort.' From there, Tempestia pulled the strings in any way that suited the Servants of Midnight. Ultimately, the Order would be brought into alignment with the Servants, who'd simply assume their 'rightful' place at the top of the hierarchy. But happenings in the Circle of Magnus changed everything."

I started, sitting bolt upright. "Azon used that name back in the keep!"

"A pity your friend Wade isn't here. He could tell you better than I could, at least if Tempestia was on the level," said Caleb.

When Katheryne's gaze came to bear on him, he quickly continued. "The Circle of Magnus was essentially a European vampire secret society at roughly around the same time as the blood alchemy experiments. It was said they also conducted their own forays into the area of blood alchemy, though for different purposes than groups like the Servants of Midnight. If what I've heard about them has been correct, they were actually the ideological forebears of the LA vampires, believing we should fade into myth and live out our lives the way we want to, without a Goddess in sight," Caleb said. "The Circle was formed by at least a dozen vampires of considerable age, all sick and tired of the antics of *Covenant*-inspired groups. They set out to subvert the *Covenant* groups in a number of different ways. There was subtle and complex sabotage on the larger, more powerful groups to completely unravel them, and raids against smaller, less defensible groups and killing them outright. That's more or less what happened to the Servants of Midnight shortly after Tempestia infiltrated the Crimson Order."

"More or less?" Clarisse asked, looking skeptical.

"I don't know precisely how the Servants met their end,"

admitted Caleb, "Some say the Circle itself went out and destroyed them in a raid. Others say the Circle managed to create Archangel, a super-vampire who annihilated the Servants of Midnight. Problem was, he apparently went insane and wiped out the Circle of Magnus afterward, before completely disappearing. According to Tempestia, Wade was a member of the Circle of Magnus."

I scowled. "I'm having a hard time buying Wade being part of a group who'd perform experiments on other vampires, even if it was for good reason."

"He wouldn't," said Katheryne firmly.

Stacey and Clarisse also made sounds of agreement.

Caleb held up his hands to quiet us down. "I never said the Circle's experiments were exactly along the lines of those done by the Servants. From everything I've heard from various sources, Archangel was actually a member of the Circle and a willing subject. The destruction of the Servants was supposed to be his trial run, after which he was going after the Crimson Order, but things didn't turn out as planned. I didn't think there had been any survivors of the Circle until Wade was brought in and Tempestia went wild.

"There's a distinctive tattoo on one of his shoulders that marks him as a member of the Circle, and once she saw it, she started endlessly babbling to me about her Dark One and how he was another sign of her eventual victory over all of the heretics of the world. He was brought back here originally because of his great strength—Barzai thought he'd be a good meal for Tempestia—but once she saw he was a member of the Circle of Magnus, she took it as a sign. One of Tempestia's quirks," Caleb said, "is that she sees almost everything in a symbolic manner, just like metaphors and symbols are used extensively in the *Covenant of Blood* to help get its message across. She not only sees Wade as a symbol, but Steele and Stacey as well."

"Symbols?" asked Stacey with a scowl. "I've got a symbol for her." He held up his middle finger and shook it vigorously. "I ain't nobody's symbol. Stacey don't serve."

"True enough," Caleb agreed. "But Tempestia sees you three as part of her destiny, and won't be swayed. It was when the Servants were destroyed that Tempestia became convinced she was meant for tremendous things."

"Like taking over the Crimson Order and becoming *the* authority on all things Goddess?" Clarisse asked, and Caleb pointed at her.

"Exactly," he replied. "It was through the actions of the Circle of Magnus—and thus Wade—and Steele and Stacey's assault on the Order's keep that all worked together to put her in her current position. As far as she's concerned, you three are meant to stand beside her as she takes the Order to new levels of insanity and aggression."

Clarisse leaned even closer now and put her arms around me, and I had to admit I was grateful for it. "She shouldn't even be alive." I grunted. "I killed that bitch."

Caleb sighed. "Not nearly enough, it seems. You came close to killing her, so close it makes me sick. In the chaos of the keep's collapse, one of her loyal Order soldiers, drawn by the mental calls for help she'd been sending to all those connected to her, managed to revive her with his blood and life. Somewhere deep down she knows she almost died because of Steele, and knows Stacey would have done the same thing, and that doesn't sit quite right with her. While she's intent on Wade being her right-hand man, since he never actually raised a hand against her, she mostly just wants to own Steele and Stacey, both as symbols and to prove to herself she's better than them. I doubt she'd be terribly disappointed if she had to kill you off, either. In fact, even you two *did* join the Order, you'll likely be dead within a year or less simply because some part of her mind will keep wondering whether or not you'll try to get rid of her again."

We sat and digested this, Caleb taking a short break from his storytelling.

After a time, I said, "So why does she think she's *the* Goddess? You kept saying she thought the Goddess had a special plan for her, so how the hell did she go from being a faithful servant of the Goddess to the main woman herself?"

"Good question." Caleb nodded in approval, reminding me of Tommy and his college professor mannerisms. "You actually have yourself to thank for that, sad to say. According to what she told me, the Goddess came to her when she was near death in the keep and told her it was time to ascend to the next stage of her destiny. When she woke up, she'd have the privilege of serving as an avatar for the Goddess, who would help her resurrect the Crimson Order from the ashes.

"So when Tempestia awoke, the Goddess supposedly took control of her body, speaking through it and using her powers to help persuade everybody that she was the genuine article. Tempestia used her half-blood magickal abilities to present herself with the same song and dance I'm sure she gave you all today. As far as I know, she hadn't even been aware of any inherent magickal tendencies before she first acted as the Goddess, but the need for flash and flair must have brought them out. From what I've seen, she can't fire off any sort of blasts or do a lot of the things skilled magick-users can do. Tempestia isn't even aware she's using magick—she just thinks she's doing what comes naturally to a Goddess, like flying, igniting candles and fires, plus a few other odds and ends. She's also *really* strong, so I'm thinking she's somehow unconsciously directing the magick to augment her physical strength."

"Probably," Katheryne said. "It's not very hard to do. Donita does it often enough, and I do it every time I get into a fight."

Caleb nodded. "I don't know exactly how strong she is, but I've seen her take down recalcitrant revenants and troublesome werewolves as though they were nothing. She's plenty powerful, just so you know, in case you decide to go toe to toe with her."

"I'm sure that'll happen sooner or later." Clarisse looked at me affectionately. "Some of us here have incurable hero complexes."

"Feh! Just wait'll Brandi gets here. She'll mop the floor with that dumb broad," Stacey declared with total certainty.

"Providing she, or anybody else, can find us," said Katheryne softly.

We all fell silent as the truth of the witch's words sank in. Though the arrival of the cavalry was at the back of all of our minds, we were all on our own until that actually happened, and we had to operate on that assumption. Anything else would have been a fatal mistake. Two of us had taken out the original Crimson Order, so hopefully five of us would be more than enough to destroy the new one. We had to, because if we couldn't, Los Angeles and every vampire in it was fated to either die or be brainwashed.

The thought of brainwashing jogged a part of my brain, and I asked the question I'd almost forgotten about amid everything else.

"So how the flying fuck did a little peckerhead like Frizz end up being called Barzai the Wise and having some sort of authority in the Order?"

"Or at least he did, until the big bosswoman sent him to his just rewards," Clarisse said with a smirk. "The little prick."

Caleb looked mildly curious. "Got rid of him, did she?"

"Drained him dry in front of the whole congregation, after thanking him for bringing us to her. I took it that she kept him around just to get us, and once that was taken care of, he was of no more use to her," I said.

Caleb pointed at me as though I'd just earned an A in class. "Precisely. He was found during one of the advance scouts' earliest runs into the city, looking for potentially useful converts the Order could use to get the wheels rolling on the coming campaign. When the scouts brought back a couple of likely turncoats, Akrath pumped them for information, making sure to ask about his old friends Brom and Jules—standard operating procedure for a new territory. Though your names were different now, it didn't take the new converts long to figure out who Akrath was looking for. All of them knew of you two, but Barzai—or Frizz, whichever you prefer—made mention of knowing Steele fairly well, though he wasn't too fond of Stacey. That was good enough for Tempestia. Akrath took him to her, and she of course appeared as the Goddess, and gave him the big presentation about destiny, eternal rewards, and being hand picked by the Goddess Herself. He ate it right up."

"He would." I snorted. "He's been a useless, sycophantic piece of shit for as long as I've known him, always trailing behind somebody or another, never trying to do much of anything with himself, a paragon of mediocrity. Tempestia's line of bullshit was probably the best thing he'd ever heard. Yeah, he'd suck that right up without question."

"That's exactly what happened," said Caleb. "He was supposed to get you and Stacey in Tempestia's hands during the battle in Los Angeles, but he obviously didn't pull it off. Whether that affected her decision to ultimately liquidate him or not, I don't know. She'd probably intended to get rid of him from the very beginning. He may have been a devoted follower, and actually turned out to be pretty effective in reeling in new members by preaching the rhetoric to the right candidates, he was weak of mind and spirit. Intelligent, but...well, soft."

"If he was trying to capture you two during the battle, then why did you guys' names end up on the lists of those who were supposed to be part of the Order?" Clarisse asked, looking puzzled, which made her quite adorable. "You could've gotten killed by your own team. Pretty counterproductive."

Caleb rolled his eyes. "From what I gathered, it was something he made up on the spot, to try endearing himself to you, and didn't stop to think what would happen if it didn't work out the way he planned. Sloppy leadership breeds even sloppier leadership, and Tempestia's sloppy as hell: just tell them the Goddess is supporting them, give them a vague idea of what to do, and then turn them loose and expect them to bring the world home to her. The only really clever bit she's pulled the entire time we've been in this country has been tricking the werewolves into joining with us, uniting against a common foe. She botched that up when the elders escaped. If it weren't for the sheer might of the werewolves and the revenants, the Crimson Order probably would've been overrun by now."

"Whoa, whoa, whoa!" Stacey waved his hands around. "According to Red and the furry friend she made during the battle, the Order killed off the elders to instigate the bad blood between the Los Angeles vampires and the werewolves. And now you're telling me they *escaped*?"

"For the record, I never said they were definitely killed—that was what Lassic and I assumed after comparing notes. An educated assumption, yeah, but still just an assumption," said Clarisse, giving Stacey a little shove.

"Oh, they escaped all right, though the werewolves didn't know that," Caleb said. "The original plan was to keep working on the elders, giving them more and more of her blood, until they became totally bent to her will—as opposed to merely passive—and then have them lead the werewolves into combat themselves. They'd been acting *really* strangely for a while, and one night they just... went nuts. They attacked their keepers while out hunting and just took off into the night."

Clarisse shook her head sadly. "There's no telling what the mixture of vampire blood and Tempestia's influence might have done to them. Poor bastards."

"After some quick thinking by Akrath, word was spread that the LA vampires had discovered the elders and killed them, which really got the werewolves going. Tempestia was so furious at the revenant masters who were supposed to be keeping an eye on the elders that she ripped them to pieces *and* killed their revenants. It doesn't pay to cross the so-called Goddess around here."

Clarisse snorted. "What an idiot. Revenants can't be easy to come by."

"Not at all," replied Caleb, "Tempestia made them."

He paused, obviously expecting one of us to say something to the effect of how impossible that was, but after all we'd heard already, the revelation didn't come as much of a surprise.

Her eyes narrowing, Clarisse said, "Do tell."

Caleb—though clearly disappointed at the lack of reaction—continued anyway. "During the first couple of years she was leading the Order, Tempestia operated very quietly, slowly accumulating followers, converting a vampire here and there, occasionally turning a mortal, taking in any willing vampires she ran across. Even though she was acting almost entirely as the Goddess, she still had her cunning about her, and was patient and resourceful, biding her time until the new Order had gained enough strength to operate on a larger scale again. From what Akrath has told me, in those days she was a driven and competent leader. I'm willing to wager that, even as crazy as she's become, Akrath's still holding onto the hope she'll revert to what she once was. If I had to guess, that's what keeps him around regardless of how reckless she's getting."

As Caleb spoke of Akrath, a gleam of respect came into his eyes. "A fundamentally good heart beats in Akrath. He's a fool for what he believes in, true enough, but he's loyal and consistent, and will never back down from his beliefs no matter what happens. Under different circumstances, he could have been a great man. There are times I pity him for what he has to deal with..."

Part of me wanted to agree with him, but the other part just couldn't do it. Stacey summed it up neatly. "He chose his path on his own, without Tempestia pulling his strings, so fuck that guy. Back to the story."

Caleb continued, "In those early days of the new Order, Tempestia and her followers ran into a crazy old vampire somewhere in the Carpathian mountains. He was ancient, possibly even old enough to have come directly from the primordial line of *vampiri*, our ill-tempered progenitors from the northern lands. But he wasn't just an old hermit—when Tempestia and Akrath spied him hunting food in the woods, they saw he was accompanied by three revenants who obeyed his every beck and call."

"Like revenant masters," I said.

Caleb shook his head. "No. Akrath's told me the masters have nothing on this old fellow. The masters, through a crude blood-bonding process, can barely hold the revenants in check. They can direct their actions just enough to make them useful and that's it. This old vampire had the revenants wrapped around his little finger. If he told them to touch their noses and hop up and down on one foot, they would have done it without hesitation. The beasts were truly and utterly his to command, and when Tempestia and Akrath tried to speak with him, they came *this* close to getting killed.

"It wasn't like how the revenant masters need to stand away and concentrate on their charges, not at all. He was right there in the thick of it, snapping and snarling, his revenants swarming around them like a well-oiled combat unit. Akrath was badly hurt, but Tempestia just barely got the situation under control. She was nearly ripped to pieces, and didn't even bother trying to convert the old vampire, who was near death after she'd gotten hold of him. He'd made her mad enough that she didn't want him in the Order; she just wanted to figure out his knack for the revenants and then make a good meal of him.

"She dragged him and Akrath back to where the rest of the Order was stationed in some caves, and fed from him to find out his secret. After some probing, she discovered that not only could he control revenants, he could *create* them as well. So of course, Tempestia had him bound up, and turned herself *again* with the poor old vampire's blood," said Caleb.

Clarisse made a sound of astonishment. "She's a fucking maniac."

"I'm not arguing," replied Caleb.

"Turning herself a third time couldn't have been good for her," I said.

"Akrath's hinted as much here and there," confirmed our historian. "Like before, the newfound powers didn't fully take in Tempestia. It was a vast improvement over the revenant masters of the past, but still fell far short of what the old vampire had. It also took her several decades to master the skill of creating revenants enough to finally start amassing a good collection of them...and there were some serious failures along the way. Akrath wouldn't give me exact details, but he shuddered when he mentioned them, and Akrath *never* shudders like that."

Clarisse leaned forward, her eyes taking on the particular sheen they always do when she's about to learn something new and interesting. "So how does she do it? What's the trick?"

"I have to admit I don't know the precise procedure. Tempestia's the only one who knows that," Caleb answered. "But as far as I've been able to figure out, the process of creating revenants is similar to that of turning someone into a vampire, though it involves a much more exact manipulation of the subject's blood chemistry and implantation of a certain mindset to make the new revenant malleable to the whims of its creator. It can only be done by Tempestia, too—the biggest secret lies in the old hermit's blood. Not just anybody can create revenants, fortunately."

"Well, thank fuck for small favors," Stacey grumbled.

"There's more," Caleb continued. "The more revenants Tempestia has running around, the more tenuous her influence. Once she's got several dozen going at once, she's got to stop, because any additional ones come out completely uncontrollable, revenant masters or not."

I whistled softly. "Otherwise she would've just overrun us with revenants."

"No shit, dude," Stacey said. "She doesn't seem like someone who knows when to quit."

Caleb gave a short bark of laugher. "Try living with and working for her for a century. You don't know how true that is." The vampire historian shook his head, his eyes glazing over slightly. "I was out traveling by myself when I ran afoul of the Order while they were passing through. I had no choice but to make myself useful to them. It was either willingly play their game, become a slave, or die horribly."

He looked toward Stacey and I, and there was defiance in his eyes. "Even if my life was spent in servitude to the Order, I was still alive. If I was alive, there was hope to escape someday. Condemn me for playing along, I don't care. Out of the billions who've lived and died, only a handful has been given the gift of eternal life. I wasn't going to let mine be wasted at the hands of a group of lunatics; if that meant becoming the Crimson Order's historian, then so be it. I never executed anybody. I never lifted a finger against anybody who stood in opposition to the Order. I just wrote down what I was told and helped where I could."

The defiance faded and pride began to glow. "By my count, I've helped more than fifty vampires escape, and have even managed to persuade Tempestia that some villages and other places didn't need to be destroyed in order to achieve her goals. Other times, I got out word of the Order's approach with vampires I'd helped escape, so any vampires in the area had time to flee. I've been waiting for an opportunity to escape myself for decades, and Los Angeles was the best chance I'd ever had."

"Why didn't you just get out before, if you helped so many other make tracks?" asked Stacey.

Caleb sighed. "It's one thing when one of the rank and file slips away, another if the historian runs off. I couldn't help anybody Tempestia had 'converted' through her blood—they didn't want to leave anyway. But the ones like me, who were playing along for survival, she didn't notice. While we were traveling, if a few mysteriously disappeared here and there... Hey, it happened. Akrath never mentioned it to her after the first time. The tantrum she threw was epic in nature."

"Petulant god-child," Katheryne growled, barely above a whisper. "Doesn't notice them when they're there, but has a fit if they decide to leave."

"Right."

"So LA it was, huh?" Clarisse asked.

"It had to be," said Caleb. "Our fearless leader had finally gone 'round the bend. Before, she'd act as just plain Tempestia, with the *Goddess* coming through to offer advice and occasionally take over whenever we got into a tight situation. She was cracked, but manageable."

"Even with an atrocious command of old formal English,"

Clarisse said with a roll of her eyes. "Her 'thees,' 'thys,' and 'thous' were driving me crazy."

Caleb laughed. "Just one more reason it was a mercy the 'Goddess' only came out to play every now and again. But once she heard of Steele and Stacey here, her *Goddess* persona took up permanent residence, and she's been slipping further and further into her own craziness ever since. I think once she realized she was going to crash headlong into two destroyers from her past, that broke the dam keeping the Goddess in place."

Stacey ground his teeth. "Shit got serious."

"More than you might realize," the historian said. "I've seen the plans and projections. Los Angeles is where the Order will gain the momentum and troops it needs to *really* get going in America. It's bad enough overseas—there's near-total domination in Southeast Asia and large portions of China and Russia. In saner times, Tempestia decreed we'd keep a relatively low profile until we got an unbreakable foothold in America, and then…go nuts."

"What do you mean," I asked, slowly and carefully, "'go nuts?'"

Caleb looked at me earnestly. "Start an all-out war with the mortals. Let them unequivocally know that vampires exist, are dangerous, and must be stopped by any means necessary. You contained the information flow to the outside world during and after the Battle of Los Angeles, but don't you think if Tempestia *really* wanted to start large-scale trouble with the mortals, she would've done it in grander fashion…or somewhere you couldn't hope to stop her? Why not just slaughter Las Cruces, New Mexico—where there wouldn't be any opposition?"

His question hung in the air and I felt my stomach fall completely out. All the back patting we'd been doing since the Battle of Los Angeles seemed so naïve, and I was painfully reminded that no matter how old and experienced you were, you could still be hoodwinked with the best of them.

"Showing our supernatural asses to the world during the Battle of Los Angeles was merely Tempestia going for the dramatic, and not a primary goal. The original battle plan for Los Angeles was *much* more covert—a systematic assassination and subversion that came to a quiet victory and never culminated in an outright invasion. But the Goddess wasn't having that—she wanted to do it in grand fashion, and nobody but Akrath had the stones to tell her the initial plan was the better idea. She just ignored him and told him to have faith."

"Probably just as well she did," I said. It was unsettling to know that the reason one was alive was likely because somebody else was batshit insane.

"So the plan was adapted to accommodate a full-on invasion with blood, fire, screaming, and explosions. Akrath told me there would be much more risk with the modified plan, but that it was containable. If the Order had won in Los Angeles, it would've stirred plenty of things up, and the world would have known there were vampires and werewolves running about. They would've known that an entire population of them had lived in LA," said Caleb. "But after that the idea—as Akrath modified and sold it to Tempestia—was to fade and stay quiet, let the mortals stew in their own suspicions and doubts. The occasional vampire or other supernatural would be discovered, maybe a few nests here and there, but nothing major. The population would be allowed to come to grips with the idea…"

"And get good and nervous about it," continued Clarisse.

"While the Order continued to build strength and overtake other large vampire communities, such as New Orleans and Houston," said Caleb. "Until the pieces were all lined up for a Night of Terror the likes of which the world hadn't ever seen. Then the whole world can go to war with vampires, wipe them off the face of the planet, and send them all to their reward with the Goddess."

"*Fuck*," Stacey growled.

"Yes," Caleb agreed. "Fuck. Los Angeles isn't the Order's endgame in America—it's the first step. The idea, regardless of the original or current configuration, is to gather followers and gain territory, to subjugate the vampires most likely to be a thorn in the Order's side, and—*and*—it comes back to Tempestia's love of symbols again. Los Angeles is notorious around the world for being such a liberal, free-wheeling community. Whether you know it or not, you inspire other vampires worldwide, and the way you accept *any* species of vampire in LA puts the idea into others' heads that maybe someday vampires can truly let go of the old ways and move forward."

"If the Order crushes LA, they'll be sending a message to

vampires across the world," Clarisse murmured.

"Got it in one," Caleb said. "It was a precisely calculated plan when we first landed here from Kamchatka, and though Tempestia went off the rails when she found out about Steele and Stacey, Akrath's managed to keep things going more or less the way they were supposed to. I tried to escape just before the attack, to warn you of what was coming, but a couple of werewolves caught me just before I got through a wooded area and onto a highway. I was so close!" He hissed and smashed his fist against his knee.

"Tempestia decreed that since I'd been so faithful in the past, I'd be granted a shred of amnesty and would be given some time to see if I wanted to recant my error. Meaning she was going to wait and see if I'd come around enough that I could finish working on the *Covenant Novum*. That's the only reason she didn't kill me right there; that lousy *Covenant Novum* is so important to her she was actually willing to give me a second chance," he snarled.

"Never underestimate a despot's love for self-congratulation," I said.

"Indeed. I was left to rot in a cell, with Akrath or somebody else coming by every day to ask me if I was willing to repent. I always refused, hoping that the pair that had brought down the Order before would make a repeat performance, or somebody else would, and I'd get free that way. I didn't want to die, but I just couldn't play the part anymore. Tempestia didn't try to forcibly change me, either, which had me wondering for a while, but now I think she intends to make an example of me. Sooner or later, unless I recant on my own, I wager Tempestia's going to put me through a very ugly reconversion—or kill me right in front of the whole Order—just to show to everybody that rebelling against the Goddess doesn't pay. But as to why I was transferred from my old cell to this one, I have no idea. But then again, Tempestia doesn't work in the most logical fashion these days."

Caleb fell silent following his last statement.

Katheryne got up and started slowly pacing, restless in a way I'd never seen her before. Considering the current situation, I wasn't surprised. It also wouldn't have surprised me if I ended up pacing myself in the near future.

For the moment, I stayed where I was, holding onto Clarisse, the two of us silently comforting one another and steeling ourselves for what was to come. Then there was the other thing, the thing we wouldn't say aloud, or even allow ourselves to think—that this might be the last time we were able to hold on to one another like this.

"Silence yourselves! Cease this pointless clamoring!" Akrath snapped at us though the bars. Naturally, Stacey, Clarisse, and I continued caterwauling our way through "Overdose," the sixteenth straight AC/DC song we'd gone through during the past hour or so.

After some brooding on our part, we decided if they were going to make us stew in our own anxiety by locking us up, we were going to make nuisances of ourselves. As Stacey so succinctly put it, "Fuck those guys."

Not only did our incessant singing annoy our captors, it raised our attitudes out of the dark abyss they'd been sliding toward since Caleb's storytelling had finished. Better to die laughing and acting like an ass than wallowing in one's own fear and misery.

Caleb wasn't singing—he didn't know the words—but been raptly listening, fascinated and delighted by the lyrics, the likes of which he'd never heard before. Katheryne, on the other hand, hadn't shown much of a change. She was leaning against the wall in the darkest corner of the cell, arms crossed over her chest, a soft blue glow diffusing the air around her. She was "simmering" as Clarisse had said, getting herself ready for whatever the Order was going to put us through when they'd finally decided we'd waited long enough.

I didn't know whether it was due to our singing, but Akrath's appearance at the door was the end of our wait, I assumed. He wouldn't have taken the time to travel all the way down here to tell us to knock our shit off—that's what underlings were for. Not that telling us to stop would have done any good; the werewolf guards had been trying to since we'd started. They'd made a lot of noise and threats about shutting us up personally, but hadn't accepted our invitations to come inside and make us stop.

Now it was Akrath's turn to holler. Then he did the guards one better and actually opened the door and strode in.

Naturally I thought about jumping him, but there was a veritable horde of werewolves, revenants, revenant masters, and covies waiting out in the corridor, so that wouldn't have been the brightest idea in the world. Not only that, but we weren't doing anything drastic until we could get hold of Tempestia. Before this was all over, either she was going to die or we were, so we bided our time and sang.

Akrath stood looking at us, arms clasped behind his back, like a particularly dangerous schoolteacher waiting for his students to bring their antics to an end, after which he would *really* put the screws to them. We didn't let that stop us, and we finished up without missing a beat.

When that was done, Stacey leaned toward Akrath and disarmingly asked, "You wouldn't to want to join us in a rousing rendition of 'Big Balls,' would you?"

"Not hardly." Akrath's voice oozed contempt. "You will have to excuse me if I have much more important and pressing concerns on my mind."

"Like our imminent deaths, perhaps?" I asked coolly.

Akrath gave a minimal shrug. "If that's what it leads to, so be it." From the tone of his voice, that's what he was hoping for. "For the moment, nothing has been decided. However, your presence has again been requested by the Goddess."

Caleb got to his feet and stretched a little bit. "Tempestia decided it's time for another kangaroo court session?"

Akrath's bearing was stiff as he speared Caleb with a sharp glare. "If the Goddess must hold court, it's because you gave her no other choice."

"You should really look into a new line of work, my good man," Caleb said. "I know how much you chafe at Tempestia's methods of late, since you know her lunacy's going to run this whole operation into the ground sooner or later. Your loyalty's to be admired, but it's going to be your downfall someday."

"Maybe sooner than later, eh?" Stacey added, waggling his eyebrows. Akrath didn't dignify either one of them with a response.

He raked the cell with a withering look. "Please fall into order and allow yourselves to be escorted to see the Goddess."

Eager to get out of the wretched cell, Stacey, Caleb, Clarisse, and I moved toward the door then we noticed that Katheryne wasn't with us. When we looked back, she was still standing in the corner of the cell, still emitting her soft blue light.

Akrath moved past us. "That includes you, my dear. Just because you are a half-life does not mean you are below the considerations of the Goddess. She has time enough for all of her guests...even the abominations."

Every muscle in my body tightened up, as did Stacey and Clarisse's. I was getting so bloody sick of hearing these bitch-bastards running Katheryne down. Why couldn't they just leave her alone?

Katheryne said nothing in response, but fixed Akrath with a stare that went right through him. She slowly brought her hand up in front of her, her glow noticeably strengthening, and she flexed her hand once—slowly, deliberating moving each finger, as if testing it out. Then she bent it backward until her palm was aimed straight at Akrath.

The glow spread to her eyes, turning them into gleaming sapphires, but her expression didn't change; it was as though she were in a trance. Akrath didn't back down, didn't even flinch, and after aiming her hand at Akrath, Katheryne didn't make a move either. The two stood transfixed, a pair of living statues.

"Jeezum crow," Stacey softly hissed, "I think she's gonna blast him!"

I didn't reply: I was holding my breath too tightly.

All was dead silent—not even the revenants in the corridor made a sound. I'd seen the power Katheryne was capable of unleashing; she was a living dynamo of magickal energy. At the range she was from Akrath, she could have vaporized him without breaking a sweat, but she held off, not saying a word, her eyes and posture relaying everything.

Had Akrath finally pushed the witch over the edge?

Just when I became certain Akrath was about to die, Katheryne's eyes shifted to meet mine, and in them I saw a question. I shook my head almost imperceptibly, and she returned her gaze to Akrath. After several long moments, she lowered her hand and the light glow around her began to fade.

Their gazes remained locked on one another for a while longer, and after a dozen rapid-fire heartbeats Akrath broke contact, turned around, and walked away from the half-blood. He pushed past us, stepping back out into the corridor, and said, "Do not trifle with the blond one. Treat her with care."

Out of the corner of my eye, I could see Caleb gaping at first Akrath then Katheryne as she joined us.

"I don't believe it!" he whispered. "I don't *believe* it!" When Clarisse put her arm around the witch, Caleb whispered, "You *scared* him! I've never seen that before!"

Katheryne didn't say anything, but Clarisse gave her a hug and kiss on the cheek. "That's because she's something special."

"No, because she's one bad motherfucker," Stacey said, giving Katheryne a punch on the shoulder.

"Thanks for holding off," I said to Katheryne as we stepped out into the corridor, where we were promptly surrounded by our escort.

"This is your show, I didn't want to step on your toes," Katheryne replied softly.

I shook my head. "This is your show too. You just have to wait until it's your proper time, and *then* you let it rip," I whispered as we started down the corridor. I chuckled. "If you want to be a legend like me, you need to wait for just the right moment to do your thing. It's all in the timing, kiddo."

She gave me a little smile. "I'll keep that in mind...old timer."

I returned the smile and took Clarisse's hand. Even though we were on the way to what was supposed to be our deaths, I felt good.

II

We heard the chanting—a form of Latin adopted and modified by covies long ago—long before we reached the cavern where we'd last seen Tempestia. It was heavy, sonorous, and repetitive, echoing endlessly down the stone tunnels of the Order's lair, almost hypnotic. I suppose had I been more receptive to the Order's bullshit, I *would* have found it hypnotic, even relaxing. As it was, it only annoyed me. I wasn't the only one.

"Hey Baldo, tell the stinking monks to shut up. That chant shit stopped selling albums a long time ago," Stacey barked at Akrath, who didn't even bother acknowledging him. My lean counterpart had never taken well to being ignored, and he turned to the brindled werewolf walking along next to us. "What about you? Doesn't that crapola get on your nerves after a while? You seem like a happening sort of guy. Wouldn't you much rather they just cranked some of Elvis's gospel numbers and left it at that?"

The werewolf—fairly short as werewolves went but stocky— gave Stacey a long, hard look with a set of green eyes. "Hush," he snapped. Curiously his tone didn't sound all that irritated...more amused than anything else, actually. "Mind your own business."

Stacey apparently hadn't sensed much hostility, either, and he pressed onward. "I bet you think I'm right, don't you? You'd much rather be jamming to Elvis than this medieval chant bullshit, wouldn't you?"

Now the werewolf looked mildly annoyed. "You would do well to silence yourself, blood-feaster. Now is not the time for fun, regardless of what side you may be on." When Stacey opened his mouth to say something else, the werewolf growled at him.

Now it was Stacey who was annoyed, and he started to growl right back. Clarisse beat me to the punch and put her hand over his mouth.

"Ixnay, ixnay," she said as he tried to mumble around her hand. "He gave you an opportunity to shut your yap. If you don't stow it now, he's gonna take it as his right to bite your face off since you're not bright enough to know a warning when you hear it."

When I looked from Clarisse to the werewolf I could have sworn I saw a faint smirk on the werewolf's face.

"You are most wise," the werewolf said approving. "A pity you and your kind saw fit to disobey your Goddess and kill our elders."

"We killed none of your people, save in self-defense." Clarisse made and refused to break eye contact with the werewolf. "Why don't you ask Akrath about that?"

"She's right," Caleb added. "If anyone would know, it would be me."

"And *you* are a traitor," the werewolf said, giving the robed vampire a suspicious glare. "Why should I trust your words?"

"Why should you trust anything Tempestia and Akrath tell *you*?" Clarisse asked the werewolf, her voice cast from iron.

From her tone, set of her jaw, and the sparks in her eyes, Clarisse was ready to turn this into a full-on argument. When the werewolf turned back to her, they dueled with their eyes and I squeezed her hand. *Not now, babe, not now.* But then, I didn't know werewolves the way she did. For all I knew, picking a fight with a werewolf in a certain way would garner one—even a vampire—respect.

"You would be wise to silence yourself, as well," the werewolf said after a long moment of consideration. He turned to look at the rest of us. "*All* of you. Judgment will come soon enough, and then all will become clear."

He moved his gaze from one vampire to the next, as if daring us to retort, but Stacey had learned his lesson, and Clarisse herself seemed unwilling to push her challenge any further, thankfully. I also wasn't too keen on the way the other four or five werewolves in our party were looking at us, and the revenants were picking up on the lycanthropes' discontent, growing restless themselves.

The tension ratcheted up notch by notch, and I was painfully aware that if a fight erupted in the confines of this tunnel, things wouldn't have gone well for us. It would have been a massacre, to be honest. After watching us for a long time as we walked, the brindled werewolf turned his gaze from us and we resumed our trip to go see the Goddess, the wonderful fake Goddess of the Order.

"The next time you get it into your head to start up a conversation about Elvis with a werewolf when you're deep in the belly of the beast, *don't*," I advised Stacey, cuffing him on the back of the head. "Remember when Dorian got so mad at you he ripped your pants off? I'd hate to have to do it, but I will."

"I was just trying to be friendly," Stacey protested softly. "You know how I am, I'm as cuddly as they come. Besides, I had to do *something* to get that lousy chanting out of my head—it's driving me batshit."

"Just be happy they're busy chanting instead of trying to forcibly recruit us," I said.

Though he scowled, he kept his trap shut.

The chanting that had started the whole conversation was now considerably louder than it had been when Stacey had first started to babble to the brindled werewolf. I could feel it in the air, like picking up the bass beats from someone's super-powered car stereo. Except this wasn't rap or one of those stupid bass albums, this was part of the preparation for our impending doom.

A doom that would be cancelled as soon as a good opportunity presented itself to us… It wasn't *if* the opportunity presented itself, it was *when*, dammit. We'd get out of this one way or another, I certainly didn't intend for the grand adventure of my life to be stopped by a bunch of mad religious nuts. I'd rather be killed by a toilet traveling at mach speed after falling out of the back of a 747.

After an interminable trip, we emerged into the cavern, which was brighter than before, lit up with so many candles it had become a monstrous, primitive cathedral. That effect was heightened even further by the black robes in attendance and the obnoxious chanting. Yep, this was something right out of the Middle Ages, all right. It was moments like this that made me realize civilization actually had made some genuine progress, though reality TV made me wonder.

The cavern floor was awash with a sea of black-robed followers swaying as they chanted, and the hypnosis notion came back to me again. They all looked as though they were under some sort of trance, their minds not entirely their own. From what Caleb had told us about Tempestia's blood, that probably wasn't entirely inaccurate.

Dozens of eyes glittered at the outer fringes of the cavern:

werewolves. Apparently they weren't up on the chanting, so they hung in the shadows with only their shining eyes giving away their presence. I was sure there were more werewolves here than before, as though they'd called in all of the legions for this event. Great.

At the far end of the cavern stood Tempestia, a huge flame erupting forth from the saucer-like platform to which Frizz's body had been committed. It was an impressive backdrop as she stood with her arms out and her head thrown back—as though crucified herself—while she lead her loyal followers in their chanting.

I could just see Wade, still on the cross, the flames lighting up his motionless form with a reddish-orange glow. Katheryne tensed and I felt the fine hairs on my arms and on the back of neck go up, as though from static electricity—she was having a hard time holding herself back. She wanted to act and act *now*, and I couldn't blame her. But we had to wait until the right moment. If we went for the throat too soon, all would be lost. Whoever said that waiting was the hardest part was a very, very wise individual.

Akrath strode forward without pause, the crowd of followers parting like the proverbial Red Sea before him, creating a wide enough gap for our procession, though it was a tight fit. Once we'd passed, the crowd moved back like loose jelly oozing back to an indentation made by a finger—they never stopped chanting and swaying, not even for a second. Fuckin' eerie.

It seemed like only seconds later we were once more standing before the self-proclaimed Goddess. She paid us no mind and continued chanting for a good long while as we stood there, wishing she'd just get on with it.

"Any time now," I muttered, tapping my foot.

"By the Elements, *silence yourself*, blood-feaster," the brindled werewolf snapped softly, meeting my gaze. "Do not anger her—that will only make this more difficult."

"Indeed," said the one on the other side of us, a brawny grey-and-white specimen, fixing us with brilliant yellow eyes. "Hold your tongues lest they be pulled out by less tolerant ones than ourselves."

"You know what's really sick?" Stacey whispered furiously, tugging on the sleeve of my leather jacket. Before I could tell him to stifle himself, he spat out, "Werewolves have a better command of the English language than most Americans do. There, I just wanted to say that, and I'll shut up now."

I rolled my eyes while the werewolves gave him some harsh warning glares. Nobody else in our procession save myself, Clarisse, Katheryne, Caleb, and the pair of werewolves flanking us seemed to have noticed anything. The revenants had fallen dead silent, quite possibly taken in by the relentless chanting, not to mention their masters were starting to sway a little too.

I looked to the rest of our party, and saw that Clarisse—while still holding tightly to my hand—was fascinated by the chant and the effect it was having on Tempestia's followers. Clarisse was interested in almost everything; even in a situation such as this, her naturally inquisitive mind wouldn't stop for a moment as she took mental notes for later perusal.

Caleb had his arms folded over his chest, his face holding a mixture of fear and hope. He knew tough times were ahead, but that didn't necessarily mean he was doomed.

Katheryne was staring intensely at Wade, tightly hugging herself, and I saw the knuckles clenching her arms were trembling ever so slightly. I took a cue from her and looked toward our captive comrade, both grateful he hadn't disappeared into that hateful tunnel beneath the city and enraged at the indignity of being strapped to the cross like a trophy. At least they hadn't nailed him to it; thank the stars for small favors.

Another flash of anger surged through me as I saw a big rat perched on Wade's shoulder, sniffing at his neck. What the hell was *that?* Didn't they even have enough care for their so-called Dark One to ensure vermin didn't crawl all over him? I normally didn't mind rats—they're clever, determined survivors like any good vampires— but it was a respect thing in this instance.

I nearly objected aloud as the rat nosed through some of Wade's hair, then went back to poking at his neck and the tattered collar of his shirt, but ultimately let it be. Truth be told, the rat was the least of Wade's and our worries at the moment. The primary worry was the big, half-vampire vermin leading the Crimson Order Chant-a-Long less than twenty feet from us.

Speaking of that particular vermin, she must have mercifully gotten bored of her own voice, as she started to wind things down.

The repetitive chants came to a sudden end with a synchronized foot-stomp from every vampiric disciple in the room, including Akrath. Tempestia slowly lowered her arms and tilted her head forward to look at us, gracing us with that unpleasant "I'm the Queen of the World" smile she pulled off better than just about anybody else I'd ever seen.

"I welcome thee back, yes," she said in her smooth, utterly confident voice. "I trust thou have enjoyed a most comfortable stay, with plenty of time for reflection and contemplation."

I hardly looked at her as she spoke, my gaze going back to the rat on Wade's shoulder. It made for an interesting parallel to our situation: we were like Wade, trussed and helpless, lacking the strength to free ourselves, while the vermin sat on our shoulder and prodded at us, enjoying every moment of it, knowing it was safe to do whatever it wanted.

I kept staring at the rat as Tempestia prattled on and on about destiny and what it meant to her and us. I'd heard it all before from other tin-plate dictators and would-be gods: *follow me and prosper, cross me and die, I'm right, you're wrong, end of story.*

She wasn't even addressing any of us directly, she was just babbling the way religious figures like to do when they've got a captive audience. I was sure actual threats and promises would come later, but at the moment she was just endlessly running at the mouth, enjoying being the center of attention. The crowd would occasionally make loud rumbles of agreement with whatever drivel she was spewing, and she kept on droning and droning and droning. The werewolves, at least, were quiet.

Clarisse tightened her grip on my hand, and still I watched the rat, my vampiric vision enabling me to see every detail. I saw its twitching whiskers, its sleek brown fur, and its bright, oily eyes. I didn't need to hear Tempestia, so I watched the rat. Maybe I needed to do it to maintain my sanity, maybe I just preferred a simple survivor over a false god, I didn't know then and I don't know now; I just felt the need to watch the rat. Then the rat noticed me.

It sat up on its haunches on Wade's shoulder, its little feet holding onto Wade's shirt, and it looked right back at me, as if daring me to do something about it. *What'cha gonna do about me, buddy?* it seemed to be saying. *Looks like you've got more than enough to keep you busy right now.*

Smartass rat. I thought about hissing at it just for the hell of it. I never got the chance as I vaguely heard Tempestia say something about a returning member of her flock, one who'd been presumed dead. At least everybody else had presumed him dead. She, on the other hand, knew all about it and had just kept quiet, waiting for the moment when his return would bring the most joy to him and everybody else. Now was the time, apparently.

I didn't see him when he first came out—the rat and I were dueling with our eyes—but as soon as I heard Stacey hiss, "Ohhh *fuck me*," my concentration on the rat shattered. I turned my eyes to Tempestia again, feeling a little off for a few seconds as I widened my focus from a single rat to the rest of the world.

Akrath had taken a place standing a behind Tempestia, his hands clasped together behind his back, and another vampire stood next to Tempestia, visibly shaking and jittering. He was dressed in a black robe like everybody else, and for a few seconds, I couldn't understand what had caused Stacey to react like he did. Then it hit me. The tunnel under the city.

"Monsters down below," the new vampire mumbled. The quaking individual standing next to Tempestia was the one Wade had dragged back up from the depths beneath the city and Catacombs, the one who'd escaped in the pandemonium following the attack of the unearthly beast and Wade's assumed death...the one we hadn't found afterward.

From the looks of it, he'd managed to make his way home well enough. Shitfire and fuck me running. What Wade had said about that tunnel, the underworld it opened up to, and the covies came back to me.

The *Covenant* idiots mustn't know about this. They're too stupid to leave it alone and would get us all killed.

From the way Tempestia was smiling at me, I would have sworn she'd just read my mind.

"Sorry, Wade," I whispered, casting a glance in his direction.

He hadn't heard me, and was still hanging quietly, the rat nosing at his cheek now. This time, however, the rat didn't hold my attention, and when Tempestia spoke, I listened closely.

"This wonderful lover of his Goddess, known as Dactius, who now stands before thee, has told me a most disturbing tale regarding a sickness sitting underneath thy infested city, as though thy madness and heresy has bred its very own monsters," she said, sweeping her gaze over us, one by one. "I believe this to be true, as I, who have created all that creeps upon the earth and soars through the skies, have never brought into creation such monsters as this poor one has described to his Goddess. What dost thou have to say for thyself in respect to these abominations?"

"Stay the hell away from them," I snapped, fixing Tempestia with my glare. "They're far beyond anything you've got the capacity to handle."

Tempestia giggled at my words, then waved a dismissive hand at me. "I would not have expected anything less from the likes of thee, Steele. Of course thou would seek to protect thy interests beneath the city, the products of your heresy and lack of faith in your Goddess. Perhaps thee and thy kind thought to play Goddess, to create your own life where there was none before, to deepen thy blasphemy even further, to attempt to raise thyself to the lofty heights occupied only by myself. But thee could not do it, now, could thee? Thy attempts at creating thy own life has resulted in those foul creatures as described to me. Thou could not create the beauty that I am capable of, could thee?"

I glanced over at a revenant, making sure she caught my movement then looked back at her. "If *that's* what you consider beauty," I said, "I'd hate to see your definition of ugliness. But whatever it is under the city, you'll leave it alone if you've got any of your mind left."

Tempestia giggled again, her eyes dancing merrily, her long hair and dress swishing around as she took a step closer to us. "Why dost thou continue to push forward with thy lies? I can see through thee, Steele—I see right through thy lies and blasphemies to see the truth within your heart and mind, yes. Thy kind created those creatures. I *know* this to be true. Once the business at hand has been taken care of, we shall descend upon your city once more to destroy those mockeries of life. They will not be allowed to exist any longer. Just as those who refuse to believe in the love of the Goddess shall cease to be, so shall those monsters."

"They're in the dark, in the dark," the jittering vampire mumbled, his eyes furtively snapping back and forth in their sockets. "The shattered moon rises high above the death fires."

"You'll be dooming us all, you dumbass!" I snarled at Tempestia, letting go of Clarisse's hand and stepping toward the "Goddess."

Our guards—who'd stepped aside when we'd arrived so they wouldn't block view between Tempestia and ourselves—moved as if to stop me, but a motion from Tempestia instantly froze them in their tracks.

I pointed to where Wade hung on the cross. "Why don't you ask your Dark One? He'll tell you plenty about what's under the city, and he'll tell you that you'll be fucking all of us if you turn that shit loose on the world!"

"*Ku'lhtklk!*" screeched Dactius before lapsing into a fit of trembles. Tempestia put a comforting hand on his shoulder, which settled him down a little.

"There are things, *dark things*, beyond our ability to understand and cope with," said Caleb solemnly. "I've lived in a bubble for a long time, but not so much so that I don't know there are matters which shouldn't be taken lightly, or trifled with at all. This could be one of those matters."

"He's right," Clarisse added, defiantly glaring at Tempestia. "There are instances of haunters of the darkness and forbidden things in countless ancient texts from around the world. If you know where to look and what signs to interpret, you can see there's a thread of commonality telling us there are things out there you shouldn't screw with if you've got a brain in your head."

"Listen to them, Tempestia," Caleb said. "Even if it's the only thing they say that you *do* actually acknowledge, listen to this. These aren't a bunch of screaming, idiot heretics like you might think. If you'd taken the time to actually learn about the secrets of this world instead of playing Goddess, you'd know they were right."

Tempestia gave Caleb an arctic glower. "You shall refer to me as 'my Goddess,' Caleb. Thou should know that by now. Tempestia is serving as my vessel for the time being, so do not call me by the name of my vessel. And there are no secrets of the world to me—I created all of this! Do not presume that thee know more than I do, because thou does not!"

"Oh, would you just shut the fuck up?"

All heads whipped around toward the unexpected snarl, and Tempestia's eyes narrowed to angry slits as Katheryne stepped forward, head held high. She strode right past me, not stopping until she was only about eight feet from Tempestia. The guards again moved as if to protect Tempestia, and she again waved them off as she speared Katheryne with her gaze.

"What didst thou say?" she asked slowly, as though she couldn't believe what she'd just heard.

"You heard me...*half-life*," Katheryne sneered, fists clenched at her sides.

A collective gasp shot through the cavern at the sheer contempt loaded into the word that Katheryne had endured so many times in the past. The witch had hit a nerve somewhere in the supremely confident, self-proclaimed Goddess.

Tempestia's voice dropped to a low, deadly tone. "What didst thou call me?"

"Are you deaf as well as dumb?" snapped the half-blood, taking another step forward. Tension and electricity were in the air now, and the cavern had fallen into total silence as everybody goggled at the half-vampire standing up to the 'Goddess' Herself.

"Do you think this is the best of ideas at the moment?" Stacey leaned over and asked, and all Clarisse and I could do was stare by way of reply. I couldn't remember the last time Stacey had asked that—as far as I knew, Clarisse had never heard him say it. "*Well?*" Stacey prodded.

"I think the point's moot," Clarisse said, eyes back on Katheryne. "There's no going back from this."

I had to agree. "To paraphrase a certain one-eyed sailor, I think she's had all she can stands and she can't stands no more."

I wasn't sure if this was the brightest move on Katheryne's part, but then, realistically, when *were* we going to have a truly good moment to strike? Furthermore, I didn't know if we'd have even been able to stop Katheryne.

Katheryne took yet another step forward, focused entirely on Tempestia, and I knew that if any guard dared to lay a hand on her they would've been incinerated. "For someone who's supposed to be omnipotent, you're pretty stupid, you know that?" she growled at Tempestia, who was looking positively pissed. I wonder how long it had been since a half-blood—how long since *anyone*—had spoken to her like this.

Katheryne's eyes began to glow with electric blue light, and I knew without question that we'd crossed the Rubicon.

Tempestia started to yell something back at the blond witch, but Dactius interrupted as he caught sight of Katheryne's eyes. "It's *her!*" he cried, pointing at Katheryne. "She's the one with the light who destroyed the monsters in the dark! I saw it with my own eyes before I escaped!"

Without hesitation he then ran over to Katheryne, dropped to the ground, and wrapped his arms around her leg. "Protect me from them, *please!*" he beseeched her, looking up with eyes like saucers. "I'll worship you and your light forever! I'm sorry for running, my Goddess, I was so scared and I didn't know what I was doing! Please forgive me!"

Katheryne spared him the merest of glances and nodded slightly, which seemed to mollify the befuddled vampire. He stopped shaking altogether and peacefully held onto the half-vampire's leg.

Tempestia gaped at how suddenly her follower had converted over to Katherynism, and when the witch again locked eyes with her, there was a faint smile on her lips and a hint of smug humor in her voice. "Well, it appears it's not too difficult to ascend to godhood, now is it?" she sneered at the fuming Tempestia.

"You're no deity!" she screamed at Katheryne. "You're nothing but a filthy half-life, a mockery to the covenant formed between myself and Brahman! You dare to walk under my light in your selfish heresy and blasphemy! You are nothing compared to me, *nothing!*"

"But to him," Katheryne replied smoothly, patting the now-placid Dactius on the head, "I'm everything. With the right words and circumstances, anybody can be a god. It's not that hard."

"You'll never be a deity, *half-life!* You'll never be *anything!*" Tempestia roared, and the flames on the saucer behind her raged up as though hit with a load of fuel. Her eyes were glowing a deep, angry red in contrast to Katheryne's electric blue.

Katheryne gave a short, contemptuous laugh. "Look who's talking. *You* were nothing until you turned yourself over to the Servants of Midnight. *You* were nothing until you turned your back on the rest of us half-vampires. *You* were nothing until you sold out people like me to lick the boots of the covies! *Nothing!* And you're still nothing! You're just a half-vampire who got lucky enough to get the power to slaughter anyone and everyone who thought differently than you!"

"*I am the Goddess!*" Tempestia shrieked, and the two were almost nose to nose. Clarisse and I were nearly crushing each other's hands, while Stacey just about hopped up and down in excitement. Caleb simply goggled as the two women stared one another down.

Then Katheryne spat right in Tempestia's face.

Time completely froze. Nobody moved, nobody even breathed. Then Tempestia backhanded Katheryne and sent her flying backward, head over heels.

The half-blood crashed against the floor none too gently, black-robed covies scurrying away. Dactius also went flying, and when he recovered, he hurried back over to Katheryne and started to help her up. We also moved to help our friend, but Katheryne held out her hand.

"I'm fine, I'm all right," she said as she sat up, blood flowing from her mouth. She looked vaguely dazed, but the anger was still very much there.

"Katheryne, are you—" I started to ask, but she cut me off.

"I said I'm *fine!*" she snapped as she shakily got back to her feet. Though her legs were wobbly, Katheryne immediately re-locked glares with Tempestia, who was looking less like a goddess and more like an angry child, complete with fists clenched in front of her chest.

"You'll suffer for eternity in Terminus for that, I swear it, yes!" Tempestia snarled as she pointed at the witch. "How *dare* you!"

"How dare *you* try to tell anybody what to think!" I yelled at Tempestia, trying to draw her attention away from Katheryne. The hit had taken a lot out of her, and if I could give her a precious few moments to recover, I'd gladly take one for the team. "How dare you dictate what's right and wrong! You've got no authority and no right to tell the world how it should be!"

"I am the Goddess," Tempestia informed me, looking as though she'd much rather just rip me to shreds than try to convert me in any capacity.

The climate of the cavern was descending into confusion, and the disciples weren't quite sure how to take this. They'd known Tempestia as a fount of confidence and absolute control—some of them for decades or more—and now they were watching her lose her grip on a situation. Doubt—that most toxic of elements to religion—was starting to whisper to them.

They were waiting for her to wipe all of us from existence or to simply *make* us obey, and it wasn't happening. They had no idea how to react. Were the heretics right, or was this all part of some clever ploy of hers? Perhaps she was trying to test their faith, yes, that could be it. But then again...

What if she really wasn't as all-powerful as she claimed to be?

It wasn't just the covies, either. The werewolves were on the edges of their figurative seats, exchanging glances and speaking with their eyes. Was this blood-feaster truly all she purported to be, or just a good trickster?

From the look in Tempestia's eyes, she could feel the seeds of doubt, and she was going to have to rein this in as soon as possible before permanently losing face with her followers. Katheryne knew it too.

"If you're really the Goddess, and you're really all-powerful, then I shouldn't pose much of a threat to you, if any," Katheryne said, challenge in her voice. "How about this? If I best you in a one-on-one duel, you free myself, my friends, and turn the Dark One over to me."

Tempestia shook her head, the confident Goddess once again. "Never. The Goddess will not lower Herself to a fight in the dirt with one as lowly as thee. Take thy place amongst thy fellows and prepare thyself for my judgment. If thee obeys, I will show thee mercy."

Katheryne threw back her head and laughed while Dactius smoothed down her hair and straightened her sweater as much as he could. "Do you expect me to roll over and die like a whipped cur? Not hardly. I don't care if you're afraid or not, I'm taking the Dark One away from you. If you want me to just go up there and take him, that's fine, but if not, you're going to have to fight me."

"Fight her!" roared the brindled werewolf standing next to Stacey. "A goddess should not have difficulty with a mere blood-feaster!

Show us your power—show us your worthiness to lead!"

"We will not suffer cowardice, not from blood-feasters or goddesses!" added the one on the other side of us. "We do not follow cowards!"

Barks and howls of assent came from the other werewolves assembled in the cavern. As far as I could tell, they were all spoiling for a good fight.

Clarisse whispered, "I don't know if Katheryne knew how the werewolves would react to her challenge, but she's played the situation so Tempestia can't get out without fighting her. If she backs off, the werewolves will call her a coward and either turn on her or simply leave. A challenge to her authority's been made, and to a werewolf, shrugging that off is indicative of cowardice and a lack of confidence."

"Fight! Fight! Fight!" Stacey shouted, banging his fist in the air like he would have at a rock concert.

I joined in, as did Clarisse and Caleb, and—amusingly enough—so did the brindled werewolf. Soon the four of us and all the werewolves were shouting in unison.

Akrath—who'd done an impressive job of remaining impassive throughout this—was looking frantic. I had no doubt that if he took command of the situation, he'd quickly have things under control. *But* that would undermine Tempestia further, putting deeper cracks into the foundation of the new Crimson Order, which had been built upon Tempestia's strength and charisma. So he had to stand there and do nothing, hoping for the best. Sucked to be him.

Tempestia looked like a cornered animal, unable to find her way out of the trap into which she'd stumbled. Holding hands above her head, she bellowed, "*Silence!*"

The cavern fell quiet again, save for a few yaps and barks from the werewolves.

She pointed at Katheryne, her fangs bared in a grim smile. "Very well, as my followers wish me to prove my power, I will fight with thee to put an end to thy impudence. Thy fate was sealed anyway, as I would not have suffered a half-life such as yourself to exist any longer, no. It is thy friends that I am interested in… What happens to thee is inconsequential, yes."

"If I beat you, we all walk free and the Dark One is turned over to me. If I can't beat you, then I'm not worthy of him," Katheryne said, casting a final glance up toward Wade. She took off her sweater, leaving her in just a gray tanktop, clearly not wanting her keepsake of her time in Las Vegas with Donita to get ripped up during the coming conflict. She handed it to Dactius, who gratefully hugged it to his chest.

"Agreed," Tempestia said. Then she turned to look at the four of us, as well as the rest of her followers, and said, "Never doubt thy Goddess, never *ever*, no. A lack of faith could land thee in Terminus, yes, and I will prove beyond a shadow of—"

A brilliant beam of magickal force energy blasted Tempestia right off her feet, sending her tumbling through the air for a respectable distance before she lost momentum and smashed into the cavern's stone floor.

Katheryne was already striding toward Tempestia's fallen form as Akrath hurried out of the way of the angry half-blood. Call it dirty fighting if you will, but you will rarely ever find a vampire who fights fairly in a life-or-death situation. When our very existence is on the line, we're the dirtiest players in the game, bar none.

"Go get her! Kick her ass!" I screamed at Katheryne, but she was too focused on Tempestia to acknowledge me.

"Wanna make a little wager on the outcome of this little brawl?" Stacey asked the brindled werewolf, who perked up his ears in confusion.

As Katheryne closed in, her magick crackled over her like electrical current, getting wilder by the second. Four spheres of energy separated themselves from that current and began spinning around the witch like moons tumbling around a planet. Clarisse hopped up and down in excitement.

"She's letting it all go, she's not gonna hold back anything!" she crowed. "She's gonna *demolish* the bitch!"

Tempestia was back on her feet, but as soon as she'd gotten upright, Katheryne blew her on her ass with an energy bolt once more, knocking her even farther across the cavern.

"Come on! *Come on!*" Katheryne roared at the half-vampire leader of the Order as she scrabbled to get back up. The witch's eyes had become suns, blue smoke trickling out of them—for the first time, I truly understood just how much power the gentle half-blood had at her disposal. "Get up, *half-life!* Damn me to Terminus! Come on, *Goddess!*"

Ka-blammo, Tempestia went flying again.

"I do believe you chose the wrong side to hook up with," I called over to Akrath, who looked like he was torn between screaming and throwing up. He spared me a venomous glare then returned to watching Tempestia get her ass stomped.

The werewolves were all barking and howling, clearly enjoying a good row, while the rest of the covies simply looked nervous as hell.

Back on her feet, Tempestia was a blur as she blindly rushed Katheryne, not giving the witch time to fire off another blast. She hit her with a solid tackle to the waist that sent them both tumbling back the way they came. The tackle turned into a roll, and both women started pummeling each other with their fists, which Katheryne—the physically weaker of the two by a good margin— got the worst of. The witch staggered to her feet, extricating herself from Tempestia, and the self-proclaimed Goddess delivered a haymaker from Hell that spun Katheryne around in a one-eighty, after which she fell flat on her face.

"Get up, Blondie! Put that whore in her place!" Stacey cried out. "You can do it!"

Tempestia took a step toward Katheryne's face-down form, and one of the half-blood's feet shot out and slammed into Tempestia's knee, causing it to bow backward as Katheryne's foot pushed the joint to its limits and beyond.

With a shriek, Tempestia stumbled away, flailing her arms, and Katheryne was drunkenly pushing herself back to her feet, blood dripping from her mouth again. She shook her head, trying to get her bearings, then put her hands side by side and let fly a double burst of energy, intent on frying her foe.

But Tempestia shot up off the ground and above the blast, laughing heartily. "I am through toying with thee, blasphemous half-life! Now is the time for retribution!"

With a motion of Tempestia's hand, the flesh on Katheryne's left forearm burst into flame. "By the stars, no!" Clarisse screamed as I gasped in shock.

The half-blood shrieked bloody murder and slapped at her

burning arm. Cackling madly, Tempestia moved her hand again, making a patch of the fabric on the right leg of Katheryne's jeans catch flame too.

"Such is the price for crossing the Goddess!" Tempestia laughed, her arms held triumphantly above her head. The covies were now cheering wildly, happy their Goddess was in control and thus relieving them of a situation where they'd potentially have to think for themselves.

Clarisse lurched forward to help Katheryne, but I held firmly to her hand. "What the fuck are you doing?" she demanded, shoving at me. "Let me go help her!"

I shook my head, watching Katheryne as she struggled to put out the flames. "She doesn't want any help. This is her fight, and we've got to let her take it through to the end. She *needs* to do this. I'll step in if she's going to get killed, but until then, she's on her own. She has to prove herself."

"But she doesn't need to prove anything!" Clarisse insisted, trying to pry my fingers loose.

"Not to us, never to us, but to herself, she's still got plenty to prove. This is her redemption," I said, and Clarisse stopped as my words hit home. She understood now, I saw it in her eyes and felt it through our bond. She hated it as much as I did, but she understood. We turned as one to watch Katheryne.

"Come on, I believe in you, kid," I whispered. "Show her who's the boss."

"Surrender now and I'll make thy death painless!" Tempestia called down to Katheryne, who was still trying to put the flames out.

At Tempestia's words, Katheryne's head snapped upward, toward Tempestia, and she screamed, *"Shut up!"*

Then the half-blood's form blurred, and Tempestia was the one howling in pain and surprise as she fell backward through the air. Katheryne was above her, and with another two-handed blast, she sent Tempestia rocketing toward the ground.

The so-called Goddess hit with a tremendous crash, creating a body-shaped crater on impact. Katheryne laughed down at Tempestia—the flames extinguished by her headlong rush through the air—who lay in her crater, barely moving.

Katheryne landed next to her fallen enemy then yanked her out of the impact crater by a handful of raven hair. All Tempestia could do was hang limply in Katheryne's grasp, weakly trying to claw at her with one hand. In sheer physical strength, Tempestia had Katheryne beat by several country miles, but she couldn't cope with Katheryne's magick, especially when the witch was fighting for the lives of her friends.

Katheryne wisely didn't waste any time grandstanding. She cocked back a blazing blue fist and drilled Tempestia square in the face with a punch enhanced by the magickal equivalent of brass knuckles. As soon as Katheryne's fist made contact, all the stored magick broke loose and hammered Tempestia with a great deal more force than the punch could generate on its own.

The Crimson Order's leader was torn from Katheryne's grasp by the punch, bounced off the still-burning saucer platform then landed face-down a short distance from us.

"You got her down, now finish her off!" Caleb yelled, ecstatic at the sight of his former boss hurting and at the mercy of the avenging half-blood.

The cavern was a cacophony. Tempestia's followers yelled for her to get up, while the werewolves howled and snapped in appreciation, and we cheered our friend on. Akrath was the only quiet one, standing back and looking positively ill at the proceedings. I almost empathized with the prick.

After all, the Order had had us dead to rights and could have disposed of us with no trouble. But Tempestia's clowning around had brought them to the painful scenario of the Goddess getting her ass handed to her by a half-vampire. If I were Akrath, I would've killed Tempestia myself.

Katheryne, burnt and bloody but far from beaten, grabbed Tempestia's hair again, pulling her up so she was on her knees. Tempestia, hissing like a snake, lunged forward with her hands bent into claws, intent on ripping the witch to pieces. I started to shout out a warning, but I needn't have bothered. The witch neatly grabbed Tempestia's hands in her own, lacing their fingers together like wrestlers going for the classic test of strength.

Katheryne wasn't concerned with testing her strength against Tempestia. Instead crackling magickal force energy began surging through her arms, running through her fingers and arcing onto Tempestia's own hands and arms. The blond half-blood clenched her hands ever more tightly on Tempestia's as the "Goddess" got a taste of what Katheryne had to offer and tried to struggle away. The witch's lips peeled back in the most wicked grin I'd ever seen her wear, her fangs fully extended and her eyes burning brightly.

"How long do you think it'll be before your precious leader gets turned into blooey juice?" Stacey asked the brindled werewolf.

"I take no orders from her, not now, not ever," the werewolf replied with a derisive snort.

"Neither will anybody else once Blondie's done with her," Stacey crowed. "Go Katheryne!"

I was crazily grinning at Tempestia's predicament, savoring the image of our Katheryne putting the screws to the big bad Goddess, and I gave Clarisse a kiss on the cheek. "Looks like we'll pull out of this one yet, eh?"

"I certainly hope so," Clarisse replied, not taking her eyes off the two combatants for even a second. "I certainly hope so."

"Unhand me or suffer my wrath, foul half-life!" Tempestia screamed, her voice ragged as Katheryne pumped more and more power into her with each passing second.

Katheryne wasn't the least bit impressed with the promised wrath. "Suffer *this*," she hissed, and the energy doubled in intensity, eliciting a shriek from Tempestia.

The electric blue energy was crackling all up and down the arms of both women, and the leader of the Crimson Order looked as though she were starting to collapse in on herself, growing smaller. Katheryne on the other hand seemed to be getting bigger, bearing down on her faltering enemy with everything she had.

"Pure energy, burning through your twisted, hateful heart!" the half-blood snarled, her eyes shining with the brilliance of twin blue suns. "It's only a fraction of what our people have suffered because of the likes of you, and I'm giving it *all* back! Take it, *take it!*"

Tempestia threw back her head and screamed in wordless agony. I think she knew the end was near, and the Grim Reaper was probably even now whispering sweet nothings into her ears.

Then, as the old saying goes, all hell broke loose.

Akrath exploded into action, and before any of us could do

anything, he'd crossed the distance between himself and Katheryne, slashing her across the face with his nails.

"For the glory of the Crimson Order!" he roared, his eyes bright and wild. "It shall yet live on!"

Katheryne screamed as blood sprayed, and all the energy she'd been pumping into Tempestia arced out all around her like an electric bomb. A solid blue bolt shot blasted Akrath squarely in the chest, flinging him head over heels.

When Katheryne covered her wounded face, the leader of the Crimson Order moaned loudly and slumped to the floor in a boneless heap.

Several of the black-robed covies lunged forward, one of them tackling Katheryne while two others ran over to Tempestia. Katheryne, her hands covering her eyes, didn't make a sound.

It had all happened so fast even my vampiric senses were swimming, and my nerves weren't helped when a high-pitched squeak came from the air above us. When I looked up, I saw the big rat fling itself off of Wade's shoulder, flying much farther than a rat had any right to leap.

Before my very eyes, the rat grew larger as it hurtled through the air. Its short little legs lengthened and stretched, fur disappeared, the face blunted, and the tail disappeared. The rat's colors changed until it had gone from an earthy brown to bright purple and green, then long hair appeared on its shifting and morphing head, long brunette hair topped with a purple bandanna. My jaw dropped. I'd seen such things before, but hadn't known *she* was capable of it.

During the seconds-long flight, the unnamed big rat had transformed into a full-sized and *very* angry gypsy.

"*Katheryne!*" Donita cried, fear and rage in her voice as she cut through the air, aimed straight at the bastard who'd taken down the witch.

After Katheryne had crumpled from his tackle, Akrath had grabbed hold of her and started to get back to his feet. Donita hit him like a charging elephant, sending the two of them tumbling across the floor. Purple energy crackled and snapped angrily all around them as they rolled, and when they came to a stop, Donita had her hands on either side of his head and was running as much power between them as she could. She was burning his hair, flesh, and ultimately his entire head, to a crisp.

Donita, her eyes blazing every bit as bright as Katheryne's had been, except in purple instead of blue, said nothing during the brief roll and execution, nothing save for furious snarls, like an animal.

Clarisse and I were at the fallen witch's side a second later, Clarisse scooping Katheryne into her arms like a mother picking up a hurt child, while I dropped into a crouch, expecting an attack at any second. The situation had gone from controlled to organized chaos to all-out nuts in a short length of time, and the covies were going to react in the same way so many other confused, weak-minded fools did when a group of freethinkers fucked with their perfect vision: kill everyone who's not one of them.

I was proved correct. The crowd of covies had become a tide rushing toward us, and I let out a small groan of despair when I got a good look at just how many black-robed ninnies, revenants, and werewolves there were.

I was shocked when our brindled guard from earlier slammed into a revenant that had surged up ahead and was on a collision course straight for me.

Snarling and snapping like a lycanthrope possessed, the werewolf attacked the revenant with the relentless fury of a chihuahua after a mailman, clawing and biting the big bastard to bits in almost no time flat. The gray-and-white werewolf who'd been on the other side of us was tugging at my arm, just about shoving his snout into my face. As he spoke I caught the hot, decayed meat scent of his breath, the smell of a carnivore. But he wasn't interested in eating me, not anything of the sort.

"Hurry. You must fall back if you are to survive this!" he barked at me, trying to drag me backward. He turned his head to Clarisse and snapped off a quick series of barks and yips that were unintelligible to me but made a great deal of sense to Clarisse.

"Trust him! He just told me the name and title of my father!" she said. Through our bond, I could feel she did indeed trust this brawny werewolf, so I didn't fight it when he yanked on my arm and dragged me backward across the floor.

"There is a small passageway you can shelter in!" he said.

But I pulled against his grasp as I remembered Stacey. Where the dickens was he? I looked around frantically, trying to find him amid the growing riot, and I couldn't see him anywhere.

"Go on! I gotta find Stacey!" I yelled at the werewolf as I flung myself into the crowd, clawing and biting at everything that got near me. I felt a pang for leaving Clarisse and Katheryne to his care, but if Clarisse trusted him, that was good enough for me. He must have been on the level somehow, as the only people who knew the name and title of Clarisse's father were Brandi and myself.

I only hoped the werewolves were fully up to the task of protecting them. Clarisse was a ferocious fighter, one of the best, but she had Katheryne to look out for, and I had no idea how severe her injuries were. I found myself whispering prayers to whatever gods existed—if any—that Katheryne would live to fight another day.

III

It was an utter madhouse inside the cavern.

Werewolves were attacking revenants and covies, who were fighting back with varying degrees of success. Snarls, screams, roars echoed through the vast space as claws and fangs rent flesh in a bloody game of supernatural grab-ass.

I briefly wondered if all the werewolves were friendly like "our" two werewolves had been. I got my answer when a werewolf leaped on my back and drove me to the ground, snarling menacingly into my ear. Well, it had been a nice thought, at least.

As soon as I'd slammed down, a skull-shattering explosion rocked the cavern, shaking the very ground and causing rocks and stalactites to fall from the ceiling far above. A collective shout filled the air, sounding like a battle cry, and I had a bad feeling the covies were rallying.

The werewolf on me yipped in surprise at the explosion, but it didn't slow him down any. His teeth effortlessly tore through my leather jacket and sliced through the flesh and muscle of my shoulder, throwing me into a pain-fueled rage. I shot an elbow backward, thumped the werewolf hard in the shoulder and tipped him off me. His teeth ripped at my skin as he fell, but considering what he *could* have done with those big choppers, I got off easy.

I pushed myself up and sprang on the werewolf, sending us rolling across the ground, clawing, biting, and tearing at one another. I should have gotten back to my feet then kicked the dogshit out of the son of a bitch—trying to best a werewolf at straight-up savagery was a fool's game. But I was too hyped up and sick with worry for Clarisse, Stacey, and Katheryne to think clearly.

And what about Donita? Where the hell had she gone? And Caleb? Fuck, fuck, *fuck!*

I hammered at the werewolf's head with a fist, trying to convince him to give up the ghost, but he wasn't having it. With a twist, he was on top and pinning me to the ground, but I kept clubbing away at his cranium. He held me in place with a powerful forearm across my chest, so I simply chomped down on that big, meaty arm, biting as hard and as deeply as I could. The werewolf let out a surprisingly high-pitched yowl, and I took the opportunity to crack him one across the snout.

"Move over, Rover, and let Dorian take over!"

All of a sudden, the werewolf flew backward off me so forcefully it left a big chunk of meat in my mouth, which I spat out in disgust.

A hand grabbed my arm and helped me up quick as a flash, and I was looking right at grinning Dorian. He was dressed in a black covy robe, which stopped me dead for a moment as I sorted out the friendly face mixed with the clothes of the enemy. A shot of relief coursed through me, but barely touched the gale-force anxiety whipping around my guts.

"The cavalry has arrived!" he gleefully announced. "Talk about timing, huh?"

Behind him, a robe-clad Tommy was busily clubbing the werewolf down with an aluminum baseball bat, whistling as he worked, no less. The werewolf was getting sluggish, but still snarling fit to beat the band. After a final whack, Tommy pulled his .38 out from under his robe, stuck it right up against the werewolf's head and pulled the trigger. Ka-blammo.

"Quiet, you," the blond professor admonished the now-silent werewolf. He stuffed the .38 back into its neat little holster and joined us. "As usual, you get the business with a rough-and-tumble type started, and leave me to take care of it," he said to Dorian, who rolled his eyes.

"Hey, I had to make sure he was all right," Dorian said.

Tommy made no reply other than grabbing Dorian's ponytail and giving it a solid yank.

Dorian gave Tommy a shove then excitedly informed me, "Everybody's here! The city's probably never been so clear of vampires!"

I had about a million questions going through my head, but they were superseded by worry over my longtime pal. For the moment, all that mattered was that backup was here, and I wasn't worried about the details. I didn't even care how they found us, just as long as it meant the odds were much more even.

"While I totally appreciate the save and I'm happy as fuck to see you guys, I've gotta find Stacey. Have you two seen him?" I demanded.

"Not yet," Tommy answered. "We ran into you purely on accident, since you happened to be the closest to us. We saw you and the others go by when the procession went through, but we couldn't follow without arousing suspicion. And speaking of suspicion," he said, ripping the robe off and tossing it aside. "In all this ruckus, I don't wish to be attacked by an overzealous werewolf who hadn't taken the time to memorize the features of all of the moles that got planted."

"Good idea," Dorian said, tearing his robe to pieces in his hurry to get it off. He gave me his winning grin again and said, "Brandi and the head werewolf have gotten really chummy, and so we've got ourselves a whole mess of 'em to counter whatever the Order's got! We've been busy since you've been gone, eh?"

"I'll say," I replied with a grin, looking around again.

Dorian's features went serious. "Katheryne?"

I shook my head. "Clarisse has got her, and has a werewolf escort. I don't know anything else."

"Shit."

"Yeah."

A small lull had formed in the area where we were standing, as the battle in the cavern had started to break off into pockets of one group fighting another, and we happened to be in one of the clear areas. At least it was clear for the moment. Things were flowing and moving around like a huge horde of amoebas running amok, and an empty area could become full of combatants at any second. Now where was my mouthy compatriot?

Not only that, I didn't want to leave Clarisse for long if I could help it. As I thought of Clarisse and her new werewolf guardians, I looked around and saw all the werewolves fighting revenants, vampires, and one another. By damn, there were a *lot* of them.

"How am I supposed to know which werewolves are friendly and which ones aren't?" I asked. "It's not like they're wearing nametags or anything like that."

"A code signal has been devised, to be given to any vampire clad in street clothes like ourselves, to let us know they're friendly," Tommy answered, "It's probably something you could appreciate, and I know for a fact Stacey would approve—"

Tommy's sentence—as well our brief reunion—came to an end when one of the aforementioned groups of fighters violently engulfed us. One second, it was clear, and the next I was knocked on my face by the flying body of another vampire, then nearly got trampled in the wild scrabble of feet that accompanying the roving battle.

I called out for my friends, and I heard Dorian respond amid a stream of cursing. Tommy's .38 went off, followed by an inhuman scream and a foot that crashed into my head. I had no idea if it was intentional, but it reminded me of how vulnerable I was on my stomach, and my survival instincts took over. I crawled like crazy and got the hell out of there.

Though I felt like a heel leaving them behind, Tommy and Dorian were most definitely *not* pussies—Tommy was coldly vicious and downright dangerous when the situation called for it—and I knew they'd be all right. It was the kind of triage you had to stomach in the middle of a full-on battle. It sucked, but you gotta do what you gotta do.

Glancing around in the pandemonium, I caught sight of the still-burning saucer, and saw a big knot of fighting in its vicinity. That's where I'd last seen Stacey—as well as Donita and Caleb—so I fought my way through the seething, struggling masses in search of my friends.

A black-robed covy charged me, fangs bared and his hands bent clawlike. I took a moment to put him down; one at a time, these little bastards weren't much trouble, as most of them were still very young and weak. As long as I didn't get tangled up in a dog-pile of them, I would be okay.

I neatly snapped the covy's neck then almost absentmindedly ripped his heart out of his chest and crushed it to a pulp. I only gave it part of my attention, as a large grey-and-black werewolf barreled toward me.

I dropped the covy's body and dropped into a fighting crouch, ready for the big bastard. "Come on, fucker," I hissed. "Show me what you've got."

The werewolf brought himself to a stop just outside of my lunging range, and left me flat-footed when he gave me the finger. What the *blazes?* Then what Tommy had said hit me.

"Who the hell taught you *that?*" I asked, fighting back laughter at the sight of the primeval creature flying me the bird.

"Klaarras's sister," he answered, looking amused himself. "She said it was a signal no one fighting for Los Angeles would miss."

"She had that right," I affirmed. "Where is she, anyway?" In this clamoring mayhem and madness, Brandi would be a damned good vampire to have with me, especially since she'd be looking for Stacey with as much fervor as myself.

The werewolf turned and pointed to our right, where I could see Brandi and Lassic completely demolishing a horde of revenants and regular covies. They moved as though the battle had been choreographed a thousand times, neatly and efficiently battering the revenants back with channeled ferocity. When it came to fighting, Brandi and Lassic were two of a kind, sharing warriors' hearts, and though they'd only known each other for a few days, they already moved as one. Pardon my French, but it was fucking impressive.

"Brraandi sent me to get you. I am Grrhaash," he said then put his big, clawed hand out as though he wanted me to shake it.

I looked at him curiously, and he shook his snout slightly. "Donita told me it is the polite thing to do when meeting somebody for the first time."

Now I really did laugh, and grabbed Grrhassh's hand and shook it heartily. "I'm Steele," I said. "Pleased to meet you."

"Agreed. I wish it were under better circumstances," he answered, meeting my eyes with his own deep brown ones.

By this time, Brandi and Lassic had finished off the revenants, and they hurried over to us, Brandi snatching me up in a quick embrace that blew the air completely out of my lungs.

"Damn, am I glad to see you!" she exclaimed. When she set me back down, I saw her eyes were nearly glowing with battlelust, while her hair was already a tangled mess and her clothes were liberally splattered with the blood of everyone who'd gotten in her way thus far.

Lassic was in agreement, giving me a shove with his shoulder that I took as a friendly gesture, at least among werewolves. "As am

I," he said. "Is Klaarras well? Where is she?"

"And where's Stacey?" Brandi asked, and I felt a wave of anxiety rush out from her. "Where's my baby?"

"Clarisse is somewhere over that way, along one of the walls, I think." I pointed toward the back of the cavern. "Katheryne's been hurt, but the two werewolves who'd been guarding us earlier were watching out for them when I took off to find Stacey."

"They were among the spies I sent back with the Crimson Order after the Battle of Los Angeles. When they passed us word of your capture, they were assigned to protect you should the situation grow desperate," Lassic said, a hint of pride crossing his canine face as he spoke of the two werewolves. "Cindrraas and Larrthgraag are good men and good warriors. They will protect Klaarrass and Kaatherryne well." His voice was etched with certainty.

"But what about Stacey?" Brandi sounded almost frantic. "Is he okay? He's here and he's alive, but I don't know anything else. It's hard to pick him up out of all this shit!"

All the combatants running in emotional high gear created a lot of empathic "static" that made it difficult for me to feel much from Clarisse through our bond. Brandi was having the same problem.

"The last time I saw him, he was over by the flaming platform," I said. "I lost him in all the confusion after Akrath attacked Katheryne, and haven't seen him since."

"Is Katheryne all right?" Brandi asked, her eyes flashing red. "If that son of a bitch hurt her, I'll fucking *kill* him!" Brandi looked over the other female vampires in our group like a big sister, not just Clarisse—to harm any of them was to incur the terrifying wrath of big sis.

I felt like ripping Akrath's spine out through his ass myself. "I'm not sure how bad it is, Clarisse was taking care of her at last count."

"That platform is in the direction he said he thought Klaarras was," Lassic said, pointing. "We can push through there and find your mate and Klaarras in the same maneuver. If Tempestia is in the way, all the better." At a curt nod of agreement from Brandi, he turned his head and began barking out orders to nearby werewolves.

"Tempestia..." Brandi growled, smashing her fists together, making me notice she was completely unarmed, save for them. Of course, her fists were better weapons than most bazookas. "I hope she gets in my way, I really, *really* hope she does." Brandi's fangs were out, and she looked totally feral in the flickering light of the cavern, a wild warrior from ages past. Woe to anybody dumb enough to get in her way.

"I hope she does, too," I said, and meant it. If Brandi got her hands on Tempestia, she'd very likely finish what Katheryne had started.

A group of werewolves—with several friendly vampires I recognized from LA—assembled around us. A few more orders from Lassic and Brandi, and the group formed a wedge, with the warrior pair at the head. Not wanting to be left out of the brunt of the carnage, I took a place next to Brandi then laughed when she protectively put me between herself and Lassic.

There was something oddly endearing about the way the powerful and foul-mouthed vampiress mothered us. I was glad to have her for a friend for many more reasons than just the overwhelming strength she brought to bear in troubled times.

Brandi pointed ahead and roared, *"Rip and fucking tear!"* Not very eloquent, but judging from our group's enthusiastic response, it was effective nonetheless.

We moved forward at a jogging speed, mowing down revenants and covies when they attacked. Any enemy werewolves were smart enough to steer clear, so we didn't have any problem with them, at least at the moment. There were only about a dozen of us in the group, but we were tightly packed and fought as a unit, so we fended off every attack thrown in our way.

My heart was beating a mile a minute as we moved inexorably forward, and I scanned for Stacey, Clarisse, Katheryne, Donita, Caleb, and that bitch Tempestia. I wanted to tear Tempestia to shreds—so badly I could taste it—but the desire to see her go toe to toe with Brandi was almost as strong.

Personal vengeance would have been incredibly sweet and satisfying, but I wasn't so stupid I'd let it blind me to what needed to be done. It ultimately didn't matter who took down Tempestia and the Order—Ernest P Worrell could've run her over with a tank for all I cared—so long as they were wiped out and my city and my friends could be left in peace.

Well-considered vengeance, exacted with finesse and intelligence, could be a wonderful, even beautifully poetic thing, but a blind desire for revenge usually created a bloody damned mess. In fact, my botched attempt at killing Frizz in the alley was a good example of that; if I'd simply ripped his head off instead of being an asshole, we would never have been captured.

Lesson learned. It didn't matter how Tempestia died—just so long as she died.

If it came down to it, I wasn't going to do the bold, heroic stand-off against Tempestia. Hell, if I had the chance, I'd skewer her through the heart from behind without saying a word. Cowardly? Yeah, maybe. But ultimately, I didn't give a shit as long as we got out of this whole sorry mess without anybody I cared about getting hurt. At the end of the night, whatever got the job done was what I was gonna do.

My heart nearly leaped out of my chest when—after our group had smashed its way through a particularly thick mob of covies and revenants—I caught sight of Stacey, Donita, and Caleb slugging it out with Tempestia not far from the saucer. Rather, Stacey and Donita were spewing profanity and duking it out with the "Goddess," while Caleb and a couple of werewolves and four LA vampires were doing their best to fend off the covies, revenants, and werewolves trying to help their leader.

Donita was on Tempestia's back—legs around the bitch's waist and arms wrapped around her neck and under one of her arms—biting at her shoulders and neck and zapping her with purple magick energy every chance she got. Meanwhile, Stacey was savagely twisting one of Tempestia's arms and wildly kicking away at her knees, trying to force her down.

Tempestia was staggering around like a drunk and screaming bloody murder at her two assailants, trying to get away, but with no real luck, thanks to the swiftness and determination the duo possessed. Every time Tempestia tried to rise into the air, Stacey yanked on her arm and pulled her back down while Donita give her a hard burst of magick, keeping her in place and off-balance.

While the duo was fighting admirably, it was little more than a holding action—neither of them had the sheer strength and power needed to truly damage Tempestia. They were stinging her plenty—and frustrating the hell out of her—judging from the way she was hollering at them.

We got there just in time too. Tempestia let go with a long, enraged bellow and started wildly swinging around the arm onto which Stacey was holding, so much so it took him off his feet, like in those cartoons where some poor sap gets hold of a fire hose spraying all over the place. Stacey was whipping in all directions as he stubbornly held on. If it weren't for the situation, I would have been in hysterics due to how ridiculous it was.

Tempestia started spinning as she tried to remove Stacey, and instead of trying to grasp at Donita with her free arm, she threw punches in Donita's general direction, catching the gypsy with several hard blows that forced her to lighten her hold on the ideological tyrant. Then Tempestia slammed Stacey against the stone floor of the cavern with a sickeningly loud *thump* and blood sprayed from his mouth, making my heart freeze. Her arm free, Tempestia started hammering away on Donita with both hands, yelling in triumph and rage. But Donita didn't have to take too many hits.

As soon as Stacey's feet left the floor, Brandi charged; the moment Tempestia slammed him down, Brandi went *berserk*.

It'd be impossible to stress how deeply the attachment between Stacey and Brandi went. The love between the two of them was boundless, and they were ferociously protective of one another, Brandi especially so. I'd seen her batter, maim, and dismember those who'd tried to hurt Stacey. Her nearly childlike adoration of him transmuted into a complete and total killing rage aimed at his tormentors when he got himself in trouble. When she got into that state, there was nothing that could stop her...*nothing*.

When Stacey hit the ground, Brandi roared, her burning anger at Tempestia a nuclear wildfire that sent her shooting forward like a cruise missile fired straight from Hell.

I was hot on her heels, heading for my fallen friend. It was easy enough getting through the crowd, as Brandi simply plowed through everything between her and Tempestia. She flung revenants and werewolves aside, sending them flying through the air with wild swings from her mighty arms, and several covies were simply pulped from piledriver punches. I almost laughed when I saw how quickly Donita scrambled off Tempestia's back when she saw Brandi coming. Donita knew the face of doom when she saw it.

Tempestia stood defiantly for a few seconds, and even started to yell something at Brandi, but when the Valkyrie smashed into her like a bullet train, the only thing coming out of her mouth were shrieks of pain and surprise. The impact sent them both tumbling end over end across the cavern floor, and they ran over several covies before they came to what amounted to a stop. Brandi grabbed Tempestia by the hair and plowed her jaw with a jackhammer knee, and Tempestia *screamed*.

I saw that much before I reached Stacey, who was already sitting up and shaking his head like a cartoon character getting rid of all the cobwebs. Despite the blood on his mouth, he seemed perfectly fine, especially when he grinned as he watched Brandi tearing into Tempestia.

"Damn, she's something, ain't she?" he asked me, sounding dreamy as I dragged him to his feet. "The viciousness of a Tasmanian Devil on meth, the unstoppable strength of a Mack truck on nitro, and the ass of a goddess. A real goddess, mind you, not the loopy pretender type."

When he looked back at me I saw his eyes were slightly unfocused, and I figured he'd gotten his brain rattled loose—in other words, no damage done. He glanced around and saw we were in the center of a momentary peaceful zone, as the squad I'd been moving with was handily keeping the Order's troops at bay.

Donita came running up, somewhat torn and battered but otherwise okay. After giving me a quick hug, she grabbed the front of my jacket and shook me vigorously. "Where's Katheryne?" she demanded, her eyes wide. "Is she okay?"

"I'm guessing so," I replied. "I left her with Clarisse and two of Lassic's boys while I went looking for our resident wild-hearted son here," I said, giving Stacey a punch on his arm that he quickly returned. "And yourself and Caleb."

"Who's Caleb?"

"That would be me," said Caleb from behind us, and we turned to see the Crimson Order's former historian jogging toward us, a big werewolf in tow.

As soon as Caleb had joined our group, the werewolf nodded curtly at him and said, "You would do best to remain with them. A great historian you are, but a warrior you are not." With that, the werewolf bounded away and sprang back into the battle raging around us.

Caleb shrugged. "Nobody's perfect." He was looking a bit worse for the wear, as though he'd gotten dragged behind a car for a block or so, but his spirits were in good-enough shape. He smiled at Donita and gave her a little respectful bow of his head. "Caleb, ex-historian of the organization known as the Crimson Order and current heretic sympathizer, at your service."

The gypsy nodded. "Donita, worried sick about her kitty-Katheryne, at your service," she said then grabbed my hand. "Take me to her, I have to see her! I spent too much time fooling around with Queen Bitch when I should've gone to her right away, so let's go!"

"It wasn't wasted time, though. We kept her in place until the big red cavalry arrived," Stacey said, his eyes on Brandi again. The Valkyrie was incredible.

Every time she got hold of Tempestia, the so-called "Goddess" got the stuffing knocked out of her. Every time the bitch tried to escape, Brandi pounced on her and let her have it even harder. It was a testament to just how strong Tempestia was that she wasn't dead yet: anybody else and Brandi would already have been scraping them off the ground. But Tempestia was holding in there, and while she was getting a mudhole stomped in her, she was still surviving.

Caleb was seriously impressed. "Who is *that?*"

"That's Brandi," Stacey replied proudly. "She requires no introduction."

"Shut up and let's go, dammit!" Donita bellowed, stomping her foot and nearly yanking my arm out of the socket. "I love Brandi to death, but she's not hurt and she can take care of herself right now. Shit, there's *never* a time when she can't take care of herself, so let's fucking go! Which way?" Her exotic features were tight with worry.

I pointed straight ahead of us, in the direction of where I'd last seen Clarisse, Katheryne, and the werewolves. Without another word, Donita started dragging me across the cavern floor. Caleb followed right along, while Stacey hung back a moment, watching Brandi.

I looked behind me, wondering if he was still loopy enough from the hit Tempestia had given him that he'd need me to yell at him to get him going. But when I caught sight of him, he was blowing a kiss in Brandi's direction. Brandi—who had both hands around the other woman's neck—actually stopped screaming at Tempestia long enough to look at Stacey and make a single kissing motion, her face melting into an expression of gentle sweetness for a few seconds. Then her eyes blazed red again and she blasted Tempestia with a headbutt that slammed the other woman to the ground like a cannon blast.

"She'll be fine," Stacey said as he scurried over. "There's nothing she can't handle, and every time anybody tries to interfere in the brawl between them, Lassic or one of his guys gets in there and puts a stop to it before they even reach my baby or Tempestia. These friendly werewolves have reminded me why I'm such a dog lover."

"They're all a bunch of big sweethearts," Donita said as we hurried through the swirling mass of fighting, sidestepping as many combatants as we could.

As I searched around for the side tunnel the werewolf had told me about, Donita continued, "Lassic's werewolves planted a number of spies in the Crimson Order after the Battle of LA, so they could get the lay of the land and look for the right time to finish off the Order themselves. They didn't want to get us involved any further, and wanted to avenge their elders on their own. Essentially, the Order fucked with their family, so the werewolves looked at it as being their responsibility. But as soon as the spies found out you guys had been captured, Lassic himself came to LA looking for Brandi. The Order had once again involved our family, and he couldn't let that stand. He told her what was going on, and flat-out told her that the werewolves were going to help us get you all back and bring the Order down, and they weren't going to take no for an answer."

"That doesn't surprise me in the least. Werewolves are among the most honorable people you'll ever meet," Caleb said. "I despised how Tempestia was using them to her own ends."

"That's because you're a weak-willed fool, unable to recognize useful cannon fodder when you see it."

Caleb—who'd been bringing up the rear—let out a squawk, and we all whipped around. *Son of a bitch.*

"Wilkesdon," I growled, my fangs extending. Donita made a soft sound of pain when I squeezed her hand too hard in my sudden flare of rage.

"The one and only," sneered the revenant master. He had three revenants with him, and one of them was holding onto Caleb tightly, its long, powerful arms wrapped right around the vampire historian, Caleb's back pressed against its chest. There were also three covies—two women and a man—all of whom looked like they'd seen better days, though Wilkesdon himself looked pretty happy with things at the moment.

"Now, I'll only tell you once: surrender yourselves and call that maniac off the Goddess, or we'll kill your new friend here. Wouldn't want to have that hanging on your conscience, would you?" Then everybody started to talk at once.

"Maniac? *Maniac?*" Stacey demanded. "*I'm* the maniac in the relationship, and she's the sensible one, *stupid!*"

"You're a fool if you think they'll let a lone expatriate like myself stand in the way of their survival, you idiot!" Caleb snapped, uselessly struggling against the revenant.

"So how'd it feel to see Katheryne beat the fucking dogshit out of your Goddess until Akrath stuck his nose into things, you little twerp?" I demanded, the vision of my thumbs going into Wilkesdon's eyes running through my head.

All three of us had just about finished our sentences when Donita went off.

"*Shut the fuck up!*" she screamed, stomping her foot and crushing my hand in hers. "All of you! We don't have time for this!" Her eyes were starting to glow purple, and my hand tingled as she started winding herself up to unload on somebody.

"You shut your mouth, bitch, or I'll have my big friend here put an end to your buddy," Wilkesdon snapped. Caleb groaned in the revenant's grasp as the monster squeezed him tighter. "I'm the one in charge here, I'm the representative of the Crimson Order, and I'm the one with the power, so I suggest you all fall into line before you all wind up dead!"

"Fuck you, asshole!" Donita roared.

"I said shut up!"

"*And I said fuck you, asshole!*"

As Wilkesdon was spitting orders and Donita was screaming at him, a shadow was slithering in from behind. Backlit by the flaming saucer's light, the front of it was lost in inky blackness. None of the revenants or covies noticed it as it stealthily moved closer and closer, moving more swiftly the nearer it got. My rage was momentarily defused as a chill went through me at the sight of this big shadow.

It came up close behind Wilkesdon, seeming to disappear for a few seconds. Just when I was wondering if I'd been seeing things, the shadow drew up behind Wilkesdon, dark and huge. Two arms, tipped with clawlike hands, crisscrossed Wilkesdon' chest, their nails digging in and holding him in place as a hooded head locked down on his neck.

Wilkesdon's scream was truly horrible, the sound of painful Death itself, lacking mercy or compassion of any sort. I watched, fascinated, as Wilkesdon's skin was pulled tight against his face, rapidly paling to near-transparency. His eyes bulged and his mouth was frozen open in a rictus of soul-sucking horror. His hands struggled with the claws across his chest, shriveling and withering before our very eyes, as though he were aging decades in seconds.

The revenants all howled in distress, not knowing what to do, and they writhed in sympathetic pain with their master as the shadow drained the very life essence from his body. Caleb pulled free of his oblivious revenant captor and hurried over to us to watch the spectacle, which had us all wide-eyed.

Every bit of Wilkesdon's visible flesh tightened and stretched against his bones, and his face was that of an ancient mummy. His eyes had rolled completely back into his head and while his mouth was still open, he wasn't making a sound. As the revenants helplessly flailed around, the other covies ran for their lives... probably not a bad idea.

What was more was that as Wilkesdon shriveled, the gaunt claws on his chest filled out and gained substance. They stopped resembling claws and began looking like hands—big, strong hands. After what seemed like ages, those hands let go of Wilkesdon and he fell to the ground, a bag of dry leaves. Parts of him crumbled, as though he were a sculpture made of sand.

The flesh peeled free of his gleaming bones like scales, and he was little more than a skeleton covered with dark clothing and bits of dried-out skin. He'd been drained so totally that even the water in his cells had been leached away. I'd been around long enough that I'd seen things like this a few times before, and it always gave me a chill. Even when you've been knocking around the world for two millennia, some things are *still* freaky as hell.

Their leader done and dusted, the revenants all let a final shriek and collapsed, as dead as the proverbial doornail. They'd been hit with a mental feedback loop of flaming agony—Wilkesdon's pain was so terrible it must have jumped over to the revenants, burning their brains even as every useable particle of their master's body was absorbed into the shadow and leaving nothing behind but a dry husk. The bond between the master and revenants was a double-edged sword in certain circumstances, it seemed.

Now the menacing shadow stood before us, holding its hands out, turning and flexing them, as though seeing them for the first time. It was dressed in the black hooded attire of the Crimson Order, but it had just killed a revenant master and three revenants, saving Caleb in the process—we didn't know what to think.

Donita held up her own hands, which crackled purple, and she growled in warning. "Whatever you are, you're *not* stopping me from seeing Katheryne."

At the gypsy's words, the figure—whose face we still couldn't see—clearly aimed its attention at us, and I could feel its gaze on us, taking our measure. It was an eerie, unsettling feeling, and it ended just as suddenly as it began. It reached up with restored hands and pulled back its hood.

Though the face was gaunt and the hair a tangled mess, it was totally Wade.

I don't know who made the first whoop of joy, but we were all shouting with delight as we rushed over to him, clapping him on the shoulder, shaking his hand, and Donita even hugged him. Normally he wasn't fond of physical contact, but in this case, he clearly didn't mind.

"Good to have you back, big guy," I said, giving him a hug as well, which he returned.

Though he never said much and was often just a strong, silent presence, he was a member of our family, a good vampire, and a good friend, and he'd been missed. I hadn't realized just how much we'd missed him until we had him back.

"Good to be back," he said, his voice raspy and tight, but considering what he'd been through during the past week, that was no surprise. "Damned good. That bastard was just what I needed."

Knowing the ins and outs of torpor myself, he wouldn't be back up to full strength until he'd had more time and plenty more blood, but he was on the right track. Compared to hanging on a cross only a few minutes ago, he'd made a world of improvement.

"Not to cut this short," he said softly. "But where's Katheryne? I need to see her...please." There was an urgency to his voice, something I'd rarely heard before.

"That's where we were going when we got interrupted," Donita said. "Looks like all the nipping and screeching into your ear did you some good, after all."

Wade smiled faintly at the gypsy. "Very much, thank you. I started coming around just in time to hear Katheryne step up for all of us. She was magnificent."

Donita nodded and sniffed a little, her emotions getting the better of her, and making her eyes glisten. "She's so brave and so loving," she whispered. "She thinks she's the least of us, but no matter what she does, she never sees how horribly wrong she is."

"Therein lies her greatness; therein lies her strength," Wade said, so softly I think only Donita and I could hear him. "Take me to her."

It didn't take us long to find the side passageway where Clarisse and Katheryne were. Thankfully, the brindled werewolf—Cindrraas by name—was crouched in the shadows behind a rock outcropping by the opening of the passage, standing guard.

He popped into view when we approached then shrank back slightly when he saw Wade. "The Dark One walks," he growled, looking cautiously at the big vampire dressed in robes he'd appropriated from the first covy he'd encountered after he'd broken free. Cindrraas studied us carefully, uncertain. Wade tended to have that effect.

The big vampire could be spooky—even downright imposing— for those who didn't know him. I suspect it wasn't helping matters for Cindrraas that Wade was dressed like a covy.

"It's okay," I said to the wary lycanthrope. "He's back with us again. He just killed Wilkesdon *and* his revenants, if that tells you anything."

The werewolf made a grunting noise that sounded a whole lot like a snort of disgust. "I despised Wilkesdon... He richly deserved death."

When we reached the werewolf, he looked at Wade. "If you are the bringer of death for Wilkesdon, I salute you." He gave a slight raise of his chin, which Clarisse had told me was their equivalent of a polite bow.

Wade nodded, saying nothing, though I knew the werewolf's gesture of respect was appreciated. The big vampire said a hell of a lot without speaking, changing his facial expression, or doing anything with his body language—one just had to know him. He was a dark, enigmatic sort, but dammit, he was *our* dark, enigmatic sort.

"We need to see Katheryne and Clarisse now," Donita said without preamble.

Cindrraas motioned toward the passageway. "They are down the tunnel with that strange bloodfeaster. Larrthgraag is guarding the other end, so that no one may sneak up on them... Few have tried to enter the tunnel, but those who have were dealt with accordingly."

It was then I noticed the numerous blood spatters on the werewolf's fur, though beyond a few scratches and scrapes, he himself was unhurt. He must have been busy.

"We thank you, Cindrraas. You and Larrthgraag are a tribute to your tribe," Donita said, apparently having been somewhat schooled in werewolf-isms. She even gave the brindled fellow a shove with her shoulder, similar to what Lassic had done to me, and that appeared to please Cindrraas.

"You are too kind," he said, giving her a raise of his chin.

"As much as I wanna go in and see Blondie," Stacey said, "I gotta get back into the action. I don't wanna miss Brandi tearing that mad bitch to pieces."

I was torn. Badly.

I wanted to go be with Katheryne—and Clarisse—but at the same time, I didn't want to leave Brandi to deal with Tempestia alone. Granted, Brandi by herself was worth more than a small army, especially when she had the likes of Lassic to back her up. But with Katheryne and Wade both out of action, I was the other heavy-hitter, and if shit went south, I needed to be there.

But Katheryne...I remembered the look in her eyes on the rooftop—had that been just last night? And then the look in them when she'd squared off against Tempestia. Then Akrath had tried to claw them out, the motherfucker, and robbed her of her victory. Had Katheryne found her redemption anyway? Had she given enough of herself that she'd come back to us?

Wade was here, he was alive, and he was free...all because of Katheryne? That was enough, right? That had to be enough. But she'd just crumpled when Akrath had attacked her, like she'd totally given up. She wouldn't do that, not when she'd clearly been the victor.

Would she?

Nobody was harsher on Katheryne than Katheryne herself. I *had* to know. It was selfish, maybe even irresponsible, but after what Katheryne had gone through, I couldn't just run back into battle now. I was getting sentimental in my old age.

And I loved the hell out of that kid. If there was any hope for the world, it was because of people like Katheryne. I'd only take a few minutes, just to know, just to help, if needed.

"If Brandi tears off one of her arms, save it for me, huh?" I gave Stacey a friendly shove, which he returned with a smack on the side of my head.

"I get first dibs on body parts, dude," he said then took off.

I turned to Caleb. "If anything, *anything* looks like it's getting out of hand, you come and get me, yeah? Doesn't matter what it is."

"Understood," he replied, taking a spot close to Cindrraas.

With one last glance back at the battle, I followed Donita and Wade into the passageway, hoping nothing would happen in these scant few minutes I was stealing.

The passage was wide enough for three people to walk abreast, and as soon as we entered, I could see Clarisse and Katheryne on the floor a short distance in. Clarisse was holding the silent witch like a mother holding a child, rocking her gently and whispering to her, while Katheryne clung to Clarisse tightly, her arms around my lover's neck. Dactius was sitting next to Clarisse, wringing his hands fearfully, and hope sprang into his face when he saw us arrive. He nudged Clarisse excitedly and she quickly motioned us over.

It was much quieter in the tunnel, though the sounds of battle echoed within, so it wasn't so much an escape from the chaos as a temporary reprieve. When we reached the pair, Katheryne hadn't stirred. Clarisse had torn strips from Dactius's robe and had wrapped them around the witch's head, and I shivered at what might be underneath, especially after seeing how much blood was down the front of Katheryne's tanktop.

How much damage had the bastard done? Eyes could be healed in time, but if he'd broken through her skull and gone deeper... No matter how tough a vampire was, if you hit us in the brain just right, that was it.

Donita dropped to her knees next to Katheryne, making soft sounds of concern. Clarisse gently handed the witch to Donita, carefully pulling her hands loose and putting them around the gypsy's neck instead. Donita leaned against the opposite wall now, rocking slowly, crimson tears running down her face as she smoothed Katheryne's hair with shaking hands.

"Oh baby, what did he do to you?" she rasped, her voice hitching. Katheryne made no reply, and I didn't think she'd even heard the gypsy.

"Can you help her?" Dactius asked Donita worriedly, sitting next to her so he could keep an eye on Katheryne. "You *must* help her, she saved me, and she saved us all!"

"I'm going to do everything I can, and that will be enough... It's *got* to be enough," the gypsy murmured.

Clarisse stood and immediately put her arms around me, hugging me tightly. I returned the gesture, lifted her up off the ground for several seconds, and wished this was all over and that we were safely underground in the Catacombs or aboveground in a club somewhere, life proceeding as normally as it did for a vampire in Los Angeles.

"Glad you made it back to me in one piece," she whispered in my ear. I squeezed her even tighter, wordlessly telling her the same thing. What a bloody, sorry mess this all was.

"How is she?" asked Wade softly.

Clarisse started a little then lifted her head from my shoulder to look toward the source of the unexpected voice.

"Long time no see," she said to him. "Glad you could make it here in one piece too. You've been missed."

But as happy as she was to see our lost comrade again, she got right to his question. "She hasn't said anything since I brought her here—it's like she shorted out when Akrath attacked her. I cleaned her up as best I could and gave her some of my blood. She drank, slowly, but she took everything I could give her. Dactius was willing to let her drain him dry if that was what it took, but I made him pull away after a while. She got plenty of blood, at least."

That Katheryne had drunk their blood in and of itself didn't say much about her condition. A vampire, even one who's beyond all help will almost always drink blood when it's put before them, their instincts taking over. But drinking Clarisse's strong and vital blood was good—it'd help the healing process.

"I don't know about her eyes, though. They were…pretty bad. I don't know how deep it is, I didn't want to go digging around in here, and—" Clarisse shook her head. "If I had my hands on Akrath right now, I'd eat his fucking heart right in front of his dying eyes, the bitch-bastard motherfucker." It was rare for Clarisse to swear so violently, and it told us just how worried she was over poor Katheryne.

"Thank you," Wade said. He stepped past us and went over to Katheryne and Donita. Dactius protectively leaned closer to Katheryne—probably remembering the last time he'd been close to Wade—but after a few moments, he leaned back again, realizing that the big, dark figure meant no harm.

The gypsy had removed the makeshift bandages and had her hands over the witch's eyes, a soft purple glow emanating from underneath them. Donita's eyes were shut and her head was tilted back a little, as though she were in a trance. She was focusing everything she had into healing her best friend and lover as quickly as she could, trying to ease the pain of injury and restoration as much as possible. If Donita could, she would have given her life to spare Katheryne even a pinch of pain. When Katheryne hurt, Donita hurt.

The big vampire knelt and slowly brushed his still-bony hand against Katheryne's cheek. Donita's eyes opened and she gave Wade a slight nod as he held his hand to the witch's face, and I saw her whisper, "Please." Then her eyes slid shut again and she turned her face upward once more, the glow beneath her hands intensifying.

"Katheryne," Wade whispered. He took hold of one of her arms, putting her hand into his own and squeezing it. "Katheryne…it's me."

The blond witch stirred then slowly turned her head in the direction of Wade's voice, Donita moving her hands so they stayed over Katheryne's eyes.

"Wade?" Katheryne's voice broke on the single syllable.

"Yes." He put his free hand to her cheek again.

"You're alive," she murmured, shifting around further in Donita's arms so she could reach out for him. She blindly groped at the air with her other hand for a few seconds, and when she found his face, she sobbed once. "It's really you."

"Yes," he said. "Thanks to you. I owe you my very existence. I wouldn't be here now if it weren't for you."

"I thought I'd killed you," whispered Katheryne, and she sobbed again.

"No. You hurt that thing so much it sidestepped—teleported— back into the tunnel to try to save itself, and because I had hold of it, I was taken too. Though it hurt me a lot, you'd dealt it a mortal blow, and I was able to finish it off. You saved my life, Katheryne. I was lost in the tunnels for a time, and eventually went into torpor. The next thing I knew, there was a big rat nipping at my ear, and I could hear your voice, challenging Tempestia not only for myself, but for everybody. You were *incredible*. I'll never be able to tell you how much that means to me, no matter how long I live," Wade said, and I thought I heard his voice crack, ever so slightly. "I can't tell you how much *you* mean to me, my avenging angel."

The witch sobbed again, and took her hand from Wade's then reached out with the both of them, circling them around his neck. Donita lifted her hands from Katheryne's face and leaned back against the wall, trembling from exhaustion, enabling Katheryne to fully lean forward to embrace Wade.

I could see her face as it rested on Wade's shoulder as he wrapped his strong arms around her, and tears freely streamed down from eyes that were whole again, if still reddened and painful. She started to say something, but her voice caught and was lost in sobs. Wade made soft shushing sounds as he smoothed her hair.

"It's okay," he said. "You did beautifully, just like you always do."

"He's right," Donita said, "You don't know how right he is, baby, just listen to him." Then Donita totally broke down too, and her sobs were added to Katheryne's.

Wade held one of his arms open, and Donita needed no other invitation. She moved over and put her arms around Katheryne, and Wade moved his arm back in place, holding all three of them together.

A quiet sob escaped from Clarisse while we held onto each other, and I'll be damned if I didn't have tears running down my face as well. I fervently hoped that maybe some of Katheryne's inner demons had been exorcised on this day, and that perhaps she'd be able to rest a little easier now.

IV

"How goes it?" I asked Caleb when Clarisse and I reemerged into the cavern.

"As well as can be expected, I wager," he answered.

I looked around the cavern at the fighting. Things were starting to taper off slightly, at least compared to earlier. The bodies were piling up as the number of combatants dropped, and as the numbers of fighters went down, the sounds of the battle were ebbing.

Vampires and werewolves from both sides were up against the walls of the cavern or partially concealed in the shadows, trying to take breathers, battered and bloody. The conflict was taking its toll on everybody. Even those who were still up and fighting like mad were showing signs of injury, and I was hard pressed to find anybody—vampire, werewolf, or revenant—who wasn't marked by this fight. What a waste this all was, I reflected with a shake of my head.

The primary instigators of this conflict, the vampires, were the ones with the gift of immortality, the ones who could live through the ages and could only die by misadventure, the ones that should have seen the stupidity of this whole mess. Yet here we were, squabbling among ourselves like common mortals, killing one another wholesale.

Granted, the Crimson Order hadn't given us much of a choice, but I would have thought that out of all of us here, all of the great minds, that one of us would have been able to figure out another solution to this. But that wasn't to be. A lot of us liked to think we were better than the mortals, while the Order thought us to be worse than the mortals, but when it came right down to it, we were no different.

People were people, whether their lifetime was finite or endless, and people were prone to stupidity and savagery. That was simply the nature of things. While some of us were capable of minimizing our stupidity and harnessing our savagery to more constructive means, the vast lot of us couldn't. It was up to those of us who could admit to and deal with what we were to pick up the pieces and figure out what to do with them. Was the true test of our mettle here in this battle, or was it going to be in the days that followed?

This conflict in itself was difficult, more trying on the spirit and soul than nearly anything I'd ever encountered before in my long nights, there was no doubt in that, but what would things in Los Angeles be like once this unholy war was said and done? Would we continue with the peaceful, though rambunctious, existence we'd enjoyed before, or would xenophobia and rage become the new language of the streets?

I sighed, feeling tired, but I wasn't so tired I wouldn't stand up for what I believed in. When the night came that I wouldn't stand up for what I believed in, it was time for me to die. But that night was a long time in coming—if ever—and I wouldn't let my weariness with this whole mess eat away at me to the point where I'd become a liability. I'd stolen my time to see Katheryne, and now it was time to fight.

After bidding a quick goodbye to Caleb and Cindrraas, Clarisse and I ran across the cavern, hand in hand, heading toward the largest source of mayhem—where Brandi was going toe to toe with Tempestia.

It wasn't hard to find, as the entire battle was starting to focus around them like the winds surrounding the eye of a hurricane. In the wake of that brutal hurricane were piles of corporeal wreckage, vampire and werewolf alike, and as we got closer to the epicenter of it all, Clarisse and I had to step around and over countless corpses in a macabre obstacle course.

I recognized familiar faces among them, and each time I saw one I felt a chill, and Clarisse and I held onto each other's hands even tighter. This was far from the first time I'd seen my friends hurt, terrorized, and killed, and if I survived this, it wouldn't be the last. It never got easier. Immortality had its ugly side, and it was brutal as hell.

The fighting had moved closer to where the LA vampires had

blown a hole in the side of the cavern. As we got nearer, I could see out the hole, which was big enough to drive a few semis through, and I almost stopped for a moment as I caught sight of the beautiful night sky hanging star-studded and bright over acre after acre of slumbering trees.

It made what was going on inside the cavern seem less real. What was outside of this battle was reality—not this terrible bloodbath—and I longed to leap out into the cool night to fly across the forest, soaring underneath the stars and moon, Clarisse with me. I wanted that so much it hurt, and I longed for this to be over, just so I could savor something as simple and primal as enjoying the night.

It didn't seem like all that much to ask for, did it?

But in order to enjoy the beautiful California night, I had to maim, mangle, and spill buckets of blood until this came to an end. Life was so fucked sometimes.

I did my best to forget about my desire to spring into the night and take care of the matter at hand first. And the matter at hand began to get *out* of hand just before we reached the fringes of the worst of the fighting.

From what we learned later on, the fighting between Brandi and Tempestia had been largely hit and run. In other words, Brandi hitting the living daylights out of Tempestia whenever she got hold of her, and Tempestia running from the Valkyrie at every chance she could, trying to get her followers to take as much heat for her as possible.

Lassic said Tempestia tried to fight Brandi at first, but after she'd gotten her arm nearly ripped out of its socket, she'd apparently decided getting away from the rampaging redhead was a much wiser tactic. Brandi wasn't having it. Tempestia had caused Stacey pain, and even if it clearly hadn't been fatal, that was more than enough reason for Brandi to destroy her.

Lassic and his werewolves, along with many of the LA vampires, had done what they could to keep the ranks of the Order away from Brandi and Tempestia, but they could only hold off so many at once. Thus Brandi also had to deal with revenants, werewolves, and regulation covies, not to mention Tempestia getting in any sort of dirty attack that she could. Despite all of this, Brandi was still going.

When I caught sight of her, her blazing emerald eyes told the story better than anything else: she was prepared to go for years against Tempestia if she had to. It wasn't just because she was avenging Stacey and fighting to save her city and her friends…she was also *enjoying* herself.

I looked for Stacey, and just when I spotted him pummeling a covy, Brandi and Tempestia both went flying up into the air as though launched from a catapult. The "Goddess" was trying to escape via flight, while the Valkyrie was holding on and clawing away with everything she had. Nothing coherent was coming out of either combatant—Tempestia was screaming in distress and anger, while Brandi was roaring from adrenaline-fueled fury. They both looked as if they'd been run through the wringer something fierce.

Everybody in the vicinity turned to follow the two women, and when they hurtled in our direction, the crowd moved like a wave. When this happened, Clarisse and I went from the fringes to being right in the middle of the battle. Pandemonium ensued.

We scrapped with whoever wanted to cause us trouble in those frantic few moments, and when I felt the hand clamp down on my shoulder, I nearly took its owner's head off, I was so hyped. Fortunately, it was a grinning Stacey.

He grabbed my hand and bellowed, "Come on!" When he gave a tug, I took Clarisse's hand, pulled her close, and held on as my friend dragged us through the crowd. Surprisingly, we got through with hardly any further incident, save for a few swipes at us, and when we got some breathing room, we were over by the flaming saucer once more.

"Did you see her?" Stacey exclaimed. "Every time my baby gets hold of that bitch, she takes her straight to school! We've got this motherfucker in the bag! Tempestia knows it too—she won't stand and fight at all!"

He turned and watched as Brandi pounded away on Tempestia while the would-be Goddess weaved and swerved through the air like a drunk. The racket the two were making was tremendous. The fighting had slowed down as everybody gawked at the spectacle.

I held my breath as the battling women crazily swooped through the air, Tempestia screeching angrily and Brandi snarling back, refusing to let up for even a second. The only thing stopping Brandi from ripping Tempestia to pieces was that she couldn't get a good grip on the bitch. If they'd been on good old terra firma, there'd be no chance in hell of Tempestia getting out in anything less than a dozen pieces.

Tempestia dived, trying to get Brandi to let go. Instead of loosening her grip, Brandi got hold of her even tighter and jerked Tempestia off course, aiming them right for one of the walls, not far from the tunnel where Katheryne, Donita, and Wade were at.

Tempestia screamed, and even above that and the racket of the ongoing struggle, I could hear Brandi laughing.

As the two madly careened toward the wall, the three of us took off in that direction. From where we'd been by the saucer, it wasn't that far, so we got a head start on everybody else. I desperately hoped no covies figured out there was anybody in the tunnel when they got near it: Katheryne, Donita, and Wade had been through far more than enough during these past several days. If anybody deserved a rest from this madness, it was they.

Tempestia tried to turn away from the wall, but Brandi forcibly kept her on course. Tempestia barely managed to steer away enough that the both of them hit the rock wall on their sides, instead of Tempestia plowing into it headfirst, which I assumed was Brandi's original plan.

Stacey yipped when the two women smashed into the wall far above us, and a hush fell over the cavern as the two plummeted then slammed into the unyielding ground with a cringe-inducing *thud*.

We ran right past the tunnel, where both Caleb and Cindrraas were watching the battle in mingled horror and exhilaration. Donita had joined them, looking drained and weak, but determined as ever. When she saw us coming, she waved then hooked up with us when we barreled past. I didn't have the time to ask her how Wade and Katheryne were doing, but if she'd come out to see the festivities, I assumed everything was relatively okay, and didn't push the issue. Not to sound cold—especially since it involved Katheryne and Wade—but at the moment I was far more concerned about Brandi.

I shouldn't have been. Just scant seconds after impact, Brandi was getting to her feet again, albeit slowly. She looked as though she'd been through a four-year war in a matter of minutes: her hair was matted with blood, and there were slashes, cuts, and scrapes nearly everywhere skin was visible. Her clothes were not only torn, but burnt in places, and her right leg was giving her a hard time when she tried to stand on it, understandable considering the massive, bloody rip visible on her thigh.

But Brandi wouldn't stop. She'd keep going until she was dead, and I hoped with all of my soul it wouldn't come to that.

The Valkyrie stood shakily for a second then turned her slitted eyes down toward Tempestia, who was just starting to get up onto her hands and knees.

"Fucking...*bitch,*" Brandi snarled, her breath coming out in pants. She viciously brought her foot down between Tempestia's shoulder blades, smashing the faux Goddess to the ground on her face. The only sound that came from Tempestia's nearly shattered form was a low moan, and a puddle of blood started to form beneath her head.

We stopped a short distance away from Brandi, not wanting to do anything that would draw her attention away from her enemy. The battling crowd came to a stop not far from the two combatants, taking in the spectacle of Brandi standing over Tempestia. While almost everybody was motionless and staring, several covies—mostly revenant masters from the looks of them—started yelling challenges and insults at Brandi, who slowly looked up from Tempestia to them.

"If you think you can do it...*do it,*" she growled softly. Then she doubled over and hacked up a spray of blood, like a mortal vomiting, and there was a lot of it. Stacey's eyes grew huge. Brandi had some serious internal damage, which was never good, regardless of whether one was immortal.

"Brandi," he called out, sounding like he was being torn apart.

Brandi turned to look at him, and once again her eyes went soft. "Baby..."

She gave her head a quick shake. "I'll live," she said, then turned her attention back to the covies. She held out her hands in a challenge, and her voice gained strength with each second, going from a harsh rasp to one of power.

"Bring it on," she growled. "I just beat the fuck out of your 'Goddess,' like Katheryne did before me. If you think you can stand up to me after I've damn near killed your precious deity, go right ahead. Come on, avenge your Goddess!"

Brandi stomped on Tempestia's back again, driving her against the ground with merciless force. Then she kicked her in the side, causing Tempestia to roll over on her back, blood spraying from her mouth. The big vampiress put her foot to Tempestia's throat.

Feebly, Tempestia reached up and grabbed Brandi's ankle, but couldn't do a thing to remove the Valkyrie's boot from her neck. Brandi spat blood into Tempestia's face then looked back at the crowd.

"Is this your Goddess, helpless beneath my foot? *Is it?* If she brought all of us into creation, if she was the one who damned all of us to be what we are, then why is her very existence beneath my bootheel?"

"She's testing our faith," called out a female covy near the front of the ranks, though her voice lacked the strength and fervor I would expect from a fanatic.

Brandi gave her the finger. "Fuck you! That's what morons like you always say! You can't accept what you're seeing with your own eyes, so you make up lies to explain what you think is an impossibility! I've got news for you, you pack of idiots, this is *reality*, this is *real life*, and this piece of *shit* under my foot is no more special than any of us. And you follow her! Why? Because she's bigger and stronger than you? Because she pretends she's the Goddess from your little storybook and has enough tricks up her sleeve to get you to obey her? Well fucking guess what? If that's all it takes, then I decree *myself* to be the Goddess because I've beaten this one to pieces, and not only that, I guess that makes Katheryne the Goddess too!"

She let this sink in for a few beats then shrieked, "*Don't you realize how fucking stupid you all are?*" She took her foot from Tempestia's neck, lifted her off the ground with one bloody hand, and held her up above her head.

"I give you your Goddess!" she screamed then flung Tempestia toward the covies.

The self-proclaimed Goddess landed facedown halfway between Brandi and her followers with a wet splat. She weakly scrabbled around trying to get up, but only made it as far as her hands and knees. Her whole body was shaking as she moved, and it was obvious she was close to her last legs. Nobody moved to help her.

Several covies sat and put their heads in their hands, while some werewolves took off running across the cavern, heading for the safety of the tunnels or the freedom beyond the hole in the cavern wall. My heart started to beat faster as I watched the Order begin unraveling in front of me. Now all Brandi had to do was smash the ringleader, and it wouldn't be long until we could all go home.

Brandi strode forward, until she was standing right in front of the trembling, bleeding, hurting Tempestia, who couldn't even lift her head to look up at the Valkyrie.

"Get up," Brandi snarled. "Get up and show me you're truly the Goddess. Get the fuck up!"

I was wondering if Tempestia was even capable of getting up at all, and I realized that's exactly what Brandi was going for. Not only was she going to kill Tempestia, but she going to break the faith of as many covies as she could by showing them that Tempestia was a fraud.

"*Get up!*" Brandi roared.

Tempestia slowly shook her head.

"*Get up now!*" screamed the Valkyrie.

Tempestia shook her head, her long hair sweeping the ground.

Brandi spat at her once more then took a step forward, "Into eternity with you, then!"

She reached down and grabbed Tempestia by the hair, and a cheer rose among the LA vampires and our werewolf comrades. This was it. It was finally over.

"Do it!" I shouted in joy. "*Do it!*"

Then a shadowy form leaped from a crevice in the wall and landed right behind Brandi.

We yelled for her to turn, but she was already on it, and now she had Akrath by the neck with her other hand. The baldheaded vampire let out a strangled cry and slashed at Brandi's forearm with a dagger. Though he cut through the leather of her much-abused jacket and the flesh of her arm, it wasn't going to do him any good. Brandi had locked down on his neck tightly enough that his eyes were already bugging out of his head.

"I've been expecting you, you little fuck. I owe you one for Katheryne," Brandi snarled. With a twist of her arm, she nearly brought Akrath to his knees. The only thing keeping him on his feet was Brandi holding him up. Akrath squawked and his dagger fell to the ground with a metallic clatter. "Into eternity with you as well!" the Valkyrie roared, her eyes blazing red.

Tempestia, weak as she was, had enough left to take advantage of Brandi's divided attention. She lunged forward, pulling her hair from the Valkyrie's grasp, and sprang onto her back. Stacey shrieked a warning, but it was too late, and Tempestia sank her fangs into Brandi's neck, latching on tightly, holding on even when Brandi flung Akrath aside and tried to rip Tempestia off.

We rushed forward to help, but in the few seconds it took us to get there, Akrath retrieved his dagger from the ground and jammed it into the left side of Brandi's chest...where her heart lay.

"*You motherfucker!*" screamed Stacey. It hurt to hear the pain in his voice—he'd been stabbed through the heart as much as his beloved. "*Brandi!*"

His shriek was agonized, and I felt like my soul was being flayed alive. That single thrust had done more damage than Akrath could have suspected, and that made me hate him even more.

The Valkyrie dropped to her knees—speaking volumes of how bad her wound was—and I slammed into Akrath as hard as I could, knocking the dagger from his hands once more. When he crumpled against me, I smashed him in the head several times, wanting to rip his face from his skull.

As I pounded Akrath, Stacey, Clarisse, and Donita hit Tempestia, and when Stacey shoved his thumb into Tempestia's eye socket, she let go of Brandi's neck and screamed bloody murder. Donita blasted her in the face with a jolt of purple magickal energy, knocking her off Brandi entirely, and Clarisse, my brave, fearless Clarisse, sprang on Tempestia and started to wail away on her with everything she had. I saw all this out of the corner of my eye, and when Clarisse leaped on Tempestia, my stomach dropped completely out of me. Oh no.

I gave Akrath a final, savage kick and got to my feet, trying to cross the distance between Clarisse and myself as quickly as I could. It wasn't enough.

As furiously as Clarisse was dishing out the punishment to Tempestia, the bitch had been revitalized by the dose of Brandi's incredibly potent blood, and was faster and stronger than my lover.

Clarisse drove a fist straight into Tempestia's face, screaming in rage for her big sister, and Tempestia didn't even try to block it. Instead, she took the punch and shot her arms up so she could claw at Clarisse's chest, rending her ivory flesh. When Clarisse howled in pain, Tempestia lunged forward and sank her fangs into Clarisse's neck. *No!*

Clarisse frantically slashed at Tempestia, desperately trying to get free, and Donita, who'd been trying to help Brandi, and I both hit her at the same time. The gypsy zapped the "Goddess" while I slammed my fist into the side of Tempestia's head.

"Get off of her!" I howled.

The half-vampire's head pulled away from Clarisse's savaged neck, and when she turned to snap at me, I fired off another punch at her mouth. It felt as if my whole arm had been struck by lightning, hurting for a split second then nearly going numb.

But it was enough, and Tempestia was slammed back to the ground, her head cracking against the stone. I snatched Clarisse up in my good arm and pulled her away.

Tempestia scrambled to her feet and snarled at us, and I could see why my hand and arm had gotten such a jolt when I'd punched her—I'd jaggedly broken off Tempestia's left fang, just below the gum, which was nearly impossible to do on a strong vampire or half-vampire. Our fangs were almost diamond-hard, and it was rare when a vampire broke one. That busted fang went quite well with Tempestia's gaping, bloodied left eye socket, where Stacey's thumb had squished her eye to ocular slime.

Tempestia charged at Clarisse and me, but Donita hit her with one more blast of magickal energy fired from her clenched fists. When it connected on the right side of Tempestia's chest, her tattered and bloodstained gown burned, her flesh sizzled, and her hair fried. Though it wasn't much more than cosmetic damage, there was enough kick behind it that it knocked Tempestia back to the ground.

Stacey, who'd been holding onto Brandi—who was incredibly back up into a crouch when she should've been flat on her back—exchanged glances with Donita. Then he ran over and grabbed Akrath, while the gypsy took his place by Brandi's side.

Brandi wasn't looking good. Her face was unnaturally pale for a vampire, at least in the places where it wasn't covered with grime or blood, and her breathing was labored. She was on her feet after a fashion, true, but she was wobbly even in a crouch, and slumped against Donita. Clarisse wasn't doing great, though at least she was better off than Brandi, even if Tempestia's claws had come painfully close to her heart.

I held my lover close to me, visions of Runquist and Alena running through my mind. It was happening all over again.

"I'm sorry, I'm sorry," I whispered to Clarisse again and again as I held her, and she weakly put a hand to my cheek, as though to tell me it wasn't my fault. Somehow I couldn't bring myself to fully believe that.

It was a different scenario this time, but the Order was still tearing away at everything I cared about, no matter what we did to them. We'd smashed their forces in Los Angeles and here in their home base, and it looked as though the damage Brandi and Katheryne had dealt to Tempestia had eroded or outright destroyed the faith of the Order's followers, if the number of covies who were now sitting down or taking their robes off was any indication. But the heart of the Order, Tempestia and Akrath, kept right on hurting those who meant the most to me. What would it take to bring this to an end?

Stacey dragged Akrath to his feet while beating the shit out of him, screaming his head off, crimson tears running down his normally jovial face. As he shook Akrath by the neck, he kept demanding, "Why? Why?" over and over again.

"After all of her stupid bullshit, why do you keep helping her? She treats you like shit, she walks all over you and everybody else, she doesn't even follow the fucking tenets of your fucking stupid religion, and you still defend her! *Why?*" He slipped behind Akrath, locked him into a full nelson, and hissed, cold and mean, "You're mine now, fucker. You tell me why, or your head's gonna come off nice and slow."

"Why?" Akrath repeated in his cultured voice, angry and weary at the same time, soft enough I could barely hear it. But as he talked, his words gained strength and force as more and more emotion welled to the surface. "Why? If the Crimson Order is to survive, it needs a powerful, charismatic leader who inspires devotion and fear in the hearts of its followers. That's not me. Tempestia's what the Order needs, despite her idiocy. While she stuns and impresses them, I control things from behind the scenes, guiding the Order by the true Will of the Goddess, not that fool's mercurial whims. She couldn't lead a parade on her own, but she *listened* to me when it was important. Everything was fine until we came to this wretched country. That's when it all fell apart...all because of *you!* Damn you all to Terminus! Damn you!"

His eyes were wild with rage and spittle flew from his mouth. I was willing to bet that the way the Order had gone to pieces so quickly after a century carefully rebuilding it had snapped something deep and fundamental in him.

By this time, the nearly shredded Tempestia had pulled herself to her feet again and was shaking her head as though trying to regain her bearings.

Nobody moved to attack her. Donita was tending to Brandi, I was holding onto Clarisse, and Stacey had Akrath. The Los Angeles vampires—Tommy and Dorian visible among them—and Lassic's werewolves mingled among the defeated covies behind Tempestia, looked ready to spring at any moment.

She fixed her remaining eye on us and growled softly. Her glare raked over all six of us, and as mad as Akrath's eyes had been, this lone one was far worse. It burned red and angry, and as blood slowly oozed from Tempestia's mouth, she looked like a rabid animal, ready to attack. I held Clarisse closer and turned so more of my back was in her direction, ready to defend Clarisse with my body if I had to, and Donita moved more between Brandi and Tempestia as well.

"Don't make another move, bitch," Stacey growled, stepping forward and dragging Akrath with him. "I wouldn't want to have to do something extreme, seeing as how I've got your main man right here where I want him."

Tempestia's mouth slowly twisted from a snarl to a wicked smile, and her eye narrowed as she softly laughed. "Well," she purred, her voice having regained most of its imperious regality from earlier, "so you do."

Akrath began writhing in Stacey's grasp, fighting like a wildcat to get free.

"My Goddess, no! *Tempestia... Don't!*" he shrieked. That was the last coherent thing to ever come out of his mouth as he burst into flames in Stacey's arms. Tempestia sagged, as though about to drop. That hellish power must've taken a lot out of her to use; though as much as it might have cost her, it was far worse for whoever was on the other end.

Akrath took the brunt of it, but Stacey got it pretty bad too. When he shrieked, I couldn't do anything by cry out in anguish.

Thank the stars for Donita. She slammed Stacey away from Akrath as the other vampire screamed and burned then hit him with some sort of magick that put out the flames almost instantly. But the damage had been done.

My dearest friend in the world curled up on the ground, smoke pouring from his seared flesh, convulsing uncontrollably and howling in agony. I wasn't sure when the tears started to fall from my eyes, but my face was soaked with them, and I moaned helplessly.

Akrath, wailing like a siren, dropped to his knees and fell on his side not far from Stacey, twitching and thrashing as the flames consumed his immortal flesh. Smoke wafted through the air, tinged with the acrid stench of burning meat. It could just as easily have been Stacey on the ground burning alive...or Clarisse...or Brandi... or Katheryne...or any of my friends.

Brandi, who'd fallen when Donita had moved to save Stacey, started crawling toward her lover, softly calling his name as he bawled. Donita knelt next to Stacey, frantically glancing between him and Brandi, not knowing who to help first, and I could see it was breaking her heart. Tears glistened in Clarisse's eyes and ran down her cheeks, and something inside me started to scream and rage.

I began trembling as though I had electrical current running through me, and I couldn't take any more of this. I'd had *enough*.

"Don't think that I didn't hear thee and thy blasphemous words, Akrath, no." Tempestia laughed at the fallen form of her former right-hand man, having straightened again. "I heard every last one of them, and I have given thee thy proper punishment for thy blasphemy and lack of faith. Now I must deliver this holy punishment to *all* of the traitors to the noble Crimson Order!"

She spun and turned her one-eyed gaze to the rest of the cavern. Everybody backed up a few steps, but nobody—not even those still wearing the black robes of the Crimson Order—made a move to cower or beg forgiveness.

"Kneel before thy Goddess, ye faithless fools!" Tempestia raised her hands above her head, trying to look dangerous and impressive. But, judging from the angry and indifferent looks the covies were giving her, I suspect they'd realized what we had a long time ago: she was nothing more than another vampire with delusions of grandeur.

"*Kneel!*" Tempestia screamed, stomping her foot. Still, nobody moved.

Then Tommy, who was standing in the front ranks of the crowd, pointed and laughed at her. His laugh cut through the air of the cavern, above Stacey and Akrath's cries, and echoed long and loud. The professor—a monk during his mortal life—knew better than most how to cut off a religious figure at the knees.

Dorian joined in, then Lassic, then another werewolf, followed by several more vampires, and then a few covies joined in. Soon, the entire crowd, composed of LA vampires, werewolves, and covies were laughing hysterically at her, pointing and jeering.

Tempestia jumped up and down and screamed, "Cease this now! I command thee!"

Nobody did. If anything, her orders made everybody laugh even harder. This went on for almost a minute, and just when I'd hit my breaking point with Tempestia's foolishness, she roared, "*I'll damn all of thee straight to Terminus for eternity! I guarantee it!*"

She launched herself into the air and looked down at the crowd, then spun to look at us and cackled. "I'll leave thee to thy own devices, as my test of thy faith has been completed and my judgment shall soon come to pass. Enjoy thy last days of life on this plane of existence, for thy ends shall all come swiftly!"

With a final laugh, she turned and sped across the cavern, then shot out of the hole in the wall and into the night sky. She was gone, and we'd won, the Crimson Order had been beaten soundly and Tempestia had fled with her tail between her legs. But it wasn't over, not at all. My seething heart told me as such, and I knew it wouldn't be over until I'd seen that *all* had been said and done.

I silently walked over to where Donita was busy working on Stacey with her magick, doing whatever she could to get him back together, and I gave Clarisse a soft kiss on her lips before gently setting her down next to the gypsy.

"Steele," she whispered, reaching out and grabbing my shoulder with a weak grip. "Don't go. We can get her another time, we—"

"Couldn't get to her before she starts this madness all over again. It ends tonight, no matter what. Nobody else is going to die or have their lives wrecked because of her," I said, then I gave her a last kiss and stood.

Though it pained her to do so, she sat up. I could see in her eyes and feel through our bond how badly she didn't want me to chase after Tempestia, but she also knew there was no stopping me. The only thing that would bring me to a halt would be death...either Tempestia's or my own.

"Promise me you'll come back," she whispered, her voice steady but her eyes pleading.

I looked into her crystal eyes for a long moment, wishing I could lose myself in them forever, wishing that the world that kept fucking with us would cease to exist and just let us be, but I knew that'd never be the case. If we wanted happiness, we'd have to fight for it...even die for it, if necessary.

That was why I was now leaving the woman I loved most of all to chase after the woman I hated more than anything, that was why I wasn't holding Clarisse to me as tears flowed down her cheeks, that was why I couldn't help Stacey when he was in pain. If the little world and people in it I loved were to continue, I might very well have to sacrifice myself for it and them.

"Promise me," she pressed, and I looked into her eyes for a few more seconds, wishing that I could.

There were a million things I wanted to say to her right then, but there was no time, no time at all. Each second I stayed, Tempestia was getting farther away. I would never lie to Clarisse—that was a promise I'd made to her long ago in that wicked, magickal summer when our paths had first joined as one, and it was something I took seriously; that was why I now said nothing to her. I gently shook my head, but there were no more tears. I had to hold onto myself so tightly now it was painful. I hated that I couldn't promise her, but I couldn't lie to her either.

"Forgive me," I said then I turned on my heel, focused my eyes on the night sky beyond the hole in the cavern wall, and I started walking.

I could feel Clarisse's hurt through our bond. That nearly killed me on the spot, but I kept going; I picked up my pace, as a matter of fact. I strode past Tommy, Dorian, and Lassic, past the covies and the rest of the LA vampires, not looking at them, not turning back to look toward Stacey and Clarisse. If I did, I wouldn't be able to leave.

Love was a beautiful, wonderful thing, but it could also be the most painful, cruel thing in the world, like when your love for someone forced you to hurt them or even to leave them. Love could be the most brutal, double-edged blade in all existence.

I didn't even try to shove such thoughts aside, I let them wash through me and drive themselves deep into the very core of my being, burning and stabbing me down where no flame or knife could ever reach. I let it fill me and overload me, and my weariness melted away. I was ready for war. The world had narrowed down to two fine points, Tempestia and myself, and those two points would either be down to one or none before long.

I came to a stop at the edge of the hole in the cavern wall, pausing for the briefest of moments. Just before I took flight I heard Donita yell, "It's your blood! The way to destroy her is in your blood!"

Donita's words skipped across the surface of my mind and slipped into my subconscious without registering. My focus was too fine, too tight, and I flung myself into the cool night air.

Just a short while ago I'd badly wanted to toss myself into the sky and fly under the moon and stars, and now I was doing just that, except I didn't want to be here. I just wanted to be in Clarisse's arms.

Damn Tempestia.

Part Seven:

Crescendo

I

At least the car I slammed into was a cheapie foreign model, which collapsed beneath my impact almost instantaneously. If it had been an old Roadmaster or Cadillac, it would've hurt a hell of a lot more. As it was, it certainly wasn't a tumble on the satin sheets with Clarisse, and as ripped up as I was already, it still hurt a lot. The glass really sucked, cutting right through my leather jacket and slicing into the aching flesh underneath.

After the inertia of my impact had been spent, I tumbled forward onto the inconsiderately hard pavement from the wreck of the little Toyota, some of the aforementioned glass tinkling onto the asphalt around me. I was in a world of hurt, so much so that even the pavement felt like a bed of nails, but I didn't even hesitate in first pushing myself to my hands and knees, and then getting back onto my feet.

I couldn't let myself even take a breather. If I did, my body might take it as an invitation to shut itself down for a while. That would have been fatal—or worse.

I shook the glass out of my blood-slicked hair then leveled my gaze on Tempestia—who looked just as bad as I did—across the street. She was furious, and if I'd had the energy, I would have grinned. I strode toward her—slower than I would've liked—and she snarled. I would have if the situation had been reversed.

We'd been duking it out in this part of the city for at least five minutes, and though she'd put the hurt to me in a bad way, nothing she did could make me stay down for more than a few seconds. She kept dishing it out and I kept getting right back up. I'd even managed to get in a few punches, kicks, and slashes, though thus far I was still behind in the "damage dealt out" contest.

To be honest, she was beating the shit out of me, but thankfully I was too dumb to stay down.

"Blasted fool, why do you persist?" she snapped, shaking her matted black hair in disgust. She'd dropped all the "thees" and "thous" for the time being, and I wondered if the seven-story drop onto the car a few minutes back had rattled something loose in her. I desperately hoped so.

I'd thought I'd lost her after taking off from the order's lair and flying over the forested area over which I'd last seen her, but after fighting down panic and hopelessness, I'd caught a dot on the horizon that had to have been her. I'd poured on as much speed as I could, keeping her just in my range of sight but staying far enough away that she wouldn't notice me right off.

Not long after, she'd hit the outskirts of LA and had slowed considerably. I suspected the vastness of the city I took for granted had taken her by surprise. She'd dropped to a floating creep as she passed over the city and gawked at it like a tourist. It was in the wee hours of a Tuesday morning in early spring, and was pretty much as quiet as LA got—I'd have loved to see her reaction on a Friday night in the middle of the summer.

After cruising for a couple of miles, Tempestia had landed on the rooftop of an apartment house in midscale section of town, and had walked to the ledge to look out over the city. That's when I got her.

She had her back to me, absorbed in the alien sights and sounds, and I picked up my speed as much as I could and rammed her from behind at an angle that enabled me to drive her down into the street and plow her into a car, which got flattened when we hit it.

Before we landed, I'd wished it were a dump truck I was aiming her at. But afterward, when we were clawing away at each other while trying to extricate ourselves from the wreckage of the car, I was almost grateful it had been an old-model Ford Ferret. Just smashing into the little car hurt like a bitch, even with Tempestia taking the brunt of the impact. I wasn't up to hitting a dump truck tonight, no sir.

We'd traded blows, and she'd stopped me every time I went for her throat or heart, and I managed to keep her away from my vital places as well, though she seemed to get me everywhere else. The blood she'd stolen from Clarisse and Brandi had put some spring back into her step, though she was clearly still hurting.

She'd grabbed me and slammed me into walls and against the street and sidewalk, and then had tossed me across the street into the Toyota, but I wouldn't let it stop me. If she wanted me to stop, she'd have to kill me.

"Why do you persist?" Her tone was petulantly pissed.

I gave no answer, and I doubt she'd expected one. I hadn't said anything to her at all thus far, and I didn't really intend to: what was there for me to say? Words couldn't express my hatred of her—no matter how much I said—and I was just going to let my actions speak for me. Besides, I didn't want to waste any energy by speaking to her. I needed to focus everything I had onto bringing her down.

So I said nothing, and just kept coming, ignoring the screechings of my abused body.

I needed to get her out of here too. Lights were on in the apartment building off which we'd plummeted, and in some of the other buildings up and down the street. While there wasn't anybody outside watching us yet, it was only a matter of time before a crowd assembled. If there was a crowd, there was sure to be cops, and if there were cops, there was sure to be the damnable media, and if the damnable media came around, there was going to be trouble. So I kept going.

Tempestia snarled and took a step forward, raising her hand. With a gesture from her, my jeans and jacket were on fire. Though she wobbled at little at this lesser use of her fire power, the bitch started laughing her ass off nonetheless.

Without even thinking about it, I lashed out with my foot and kicked the fire hydrant on the sidewalk in front of me. I knocked it completely off of its moorings, releasing a powerful geyser of icy cold water into the cool night air. I stepped forward, going right through the spray. It nearly threw me off my feet and chilled me to the bone, but it completely put out the flames and soaked me so thoroughly that when Tempestia raised her hand again, nothing happened.

She growled and tried it once more, but my dripping clothes and flesh refused to ignite. I allowed myself a smile. Then I charged.

Tempestia was so irked that I'd foiled her in such a mundane manner that she wasn't ready for me. I hit her with a spearing tackle, launching us both backward into a brick wall that promptly gave way, and we went tumbling inside a building.

"Get off me, heretic scum!" Tempestia screamed, pounding away at my head and shoulders. I bit her everywhere I could, trying to move up her chest to her neck so I could rip her throat out.

But that didn't play out. She shoved me off and sent me flying through the air, and I came crashing down onto a solid, heavy glass case that hurt like hell to land on. It collapsed on impact and basically turned into a glass bomb that cut the holy fuck out of me.

As soon as the sound of shattering glass cleared, I heard another sound—a fast, hard clanging that wouldn't stop. After I'd shook out a few cobwebs—not to mention more glass from my hair—I saw we were in the middle of a jewelry store.

Then I heard more glass crashing and breaking. Tempestia was flinging aside the heavy display cases as she marched towards me, murder in her eye. Great.

The case I'd landed on had been a big one next to the cash register, and I was lying amid busted glass, shredded velvet, and the bent metal supports that had held the case together. I scrambled around, knocking over the register stand and a rack of little boxes beneath it, all while cutting myself up even more. When I put my hand down to push myself back to my feet, it felt like the flesh of my hand was being pierced by a thousand tiny needles. But it didn't feel like glass.

When I looked down and lifted my hand, I saw a titanium choker-style necklace embedded with what looked like hundreds of little diamonds, sparkling brightly in the strobing red alarm lights overhead. It had fallen out of a box marked "N Dorman for pickup Tuesday." The other boxes held various items, as well, but this was by far the biggest and most eye-catching.

The thing probably cost thousands of bucks—and was quite pretty—but now it was sitting amidst the ruins of its case, splattered with my blood... and I got an idea. With a silent apology to N Dorman, I grabbed the choker and wrapped it around my fist like brass knuckles. When Tempestia leaped at me, I shot forward and nailed her with a punch to her cheek.

It would have been a good, solid punch anyway, but with my expensive little enhancement, I really made it count.

The left side of Tempestia's face was absolutely shredded, and when I glanced down at the choker—which was warped but incredibly still in one piece—I saw it was covered with blood and gobbets of her flesh. Tempestia's skin may have been extremely tough, but it wasn't up to diamond hardness.

Glaring at me, the bitch slowly put her hand to her mutilated cheek, as if in disbelief I'd managed to deal her such a blow. I was down in a crouch, coiling myself after my first punch, and I wasted no time in rushing her once more to slam my diamond-wrapped fist into her stomach then crack her across the chin with an elbow. I forced her back a few steps until she headbutted me, which knocked me back just as many steps as I'd forced her forward.

As I dizzily staggered, she gave me a ferocious backhand that threw me clean off my feet, spun me like a pinwheel, and landed me on my head. Even after all the damage that had been rained down upon her, she was still a monstrous powerhouse. I would have hated to have slugged it out with her when she was fresh and at full strength; hell, I hated it *now*.

When my head bounced off the floor, I grayed out for a few seconds. The only thing that brought me back was an image of Clarisse lying bleeding in my arms and Stacey lying burnt on the ground, which gave me a jolt of strength I didn't even think I still had. I was back on my feet in a second. No matter how much I got hurt, no matter what happened, I would *not* give in, and I would *not* surrender, not to Tempestia, not to anybody.

I channeled all my pain—both emotional and physical—into one tiny, burning point that reenergized my battered, aching body. With a roar, I threw myself at Tempestia like a wildcat, hitting her with a much harder spear than the one that had taken us through the wall of the jewelry store. This time we crashed into the security grating that kept out thieves.

The grating bowed back from the impact, bending and twisting enough that it broke through the plate glass window and knocked it to splinters, adding to the evening's glass casualty count. I held onto the grating for leverage, repeatedly ramming into Tempestia with my body, forcing her against the grating even further.

When she tried to push me back, I smashed her with a diamond-wrapped fist to the face, dazing her for a moment. I backed up then ran at her full on, leaping and turning so my back and shoulder hit her like a battering ram.

Tempestia groaned, and I pummeled her with a volley of wicked elbows to her head, which gave me a few more seconds to back off and charge again, ramming her even harder this time. The bitch howled in concert with the security grating, which was being stressed in ways for which it had never been designed, and looked like a piece of abstract art...that had been hit by a truck.

I shot a few kicks into Tempestia's stomach and face then ran across the entire length of the store for my next charge. When I connected, the grating gave way, and we flew through the front window of the jewelry store, cleared the sidewalk, and bounced off the top of a Volkswagen (I hated those things) before falling into two heaps in the street.

I felt like such total shit that it was hard to even open my eyes, much less reach over and slam my fist upside Tempestia's head as I lay facedown on the pavement.

When I started to get back onto my feet, so did she, and we stared each other down, less than three feet from one another. We were both mangled wrecks, but I could see in her eye that she was far from beaten, and I knew that she could see the same in me.

"Thou art a fool to keep resisting, Steele." Her voice was a purr in sharp contrast to her bloodied appearance. "Open thy heart to the Goddess, and thou shalt see I'm right. Thee wouldn't have to suffer like this if thou stood with me instead of against me, no. Those who stand against the Goddess always pay the price in pain and regret, yes. Lack of faith carries a very high price."

Apparently she'd gotten herself more or less together despite the beating I was giving her, and was back into full Goddess mode. Lovely.

I'd thought that nothing she said could possibly make me angrier, but hearing her speak to me again as though she were a deity, with her fucking "thous" did it. I fed her a diamond-clad fist, hoping I'd break her other fang.

I didn't, but I did bloody the hell out of her mouth, and the look in her eye told me I'd put a sting to her pride as well. Good.

I swung again, but this time, she was ready for me, and I got slammed to the pavement before I could even blink. While I was down, she started to kick the shit out of me, and it was all I could to do curl up and prevent her from hurting me more than I already was. After what seemed like an eternity of kicking, she grabbed the back of my still soaking-wet leather jacket and hauled me to my feet, holding me so I was eye to eye with her. Just when my vision started refocusing, she gave me a sharp headbutt that scattered my senses again.

"Why dost thou persist? Why dost thou forsake thy Goddess? Thou hast seen what I'm capable of, thou hast seen the destruction and devastation that comes when there is a lack of faith in me, and yet thou continue to fight against me! Why? Why does thou not just give in to the comfortable path of eternal paradise? It is not hard to love the Goddess, Steele, not hard at all, and despite what thou hast done to me and the Crimson Order, I am willing to forgive thee, yes, and allow thee to take thy place at my side!"

"Because I don't fucking believe in you or anything you or your cronies tell me," I informed her through the haze hanging over my addled mind. I didn't really want to talk to her, but I figured it was best to do so, lest she just tear me to shreds before I had a chance to get my bearings or strength back.

"Why dost thou not believe?" Tempestia sounded more curious than anything now, as though she simply couldn't comprehend a vampire who didn't believe in the Goddess.

"Because the world was here long before you or your mumbo-jumbo bullshit religion, and it will continue to exist long after every last copy of the *Covenant* is ashes. Because I lived my life for years upon years before ever hearing of the Goddess and the Crimson Order, because you bring nothing but pain and ugliness to the world. You say you created the world, that you created all of us, but you don't know how wrong you are." I panted, tensing in anticipation of another beating. It didn't come, so I took a deep breath and continued.

"*You* were created by the words in a book and the beliefs of the fool vampires who read them, and you've created nothing but havoc and pain in your time on this planet—this planet that you didn't create! Whoever wrote the *Covenant* is your creator, Tempestia, and you're nothing more than a half-vampire who got off a lot luckier than most did. You think I'm a fool? At least I'm not a delusional fool like you are." I focused on her lone eye as best I could against the spinning of my head. As I went through my tirade, that eye got narrower and narrower.

"I should kill thee for such heresy right here and right now!" she bellowed, shaking me hard.

"Then why the fuck don't you?" I heard myself asking, and I couldn't believe the words had come out of my mouth. I don't think Tempestia did, either.

"Dost thou realize what thou are trifling with here? I hold the power of death over thee, Steele," she hissed.

Fuck it. What was a little more hot water?

"So what?" I crowed. "Anybody can kill anybody else on the right night. Shit, four kids and a dog could dust me if I wasn't paying attention. Hate to disappoint you, but the power of death over someone isn't special. Any jackass with a gun has that; you can go buy it in a department store, for fuck's sake. I bet it's the power of life you're after, isn't it?"

Tempestia said nothing—she just kept glaring with that lone blazing eye. I took that as my invitation to continue. Tin-plate dictators loved to hear what their foes had to say about them before they killed said foes. It made them feel better to ice someone who's got them figured out—that means that the son of a bitch couldn't go around telling everybody how fucked up the dictator was.

"Somewhere down in there, you know you can't create life, you can't make something from nothing. You can make revenants from vampires, you can make followers out of vampires, and you can make vampires from mortals, yeah. But you can't truly *create*, and even as stupid as you are, you know it. But you crave that power nonetheless, don't you? Since you can't create life, you want to control what's already there. Maybe it was about devotion to the Goddess and the *Covenant* in the beginning, but once you got yourself a good dose of power, that was it. You're not in this for love of your religion, it's for the power, and there's never enough to go around.

"When you're the Goddess, you're something more than a half-vampire by the name of Tempestia. People do what you say. People fear you. But even that's not enough. You can't be content with your little army of followers—you want me and you want Stacey, the guys who got the better of you way back when. You could've killed us in a hundred different ways when you had us in that cell, but you had to get all cute about it and try to make us part of your flock. Any jackoff can burn down a church. But it takes someone truly special to convince the churchgoers to burn their own church down. If you could make me and Stacey bend to your will and spit on everything we hold dear, then you're *finally* validated and you've *finally* beaten us, haven't you? Go ahead and do your worst. You can kill me, but you can't rule me... *I won't let you.*"

I didn't even see the punch coming, and it slammed me into the side of the Volkswagen hard enough to make me gray out again for a few seconds.

As the world swam in front of my eyes, Tempestia leveled a finger at me and snarled, "I'll be back, Steele, yes. Someday thou shalt call me thy mistress and the ruler of thy universe, and thou shalt help me crush all heretics and fools, and then all vampires shall hail the name of their true Goddess! Know that thy day is coming, Steele, know that I shall never cease, I shall never tire, I shall never rest until thou hast seen the light and known the love of the Goddess! And speaking of the light, thou must scurry underground with all due haste, as the night is coming to an end and my glory is coming to this part of the world once more!"

I looked straight up—though it felt like my head was going to fall off—and I saw that the sky behind me had been painted a light pink by the toxic rays of dawn. I heard a yell from down the street, the shout of a familiar voice then when I started to push myself to my feet again, Tempestia savagely kicked me in the head, causing me to totally black out.

"C'mon, boy...shake it off! Show me a sign there's still something rattling around in that thick skull of yours!"

Consciousness returned grudgingly, and my body fought against it as much as it could—if I were conscious, that meant I'd get back up and start doing things to get myself hurt once more. As soon as I got my eyes open and saw the pinkening sky, that's exactly what I did.

I was lying on my back in an alley, and as soon as I saw the deep blue of night's dregs giving way to the bright pinks and whites of the new day, I sat right up, though it hurt like a motherfucker. That didn't matter, and I stood up next, every cell in my body screaming at me to lie down and pass out again—if I didn't, I was going to be in a world of shit.

I told them to shut up. I didn't have time for physical frailties.

"It looks like hell, but it lives!" someone with a deep voice asked from my side.

I turned to see a stern-faced Screamin' Willie, dressed in a three-piece suit, looking at me with his arms folded over his chest.

"Where'd she go?" I asked. "How long have I been out?"

I took a step forward and nearly toppled over, so I put a hand on Screamin' Willie's shoulder to steady myself. When I pulled it away, I'd left a bloody, strangely misshapen handprint on the fabric of his suit. It was the hand that still had the choker wrapped around it, and I mumbled an apology to Willie as I pulled the warped, blood-drenched choker from my hand and stuffed it into the inner pocket of my jacket.

"Not a problem. I've bloodied enough suits to outfit an army," Willie said. "Anyway, you've been out for maybe a minute, long enough for me to drag you into the alley and give you a good yelling-at. The local constables are on their way, afraid of another 'gang war' breaking out, I wager. The smart thing to do here would be get underground, lick your wounds, and live to fight another night. No point in that, so I'll just tell you two things. One, she headed due west, toward the beach. Two...give her hell, boy. I'll round up as many half-bloods to send after you ASAP—I stayed behind with a contingent, just in case the Order had something up their sleeve while we were smashing up their home. Now go. Do what you've got to do."

I looked at Willie gratefully, and he gave me a light shove, encouraging me to go. Without another word I shot straight up into the air with everything I had.

I rose several hundred feet in a matter of seconds then launched myself forward, aimed in the direction of the last purple traces of night, with the pink of the day behind me and the delicate blue a-borning from the purple and pink above me. Time was running out, for both the night and me.

There was only a scant bit of darkness left, and only a scant amount of strength left in me. Even as I tore through the sky above

LA, I could feel my body trying to shut down. The icy fingers of torpor were starting to caress me, and I fought against them mightily. I could rest—or die—when Tempestia was gone, but until then, I wouldn't stop.

This was personal in the most intense way possible.

I could see her ahead of me, similar to when I'd chased her into the city, and this time I didn't bother holding back. I couldn't have cared less if she knew I was behind her, and if she noticed me from a distance off, so be it. The light behind me was getting brighter by the minute, and though we were flying due west, there was no way we were gonna be able to outrun the sun itself. Of course, Tempestia didn't have to worry about that, and that just made me even more desperate. Once she was gone, she was *gone*.

I had no real plan of dealing with her when I caught her, and it mostly consisted of me beating the snot out of her and trying to crash her into the ground, killing her one way or another. Very simple.

My own survival wasn't tantamount on my list of priorities, so I wasn't too worried about how I was going to survive the coming of dawn if I was stuck out in the open. I didn't want to die, not by any means, and if there was a chance of survival, I'd grasp it as hard as I could and never let go. But the desire—nay, the *need*—to put an end to Tempestia was holding priority over everything.

Even if I didn't make it, she wasn't going to hurt anybody else ever again, whether it be a stranger in the street or someone I loved more than anything.

We were flying toward the edge of the city, and I could see the beach and the Pacific Ocean off in the distance. It wouldn't be much longer and we'd be over open water.

I picked up the speed as best I could in my battered state, eating up the distance between my quarry and myself, and my heart began to race even harder than it was already. This was my final chance to stop her. There were no covies out here, no LA vampires, just me and her, and the moment was weighing down on me.

As Linus once told Charlie Brown, you can either be a hero or a goat, and I had no intention of being a goat. But I also wasn't doing this to be a hero. I was doing this because I *had* to, because I could never let myself rest until Tempestia was gone. That was the destiny

I chose for myself: the protector of the vampires of Los Angeles, and the guardian of those I loved.

I'd fulfill that destiny, or die trying.

I forced a bit more speed out of myself, and I held my body as tightly streamlined as possible. My filthy, bloody hair trailed behind me like a streamer and my tattered, still-wet clothes flapped in the wind as I cut through the air behind Tempestia. She looked as bad as I did—maybe even a little worse, since her white clothing showed blood and grime a lot more than my own black outfit did—and the shredded remnants of her train clawed at the air behind her like a hand from the grave. I fixed my eyes on the whipping train for a second, and just like that, it went out of my view.

A blink later, Tempestia was barreling toward me like a train of an entirely different sort.

"If thee wishes to die so badly, then I shall grant thy wish, blasphemer!" she shrieked as she tore through the cool air straight at me. Apparently not only had she noticed I was following, she wasn't a fan of it.

Her eye was like a bloody laser beacon, and her face was far worse than that of any devil ever depicted in medieval myth and legend. In those few seconds before impact occurred, Tempestia didn't look like anything that had once been even remotely human. I didn't even try to slow down, and instead gritted my teeth and sped up.

The force of our collision hit me like the hammer of a god, and I saw stars before my eyes as the shock tore through my body. To this very day, I can't remember what happened immediately following that.

The next thing I knew, we were wildly pinwheeling through the air, locked onto each other and clawing away at one another like rabid dogs. If I'd been mortal, I would've puked my guts out from the spectacle of the earth and sky madly spinning around on all axes. To make things worse, I had Tempestia screaming in my ears at the same time.

"Are thou so stupid that thee cannot see when mercy has been granted upon thee?" she roared. "Even when I grant mercy, thee still spite me! If Terminus is what thee wishes for, *then Terminus it shall be!"*

She was raining the damage down on me, and while I was holding on, I wasn't giving as good as I got, not even close. My bearings were too scrambled for me to really give it my all.

From out of nowhere, a palm tree appeared, and we crashed right into its upper portion and bounced off wildly. I heard a few of my ribs either crack or break outright. Whether it was a crack or break was irrelevant, as the tremendous pain that shot through my midsection told me that whatever it was, I'd been hurt.

But the pain, bless it, shook some of my bearings back into place and gave me a shot of badly needed strength. Pain could be extremely useful—even wonderful—when properly used. At that point, all my poor body had left was pain, and the addition of more got things moving again, at least.

Tumbling through the air, I repeatedly headbutted Tempestia, desperately trying to dizzy her enough that I could get her onto the ground again.

But all I really accomplished was addling her enough that we started to spin even more out of control, and another brutal impact wracked my body as we bounced off the top of a beach house. Something else in me gave way, but I kept going. I could feel my body wanting to gray out again, this time from an overload of pain. My body had already had a taste of unconsciousness and wanted it back, *bad*.

I fought it off, willing myself to focus, and things snapped into crystal clarity as I forced something within me well beyond what I should have. That was fine with me, just as long as I could still fight.

I redoubled my efforts, punching, biting, and clawing at Tempestia, and I started gaining ground on her.

The pinwheeling slowed down, and I mercilessly hammered away at her remaining eye while holding onto her by a handful of her tattered dress. I lunged for her neck, intent on ripping out her throat. One good bite and tear, and this would be over.

But just before my fangs hit her flesh, a steely hand clamped onto my own neck and stopped me dead. With a roar, Tempestia tore me loose, held me for a moment, then flung me downward, where there were plenty of large rocks at waterside to break my fall.

I'm amazed I didn't black out. I must've fallen a good hundred feet—Tempestia's throw painfully augmented by gravity. When I hit those rocks, I knew I was done.

Pain seared through me so hard I couldn't even scream. Normally the impact wouldn't have hurt me too badly, but in the condition I was in was more than enough to finish me off, at least where this fight was concerned. My insides felt as if they'd been pulped, all of my bones felt like they'd been fractured or broken, and the wetness on the back of my head had nothing to do with my walking through the fire hydrant spray earlier. She'd damn near smashed me to pieces.

But I didn't black out, not even close. Whatever I'd kicked into gear earlier was still holding on, and while I could barely move, I was still very much awake and alert.

I lay on the rocks along the water's edge, and the sky before me was a massive wall of pink and blue. The sun would be peeking over the horizon any second now, and while this ethereal wall was the harbinger of my doom, it was beautiful. I hadn't seen the sky like this in ages, and while it would never be as beautiful to me as the velvet night, I could think of far worse things to see before my death.

Up in that wall of dawn, I saw Tempestia…and she was falling.

She was plummeting toward the earth, her limbs limp, and my heart started to soar. But then it went into a sickening free fall when she righted herself and hung in the air for several seconds and turned her eye on her helpless tormentor.

She never glanced away as she slowly drifted downward, and I struggled to get up and do something. But while the spirit was willing, the flesh was broken. All I could do was lie there on the rocks, with the surf crashing behind me, watching her approach and hearing her laugh. I should've panicked, I should've freaked out, but I didn't.

After I found that my struggling did no good, I simply lay there, listening to the waves and Tempestia's laughter, waiting for her to come to me. It wasn't even a sense of resignation or being defeated. My emotions, after being on a rollercoaster for so long, had simply flatlined. I wanted to be furious, I wanted to scream and rail, but I couldn't even muster that. I was dead calm.

I said nothing as she hovered over me in triumph, cackling at my state. My gaze wasn't even defiant, but as peaceful as a monk's. When Tempestia threw her taunts at me, I said nothing, I didn't even move. I simply looked at her and the glorious sky behind her, though the brightness of it already hurt my eyes.

When she grabbed the front of my jacket and lifted me off the rock, and my entire body screamed in agony at merely being moved, I didn't make a sound. I think I even smiled at her.

But she didn't much seem to care. Her eye—marred with broken capillaries and the flesh around it raw from my earlier pounding—spoke of madness and insanity. She was totally out there now that she was certain of her victory.

She pulled me higher and higher into the sky, holding onto the front of my jacket and twirling us around in the air like a pair of ballroom dancers, laughing in my face. We pulled away from the rocks as we rose, and in seconds we were out above the ocean, the beach and morning sky somewhere behind me.

Ahead of me was Tempestia's face and the fading purple and blue shreds of the night. The night in which we'd fought the Crimson Order, when Katheryne had valiantly made her stand against Tempestia, when Wade had come back to us, when Brandi had given her all in combat, when Stacey and Clarisse had been badly hurt by Tempestia, and when I'd had my clock cleaned by her.

But I wasn't defeated yet. I was still alive, I was still aware, and though I was exhausted far beyond anything I'd ever been in the past, I still had a little left in me. Expending that little bit was probably gonna kill me, but if accomplished what I wanted, it would be worth it. I just had to wait for the right moment.

Unfortunately, I had absolutely no fucking idea what the right moment was.

"I would have let thee live, Steele," Tempestia said when we came to a stop above the ocean, and her voice was surprisingly gentle. "I truly would have. I granted thee time to learn thy folly and to correct thy ways. But thou wouldn't have it, so I must send thee off to Terminus where thou shall not be a problem to me any further."

She shook her head, looking almost melancholy, though her lone eye nearly swirled with her lunacy. "There are some who cannot be touched by the love of the Goddess, I have seen, and sadly, thou art one of them."

Then she twitched, her eye narrowed, and her expression of

near-sadness turned to one of glee. "But know this before I hurl thee off into Terminus, know that across the ocean are the rest of my followers, awaiting my return, yes. Though thee and thy friends have ran off the noble Crimson Order in California, there are still many, many more faithful out there on the other side of the ocean. In the mountains, in the caves, in the plains, in the jungles, there are so many more of the loving and the converted who have seen my love and my glory over the last century, and when I have disposed of thee, I shall journey across the ocean to—"

She paused, and we plunged about ten feet. She came close to dropping me, but then she rapidly regained herself and we rose to our original altitude. She scowled at me and clucked her tongue.

"Thou hast damaged this vessel, the body of my loyal follower Tempestia, greatly. It is all my essence can do to hold her together. But I *have* held her together. I *have* kept her body functioning so that I may use her as my messenger upon this planet, despite all of thy efforts to foil me otherwise. Just as thou have nearly destroyed Tempestia and yet I have succeeded, so shall it be in the future, yes. Thou hast crushed the new Crimson Order emerging in your country, but ultimately I have succeeded, because I have escaped with this body, so that I may cross the ocean and return with my followers, stronger than before. And, having learned from the mistakes of this failed conquest, I shall not be denied a second time around. Especially since thee will no longer be walking among the heretics of Los Angeles, no. And now, Steele, though I would much prefer to have thee alive and at my side, I must now commit thee to the light of my true form, the one from which I reach out and control loyal Tempestia's body. I regret having to do this, but thou giveth me no choice."

As she spoke, I could see sunlight touching her face and feel it starting to tickle and burn the exposed flesh of my hands hanging at my sides. The burning was weak at first, but as the seconds passed, it grew steadily stronger, and my hands were soon stinging enough that I put them against my thighs, protected by the shadow of my body.

I felt the back of my jacket and hair warm up, and tiny pinpricks of stinging occurred on my scalp where bits of the sun made it through my matted hair. But other than that, my clothing and my hair protected my back, though there were a few tears in the back of my jeans that let in the sun. The searing pain that accompanied the sunlight wasn't even enough to make me move.

I was so battered, so exhausted, that the only thing that could make me do anything was my own will. But what could I do?

I was helpless in Tempestia's grasp, way up in the air over the Pacific Ocean, with the nearest land well behind me, so I did nothing but watch her and listen. The sunlight against her face was almost too bright for me to stand, and the blood on her face shone brightly in the light, the vampiric elements in her blood giving it a supernatural shine.

I waited for it to catch flame and burn to ash, like mine would have in the same light, but it didn't. She truly was a half-vampire, immune to the light of the sun. Her blood could take sunlight all day without a problem, whereas mine would ignite like gasoline touched with a match.

And then it hit me.

It's your blood! The way to destroy her is in your blood! Donita had called out to me before I'd left the cavern. Though the words hadn't touched me then, they did now, as I stared into Tempestia's face while she gave me her little sermon on her own superiority.

Donita had a hint of precognitive ability in her, and there were times she could catch glimpses of the future. Though they were often vague, she was always on the money, and as her words echoed in my head, I realized what I needed to do. My face didn't change and eyes didn't move, but inside of me, the final gate was opened, the gate holding the vitality I needed to stay alive, and the last of my strength flowed into me silently and swiftly.

This was it, the last shot I had, and if I failed, it was my death and the survival of Tempestia. If I succeeded, she was as good as gone, and I might yet still die. Yet if it saved my friends and my city, it was a price more than worth paying.

I smiled serenely at Tempestia as she babbled away, and while holding my lips pressed together, I used my fangs to delicately slice the flesh inside my mouth so expertly that my expression didn't change an iota. The strong, salty taste of my own blood filled my mouth, and I gently sucked at the wound, pulling more and more blood out, building up a nice supply.

My cheeks began to slightly balloon out as I filled my mouth with blood, but Tempestia was so wrapped up in talking about herself that she didn't even notice. I tried to keep my cheeks as slack as possible, but the amount of blood kept increasing, and my cheeks grew more and more taut. My mouth was getting so full that I just hung my head down, as if in defeat.

That seemed to really please Tempestia, as she got an extra lilt to her voice. Good, just so long as she didn't notice I was getting chipmunk cheeks.

Finally, after what seemed like years of pointless prattling, Tempestia paused and then asked, "So, my heretical friend, does thou have any final words before I turn thee around to gaze upon my true face? I do not expect thee to beg or plead for mercy. After the lessons of tonight, I know thee will not do that, so I ask if thee has any final insults or words of defiance for me before I commit thee to Terminus. I would think that thee would want to put an end to thy existence on this plane with a witty remark or some cretinous barb."

Yep.

I snapped up my head and sprayed the mouthful of my own blood into Tempestia's face. I didn't just spray her, I *hosed* her with it—so much so I got every part of her flesh from the neck up to her hair, and the effect was explosive.

As soon as my blood hit the air and came in contact with the sunlight, it burst into flame, crossing the short distance between our faces and clinging to Tempestia's flesh like napalm. It was as though I'd spat a fireball right in her face. Holy shit, did she *scream*.

She let go of me to put her hands on her face, to claw the burning pain from it, but I was ready for that, so I hung in the air right where she left me.

Snarling, I cocked back my left fist and threw my whole body into a sledgehammer punch that snapped her head to the side and spun her partway around. As soon as I'd softened her up with that, I cocked back with my right fist—my really good one—and I let her have it with everything I had in me. My punch had an upward bent to it, and this time her head snapped back as though someone had grabbed her by the back of her hair and yanked *hard*.

Her hands fell from her burning face, the stench of seared flesh hitting me, and she screamed again. I felt my body getting ready to cash in its chips, and I let rip with a primal roar of pure will that forced my body to stay together—despite the sun, despite the damage, and despite all of the pain—long enough to do what I needed to do.

I sucked more blood into my mouth and as Tempestia hung in the air, knocked stupid by my twin blows of fury (shut up, I earned it), I drew my right hand back again, but not for a punch. My hand shot forward like a cobra strike, and instead of heading for Tempestia's face, it went for her chest. My fingers tore through the flesh, shattered bone, and ripped muscle, reaching into her for the prize I needed to claim if I was going to put an end to all of this craziness.

My hand clenched tightly around the furiously beating pump of vitality within Tempestia, and with a motion as sudden and savage as the one that had put my hand into her chest, I pulled my hand out. Her heart, still beating, was in my grasp.

In front of Tempestia's horrified eye, I sprayed her heart with the blood I'd accumulated then held it aloft, where it burst into flame in the sunlight.

The flesh of my hand burned just as wildly as Tempestia's heart, but the pain didn't touch me. I even started to laugh hysterically at the look of terror and defeat on Tempestia's face. She knew she'd been licked. She knew that even after everything she'd done to me, I'd won. Even if I died along with her, she couldn't take that away from me, and the vampires of Los Angeles would live to fight another day. She'd failed and I'd succeeded once more...

And she had nobody to blame but herself.

I crushed the burning shreds of Tempestia's heart, grinding them into pulpy ash. As I felt my strength begin to falter—my last reserves spent and beyond recovery—I flung the crap that had once been Tempestia's heart into her face and lunged at her.

She didn't even scream, didn't make a sound, when I latched onto her, holding on with a death grip, and we began to fall. I had just enough strength to hold onto her as we plummeted, determined not to let her go. I stared into her eye as we fell, and as the light in it faded, I laughed once again.

"Off to Terminus with thee," I cackled, "and don't fuck with the

Hollywood vampires!" The flesh around her eye tightened at my words then went completely lax as the last light went out of the bloodied ocular organ forever. Tempestia was dead, and with her heart gone, there was no coming back for her, not now, not ever. I'd won. *We'd* won. The reign of terror of the Crimson Order in California was done, finished. It was over.

There was a broad smile on my face as we slammed into the cool waters of the Pacific and the entire world went to black.

Conclusion:

Coming Home

I

Iheard nothing for a long, long time.
It seemed as though that nothing had existed forever, and that it always was and forever would be. But that nothing was pierced by something that wasn't nothing, as ridiculous as that wording may seem.

You had to have been there, I guess. But anyway...

After an eternity of feeling nothing, I distantly felt a soft breeze against the skin of my cheek, and I faintly smelled the salt scent of the wind. I could hear the crashing of waves, sounding as though they were miles away, and I tried to urge them further away. I didn't want to leave the warm, silent cocoon that was my existence. Inertia weighed heavily on me, and I didn't much want to argue with it. I gave in to it, encouraged it, actually, and I began drifting away once more, and the smells, feelings, and sounds of the world outside of my own little one began to fade.

But then I felt something softer than the breeze against my cheek, and my waning hearing picked up the voice that ensured I couldn't retreat into the warmth and darkness.

"Come on, big boy, you've had long enough...don't make me spend another night missing you, luv. Come back to me..."

When I heard that voice, *her* voice, I started pushing against the darkness, trying to swim upward through its currents. It was tough going. My mind was thick and sluggish, not wanting to respond, but I went inch by bloody inch, and I slowly made my way toward the voice, which kept quietly giving me encouragement.

She knew I was trying to come back, just as she always knew what was on my mind, and her voice was a lifeline. Though the darkness of my own mind wasn't bad, there were much more lovely things than the comfortable darkness.

"I know you can hear me, baby, come home...we've missed you, and *I've* missed you especially...come home, you can make it."

As I crawled upward, away from the darkness, I became more aware of my body, and I started to feel the aches and pains, and I realized I'd been hurt hideously. That made returning harder, but her voice got louder and clearer. Along with the ocean breeze, I could smell the scent of sweet cinnamon, and I could feel soft hands holding me. Despite the pain, I fought mightily to come back. The pain would be more than worth it if I could just get home, so I kept going, swimming higher and higher.

The waves and her voice got louder, the scents of the salt breeze and the cinnamon got stronger, and my aches, pains, and the feel of her soft hands grew more acute. Almost there. Soon, everything felt like it was right there at my fingertips, and with an effort, I slowly opened my eyes to see a star-speckled sky accented with the light orange glow of the city's lights...and I saw Clarisse.

She smiled down at me, and her beautiful face—so wonderful compared to the darkness—lit up like a nova. "Welcome back to the land of the living." She gently ran her fingers through my hair, and though it hurt a little where the sun had touched my scalp, it really did feel good, and when she leaned over and delicately kissed my forehead, the pain seemed to all go away. "All hail to the conquering hero," she whispered. "I love you."

My throat was full of rusty gears, and though the words came out in a harsh rasp, she understood. "I love you too."

Clarisse patted me on the cheek, and a crimson tear slipped down her own. The ocean breeze played through her hair, a brilliant shade of red even in the reduced light out on the beach. "Don't ever run away like that without telling me you're coming back. I don't care what it takes, always come back to me, baby. You can save the world all you want, but don't ever leave me, never ever. If that makes me selfish, I don't care."

She pulled me closer and hugged me tightly, sniffling a little in my ear, and I was doing the same. She held onto me and rocked back and forth for a long time, the only sounds coming from the ocean, the wind, and us. I was lying in the sand, the upper part of my body in Clarisse's arms. There was sand all over me, on my skin, on my clothes, and in my hair...add that to my already-ruinous state, and I was a total wreck.

In answer to my thoughts, Clarisse said, "You've been dug under for five days now. Donita made it here just in time to see you hit the ocean, and she went out into the water to get you. There was nowhere to go since the sun was fully up by then, so she just set you on the beach well away from the tide line, and you dug under by natural instinct while she covered you as best she could. That's where you've been ever since. I wanted to get you out on the first night, and Stacey even had a shovel out, but Donita and Tommy thought it best to let you lie in peace for a while, before we put any more shock on your system. You were messed up so badly, and you still look it, but I couldn't wait any more, I didn't want you under the sand any longer, away from us, away from me. I couldn't help it—" A tiny sob came from her, and I held her as tightly as I could.

"It's all right, don't worry," I rasped. Talking hurt, a lot, but that didn't matter. Clarisse wouldn't punish herself for not being able to wait, but I wanted to comfort her anyway. "I would've done the same. Love ain't logical."

"No, it isn't." She kissed me on the cheek, ignoring the sand on it. "But I don't care, either."

We silently held each other for a while longer, then she laughed a bit. "Donita was out here on this very spot every day, relaxing and recovering, soaking up the sun and eating like a pig, and sending healing magick down through the sand. Even Katheryne, after the first day, braved the hordes of beach bums who hoot at a pretty blonde in the sun to come out and sit too. They came out here every day, from morning to night, and they even read books out loud and played music for you too."

Clarisse's words triggered a little flood in my mind, and I heard Donita's voice as she read Steinbeck's *Travels With Charley* and Katheryne's while she read Twain's *Tom Sawyer*. Though I also heard Twisted Sister, Bon Jovi, Skid Row, and the Beach Boys, I also heard something that didn't belong...

"Donita brought her Spice Girls albums, didn't she?" I groaned, and Clarisse giggled and rocked me back and forth happily.

"You *did* hear them! We were afraid it would drive you to attack them, but Donita insisted it gave you incentive to heal more quickly.

Poor baby," she said, cooing to me softly.

"Damn gypsy," I murmured. "Her heart's in the right place, even if her musical tastes aren't." Just speaking to Clarisse was leaving me exhausted, using up what little reserves of strength I'd rebuilt, and she picked up on that.

"Speaking of tastes, maybe you'd better get a taste of me." She pushed her hair away from her neck, giving me a clean view of her soft, pearlescent skin, completely, blessedly healed from the damage Tempestia had meted out. When I saw the jugular vein pulsing steadily, that was all I needed.

Despite the ravenous hunger that had sprang up in me, I was as gentle as I could be as I slid my fangs through her flesh and broke open the vein that poured her hot, salty blood into my mouth. By the moon and stars, did that taste delicious.

I drank deeply, pulling out as much as I could as quickly as I could, and when I tried to slow down for Clarisse's sake, she patted me on the back and said, "Don't worry, I fed heavily just before coming down to dig you up, so I've got more than enough. Take as much as you need." That was all the invitation I needed, and I drank from her for a long time, taking so much I feared that I was going to drain her totally, but she kept softly insisting I keep going.

She was brimming with hot blood tonight; she must have drunk to capacity and then some before coming. As I drank her sweetness down, I could detect other flavors in there besides her own. Each blood has its own taste and bite to it, and in Clarisse's I found the hints of many others, and they were familiar. Most of them I'd never drank before, but I'd smelled them many a time, and I recognized the tinges of Valkyrie, Gypsy, Witch, Casanova, Scholar, Wild-Hearted Son, and something so different and strange that it couldn't have been anybody but our resident Enigma. All of them were strong and potent, full of energy and vitality, and mixed with Clarisse's own lively blood, they made for a powerful elixir that revived and restored the weary, battered cells of my body.

"They all insisted I take from them to give to you. They wouldn't let me dig you up otherwise," Clarisse explained softly. "They said it was the least they could do. I had dozens of other vampires, and even werewolves, offering their blood to me, but I couldn't take it all, so it was family tonight. They wanted to give back to you part of the lives you helped to save, and so did I. You're an overgrown, ancient boy scout with an overblown hero complex, but I love you. Don't you ever change, no matter how much you scare me, no matter how much you worry me, and no matter how much I want to kick you sometimes. Don't ever change, baby, not for anything in the world."

I reluctantly broke contact with her neck, and after licking the wound to close it, I nuzzled against her neck, feeling much stronger and much more alive again. This time when I spoke, my voice was back to normal. "Just as long as you don't change a thing about yourself either, darlin'."

Clarisse took my face in her hands and pulled me up so my eyes met her own, and she said, "I promise."

Then she kissed me, and the stars overhead turned to fireworks and the glow from the city became an inferno. It would be a week before I was completely back to my old self, but for the moment, I felt incredible. The kiss went on for eternity, and with each second that passed, I seemed to gain a little more strength, until finally, I swooped Clarisse up in my arms and rose on legs that started off shaky but grew steadily firmer, and I spun her around and around on the sand as we kissed.

Then we broke the kiss and she slid out of my arms, wrapped her own around me, and we continued to twirl, almost like dancers, looking into each other's eyes and laughing merrily, like two stupid kids in love for the first time. I was a total wreck, but she was stunning in her beauty, and she made up for my rattiness a thousand times over, so all was well.

When the twirling slowed and came to a stop, we stood on the beach holding onto each other, the side of her face pressed against my chest and my face in her hair, she said, "And I'm not the only one that wanted to say thank you tonight. Look."

I'd been pointed toward ocean, but Clarisse gently turned us so we could both look up the beach, and I saw everybody. They were all there, every one of them, and when they saw me looking at them, they cheered.

Stacey and Brandi both looked in tip-top form, with Stacey sitting up on Brandi's shoulders, screaming louder and harder than anybody else, clapping his hands like an insane monkey, while the Valkyrie herself clapped and hollered at me. Tommy and Dorian were both letting fly with noisemakers and New Year's party horns, Dorian dancing a dumb little jig. Wade—in a fresh duster and looking like his old self again—was shouting something that sounded like an ancient war cry and raising his fist in the air, while Donita was shooting off little sparks of purple energy with one hand and cheering like a lunatic.

Katheryne—without a mark on her pretty face—wasn't clapping or yelling; she couldn't have clapped even if she'd been inclined to, as Wade and Donita both were holding her hands. But she didn't need to clap. The small, happy smile she gave me and the bright look in her unscathed eyes said it all. When she silently mouthed the words, "thank you," that did it for me, and the tears ran down my face, and I held Clarisse even tighter.

There were others there too.

Along the beach I saw Screamin' Willie, who took his hat from his head, pressed it against his chest, and gave me a gentlemanly bow of respect. I saw Lassic and a horde of werewolves, who all howled and yipped at me, baring their throats in their own gestures of respect. There were so many others, vampires I knew and didn't know, and I even saw Dactius, now dressed in blue jeans and a denim jacket similar to what Katheryne often wore, jumping up and down wildly, yelling with the best of them.

Next to Dactius, dressed in jeans, a T-shirt, and a leather jacket, looking very much like a regulation Sunset Strip rat, was Caleb, the former Crimson Order historian. The phrase "just happy to be there" had probably never been truer than it was for Caleb right then—after being stuck with the Order for so long, he was blessedly *free.*

"Willie had some of the half-blood cops pull some strings and had this section of the beach closed off, so the werewolves could be here too. We've got the run of the place," Clarisse said then she kissed me again. "Welcome home, hero…and thank you."

The rest of the night was a blur—a happy, wonderful blur of smiling faces, congratulations, tearful and boisterous thank yous, joyful reunions, and Stacey and Donita fighting and chasing each other around and accidentally getting their roasted marshmallows stuck in some of the werewolves' fur. I was still weak, sore, and worn out, but no matter how many times Clarisse asked me if I wanted to go back down to the Catacombs to get cleaned off and rest for a while, I wouldn't hear of it.

The celebration was as much for the rest of the vampires and werewolves as it was for me, and I wanted them to have a ball. This was the closure to the nightmare the Crimson Order had brought down upon us. While I'd slumbered beneath the sands for those five days, the others had done everything they could to tie up the other details, and by the time I came back up, nearly everything was complete and getting back to normal again, or at least as normal as things got for vampires in Hollywood. They deserved it just as much as I did.

The celebration went on until it was nearly dawn, at which time the werewolves and full vampires headed down to the Catacombs, while the half-bloods squared everything else away. After I'd given all of my hugs, administered friendly punches to arms, shot off my affectionate insults, and said my good days to everybody, Clarisse and I retired to a quiet little room we'd taken all for ourselves deep within the Catacombs.

Free of my filthy rags, I cuddled up with Clarisse underneath the delightfully cozy sheets on our incredibly comfortable bed, and after some more feeding on my part, we slept for two entire days and nights, wrapped up in each other's arms, not a care in the world for the first time in far too long.

"So…where's Lassie?" Charles asked as he greeted Clarisse, Brandi, Stacey, and I as we entered his backyard through the gate, each of us bearing a cat. Once inside the yard, we let Time, Famine, Pestilence, and Death loose, where they were gleefully set upon by the big fat Mexican's three children. Ana (six), Santiago (four), and Federico (nine) grabbed Death, Time, and Famine respectively, squealing and laughing with delight, and carted the cats off for the full gauntlet of love and attention.

This left Pestilence to fend for herself against Carlitos—the Pocalotas' stocky, lovestruck pug—who came snorting and slobbering across the yard, straight for the snooty calico cat. With a yowl, Pestilence darted across the yard, Carlitos giving chase not unlike Pepe Le Pew.

"Lassie?" I asked, giving Charles a hearty handshake and slap on the shoulder.

"The wolfman!" he exclaimed, baring his teeth and making claws out of his hands. "You guys have brought all sorts of weird shit over here, but you've never brought a wolfman. Where's he at?"

"So, what? We can't just come over and hang out for a barbecue? We've always gotta bring something weird?" Clarisse asked, leaning over and giving our host a hug.

"Hey, the kids love it," he said, tousling her hair before he turned to Brandi and gave her a punch on the shoulder. "What's up, you big old bitch?"

"Not much, Chuck, you big old fuck!" With a grin, Brandi slugged him back, pulling the punch so she didn't kill the mortal, but gave him enough to let him know she'd been there. Charles grimaced, but didn't let it slow him down as he made a show of shrugging Stacey off. "I don't gotta greet *this* guy—I see *him* all the time."

Stacey rolled his eyes. "Yeah, we'll see who you come running to the next time you've got a Morlock hanging out in your tool shed."

"It was *your* Morlock! I just wanted to mow the lawn, and that… *thing* tried to eat me!" Charles exclaimed, hitting Stacey with his cowboy hat. Considering all the screwball shit Charles had gotten tangled up in since moving in across the street from Stacey over a decade ago, he would've been in his rights to just shoot Stacey with a cannon…in the face.

"You must've done something to upset him, because 'ol Moe usually just sticks to peeping in windows. And hey, I still got him down in the basement!" Stacey said. "He's gotta perform one more labor for me before he can go back to his own dimension, so maybe I'll send him over to finish the job!"

Charles hit Stacey with his hat again, and just as another loud, good-natured argument was about to ensue, the big wooden gate opened with a squeak of its hinges, revealing a large ghost. Dark, intelligent eyes peered at us through the eyeholes cut in its clean white sheet, and the figure smoothly strode forward, moving with grace and dignity.

"I'm still amazed we found a sheet in your house that didn't have cartoon characters on it," Clarisse said to Stacey as we made room for the ghost.

"I keep a few around for special occasions. Nobody gets to use my *Wacky Races* sheets but *me*," replied the slim vampire, his tone brooking no argument.

The ghost stepped up to Charles, who'd long ago lost any trepidation toward the unknown. He may have been a middle-aged mortal, but he had an unshakability that put many vampires to shame.

"Trick or treat," said the ghost in a deep, rumbly voice.

A big grin formed beneath Charles's mustache. "No shit?"

"No, there *will* be shit. A great deal of it. On your porch. In flames."

For once, Charles didn't know what to say, and there was a long pause, punctuated by the sounds of children laughing, cats meowing, and Carlitos snorting. Then Stacey made an "uh huh, uh huh" sound which rapidly mutated into great, gasping guffaws. Brandi, in spite of herself, bit her lip and fought back the giggles, while Clarisse looked as though she wanted to kick Stacey in the face. Innocent in the whole matter, I just smiled and enjoyed the scene.

The ghost looked askance over at Stacey, who was doubled over in mirth. "That's right, is it not? You told me of Mr. Robinson's Halloween lament, nineteen fifty-six. The big flaming piles of—"

"Isn't he the cutest thing?" Brandi squealed, swooping Stacey up into her arms; he was laughing too hard to protest, even as she smashed him in a crippling hug that would've killed a mortal. "Even when he's being a jackoff, you can't help but love him."

"Did you have anything to do with that?" Clarisse asked, arching a dangerous eyebrow at me.

I held up my hands in protest. "Not this, no. The Robinson thing, yeah...I was onboard for that. But I didn't think to educate the werewolves about it."

"That horrible little goddamned asshole," Clarisse muttered.

"And he's all mine!" Brandi slung Stacey over her shoulder like a sack of potatoes—or sack of shit, as it were—and hauled him across the backyard toward the kids' sandbox. "C'mon, kids. Let's see if your adorable Uncle Stacey bounces!"

Stacey tried to protest, but instead of something coherent, he sounded like an asthmatic goose making an obscene phone call.

"So do I get to see what's under the sheet, or am I just supposed to use my imagination?" Charles asked.

The ghost surveyed the backyard, his gaze lingering on the sturdy eight-foot-high fence surrounding it. Stacey, Dorian, and I had helped Charles put that fence up specifically so we could cut loose during our semi-monthly barbecues, without worry about getting the cops called because we had brought an ogre with us.

Satisfied with the weird-proof fence, the ghost turned his attention back to Charles. "Very well. I am Lassic, of the Arragus line, acting alpha of this territory. I am pleased to meet you."

With a simple flourish, the big werewolf pulled the sheet off and revealed himself, standing proudly as the bits of silver mixed in his dark gray, black, and white fur gleamed in the flickering light of the tiki torches. Charles whistled appreciatively; he'd seen enough strange sights by now that nothing ever shocked him, but he was clearly impressed. "You look like a huge walking wolf, got the snout and the ears and everything. Not at all like the old movie, huh?"

Lassic, who'd watched the old Universal *The Wolf Man* film with us down in the Catacombs, chuckled. "No. True werewolves have a much closer kinship to wolves than those who have been made."

"Made?"

"True werewolves are born, and cannot be made—we are our own distinct people," Lassic answered. "But that hasn't stopped others from trying to duplicate our abilities, through chemistry, sorcery, and other means. So there are indeed numerous kinds of 'wolf men' very much like the movie monsters, most of them just barely in control of their stolen powers, scorned by the ancient moon for their thievery. We tend to kill them on sight."

Charles considered this. "Your own family first, *si?*"

Lassic nodded. "Always. Whether blood or chosen, your family is your heart, and must always be defended and respected."

"I think we understand each other," the big Mexican said, extending his hand. Lassic took it in his own, and gave it a hearty shake. Then he turned and bellowed, "Kids! Come and see your Uncle Lassic!"

Lassic looked at us, his ears perked up in a question. "Uncle?"

Clarisse grinned and gave the werewolf a friendly shove. "You've been adopted."

"I see. And that's good, yes?"

"Very."

The kids forgot all about the cats when presented with what was essentially a gigantic talking dog. They pawed at Lassic incessantly, asking him endless questions...most of them seeming to revolve around eating people, vampires, and other werewolves. Lassic took it all in stride, with the bearing of a supremely patient family dog allowing the children to pull his ears.

At this point Pestilence—whom Carlitos had had cornered under the bushes on the other side of the yard—made a desperate bid for escape. She came flying across the yard, through the sandbox and the other three cats, who madly scattered as she and Carlitos came barreling through.

After running through the other cats, Pestilence headed straight for Lassic and scurried between his legs and under his tail, ending up on the other side of Clarisse, cowering and yowling. This left Carlitos running directly at Lassic, and the pug stopped up short, stared at the werewolf, and snorted once in surprise.

Time slowed to a crawl as the werewolf and pug regarded one another, and the backyard fell silent as we watched the two slowly advance on one another, sniffing at the air.

"I wish I had a camera for this," Clarisse murmured, giving my hand a squeeze in excitement.

The kids were watching with a mixture of eagerness and concern. "He's not gonna eat Carlitos, is he?" Ana asked, her brow furrowed.

Charles put his broad hand on the little girl's shoulder. "No. He understands family. Carlitos is totally safe."

I smiled—*that* was why we liked Charles so much. He always saw the similarities first, and while he was fascinated in the differences between people, he didn't get hung up on them. Differences were there to keep people interesting, not keep people apart.

A devout Catholic, he never objected to our own beliefs or lack thereof, and he'd once told me, "My God isn't your god, if you have any at all, so you look at things differently than me. Regardless of which one of us is right or wrong about life, the universe, and everything—for all we know we're *all* right—a true man doesn't let his religion interfere with his friendships."

Charles was everything the Crimson Order could never

understand, and was stronger than Tempestia could've ever hoped to have been. He'd just met his first werewolf, and instead of reacting with concern because of Lassic's fearsome appearance, he'd taken Lassic at his word and trusted him. Charles didn't see a werewolf, he saw a *person*.

Though what Carlitos saw was up for interpretation. Lassic slowly dropped to his hands and knees as the pug watched him intently, and then they circled one another, until...

"They're sniffing each other's butts!" Federico exclaimed before dissolving into laughter.

"That's the dog equivalent of swapping business cards, kid," I said, though I had to admit the scene was surreal as hell. I really did wish someone had a camera for this. I glanced around, looking for Stacey—this was his kind of thing, where was he? Then I spotted him and Brandi furiously making out beneath the magnolia tree, and considering where Brandi had her hands, they weren't going anywhere for a while. So much for that.

After some vigorous sniffing, Lassic and Carlitos got almost nose-to-nose and silently regarded one another. Then Lassic leaned forward and licked Carlitos's blunt snout. This seemed to please the pug, who let out a short, sharp yip and began wagging his tail. Lassic yipped in return and wagged his own tail before he gave the pug another lick.

"Are you friends now?" Ana demanded, her brown eyes huge.

Lassic reached out and gave Carlitos a pat on the head with his big hand. "Yes. He was concerned for his territory, understandably so, and I assured him I was no threat. He has welcomed me as a guest in his territory, and I am honored by his hospitality."

Charles frowned. "*His* hospitality?"

The werewolf shrugged. "The entire yard has been thoroughly scent-marked by Carlitos. As far as a werewolf is concerned, this is Carlitos's territory."

"You're kidding."

"No. Scent is very important. I understand that this is your house and yard, but my instincts keep whispering that Carlitos is the alpha, due to his copious scent-marking. I suggest you do your own scent-marking, to avoid any confusion should other werewolves come to visit."

Charles gazed at Lassic for a long moment. "Pee in my yard, you mean."

"A great deal, yes."

"You're fucking with me."

"I would not presume to do any such thing."

The big Mexican considered this, and then a slow smile formed on his lips. He put his arm around Lassic's broad shoulders and started walking him toward the house, followed by the kids and Carlitos. "Would you be willing to tell my wife that I should be pissing in the yard, for the sake of werewolf relations?"

"I would, yes."

"You're all right, *hombre*! You smoke cigars, by any chance?"

"No...should I?"

"Well, I just got a box fresh off the boat from Cuba, and I'm always up for sharing..."

Clarisse and I watched them go, and she slowly shook her head. "Who do you think Jacinta's gonna kill first?"

"Charles. Then Lassic. Then she's gonna get us for being accessories."

She considered this. "You wanna go out behind the tool shed and make out until this blows over?"

I held out my hand. "As long as that creepy Morlock's not in there, I'd be *delighted*."

I settled back into the padded lawn chair and let out a contented sigh. That had been the best time I'd ever spent behind a tool shed.

"Feeling good, lover?" Clarisse reached out and gently ran her fingers across the back of my hand, resting on the arm of the chair.

"Very," I replied.

Things were starting to really get back to normal in LA and the vital rhythm of the city's vampires was slowly returning to its proper pace again. There were still wounds that'd take time to heal—if they *could* heal. We'd lost good friends in the conflict and much damage had been inflicted upon the city and the Catacombs. But we were nothing if not survivors.

We'd make do with what was left, both materially and emotionally, and build it into something even better than what'd been there before. That would be our final victory over the Crimson

Order: we'd come out of the conflict stronger than ever, and if they ever came over the sea to screw with us again, we'd be ready for them. For the first time in what seemed like forever, two groups of werewolves and vampires were on good, solid terms with one another.

While the werewolves would be returning to their mountains and forests soon enough, a friendship had been forged between Lassic's people and the vampires of LA, and if war ever came upon either side, the other would be there to stand by them. Following the final battle with the Crimson Order, Lassic had granted amnesty to the werewolves who'd aligned with the Order, seeking to heal the schism in his tribe. Many had gratefully rejoined, but there were others who went rogue and simply disappeared, as they felt Lassic wasn't worthy to be the new leader of the werewolves, as he technically wasn't an elder. Lassic himself fully admitted that, but the majority of his people had chosen him to lead until the original elders could be located, and so he would serve until he wasn't needed anymore.

Though I knew it pained the werewolves to be without their elders, part of me hoped it'd take a long time to find them, if they were ever found. I liked Lassic a great deal, and if not for rallying his werewolves to help us against the Order, things might've turned out a whole hell of a lot worse. He wasn't just a battlefield commander, either; he had grand ideas for a future between our peoples, and I had to admit, his vision was compelling.

There was an old werewolf proverb that said, "that which doesn't grow, dies." Lassic believed in that, heart and soul, and after working with us to topple the Crimson Order, he felt that it was time for our peoples to finally put an end to our ages-old enmity. The Order had been a stark reminder of what happened when people refused to grow, clinging to outmoded ideas and trying to stifle new ones by any means necessary.

He'd been encouraging the younger werewolves—who could still shift between human and wolfen forms—to explore Los Angeles and to learn as much about the city and its vampires as possible. At the same time, he'd extended the offer to any of LA's vampires to come and visit with the werewolves in their homes in the forests and caverns.

Clarisse and Brandi both backed him one hundred percent, and the offer had been put out for any interested werewolves to come live with us in the city for as long as they wanted. Clarisse herself had told me that now was the best time to push this, while the memories of our victory were still fresh and the feelings of friendship still warm between our peoples.

We won the war, so let's not fuck up and lose the peace, she'd said, and she was right. The Order had tried to drag us back to the Dark Ages, and that was all the more reason to aggressively move forward into the future. We already had a number of werewolves looking to stay in Los Angeles, and there were numerous vampires looking to pack their bags and head out to the wilderness, including Brandi, who was quite taken with the werewolves.

Stacey, on the other hand, had shown a great deal of interest in helping the werewolves acclimate to the city. I had the feeling there was going to be some babysitting in my future, especially if Brandi was going to be away in the woods. Well, not like I hadn't already babysat him through most of the Renaissance...

"I take it I'm not the only one who likes happy endings, eh?" asked Clarisse, kissing me on the cheek as I leaned back in the chair, letting my thoughts take me where they wanted to go.

"I could just sit here and take everything in all night long and be perfectly content with it," I said. Then I looked at her and gave her a mischievous grin. "Of course, I'd be more content if we got a little time to ourselves later on..."

Clarisse chuckled and gave me another kiss, the light from the tiki torches dancing in her sapphire eyes. "We might just be able to arrange that, you know. I think I could take time away from this to show my hero how much I love him."

"I'm not a hero, I just did what I had to do, that's all." I patted her on the thigh.

Despite my protests, I'd gotten a hero's welcome by every vampire and werewolf in LA, and hardly an hour went by that someone didn't come up and congratulate me on taking down Tempestia. I always thanked them, but made sure to remind everybody that if it weren't for Katheryne and Brandi putting so much hurt to Tempestia, I would've been toast.

As it was, things had been too damned close for my comfort,

but nobody wanted to focus on that. They just wanted to thank me for killing off the big bad bogeywoman, so I let them. If that's what they wanted to do, that was fine, just so long as they didn't forget that I had a lot of help. I couldn't have done it alone.

Barth, the community's eccentric artist, had even gone so far as to paint a big picture of myself as a big black Labrador retriever—complete with a bandanna, leather jacket, and heroic grimace—leading a contingent of fanged golden retrievers, pit bulls, and Doberman pinschers in combat against a gruesome-looking horde of fanged chihuahuas and poodles. I'd loved the picture so much I'd hung it up in Henry's, with the grumbled blessing of the haunted voodoo skull himself, so everybody could see it and have a good view of Barth's warped artistic mastery.

"I know, I know, but I still think you're the cat's meow," said Clarisse, who hugged me. "Just shut up and let me gush over you, luv. I like to."

"Shucks ma'am, t'weren't nothin'," I said, imitating John Wayne.

Clarisse gave me a little nip on the neck. "You're such a goon sometimes!"

I snickered then loudly said, "Speaking of goons, here comes two right now!"

"That's not what your mom said when she saw us." Dorian threw me the finger as he came through the back gate with Tommy, who held a big brown paper bag. The latter merely snorted by way of reply.

"It's about time you two got here! The natives are getting restless! Or at least *I* am," Charles said as he came back out of the house, cowboy hat cocked back on his head, and hurried over to get a look at what was in the bag.

"Would've been here sooner, if a certain somebody hadn't insisted going to this weird slaughterhouse-looking place near South Central." Dorian shot Tommy an arch look. "Just finished up with my car yesterday, and then a fuckin' *shoot-out* happens just down the street—bullets whizzing by us while we were driving away and everything!"

Tommy regarded Dorian sourly. "You want some cheese to go with that whine? Quit being a prima donna, it ill becomes you. Actually, now that I think of it, it becomes you very well, but it annoys me to no end, so quiet with you."

When Dorian sputtered, Tommy continued, "I gave you the option to drop me off while you circled the area, for the sake of your precious vehicle, but you insisted upon going inside once you'd laid eyes upon the butcher's daughter. I seem to recall you saying there was something 'vital' about an attractive young woman who worked with bloody carcasses all day long."

"Well, I got her number, didn't I? And that's beside the point!"

"Of course it is, Dorian, of course it is. You sorry deviant," Tommy said, with his professor voice in full gear. "But moving on, my motives for going to said butcher's shop—which you seem to have forgotten in your never-ending quest to complain—was because they simply offer the best-tasting cuts of meat to be found anywhere in the city. I have sworn by that place for over a decade now, as you should well know. Once you've sunk your fangs into one of these steaks, perhaps it will cease your endless prattling. But then again, I doubt that."

Dorian cuffed him on the back of the head, though Tommy looked vindicated when Charles declared, "These steaks look incredible! They already look good enough to eat! Tommy, you've outdone yourself, *amigo!*"

Tommy handed the bag over to Charles, and gave Dorian a smug look before heading over to the sandbox to get Death. Dorian started to yell something at him, but just gave him the finger instead. Then, having put it behind him already, called out, "Hey, you guys got a cheese tray or anything like that?"

"It's in the house, on the counter next to the microwave," Donita answered, starting to fiddle with the charcoal in the old grill. She and Katheryne had already been here for hours, getting the food together inside and hanging out with Charles's wife, Jacinta. "Katheryne put it together and nobody's brought it out yet. Be a dear, and go get it, eh?" That seemed fine with Dorian, who headed toward the house.

Charles set the bag of meat down on the picnic table next to the grill, drawing the attention of both Lassic and Carlitos, who checked out the bag with a great deal of interest. Then Donita said, "Hey Chuck, check this out!"

She waved her hand around in the air, raised it up high then brought it down like she was lobbing a ball into the grill. A thick jet of fire shot up out of the charcoal briquettes as they all burst into flame. "Pretty neat, huh?" She cackled.

"No, no, no!" howled Charles in dismay, putting his hands to his face in horror. "You can't start it up like that! You need to go slow!"

"But you go *too* slow, a little bit faster is what you need. You gotta be subtle about it, but you can't dick around too long." Dorian took a detour to the grill. "This needs to be put out so we can start over and do it right."

"Yeah, but you guys don't know how to arrange charcoal for shit. I'll show you how to do it right, dammit. I got this." Brandi walked over from the magnolia tree with Stacey in tow.

"The secret is the lighter fluid, you morons! You need to use a ton of that, throw a match in, and watch it flash-fry, that's what works best!" Stacey told everybody, who ignored him.

"I can't believe you just lit it up like that!" Charles exclaimed to Donita, who had her hands on her hips, looking exasperated. "Have I taught you nothing?"

"Well, fuck all y'all, then!" Donita growled, waving her hand over the fire and snuffing it instantly. "A gal tries to do you a favor and all you assholes can do is complain about it! To hell with you bitches!"

"Ummm!" Ana yelled, pointing at Donita. "Aunt Donita said a swear!"

"Damn right I did, kiddo," Donita replied, "Because your poppa and everybody else is being a horde of jackasses about how to start a damn fire! C'mon kids, let's go back in the house and go harass your mom and Aunt Katheryne."

Before they left, though, Donita used a flick of her wrist, augmented by her magick, to knock Charles's cowboy hat off his head and across the yard. He went scurrying after it while Dorian, Brandi, and Stacey argued over the best way to start a cooking fire.

Lassic watched the argument with interest, occasionally stopping to ask Stacey or Brandi what a particular term meant. When Charles got back into the argument, it hit full, glorious swing.

After Charles pulled rank and declared that since it was *his* grill, he was going to start *his* fire any damn way he pleased, the argument turned to the proper way to cook the meat once the fire really did get going. Lassic innocently asked what had been so wrong with the fire Donita started, and all four stared at him as though he'd declared he was going to eat the children. They all started up at once about cooking fire techniques, and Lassic looked sorry he'd even bothered asking.

Carlitos, who'd lost interest in the bag of meat when nobody offered to share it with him, yawned and stretched, looking around the yard. Then he spotted Pestilence, who had settled directly underneath Clarisse's chair. The stocky pug nearly leaped in place as he caught sight of his lady love, snorting and grunting like a lunatic. Pestilence let out a long, pitiful meow when Carlitos shot across the yard toward her.

The chase was on once more, and Tommy—lovingly holding Death and talking away to her—screeched when Pestilence clawed her way up his jeans, looking for refuge. She fell all over Death, who howled in surprise and annoyance. The two started scrapping right there in Tommy's arms, while Carlitos danced around on his hind legs at Tommy's feet, eagerly snorting and leaping.

"Dammit! Take your domestic matters elsewhere!" the dark blond vampire yelled as he futilely tried to get the brawling cats off himself. When Famine saw the excitement, he shot across the yard like a bullet train and ran up the other leg of Tommy's jeans, gleefully insinuating himself into the fight between Pestilence and Death. "Cease and desist, damn you! I am not a jungle gym and there will be no monkey business here!"

I was laughing so hard I was in tears and so was Clarisse. It only got worse when a jet of water shot through the air and hit Tommy right in the chest, soaking him and the three cats.

The stream lasted for several seconds, and when it stopped, Stacey's laughter was heard. We all looked in the direction where the water had originated, and there stood Stacey, holding the garden hose and wearing a little plastic fireman's hat he'd gotten from the kids' sandbox. "That'll be enough of that, you crazy kids! You're gonna need a room if you're gonna do that!" Stacey sternly addressed them.

Tommy was quite a sight, totally drenched with three equally wet cats hanging off his New York Dolls shirt and denim jacket by their claws.

"Holy cow, all four of you look like drowned rats, especially the kitties!" Stacey howled, dropped the hose and clutched his midsection with mirth.

Tommy looked down at the cats, they looked up at him, then the felines all neatly dropped off his jacket and shirt while Stacey continued to laugh his head off. He didn't laugh for much longer, though, and let out a wail of distress as Tommy and the three cats charged after him, murder in their eyes.

Since Pestilence was part of the merry band pursuing Stacey, Carlitos took off after them, and the entire motley crew circled the backyard three times—Stacey screaming the whole while—before the wiry vampire ran through the gate, with everybody else close behind them.

"Dammit, what the hell did I ever do to any of you?" Stacey screeched as he beat a hasty retreat from the yard, with a vampire, three cats, and a pug in hot pursuit.

As soon as the gate slammed shut behind Carlitos, Katheryne stepped out of the house onto the back porch and looked around, not saying anything but looking certain she'd just missed something interesting.

"Hey! Food!" Dorian happily called out, stepping away from the heated cooking fire argument for a moment to give Katheryne a little hug and to grab a handful from the cheese tray. In the meantime, Charles and Brandi continued the argument, Charles making hostile gestures at Brandi with a spatula and Brandi waving her arms around in frustration.

Then she said something we didn't catch, but made Charles lean over and whack her on the ass with his spatula and holler, "You may be hundreds of years old, but you know squat about cookouts, *amiga!*"

"Don't *you* smack *me* on the ass!" Brandi hollered back at him. So, of course, Charles leaned over and did it again.

"Don't tell me how to cook!"

"In about three seconds I'm gonna be telling you how to get down off your roof after you've been thrown up there!"

"I'd like to see you try! I used to box when I was younger, and I'd knock your block off!"

And so it went. Charles loved a good argument—as did most of us—so there was always lots of yelling at these little gatherings. I'm sure an outsider would have thought we all hated each other.

In fact, Lassic was looking a little concerned at the vehemence with which Brandi and Charles were arguing. When Dorian had gotten his share of food from the cheese tray, he stepped right back into the verbal brawl as well, howling at the both of them.

Lassic looked over at me, as though he wasn't sure whether to try to calm everybody down or just let it go. I gave him a smile and a thumbs-up sign, and after a moment, he returned it with a little nod, apparently satisfied all was well.

Katheryne approached Clarisse and I, still holding the cheese tray, and offered it to us.

"Coffee, tea, or milk?" she asked softly, and Clarisse and I helped ourselves. Then Katheryne asked, "Did I miss something a minute ago? I heard a lot of screaming, and then the gate slammed..."

"Stacey gave Tommy and the cats an unsolicited bath," Clarisse answered.

"Ah," replied Katheryne.

She set down the cheese tray on the little plastic table set up among the chairs then took a seat next to Clarisse. The redhead took Katheryne's hand, and Katheryne graced us with her gentle little smile, and my already-good mood went up a notch.

Katheryne had seemed especially happy over the past week, and it was wonderful to see her in such high spirits, having returned to us from the dark depths. She didn't jump for joy, nor did she chatter endlessly, but she smiled a little more often and just had a way about her, of carrying herself, that said that she was content and happy with life.

There would be other trials in the future for her, I was certain, but she'd make it through anything that was thrown at her. She was stronger than anybody thought—stronger than even she herself thought—and though at times she might seem the least of us, I knew she had it in her to be the greatest of us all. But, for the moment, everything was right in her world, which made us happy, and we loved her, for she was our Katheryne.

"So Dactius decided not to come, eh?" I asked. I hadn't seen any signs of Katheryne's personal fan club anywhere near, and usually whenever he was in the same vicinity as Katheryne, he adoringly followed her every move.

Katheryne gave a little shake of her head. "No, I told him I thought it'd be nice if he helped the werewolves get their caverns and tunnels back in order, so he went and did that instead. He's a nice person, but he needs to find something else to do besides following me..."

"Ah, but you're the apple of his eye, his goddess, the bearer of the blue light that burns the evil away." Clarisse patted Katheryne's hand, and the bluestreaked blonde witch made a weary face.

"I don't want to be anybody's goddess. I just want to be me. And he's got to stop telling all the fledglings that I'm the end-all be-all of everything too." The witch sighed. "I know he means well, but..."

I chuckled.

After the Crimson Order had crumbled to ash, most of the new fledglings the Order had created had chosen to align themselves with the vampires of Los Angeles once they'd seen the Order had been full of shit about us. These were people who'd been made into vampires by the Order for the purpose of being foot soldiers, and they hadn't been given the choice as to whether they wanted to be vampires.

Tempestia had simply decreed it was the will of the Goddess that some mortals were transformed into vampires to help the Order, and then blamed it on us. It was her reasoning that if we hadn't been such a heretical presence she wouldn't have had to go to such measures to try to counter us.

There were dozens of fledglings, and they were all still going through the difficult transition between their mortal lives and their new, immortal ones. Now that they were free of Tempestia's control, they were seeing things clearly again, and while some of them were horrified by what had happened to them, the majority was dealing with it pretty well.

For the most part, these young vampires were being assigned to numerous older mentors, as the Order had taught them only enough to be effective in combat and to follow the dictates of Tempestia. Now that the Order was gone, they were adrift, searching for a purpose and direction in their new life, not truly understanding that they were now free to go and do whatever they wanted to do. Some of them followed their mentors almost slavishly, trying to regain the direction they'd lost.

Dactius was one of these, and he followed Katheryne around

like a puppy. After some of the other fledglings had heard him speak so glowingly of her, they'd started to follow her as well, and though Katheryne tried her best to be gentle in discouraging them, they drove her absolutely nuts at times.

"Once they've seen enough of how things run around here," I said, "they'll start to figure it out on their own. But in the meantime, you've got yourself your own little set of shadows."

Katheryne made that weary face again. "I don't like having shadows, and I'm afraid Donita's going to start beating them up too. You know how protective she is."

I really laughed at that, as did Clarisse. The gypsy was getting pretty sick and tired of Katheryne's little pack of shadows. She'd taken to yelling at some of them when they'd gotten especially annoying. But that hadn't deterred them, and they continued to caper after Katheryne, much to Donita's irritation.

"Speaking of the little spitfire, where'd she go?" asked Clarisse.

Katheryne pointed toward the house.

"She's painting with the kids right now. Federico got a new set of paints last week, and when he showed them to her, she had to start playing with them. She was also muttering something about nobody out here knowing how to start a proper fire, which I assume is the hot topic at the moment."

"Shut up, you know nothing!" Charles yelled at Dorian, swatting him on the arm with the spatula.

"Oh yeah, you know even less than that!" Dorian replied, removing his own cowboy hat and klonking Charles with it.

"You're both a couple of morons. If you'd let me do this from the beginning, we'd be eating right now!" Brandi growled at them.

"*Shut up!*" Dorian and Charles both yelled at the Valkyrie, who pulled herself up to her full height of six feet and four inches, put her hands on her hips, and leaned forward imposingly.

"Make me," she said, and both Charles and Dorian looked at one another questioningly for a moment then went back to yelling at each other.

Brandi nodded knowingly. "That's what I thought."

"A very hot topic," I confirmed.

Katheryne giggled, which was good to hear.

After a few more minutes of nonsense, Jacinta came out onto the porch, surveyed the argument then yelled something loudly and authoritatively in Spanish. All three verbal combatants stopped short, looked at her then seemed to shrink a few inches as the short, rotund woman crossed her arms and dared any of them to argue with her. Jacinta was a dear woman, a wonderful wife and loving mother, but when she put her voice to *that* level and started shouting in Spanish, it was time to back off.

"Now, if it's not too much trouble, we'd all appreciate it if you'd stop with the fighting and get with the cooking. No more fooling around, you got me?" she asked, giving the sheepish trio the evil eye.

"Yes dear," said Charles.

"Yes ma'am," said Dorian.

"Yes, oh killer of giants," said Brandi.

"Now, I need some help inside. If there aren't any volunteers, I'm going to pick one," Jacinta said, and the troublesome trio studiously turned their attention back to the grill. The Mexican woman folded her arms over her chest, looking unimpressed.

"I will offer my services," Lassic said, stepping forward. Smart move on his part—Jacinta had shot down the notion of Charles being given free rein to piss in the yard with a great deal of sound and fury. The werewolf probably figured this was a good way to fix his standing with Jacinta.

He was right…the woman *loved* willing helpers.

She graced the werewolf with a bright smile. "What a gentleman you are!"

"I try my best," the werewolf replied, approaching Jacinta.

"I'm sure you do. But you have to be careful about the company you keep," she chided him, taking him by the arm and leading him toward the house. "The wrong people can put some truly stupid ideas into your head."

"I am discovering that, yes."

The gate opened and in came Tommy, soaking wet and mumbling. Death and Pestilence were draped over his shoulders, panting heavily, while Famine was happily bouncing along behind Tommy, looking ready for another run around the neighborhood. So was Carlitos, who was keeping his eyes on the exhausted Pestilence.

"Now what happened to you?" Jacinta turned away from Lassic

and took in the appearance of Tommy and the cats with a mother's trained eye.

"Stacey happened," Tommy grumbled.

"Ah," said Jacinta, nodding knowingly. "That boy is *loco*. I'm amazed he hasn't gotten himself killed yet."

"Oh, I assure you, it's not from a lack of trying on my part," said the dark blond vampire. Death let out a soft mew of agreement, while Pestilence made a more assertive growl. "He's lucky he can retreat so fast, the son of a bitch."

Jacinta gave him a smack on his arm. "Watch your mouth while you're around the house. I don't want the kids picking up any of that gutter talk. Lord knows Stacey's taught them more than enough as it is. Let's get you inside and get your clothes dried off. I'm sure Donita can take care of that quicker than my machine can, so we'll talk to her. And while you're inside, you can help with some of the other food. And as for you," she said, turning back to Lassic. "You won't shed in the potato salad, will you?"

"I shall do my best not to," replied the werewolf.

Jacinta gave Lassic a pat on his shoulder and said, "Good man. Now inside with the both of you, and bring the cats too. I don't want them catching cold, being wet and all." Tommy, Death, Pestilence, Famine, and Lassic all followed after Jacinta as she headed back into the house.

After Jacinta had established law and order once more, things proceeded quietly for a spell.

Charles was cooking the steaks on the grill, filling the backyard with their wonderful aroma, while both Brandi and Dorian took it upon themselves to softly criticize Charles's technique. Charles just as softly snarled back at them, though the three settled down a bit when Charles produced cigars a cousin of his in Florida had sent, and the three contentedly lit up.

Everything was peaceful, and I leaned way back in my chair and looked up at the sky. I couldn't see many stars thanks to the glow of the city, but it was still a nice sight anyway, and I just enjoyed the moment, sitting in my chair, holding onto Clarisse's hand while she held onto Katheryne's, and the three of us sat in quiet companionship.

The kids and Donita came back outside after a while, and they ran over and showed us their paintings of the cats, who had rejoined them after Donita had dried the felines off with her magick. Then they showed us the painting Donita had done, a somewhat abstracted image of a rat lounging on a gutter outside of the Rainbow Bar and Grill cleaning his fur. The gypsy had had a thing for rodents, and was always feeding squirrels in the park, hamsters at the library, and rats in the gutters. The feeling was mutual, and the rodents would often follow her around after they'd seen how friendly she was to them. Dorian sometimes called her the Pied Piperette of LA.

Lassic soon came back outside as well, carefully carrying a bowl of potato salad in his big hands. He took it over to the picnic table near the grill, hungrily sniffing at the air and eyeing the steaks longingly.

Charles, who knew that sort of look all too well, clapped him on the shoulder, reassuring him it wouldn't be much longer, as his cooking method not only yielded tasty meat, but was fast as well. Brandi and Dorian both took issue with that, and Lassic gracefully excused himself to rejoin the kids as they played with the cats... with the exception of Time, who was fast asleep under my chair.

Pestilence kept looking uneasily over to the screen door leading into the house, where Carlitos was sitting and gazing at her mournfully, trapped inside for the moment, and she was playing even more stiffly than normal. Under regular circumstances, the haughty Pestilence wasn't much for roughhousing with kids, but her nervousness at the imminent freeing of Carlitos made her that much more reluctant to play, lest she not be able to get away when the adoring pug was freed.

Donita settled into Katheryne's lap, and the witch lovingly wrapped her arms around the gypsy's waist and rested her head against Donita's shoulder as Donita slipped an arm around the blonde's shoulders. "Nice night, isn't it?" Donita asked Katheryne, who nodded and smiled.

"Wonderful," she answered, and I knew she was talking about a lot more than just the comfortable, cool, and calm weather. She leaned over and gave Donita a kiss on the cheek, which the gypsy reciprocated with one to Katheryne's forehead.

"You've healed up perfectly, baby, I can't even see the slightest hints of any marks," said Donita, as she traced a finger over

Katheryne's cheeks and the area around her eyes. "Not a blemish to that pretty face at all, is there?"

"Nope." Katheryne blushed softly at the attention, which made Donita giggle and give her a hug, getting a gentle grin from the witch.

Clarisse leaned over and kissed me, hugging me at the same time, and I gladly returned the favor. It was a damned good moment.

Then we heard rustling coming from the fence behind us. A few seconds later a soft thump came from the grass, and when we turned, there was Stacey crouching on the grass, sopping wet and covered with twigs and leaves, furtively looking around.

"Where is he?" the slim vampire demanded, darting his gaze all over the yard.

"What the hell happened to you?" I asked.

Stacey rapidly motioned for me to quiet down. "Never mind that, you fool, where is he?" He machine-gunned his words, reminding me of Hunter S Thompson.

"I assume you mean Tommy Cat," Donita said, and Stacey rapidly nodded. "He's inside right now, talking a little about Roman history with Jacinta. She's gotten quite an interest in the topic since he loaned her that book a couple of weeks ago, so she's letting him tell her everything he knows, and you know how he *loves* a receptive audience," she said with amusement.

"Okay, I'm safe for about three hours, that's good." Stacey scurried over and hunkered down so he was hidden by my chair, but still had a good view of the yard. "I'll just have to make a break for Brandi if he spots me, and hope she protects me. She gets these ideas that occasionally getting my ass kicked by one of you guys does me some good. I need to figure out how to disabuse her of those notions."

"Now, what happened to you?" I wanted to know why he was so wet and covered with yard detritus, not to mention the reek of chlorine hanging on him.

"I hid out in old man Hoboken's pool," Stacey said proudly. Hoboken was his highly religious next-door neighbor, who was constantly bothering the vampire about the noise and decadence so prevalent at Stacey's house. "I figured my fan club wouldn't think to look there, and by damn, I was right! Then after I got out of the pool, I got tangled up in some of Hoboken's bushes, and here I am, unscathed and sound."

Stacey looked rather pleased with himself, but his gloating look turned to one of horror when Brandi looked over from the grill, directly at him, and chirped, "Oh hi *Stacey!* Where've you been, my love?"

"Oh nooo," Stacey moaned, slapping himself on the forehead. "There are times I could *kill* her if I was capable of it!"

The screen door on the porch was flung open, and Tommy and Carlitos came hurtling out onto the porch. Tommy stopped to take in the yard, while Carlitos shot toward Pestilence like a snorting, slobbering rocket. The cat wailed piteously at the same time Stacey made approximately the same sound. When Pestilence started running away from the pug, Tommy fixed his eyes on Stacey, pointed right at him, and snarled, "You lackbrained son of a whore, prepare to die!"

"Save me," Stacey whined.

I threw back my head and laughed.

Stacey was saved by an unexpected intervention when the gate rattled and a voice called out, *"Pocalota!* I need to talk to you!"

While Tommy had missed Stacey in Hoboken's pool, apparently Mr. Hoboken had not. The gate rattled once more, and then the ever-rude Mr. Hoboken simply let himself in without invitation. Clarisse gasped and hissed, "Lassic!"

But when I looked over at the grill, the werewolf had already gotten his sheet back on, and was again looking like a big, innocent ghost.

The short, pudgy man dressed in suit pants, dress shirt, and tie stomped across the yard straight toward Charles, jabbing his finger at him, sternly admonishing Charles for the noise coming out of his yard at ten o'clock in the evening then telling him that the children should have been put to bed a long time ago...never mind that the kids didn't even have school the following day.

Charles, casually chomping on his cigar, looked at Mr. Hoboken as if he was a complete idiot. The big Mexican tipped his cowboy hat back and scratched his head as Hoboken continued on about how he was tired of all the noise coming out of Charles's yard, and that he was a bad parent to expose his "impressionable" children to such "unholy" influences as us.

"I know what kind of trouble this bunch is capable of. Living next door to that *heathen* over there has been very educational." He pointed at Stacey angrily, who happily waved at Hoboken as though they were best friends.

"Hi, Mr. Hoboken! How are you tonight?"

"I know you were in my pool! You thought I didn't see you floating around in there, but I did!" he snarled, his bald head and face flaring scarlet as he yelled.

"You've got a very nice pool, Mr. Hoboken," Stacey cheerily said. "I sure do wish you'd invite me over to come swimming sometime!"

"So that's where you were hiding out, you little prick! All you did was delay the inevitable!" Tommy growled at the black-haired vampire, and started to roll up the sleeves of his denim jacket.

"That's exactly what I'm talking about!" Hoboken screamed, pointing at Tommy now. The vampire looked over at him and muttered something hideously obscene at the fat man in Latin. Then when Hoboken caught sight of Federico giving him the finger, he had a conniption.

"Look at your kids, Pocalota! You're raising them all wrong by letting them hang around with these heathens!" Hoboken yelled. "And what about those two?" he screeched, looking over at Donita and Katheryne, who still had their arms around each other. "They're living in sin, I tell you! How can you call yourself a Christian when you've forsaken the word of the Lord by associating with these cretins!"

Donita and Katheryne did the natural thing and started furiously making out.

The two half-bloods aside, we all sat and watched as Hoboken screamed and railed against us and what we stood for, and it seemed to enrage the little man even more that we weren't reacting to him. Charles would nod at him occasionally, but went on cooking the steaks, while Jacinta came out onto the porch to watch the display of the righteous jerk, arms crossed over her chest.

Then Hoboken spied Lassic and he leaned forward to look at the ghostly figure curiously. "And what manner of freak is this? What the blazes kind of party are you running here, Pocalota?"

Lassic regarded Hoboken then politely said, "I am a ghost. Trick or treat."

Predictably, everybody went into hysterics, except for Hoboken, who apparently didn't see the humor in the situation. "This isn't funny!" Hoboken screeched, stomping his foot.

Charles tipped his hat forward on his head and pointed at the fat man with his spatula.

"I think I've heard just about enough from you, *hombre,*" he said, his voice sharp. "I don't recall inviting you to this little get-together, and I don't appreciate you insulting my friends or telling me how rotten my kids are. I don't take parenting tips from guys who don't have kids of their own, and I don't take tips on how to pick my friends from a guy who doesn't have any, either. I do things my own way, you do things your way, and if you don't like how I handle myself, then stay away from me. If we're being too loud, call over here and tell us to keep it down, and we will. But if you come over here and give us a sermon, you'd better expect nothing but further trouble from us. Now that I've said my piece, *amigo,* why don't you kindly fuck off and get out of my yard before I kick the shit out of you?"

The kids, even little Santiago, all cheered proudly for their father. Jacinta, who normally tried to curb Charles's cursing, nodded in approval, and the rest of us all applauded him.

Hoboken sputtered and stammered, and just when he opened his mouth to say something else, a shadow separated itself from the darkness in one of the corners of the yard, glided toward Hoboken with fluid grace, and stood imposingly in front of him, black duster softly flapping.

"You've been asked to leave. I suggest you do so," said Wade softly. Though his voice was totally even, Hoboken looked up at the big vampire with more than a touch of fear: Wade just had that way about him.

Hoboken backed away from Wade and made his retreat, heading out the gate without another word, not even a backward glance. When the gate had slammed shut, Charles reached into his overalls and offered Wade a cigar. "Well said, *mi amigo.* If I were half the persuader you are, I'd be a rich man right now," he said. Wade took the cigar with an appreciative nod.

"Thanks," he said, and when Charles informed him that he had first choice of steaks, Wade nodded. "Now that's what I like to hear."

"Damn, if that isn't creepy how he just kind of appears from out of nowhere like that," Stacey said, hiding behind my chair again, just in case Tommy decided to continue his vendetta.

"I knew he was there," Katheryne said, a little teasing lilt to her voice.

"Well of course you did, you're just as weird as he is." Stacey poked her in the ribs and made her squirm.

"They're not weird. I think they make quite a pair," said Jacinta, who'd come over to sit with us now that she'd brought out the last of the food. "So are you two actually seeing one another yet, or are you still up in the air?" she asked. Donita giggled at the way Katheryne blushed.

"He's...special to me," the witch answered, and would say nothing more on the subject. Jacinta kept at it for a while, teasing her about how cute she and Wade would be together, making the blonde blush furiously several times, which got all of us giggling at her.

Behind the blushing I could see the twinkle in her eyes, and I knew she was enjoying herself. Hell, we were all enjoying ourselves, from Charles, Brandi, Dorian, Tommy, Wade, and Lassic over at the grill, to the kids and the cats in the yard, to our little group over by the fence.

I leaned over and hugged Clarisse as tightly as I could then kissed her, my heart riding high inside of me. Life was good.

My Chevelle came to a stop out by one of the picnic areas near Mount Wilson, not far from where the werewolves were getting their old caves and warrens back in shape. I shut down the purring engine and looked out the windshield at the trees ahead of us then at the clear night sky above. The city was directly behind us right now, and without its glow to dampen things in this direction, the stars shone much more strongly.

"Now that's more like it." Clarisse leaned forward to look at the stars through the windshield.

"Yup," I said. "What do you think, Tempestia?"

I reached over and patted the gleaming skull—which sported

one broken fang—sitting on my dashboard.

After I'd emerged from the ocean, I'd still had a death-grip on Tempestia's broken body, and Donita had separated me from her while I'd instinctively dug under. The gypsy had taken it upon herself to incinerate every last bit of Tempestia's body and scatter the ashes, except for the skull.

She'd cleaned and polished it up for me, inscribing, *Deities come and go, empires rise and fall, but vampires are forever,* on it, followed by the date on which Tempestia had been defeated. Since then Tempestia had become a permanent occupant of my car, and I tended to think of her as my good-luck charm.

"I think she probably would have claimed it was because of her that it was so beautiful out tonight, knowing her," Clarisse said, the repaired diamond-studded titanium choker around her neck sparkling in the moonlight, and I had to agree.

We crossed the grass of the picnic area, hand in hand, looking up at the sky and saying nothing. There was nothing we needed to say that we didn't already know or weren't already sensing from one another. Sometimes silence spoke more than words, so we stepped through the grass, content in our silence.

We stopped and looked at the full moon, holding onto one another, savoring it all. It was times like this that I lived and strived for, and I wished it could last forever. I'd seen some of the most spectacular things in the entire world and I'd participated in some of the most incredible events, but despite all of that, nothing compared to sitting around shooting the shit with my closest friends, winning a hard-fought race out on the highway, making a packed house of music fans scream, or standing under the stars holding onto the woman I loved.

The incredible things were great, they added variety to one's life, but it was ultimately the simple things from which one's life was built. It was those things that I remembered the most when I looked back on my long life.

Life is an adventure, a wild and wondrous thing, and when it comes down to it, it doesn't matter whether you're a vampire. It's how you live out what you've been given. Simply having immortal or mortal blood in your veins doesn't make a difference as to how good or bad your life will be.

There are vampires who squander their long existences on unrewarding, mindless pursuits, while there are mortals who make impressive use of their short time on this planet. Some, both immortal and mortal, choose to waste their time, wishing for something they don't have, wishing they were either a vampire, or wishing they were mortal again, and by doing so, they're losing what they already have.

You may choose to become one of us, and then again you might not. But regardless of your choice, I ask that you carefully consider everything I've told you, both in the words I've written and what I've told you in past conversations. Becoming a vampire doesn't automatically make your life fantastic, and staying mortal doesn't mean you're forever condemned to the mundane.

It all depends upon what you do with whatever it is that you're given.

There are benefits to being forever young and living through the ages, seeing and doing things no mortal ever could, and I've spoken to those who wouldn't give up their mortality for anything, as they enjoy growing old with their children or loved ones too much.

For me, becoming a vampire was the greatest choice I could have ever made. I know in my heart that I would never have been content to have children and grow old, and though I'll likely never see the light of day again, it doesn't bother me. What I've given up has been far outweighed by what I've gained, and I think of that every time I gaze into Clarisse's eyes or listen to Stacey laugh.

What's right for you? I don't know, and I don't presume to know. The choice is ultimately yours. I think you'd make a great vampiress, but I also think you're doing quite well as you are now, so I can't give you any further advice. Choose wisely, Michelle, for this decision is one that'll deeply affect the rest of your life, though there's no rush.

You may take years to make your decision if you like, but if tomorrow you wish to become one of us—if you truly believe that's what's right for you—that's fine too. I trust your judgment, and I'm very patient. I've got all the time in the world.

After watching the moon for a time, Clarisse and I locked gazes, neither of us taking a cue from the other, but simply *knowing* what the other was thinking. Clarisse ran her fingers along my cheek, and I ran mine through her hair, and feelings and thoughts flowed between us, things words could never express, and I felt as though my heart were about to explode.

Right then, I couldn't have been happier, and I drank in deeply of it, savoring it to the very core of my soul. When Clarisse and I kissed, my heart *did* explode, filling every cell of my body with joy and happiness, and I ceased feeling the ground beneath my feet, and I saw the moon and the stars no more. There was only Clarisse, and for her, there was only me. I knew this because our souls were entwined with one another, and we were as one.

For the moment, we were everything.

About the Author

I'm the product of a small-town upbringing wherein my parents encouraged me to pursue my interests and do what made me happy, and screw anybody who didn't like it. So I pissed away a large portion of my youth on old movies, mountains of books, EC comics, Star Trek, robots, petty mischief, Calvin & Hobbes, and an obscene amount of rock n roll. The Unholy War duology is the direct result of those halcyon days.

I'm not a drunk and have no idea how to make meth, and I didn't listen when a school chum advised me, "only stupid people read," so I think I turned out all right. Could've been worse.

Check out the ever-expanding world of the (R)Evolution By Night—Unholy War is just the beginning—at my website, which I really should update more often…

www.therevolutionbynight.com

Curious about other Crossroad Press books?
Stop by our site:
http://store.crossroadpress.com
We offer quality writing
in digital, audio, and print formats.

Enter the code FIRSTBOOK
to get 20% off your first order from our store!
Stop by today!

www.ingramcontent.com/pod-product-compliance
Lightning Source LLC
Chambersburg PA
CBHW060857250626
47159CB00008B/2783